The Background:

England in 2066, is bizarre mix of backwards ideology and innovative technology. 'The Rulers' were voted into power in 2043. Their party, The True Order, used the slogan, 'Enough is enough.' They promised to re-establish law and order, end handouts to those who wouldn't work and bring back 'good old fashioned values.' The regime seemed tough but people wanted it.

The Rulers gradually turn the country into a dictatorship, abolishing the voting system. They bring back public hangings, which are televised. They reintroduce workhouses, for those who can't work. Poverty spreads, as does disease. The New Plague, a mysterious disease that seems mainly to afflict the poor, becomes rife. People are dying in their thousands, but The Rulers do nothing to stop it.

People mainly live in Tech-Cities, where they are protected from vigilante groups who won't conform. The roads are quiet, only the rich can afford magnetised cars. International trade is limited, as travel between countries has mainly broken down in the effort to reduce carbon emissions and keep out terrorism. Everyone is forced to call their children names that teach what The Rulers consider to be valuable qualities; names su̲ _____ Silence.

Praise for Breaking Silence:

'Fantastic! I genuinely loved it! It was well written and the storyline was so creative and intriguing. Si is an ordinary boy with an extraordinary story.'

Caitlin, aged 15

'This book is amazing! So gripping, thrilling and exceedingly exciting. I can't wait 'til book two. The characters seem very mysterious and secretive, you never know what will happen next.'

Betty, Amazon reviewer

'I love this book! It's so unpredictable, I couldn't stop thinking about it for days afterwards!'

Iona, Amazon reviewer

Breaking Silence

First published 2016 in Great Britain by GoApe Books.
An imprint of:

Monkey Island Publishing
Hurgill Road
Richmond
North Yorkshire
DL10 4SZ

Text copyright © 2016 Karen Langtree
Design and typography by Gill McLean

1st Edition published 2016
The moral rights of Karen Langtree have been asserted

ISBN 978-0-9561086-7-8

A CIP catalogue record of this book is available from the British library

Printed in Great Britain

MONKEY ISLAND
PUBLISHING

Breaking
Silence

Part I

Part I

1

'If you come any closer you will end up one hundred percent dead.'

Si froze. Darkness clung to him. His torch had run out hours ago and since then he had been making slow progress, through the trees by touch alone. The girl turned on a flashlight. Si shielded his eyes, as the beam struck his face.

'Can't you make it just fifty percent dead?' he said.

'Don't push me!' the voice replied.

'So, how will you kill me?'

'With my knife.'

Si paused.

'What kind of knife is it?'

'What?'

'I said, what kind of knife is it?'

'A bloody big sharp one, so shut up!'

The light advanced. 'Turn around and put your hands on your head. Slowly.'

He did so, hoping that he was not about to feel cold steel slicing through his liver. Instead he felt her hand pushing him forwards.

'Move!'

He stumbled. He could now see the outlines of the trees

towering over him in the ghostly light. He wondered how he had made it this far without knocking himself out.

'What are you doing out here?' the girl said.

'I could ask you the same thing.' Si felt the knife press against his ribs. It was real enough.

'Shut up. Keep moving.'

They walked on in silence for a few minutes until she stopped, abruptly.

'Put your hands behind your back.'

Si did so. She pulled out some rope and tied them together. The rope burned his wrists.

'That hurts,' Si said, matter-of-factly.

'Good. Sit down against this tree and put your legs out straight; together.'

He obeyed, trying to catch a glimpse of the girl, but it was like being in a spotlight on the stage. She tied his feet together.

'You're good at this,' Si said.

'Shut up!'

She bound him to the tree with another length of rope.

'You carry a LOT of rope.'

He felt the knife then, under his chin, the point digging into the fleshy part behind his jawbone. She ran it slowly along the stubble beginning to form there. Perhaps he had pushed her a little too far. He held his breath.

'I'll be back at first light to see what's left of you.'

When she had gone he struggled to free his limbs but could barely move them. The rope cut into his ribs and abdomen making it more difficult to breathe. He stopped struggling and sighed.

Until now his fears had not been about what might lurk in the forest. But tied here, defenceless, with the girl's words in his ears, he began to think about it. He had thought he was safe when he reached the trees at twilight. With his torch, he had hoped to get as far as possible. Damn solar powered batteries! And he had not expected to encounter a girl brandishing a knife. Who was she?

Was she from one of the vigilante groups who lived in the countryside? Or perhaps she was living in an environmental commune: People who refused to be part of the tech-cities. Then there was talk of cannibalism, outside the cities, which carried a death penalty. He had been forced to witness an execution on TV a couple of years ago, whilst in the workhouse. People liked to frighten one another. He shuddered.

How he managed to fall asleep, he had no idea, but the next thing he knew was a hand shaking him and the girl's face peering into his.

'You survived!'

'Don't sound too disappointed,' Si said.

'Come with me.'

Before she untied him she took off her bandana and blindfolded him. Then, leaving his hands tied and picking up his torch, she pushed him in front of her. Si felt the knife in his back again.

'Where are we going?'

'Don't ask stupid questions.'

'Fair enough. You got any food? I'm starving. I don't eat human flesh though.'

'Don't be revolting.' She pushed him forward so he stumbled.

It wasn't long before they halted and Si heard other sounds: voices, dogs, hammering, laughter. He felt heat and smelt smoke.

'A wood fire! I've read about those. Can I see it?'

To his surprise, the girl removed the blindfold and pushed him down by the fire. He blinked hard and, immediately, his eyes began to water. He shivered as the warmth washed over his body. An old man and a small boy, sitting by the fire, stared at him.

'Can I warm my hands?' Si indicated that they were still tied behind his back. The girl untied him and he held them as near to the flames as he could. It felt good. He looked up at the girl.

'Thanks.'

'Wait here. Don't try to run. That boy could kill you in an instant with one shot from his sling.'

Si looked across at the scruffy child. As if to prove it, the boy pulled out his sling-shot and waved it menacingly. The man laughed; an aged, hacking cough of a laugh, and the boy joined in.

When the girl returned, she carried a wooden bowl of something green and mushy and a beaker of water.

'Here.' She thrust it into his hands.

'Thanks.'

'Plin will be over in a minute. He's the village Elder. You'll tell him what you're doing here.' She sat down. No one spoke.

Si ate the vegetable mush with his fingers. It felt like forever since he'd last eaten. He watched the girl and she watched him. She looked about his age; fifteen/sixteen he guessed. She had long, blond, unkempt hair, tied in a pony-tail and wore a white tee-shirt and beige combat trousers. Her blue eyes were cold and piercing like the knife she carried and her mouth was set in a thin, unwavering line. Something in Si wanted to make her smile.

In contrast, Si was bruised and dirty. His clothes, which consisted of grey, institutional overalls, were torn in places. It seemed pretty obvious that he was on the run. He swept his dark fringe out of his eyes and looked away into the fire.

A tall man with bushy hair walked up behind the girl. She stood and he smiled at her.

'This is the boy I found, Plin.'

Plin sat and spoke to Si. 'How you doing?'

Si glanced at the girl. 'I've been better I think – possibly. A long time ago. But this is good so far: Food, warmth, freedom. Thanks.'

Plin smiled. 'You're welcome.' The others watched as Si continued to eat. 'Freedom, you say. From what?'

Si scanned the camp. They were a small group, living in wooden shelters. He saw a dead animal being roasted on a spit and some children playing noisily nearby.

'Well, freedom from being tied to a tree all night. That's good.'

Plin laughed. 'We have to protect ourselves, hence the blindfold. But Chas can be a little ...overzealous.'

The girl smiled sarcastically at him.

He continued. 'People don't approve of our lifestyle. They want to 'upgrade' it and make us live in the tech-cities. But we choose this.'

'Freedom, you mean,' said Si.

'Yes.'

'So do I.' He looked down at his 'uniform.' He wanted to rip it from his body. He would rather be naked, even on this damp October day; even in front of this girl and these people.

'Can we get you something more comfortable to wear?' Plin asked.

'Please.'

'Will you tell us who you are?'

He hesitated a moment then shrugged. 'Silence Hunter

4004A50.' He recited it as he had become accustomed to in the workhouse. 'I prefer Si.'

'Plin nodded. 'Chas, take Si to my hut and find him something. I've got to see Ambi.' He turned to Si. 'We'll talk some more, later.'

Chas scowled. 'Come with me.'

She led him to a hut that was larger than the rest, walking straight inside, in a way that made Si wonder if she lived with Plin.

'Plin. What's that short for?'

'Discipline. Haven't you heard that one before? Come through here. I'll find you something. Then I'll burn those; unless you want them.'

Si smiled. 'What, like as a souvenir or something? They'll make good fuel.' He began to unbutton the overalls.' So what's your birth name?'

'You ask a lot of questions.'

'Just curious. You told me Plin's name. Is yours a big secret?'

She rolled her eyes. 'Chastity Komchenski, 4098H50. But Chas is who I am now.'

He shrugged. 'Fine.'

They went through a curtain into a sleeping area. There was a large palette on the floor covered in animal skins and a smaller palette beside it. It was so primitive compared to what Si had been used to.

'You were brought up in a tech-city, right? You've only seen stuff like this in history books; Or maybe in Regime propaganda. How the simple-minded revolutionaries live, eh?' She gave a harsh, sarcastic laugh.

'I learnt a bit about people like you - at the Bastille school,' he said.

Her eyes widened. 'You were at the Bastille? Why? I heard they only hold special cases there. Normal waifs and strays just get thrown into workhouses.'

Si stared at her, trying to see past the hard cold eyes. For a moment fear had softened her. 'I don't know why, but soon I'm going to find out. I do know one thing though. I'm never going back. I'd rather you stick your bloody big knife in me first.'

There was a hint of a smile. 'I'll remember that.' She handed him some clothes. 'I'll be outside.'

The clothes felt good; soft, natural, warm. When he emerged, Chas was waiting for him with Plin.

'I'll show you round the village. Chas has jobs to do and I can spare an hour. Then, if you want to sleep we can make up a bed in one of the huts. Chas didn't offer you our best hospitality last night.'

'Plin, I...' she began to protest, but Plin silenced her with a playful tousle of her hair.

'Ah, you're too serious Chas. I know you were protecting us. Go on, I'll take care of your friend.'

Chas frowned and left them.

Si warmed to Plin immediately and saw the respect he received from the others, as their leader. The village was a simple and pleasant place: A far cry from life in the tech-cities, or what he could remember of it. He had almost forgotten what life was like before the workhouse and the Bastille. There was a pungent smell of wood-smoke everywhere, which comforted him, although he didn't know why.

The villagers were engaged in subsistence tasks. There was an area where vegetables and crops were grown. It was a large plot and looked like old-fashioned allotments Si had seen in history books. One of the men was eager to tell Si exactly how everything was grown and how they used it. Many plants were medicinal as well as for food.

Someone was sawing wood to repair shelters. Another man was carving wood to make utensils. Some of these were intricately decorated and Si enjoyed seeing the man beam shyly, as he complimented him. A couple of women were leading a group of children in singing. Their voices meandered like a wave of happiness through the settlement. People stopped what they were doing to smile and listen. Chas was giving some children an archery lesson on the edge of the camp.

Si desperately wanted to sleep. He kept stifling yawns and apologising. Plin took him to the hut that had been prepared for him.

'You should be warm enough in there. We'll see you when you're rested.'

'Not sure why you're trusting me but thanks.'

Plin smiled. 'Intuition.'

2

Si woke up feeling disorientated by the unfamiliar surroundings. He must have slept deeply for fifteen hours or so. Emerging from the shelter, feeling stiff and a little cold, Si blew into his hands and jumped up and down, trying to generate some warmth. Stretching and yawning, he took in the panorama of the camp, breathing in the scent of the trees mingled with the wood-smoke. The ground glistened with a slight frost. A cockerel was crowing. As he lowered his arms he felt, not for the first time, a painful twinge in his left forearm. It had been bothering him on and off since his escape from the Bastille, but there had been too many other things on his mind to worry about it earlier. He rubbed at the spot looking for a bruise, but there was none. Perhaps it was something to do with all the so-called 'tests' they had been doing on him recently in the Bastille.

'If you want food you'd better come with me,' said Chas, heading towards a wisp of smoke that was emerging from behind some huts. Si followed. As they turned the corner he saw the fire with several people gathered around it. A dark haired woman tended a pot, hanging over it, and doled out porridge. Chas picked up a bowl from a pile and joined the queue. Si did the same. The woman spooned in silence, not even seeming to notice that Si was a stranger. People sat around in small groups, eating and talking.

One group was laughing as a scrawny dog furtively snatched a half empty bowl in its jaws and ran off to enjoy the lickings.

Chas sat down with a group that included Plin. 'Hey,' he said, kissing her on the cheek. She huddled up next to him and he put his arm round her, to warm her. Si was uncertain where to go, but Plin beckoned to him. 'Come and join us, Si.'

Chas glanced in Si's direction. Her face was passive but he still sensed hostility.

'So, how did you sleep? I hear you're used to the comforts of the Bastille?' said one of the other men. Plin raised an eyebrow at Si and shovelled more porridge into his mouth.

'Yeah, that's right,' Si said. 'The Bastille – comfort personified! I slept well, thanks.'

'Good,' Plin said. The others in the group watched him while they ate. Si didn't blame them for being a little suspicious of him, having come from the Bastille. He was familiar with stories of groups like this being infiltrated and got rid of.

They ate in silence for a while. 'So, do you have any plans, Si? It's just that if you want to stay with us, we need to work out what you can do. We're just trying to subsist out here on our own. We like our way of life. People join us now and again, for various reasons. Most stay. We've not had much trouble. If you're on the run from the Bastille, it makes it more complicated.' He paused. 'But not impossible.'

'It's tempting to stay ...'

Chas glanced up at him briefly.

'I need to think. I've got something...some people I want to find, but I don't know where to start. And I don't want to put you in danger.' He looked at Chas, but this time her eyes were firmly on her breakfast.

'Why were you at the Bastille?' asked the man who had spoken before. He had been openly observing Si. 'They don't send any old orphan to the Bastille. Why you?'

'I honestly don't know. All I know is that they've been doing lots of tests on me recently.' Subconsciously, he rubbed his forearm.

Plin picked up on it. 'What's up with your arm?'

'I don't know. I keep getting a twinge and there's a lump in it.'

The other man moved towards Si. The whole group looked curiously on now. 'May I?' he asked, reaching for Si's arm. The man felt the lump. He squeezed Si's skin, trying to get the shape and size of the lump. Then he pressed down hard on it. Si felt a small pulse beating against his bone. The man felt it in his finger too.

'A tracker,' he said.

The group began muttering and looked with concerned expectation at Plin, waiting for his response. All, except Chas. She stood up.

'A tracker? Didn't you realise before now, you idiot?' Mockingly, she repeated his words. 'I don't want to put you in danger! Well you can be one hundred per cent certain you have now!'

Plin pulled Chas down by the arm and spoke firmly to her. 'Chas, you're making it worse. You'll make people afraid.'

'That's not my fault. They should be afraid.'

'I'm sorry,' said Si, standing up. 'I'll leave immediately. I don't want to endanger anyone.' He looked pleadingly at Chas but her face was full of contempt. He turned to Plin. 'You've been kind, thank you.' Then, to Chas, he said, 'You brought me here. I didn't ask to come!'

'I had to!' she flared, jumping up again. 'You were snooping in the forest. We had to know why.'

'Chas, you're a great guardian of this village,' said Plin, standing and putting a hand on her arm. 'The boy didn't know about the tracker. I believe him.' She shook her arm free of his touch. Plin spoke to Si. 'If you run now, it won't be long before they find you. We can get that tracker out of your arm and destroy it, if you'll trust us to do it.'

Si looked at his arm, then at Plin. 'But won't they be on their way here right now? If I leave now, with the tracker intact, they might by-pass the village to follow me.'

'He's right,' said Chas. 'Let him leave.'

'No Chas,' Plin said. 'Is that what you really want for him – to be tracked down and possibly shot or taken back to the Bastille?' Chas bent down and drew a pattern in the earth with her finger. There was a faint shake of her head. Si was surprised. 'We're going to help you,' Plin said. 'We'll remove the tracker, then you can leave. Chas will take you to the nearest safe path. When you're far enough away, destroy it.'

Chas looked at Plin as if he'd just asked her to chop off her arm, but she said nothing. 'Get him some provisions Chas. Faith will help you.' Another woman rose and went with Chas. 'Come with me.' Plin said to Si. 'Temp, I need your help.'

The man who had examined Si's arm nodded and followed them to Plin's hut.

'Why haven't they come by now?' asked Si, as Plin rubbed some sort of ointment on his arm.

Temp replied. 'The tracker is only activated once someone crosses the Bastille fence. Then someone would have to notice (they don't really expect anyone to escape). Finally they'd assemble a party to track you. Nightfall, and your chosen route into the forest, helped you. They won't be far behind though.' The last comment was to Plin. He nodded, taking a pen-knife from a roll of cloth. He held the blade in a candle flame to sterilize it.

'This will hurt,' he said. Si nodded, and braced himself.

'How do you know all this? 'he managed to ask Temp, just before the blade made an incision. He drew a sharp breath.

'I ran from there too: Five years ago.'

The device, which was about half a centimetre square, was just under the surface of the skin, and came out easily. Temp covered the wound and bound the arm. Plin cleaned the tracker of blood and put it, pulsating faintly, into the palm of Si's hand.

He smiled. 'You hardly flinched.'

Si shrugged. 'I should get going. I'm really grateful for your help.' They headed back to the fire. 'How come they never found you?' Si asked Temp.

'I knew about trackers. I got it out before I crossed the fence. Then I kept on the move. It was over a year before I came here. Keep on the move Si. Keep your wits about you. Who are you looking for?'

'My mother and father. I don't believe they're dead, like they told me at the workhouse. It's too long to explain now. I should go.'

Plin put his hand on Si's shoulder. 'I hope you find them.'

'Thanks.'

Chas may not have been thrilled by the task assigned to her but she was ready. On her back was a rucksack. Strapped to her waist, in a sheath, was her knife. She handed another rucksack to Si and a smaller, but equally scary looking, knife. Plin laughed at Si's expression as he took it.

'Get her to teach you one or two things with that before she leaves you.' He gave Si a bear- hug, then kissed Chas tenderly on the cheek. 'Be careful.' Again, Si saw a gentle moment pass between them.

'Good luck,' said Temp, shaking his hand.

Si turned to follow Chas. 'I hope they don't come here and cause trouble.'

'We'll be fine,' said Plin. 'Don't worry about us.'

'Let's go,' said Chas, hiking off ahead.

Si jogged to catch her. She could walk at quite a pace. She didn't speak to him, just marched on. Si couldn't work her out. His arm throbbed but he didn't think she'd be sympathetic. As they walked, he kept turning over the tracker in his jeans pocket.

'How far are you taking me?' he asked, finally breaking the silence.

'It's a few miles to the track,' she said, not turning her head. 'Then it's easy to follow to the edge of the woods. It heads north. Don't destroy the tracker 'til a few miles after that.'

'Okay.'

The forest was dense around the village clearing and not much light managed to filter through the trees. The ground was overrun with brambles and Chas kept hacking them back with her knife. She knew the area very well, stopping now and again to get her bearings. Si noted that she had an amazing sense of direction. She was wearing combat trousers, a chunky beige jumper, hiking boots and a combat jacket. She had the bandana round her head. Si had been given jeans, a shirt and v- neck sweater, as well as an old waterproof jacket. The air was cold and their breath made steamy clouds as they exhaled. Tramping, slashing and breathing were the only sounds. Chas was two steps in front of Si.

After a couple of miles, Chas stopped and took a water bottle from her pack. She took a few sips.

'You should drink,' she said.

They took off their jackets and jumpers and tied them round their waists. Despite the cold they were sweating.

'What in particular don't you like about me?' Si asked.

She watched him as he fiddled with the arms of his jumper.

'Everything.'

'But I haven't done anything to you personally, have I? Unless we met in a former life and I've forgotten. Everyone else seemed willing to give me a chance.' He looked up.

'Well, they're trusting fools some of them, even Plin. People have betrayed him in the past, but he still goes on trusting.'

'Maybe he believes that not everyone is going to treat him the same way.'

Chas shrugged and looked at the ground. 'It's nothing personal.'

'Who betrayed you then?'

She looked startled, then kicked at dead leaves on the floor. 'People. Come on. We need to get going.'

They had just begun to walk again when a terrible noise ricocheted around the trees. A series of gun-shots were heard in the distance. Chas froze.

'It's the village. I've got to go back.'

She set off, running. 'You're on your own now.'

'I'm coming with you,' Si shouted, scrambling after her.

'No! Just go!' she shouted back, not stopping.

'No. I'm coming with you, Chas. I want to help.'

Si scrabbled in his pocket and threw the tracker into the bushes. There was no time to destroy it.

The run back to the village was painful for Si. He was reasonably fit from gym sessions at the Bastille, but his arm throbbed, his legs caught in the brambles and Chas sprinted all the way, crashing through the undergrowth like a wild animal in fear of its life. At one point she stumbled and fell. Si reached her and pulled her to her feet.

'You okay?'

She shook him off and sped on.

When they reached the village they were met by devastation. Huts were on fire, and debris was strewn everywhere. A dead dog lay in their path.

Si looked on in frozen despair.

'Oh God! No!'

Chas took out her knife and looked disdainfully at him.

'Keep close to me. Where's your knife?'

He fumbled for it in its sheath. His heart pounded as he looked at the deadly weapon in his hands. He'd never hurt anyone in his life. They prowled through the settlement. Apart from the crackling from the fires there was an eerie silence. No screaming, no crying, no shouting. The first body they came across was that of a young woman, not much older than them.

'Ambi,' Chas cried, stooping to take her in her arms. Si bent over the blood soaked body, feeling for a pulse in her neck. She had a bullet wound in her chest.

'She's dead, Chas.'

'I know,' she snapped. She stood up, laying Ambi gently back on the ground. Swiping at tears with the back of her hand, she moved on. Si followed, looking all around for signs of movement. They came across more bodies. Now the tears were streaming down her face and she didn't try to disguise them.

'No, please God, no!' Si chanted over and over again, like a prayer for resurrection.

'Shut up!' Chas whirled round on him. 'It's real. They're dead and it's all your fault!'

'I'm sorry. I'm so sorry. I didn't know. Please Chas...' He was crying now. He tried to take her arm.

'Shut up, shut up, shut up!' she screamed at him. 'Leave me alone.' She ran from him.

It was clear the attackers were no longer here. Si wondered how he and Chas hadn't crashed into them as they hurtled back to the village.

Chas entered the hut she shared with Plin. As Si came in behind her he found her crouched over a body, sobbing. Si looked into the staring, dead eyes of Plin, his body sprawled awkwardly on the bed.

'No!' she wailed. ' Not you Plin ... No!'

Si bent down and touched her shoulder. 'Get off me! Get out! Leave us alone!' She thrust him off and lay over the body, howling. Si backed off but didn't leave. He crouched down, buried his face in his hands, and wept. He had no idea how long he cried, but eventually, a voice in his head made him realise that they had to leave. The attackers could come back at any moment.

Chas was still howling. Si tried to prise her from Plin but her grip was fierce. He walked out of the hut and looked around. Suddenly he felt a gripping pain in his stomach and doubled over, retching violently. He walked over to a water butt to splash his face, in an attempt to bring some clarity. He must think what to do next and how to handle Chas. Should he just leave, like she kept telling him to? He couldn't. As he stood there he heard a crack behind him. He turned to see a figure disappearing into

Plin's hut. Without thinking, he sprinted back to it, his knife at the ready. The man was poised over Chas with a gun in his hand.

'No!' Si roared. The man turned.

Si plunged his knife into the man's body, he didn't know how or where. The man doubled up and fell to the ground. Chas was in shock.

'Get up!' Si urged, pulling at her arm. For once, she obeyed. She looked at the lifeless figure of her attacker, then stared in amazement at Si. Grimacing, he drew the knife out of the man's ribs, gulping back another wave of nausea.

'Come on,' he said. 'We have to get out of here.'

She took one last look at Plin, picked up her rucksack and knife, and allowed herself to be led from the hut.

*

She was still sobbing and gulping at the air. Si pulled her along, stumbling as he went. He couldn't think straight. All he could think was that they must get away from here. Chas didn't protest at being dragged along; all the fight had gone out of her. If he let go of her, he knew that she would collapse in a heap, not caring what might happen to her. In his free hand Si gripped his knife. Keeping close to the huts, his eyes scouted around for signs of movement. He knew they were not being very quiet and if someone were nearby he would have to defend them. His heart pumped fast in his chest.

'I don't know which way to go Chas. You've got to help me.'

But Chas just sobbed.

There was no sign of any other living person, so Si had to make a decision. The ring of trees that surrounded the village was about ten metres away. There was no clue as to whether anyone was lurking in the shadows there. They would have to take a chance. With one last check around him, he grabbed Chas's hand and bolted for the trees. She staggered after him.

'Come on!' he urged. She began to find her feet and tearing her arm from his grip, ran faster than him. But once beneath the cover of the trees she sunk down on her knees again, bent double with her head on the ground.

'Chas, they'll come back for us, we've got to get far away from here. I don't have a clue which direction to take. You know this forest, you've got to help.' Si was frantic.

'Plin!' she wailed into the leaves.

Si crouched beside her. Gently, he said, 'He's gone Chas.'

3

Somehow Si managed to persuade Chas to stand, although she was still doubled over. He half carried, half dragged her as far away from the village as possible, still feeling sick himself. Alert for sounds of anyone moving in their vicinity, he kept stopping to listen. Chas was softly whimpering now. She didn't even try to break free from his hold anymore. All her body weight, slight though she was, hung on his arms. After about twenty minutes they reached a large thicket of tightly knit brambles. He pulled out his knife and began to hack a hole in the brambles. Chas stood in a daze.

'Will you please help me?' he shouted at her. 'If we can hack into this we can rest in the thicket for a while and think what to do.'

She stared at him then, as if he had woken her from sleep. He stopped hacking and looked her in the eye. 'Chas, please – help me?'

She grabbed her knife and began to hack furiously. His arms were torn and bleeding; his forearm ached. Was it only a few hours ago that Plin and Temp had removed that tracker? He glanced at Chas who was suddenly behaving like the ranger she was.

It didn't take them long to carve out a small den and crawl into it.

'Pull the brambles back across,' Chas said. 'It has to look like it did before. Did you cover our tracks?'

'No … I,' Si stuttered.

'Useless!'

She climbed back out, cautiously, and pushed the brambles back across the hole. Si heard rustling gradually moving further away as Chas did her best to make them safe. He got out his water bottle and took a long drink, trying to think straight, but there was just a void. Suddenly the brambles began to quiver. He gripped his knife. But it was only Chas.

'There's no sign of anyone. I don't know why they haven't found us. They can't be far away and you didn't exactly make it hard for them to follow us.'

'Difficult, when you're dragging another human being behind you!'

Chas looked away and was silent for a while.

'You should have left me there,' she said quietly.

'I couldn't have done that. They would've killed you too.'

'Good. Then I'd still be with Plin. I'd rather be dead with Plin than alive with you!'

'Cheers.'

There was silence between them.

'Do you believe in an afterlife then?' he asked.

'I don't know. What does it matter? Just leave me alone.'

She huddled into a tight ball and closed her eyes. There was not much room in their hideout so she couldn't move away from him. Si felt incredibly tired. He wanted to be able to work out a plan. Should they move out quickly or was it wise to stay here for a long time in case the attackers came back to search for him? He guessed they must be government militia sent by the Bastille. It must be the real hardcore unit that had done this. He didn't understand why his escape had provoked such a strong response, causing this terrible chain of events. And what should he do now? What about Chas? Maybe she would be safer if he did leave her and go it alone. She could look after herself. In fact, he was probably more of a handicap, and certainly his presence put her in danger. But he couldn't abandon her when he had caused so much pain.

He curled on his side away from Chas; their backs touching. Sleep took him.

When he woke up it was getting dark. Chas was staring at him. He sat up, feeling the stiffness in every joint.

'I'm going back to bury the dead,' she announced.

'That's crazy,' Si said. 'They could be waiting for us.'

'I said, I'm going back, not we. Besides, why would they still be there? They didn't find you – they'd presume you'd moved on. And that's what you're going to do now: alone.'

'But Chas, I couldn't bear it if anything happened to you.'

'What? I'm nothing to you. We only just met. Like you said, this is my own fault. I brought you here. I should have left you out there that night. My village would have been safe ... and Plin would still be alive.'

'It's all because of me that this has happened. How do you think that makes me feel? And you ... I want to ...to protect you: to do something right.'

She almost laughed then, but shook it away.

'Nice speech, Bastille boy! But I'm not going to be your scapegoat. I'm not helping you appease your guilty conscience. I hope it plagues you 'til you die!' She started to push her way out of the brambles. 'I'm going to bury them.'

'I'm coming with you.'

'No! You're not!'

They both stood up outside the hideout. 'I am coming,' Si said.

Chas, hands on hips, pushed her face inches from his. 'Do you really think you can protect me?' Then she did laugh. It bounced off the trees and turned on him like a pack of wild animals. 'You need me, not the other way round!' She started walking back to the village.

'I do. I admit, I'll be better off with your help,' he said, running after her.

'And I'll be better off without you!'

'I did just save your life, have you forgotten that already?'

She marched on without responding. At the edge of the trees she stopped and scanned the village in the fading light. The bigger fires were still burning. The smell of acrid smoke was overwhelming and Si began to cough as he caught up with her. She gave him a cursory glance. There appeared to be no movement so Chas made her way cautiously into the village. He followed her to a shed from which she took two spades. She thrust one at him.

They worked in silence, dragging the bodies to the same place and digging individual graves for them. Chas marked each one with some stones in the shape of the person's initials. Si made no comment; he dug until every part of him ached and his hands were raw. They worked in complete darkness now but for the light of the fires. Even on this cold autumn night the sweat poured down their faces and backs. They were exhausted but Chas was determined to do this and Si equally determined to help her.

The last body was Plin's. As they laid him in the grave, Chas bent to kiss his cheek. There were no tears this time. Si crouched at the foot of the hole. His lips moved as if they wanted to pray but he had no idea what to say. He stood up and prepared to cover the body with earth.

'Wait!' Chas said. She took a leather thong from around her neck. On it hung two silver circles; one within the other. She laid it on Plin's chest. 'You gave this to me when I first came here. Said you'd look after me. You were a good man and a kind father to me. Sleep gently Plin.'

She walked away. Si covered the body, and each clump of dirt that fell was a prayer for forgiveness.

He found Chas in her old hut. They had removed the body of their attacker and she had insisted on throwing it into the woods for the animals to devour. She sat on her bed, sorting through some faded pictures and precious items, by the light of a lamp. Si stood in the doorway watching her for some time. She seemed so absorbed in her memories that he thought she hadn't heard him come in.

'It took some guts to do what you did earlier in here,' she said without looking up.

'I don't know about guts,' he said, sitting down next to her. 'It was sheer panic.'

'It was instinct, Si.' This was the first time she had used his name. 'You did save my life. You didn't need to come back, but you did.'

'You'd have done the same for me.'

She looked at him. 'You're a bit like Plin. You trust too easily. I probably would have left you to your own devices.'

'Thanks!' he said, daring to smile at her.

'You know, they took all the children, but there's someone else missing,' she said.

'I know. Temp's body wasn't there. Was he the only one?'

'Yes.'

'Maybe they took him.'

'Why? It doesn't make sense.' She paused. 'Maybe he betrayed us.'

Si thought for a moment. 'He told me he had once escaped from the Bastille. Did you know that?'

'No, he never said anything.'

'He didn't seem the type to betray you,' said Si.

'There is no 'type,' anyone is capable.' The edge was back in her voice.

Si glanced sideways at her. 'What shall we do now?'

'We might as well stay here. At least we'll have some warmth for what's left of the night. I don't think they're coming back but I can keep watch,' she said.

'We can take turns,' said Si.

'No it's okay. I can't sleep now anyway.' She picked up a blanket and sat down in the doorway.

Si couldn't bring himself to sleep where Plin had been killed. He climbed over into Chas' bed. 'Do you mind?'

She shook her head.

When he woke up, Chas was gone. Light filtered through gaps in the wooden slats. The smell of damp ash and stale smoke hung in the air. Memories of the previous day began to invade the oblivion of sleep. Exhaustion had made it easy for Si to sleep and he felt guilty. Slowly, his mind began to wonder where Chas was. Had she left him? She couldn't have been taken, as they would certainly have taken him too. Warily, he emerged from the hut, subconsciously putting his hand on his knife. The sound of his feet crunching through leaves was amplified in the stillness. Sunshine was breaking through the grey clouds that had rained on the village overnight. It was eerie walking through the place where twenty-four hours ago he had felt such warmth and vibrancy. Now only death hung in the damp morning air.

As he rounded the corner he saw Chas, with her back to him, sitting by a fire she had kindled back to life.

'There's porridge,' she said, not turning round. She was eating from a wooden bowl.

'Thanks.' He took the bowl she handed to him, filling it from the large pot over the fire. It was covered in intricate carved patterns and Si recalled the smiling face of its creator. He could almost see the woman from yesterday doling out the porridge.

'I'll take you to the nearest tech-city, then you're on your own,' she said.

'Oh, okay.'

'You can ask around about whoever it is you're looking for. But keep a low profile. They won't stop looking for you.'

'I know. What will you do?'

'I'll find something. Maybe another commune. But one day I'll hit back at The Rulers somehow for what they've done here.'

'Haven't you had enough trouble?'

'For now. But they can't keep taking people away from me. They should reap some consequences.'

'You could always come with me,' He tried to make it sound like he was offering for her sake, when really he knew his motives were selfish. She could be a massive help to him with her skills and besides, he found himself wanting the company.

'What? And get banged up in the Bastille for helping a prized runaway? No thanks.'

'But you're already helping me.'

'Yeah, well...'

Si couldn't help but grin at her. Her face remained serious.

'I can't leave you here, can I?' she said, as if attempting to justify her actions to herself.

'You could. You threatened to, and told me to leave yesterday,' Si said, still grinning stupidly.

Well, I can't. I wish I could, but I'd just ... feel guilty.'

Si almost laughed then. 'You'd feel guilty! But I'm a complete stranger. I'm nothing to you. Remember? You almost sound like you care!'

She sighed and still her serious face did not crack even the glimmer of a smile. Si frowned. 'Sorry.' He expected her to say something vitriolic and storm off.

Staring into the fire, she said, 'Plin liked you and he died so that you could have the chance to find what you're looking for.'

Si nodded gravely. 'You could help me find it – find them,' he said. 'You could help me not to get caught.' He could see her indecision. 'Maybe you'll have the chance to get back at The Rulers. I'm sure your paths will cross if you stick with me.'

'Hmm. Come on. I'll take you to the tech-city.'

She put out the fire. They collected their things and some extra provisions then Chas made a final visit to the graves. She walked around them slowly, finally crouching at Plin's grave. Si watched her from a distance. She didn't betray any more emotions.

After a while she stood up and walked towards Si. 'I'm ready.'

4

Temp's whole body ached. He groaned and lifted his head, taking in his surroundings for the first time. He was slumped in a chair with his limbs strapped to it. The room was about eight feet square and the only other object was a table, in front of him. The walls were made of steel and there were no windows. There was, however, a panel of mirrored glass in the wall straight in front of him. He looked down at his body. His clothes were torn and blood- stained. His head ached and his left eye wouldn't open properly. He knew where he was, immediately. Memories came flooding back to him. Bile rose in his throat. How had he ended up back in this terrible place? Then, the nightmare of the last few hours played through his mind like a HoloTV programme: The raid on the village, the shooting, the screaming, the bodies, Plin being shot. He saw himself being pushed to his knees and a gun being aimed at his temple. He was about to be executed. Then someone commanded them to stop. Finally - blackness.

The door swung open. The man that entered was no older than thirty. He was tall and rangy with hollow cheeks and piercing blue eyes behind his small round spectacles. Temp knew him instantly. The Commander's uniform was the thing that gave him power and authority. Otherwise he was just a man with a capacity for cruelty.

'Welcome back, Temperance Alliston. Did you enjoy your little sojourn into the outside world?' He perched on the edge of the table, in front of Temp, smiling psychopathically. 'Aren't you glad to be home, safe and sound?' Temp closed his good eye. 'Now, you're going to be very helpful to us aren't you? Shame about your friends in that commune. Lucky I recognised you. I saved your life, Temperance.'

'What do you want?' Temp said, wearily.

'It's quite simple. We want the boy. And you're going to tell us what you know about him.'

'I don't know anything about him. He'd just arrived. You know that.'

'And you helped him remove the tracker. Oh dear, naughty, naughty Temperance. Where was he going?'

'I don't know.'

'Of course not. He doesn't even know himself, does he? But which way was he heading?'

'I don't know.'

'You sent him off, didn't you? North, south, east or west?'

'I don't know.'

The Commander slapped him suddenly across the face.

'Come on, Temperance. Be helpful. Then things won't have to get nasty. You can live here in the Bastille without a care in the world.'

'I'd rather die,' Temp muttered.

'Well, that's a shame. It can be arranged of course, but not until you help us find the boy.' The Commander spoke to the mirrored glass. 'Send in the instruments.' He touched Temp's bruised eyelid curiously with his finger, then withdrew it sharply, with a shiver. Temp didn't flinch. The Commander stood up. 'You will be useful to us Temperance. I'm one hundred percent certain of that.'

He turned and left the room.

Temp knew what was coming. He'd been through it before. The boy must be very important to them. He was glad he didn't know much of any use and hoped he could hold back what he did know.

*

The Commander watched from behind the mirrored glass as the trolley was wheeled in containing various shining metal implements and syringes. 'Tell me when it's finished,' he said to another man. 'Don't kill him. We might be able to use him again. Just get all he knows out of him. I'll be in my quarters.' Taking one last look at Temp and the trolley of torture, he shuddered and left.

A few hours later the official in a white coat stood in the Commander's quarters. 'All we got was that the boy is not alone. He's with a girl of about the same age. She's good at tracking. Lived in the forest for some years. Couldn't get a name.'

A frown passed across the Commander's face. The man hesitated.

'Go on,' said the Commander.

'They headed north east, probably towards York. The village leader had friends there. Hunter doesn't believe his parents are dead. He wants to find them.'

'No, he's never really believed they were dead, despite everything the workhouse tried. Do you think Temperance knows anything else?'

The man shook his head slowly.

'He's not dead is he? I told you ...'

'No sir, he's alive. They transported him to medical.'

'Good.'

'What will you do about the boy's mother, Sir? You said she'd get to see the boy was okay if she told you where the nanomedibot was.'

'I don't give a damn about Kate Hunter. We should have used the boy years ago to crack her. And now he's escaped. That idiot who calls himself the Master of the Bastille would be next in that chair if I had my way!'

'He's got friends in higher places than you, I'm afraid, Sir.'

'Don't you think I know that! That will be all.'

The man retreated. The Commander pressed a button to activate the holophone. An image of the Master of the Bastille sprang to life in front of him.

'Yes, Commander? What can I do for you?' The rotund man, hastily brushed crumbs from his uniform.

The Commander ground his teeth. The man was a fool but he couldn't touch him. 'They're headed north east, towards York. Alert the law-keepers of the city. Get adverts on HTV telling people to look out for Silence Hunter and a girl the same age. And offer a reward; not too large, I don't want people to know quite how important the boy is. Tell the law-keepers we're on our way.'

'Right away, Commander' replied the Master.

The image died. The Commander pressed another button and the doctor appeared in the medical quarters. 'Make sure Temperance Alliston is kept alive. I may need him again.'

'He's unconscious at the moment, Sir.'

'Well don't lose him or your life will be over!'

'Of course, Sir.'

The image cut out and another was summoned. 'Sergeant Knowles, get some men ready and a vehicle, supplies and weapons, we're going to York to bring back the fugitive.'

5

They walked in silence for a long while but this time it was not awkward or hostile. Both Chas and Si were deep in their own thoughts.

Chas was remembering how she had come to the village, a few years ago, alone and afraid. Plin and the others had taken her in, looked after her, taught her many skills. She had learnt to hunt using a bow and arrow and traps. She had learnt many survival skills from Temp. He had taught her and the other youths how to look after themselves and shown them what they could and couldn't eat from the things that grew wild around them. They had learnt how to make shelters and the signs that would lead them to water. No one asked any awkward questions about the past. As Chas grew older she had taught these same skills to the younger children in the camp.

Anger welled up in her as she thought of where Temp might be. And those children– locked up in some filthy workhouse, with no freedom, no life to speak of. She knew what it was like. She just hoped that some of them would one day escape, as she had done.

And then her thoughts turned to Plin. When she had first arrived at the village, Plin had a partner, Empathy. He and Emmy had taken Chas into their home and into their lives.

Emmy was a beautiful, kind person, who suited her birth name. They gradually helped Chas to trust again. However, two years after Chas arrived, Emmy died suddenly. Chas and Plin were devastated but it brought them even closer together. And now, here she was, with only this boy (who had brought her nothing but trouble) for company. She didn't know what to make of him, or his limited story.

*

Si was thinking about his parents and trying to figure out why they had disappeared. And why were the authorities so interested in him?

Both his mother, Kate, and his father, Morgan, had been eminent scientists working in the field of nanotechnology. They had been on the verge of an exciting new discovery before they supposedly died in an 'accidental' fire at the Lab. Si was sure that his parents had been on to something that threatened The Rulers' dominance.

*

Neither Si nor Chas had been much aware of their surroundings. Chas was on autopilot. Suddenly a road appeared in front of them, breaking abruptly into their thoughts. It was full of pot-holes. Old fashioned cars were scarce, because oil was too expensive, and only the major roads were well maintained and magnetised for the new magnetic cars. Si and Chas emerged from the foliage onto a verge. This road was deserted. Without hesitation Chas turned to the left and began walking beside the road, keeping near to the edge of the trees.

'Which city are we headed for?' Si asked.

'Do you really have no idea where we are?'

'Not really,' he said, shrugging his shoulders. 'Geography wasn't my strong point at school. I know we're somewhere in Yorkshire because everyone knows the Bastille is on the Moors, but apart from that ...'

Chas sighed. 'We're heading for York, it's the nearest tech-city. Plin had a contact there. I met her a few times when we were trading.'

'I went to York a few times with my parents. My dad was from there so we used to visit his mum. He liked to show me all the stuff about the Romans, Vikings, Tudors and all that.'

Chas looked quizzically at him. 'Sounds boring to me. I didn't really do school. I learnt the basics from Plin and Emm...' She stopped. 'So what happened to your parents? They just disappeared?'

'They were supposedly killed in an accident.'

'You don't believe it.'

'Not anymore. Too much has happened. They asked me too many questions about them at the Bastille.'

'So that's who you're looking for?'

'Well done, Sherlock.'

'Eh?'

'Never mind. Yes. I'm looking for my parents.'

'This contact in York is called Meg. She's quirky but she knows lots of people. She might know something.'

*

As they turned a corner in the road, someone was coming towards them. They jumped into the undergrowth and laid low. The man was whistling as he pushed a wooden wheelbarrow full

43

of fruit and vegetables down the road. Chas suddenly jumped out, startling Si – and the man.

'Can we have some fruit and veg?'

'Oh my giddy god-fearing gooseberries! You nearly give me 'eart-attack girl! What you doing 'iding in t' bushes there?'

'None of your business. Just hungry. I've got money or I can trade?'

The man looked over to where Chas had leapt from the bushes. 'And will your friend be wantin' some too?'

Si emerged, slowly. Chas tutted at him. 'Can't you keep out of sight! Even this old guy spotted you!'

' 'Ere less of the old! I'm only twenty three!' He chuckled to himself.

'So can we have some food?'

'Aye. Help y'self.'

'Your face looks familiar lad. 'Ave ah seen you before?'

'I doubt it,' said Si.

'Eeh I'm sure I 'ave,' he said, scratching his stubbled chin. 'No I can't remember. But it'll come back to me, always does.'

Chas gave the man some coins. 'Thanks,' she said. 'We'd better get going. Like to get to the city by nightfall.'

'Aye that's right, lass. Bit dangerous out here after dark.' The man picked up his barrow and plodded on, resuming his whistling.

'Come on,' Chas said impatiently. 'You'll be back in the Bastille by tomorrow if you're not careful. They must have your face everywhere by now.'

'You didn't tell me to stay hidden,' Si protested.

'No, because I thought you had a brain in there,' she said, prodding him in the temples. 'All that education – wasted if you've no common sense!'

Si laughed. 'You're right. I am a complete dork.'

Chas looked at him in bewilderment. 'A what?'

'Aha there's a new word for you! See, an education does pay off.'

Chas shook her head. 'Idiot!'

*

The road was mainly deserted for the rest of the journey. People didn't tend to travel much these days because it was difficult and dangerous. Magnetic cars were only for the rich. Magnetised public transport was limited and unreliable. The common people had reverted to walking and using horses and carts. The internet provided most things people needed. However, despite this virtual world-wide connection, the real world had become a much more local place. Foreign travel was now so expensive that only the elite could afford it. Cutting the Carbon Footprint had become a global obsession. Most people contented themselves with watching the world on HTV.

A wagon and a few people on foot passed them but Si kept his head down and they passed unnoticed. They stopped at one point to eat.

'Do you think we'll make York before it gets dark?' Si asked. He looked at his watch. It was 3.30 in the afternoon. The sun was low in the sky and the air was starting to feel damp.

'I don't know, but we should keep going. I think I can remember the place where Meg lived, although York is a bit of a maze of streets. It'll be safer to be inside the city walls than out here though.'

The ancient walls of York still existed but The Rulers had

surrounded all their tech-cities with high voltage walls – to protect them from outsiders. At night the gates were locked and the city became yet another prison – no one in, no one out.

'So who was Emmy? You started to talk about her earlier, and then you changed the subject,' Si said.

Chas shook her head. 'None of your business.'

'True, but I'm nosy as well as an idiot.'

Chas rolled her eyes at him, then sighed. 'She was Plin's partner. They took care of me; taught me stuff.' She found herself telling him more about them.

'You really loved them, didn't you?'

'I dunno. Love sucks! You just get hurt, much worse than any physical pain. I can cope with that. I once got an arrow through my shoulder,' she pulled back her top to reveal a scar. 'It hurt like crazy but it doesn't bother me now.'

He glanced across at her. They were still walking. She didn't reply, just chewed her lip. 'Dare I ask about your real parents? Do you have any family? How come you ended up at the village?'

'You ask too many questions,' she said.

'Fair enough,' He didn't want to push her too far. 'My parents are Kate and Morgan Hunter. 'Eminent Scientists.' That's how they were always described.'

Chas screwed up her face. Si laughed and shook his head.

'I sometimes went into the Lab with them. I used to wear these ridiculous goggles that were way too big and a white lab coat they'd had made for me.' Chas looked at him. He was smiling as he remembered.

'You don't need to tell me about your people,' she said.

'I want to: Unless it makes you uncomfortable.'

'No it's not that. Look, it's getting dark. We're not going to get to York in time. We should make camp. Let's head away from the road and find somewhere half decent.'

They were now walking besides farmland. Hedges surrounded the fields. They had passed one or two isolated farm-houses. Chas led the way over a hedge and through fields of sheep who paid them no attention. They must have walked for another mile in the opposite direction to the road when they came across a dilapidated barn. There was just one other building in sight but it was a long way off. The barn had a patchy wooden roof left and some empty window frames high up in the walls. A broken wooden door was propped against the only doorway. They pulled it aside and went in. Outside, the light was almost gone so their eyes didn't need long to adjust to the dark interior. It stank of animal faeces and stagnant water. There was dirty straw on the ground and puddles where rain had penetrated the roof. They found the driest corner and made themselves as comfortable as possible. It was getting much colder so they put on a few extra items of clothing from their packs.

'I'll make a fire,' said Chas. 'Come on let's find some wood.'

They hunted around outside, by torchlight, and soon Chas had a satisfactory fire going, around which they huddled, gratefully. They ate, and drank the last of their water.

'So, how did they supposedly die?' Chas asked as they watched the flames.

It took Si a moment to realise that she was picking up their conversation from the road. He told her about the accident at the Lab.

'A couple of Mum and Dad's friends turned up at my school. It was break-time so we were all hanging around outside. They kind of loitered by the wire fence trying to get my attention.

When I went over they told me I was in danger and needed to come with them now. I trusted them so I slipped out of the school gates. They broke the news to me that Mum and Dad had been killed in an accident at the Lab, but that the circumstances were suspicious. I went to stay with them.' Si stopped; inhaling deeply. Chas was watching him intently, but she didn't say anything.

'There was no funeral. The official story was that they had been incinerated in the fire. There was this grand memorial service to 'honour' them for their 'groundbreaking achievements.' When I didn't attend they came looking for me. Eventually, they found me, arrested Dan and Elle for abduction and put me in a workhouse, where they could 'supervise my education.' But I wasn't allowed to talk about my parents. If I did I was punished and if I didn't study hard enough I was punished.'

Chas kicked at the dirty straw. Her face was screwed up and shadows, from the flickering light, danced manically across it.

'You've been there, done that, haven't you?' Si said.

She nodded.

'Workhouse?'

She nodded again.

'Did they hurt you?'

Chas squeezed her lips together tightly, then said. 'They worked us really hard. There was no learning for the likes of us. We were the 'scum': the out of control kids. We skivvied for the rich. They beat us to keep us submissive. I got extra beatings every time I tried to run away, but I never gave up and one day I managed it.'

'Did they come after you?'

'Dunno. But I'm not important like you. They wouldn't have looked too hard. I guess they thought I'd end up dead somewhere and that would be one less piece of dirt to worry about.' She was staring into the fire, her eyes hard and angry.

Si wanted to know more. How had she ended up in a workhouse? Where were her parents? Instead he let the silence swallow up the last of their words.

6

The fire hissed and spat at them. Chas poked it with a branch and sparks attacked her fingers. She didn't flinch but threw the last of the sticks and branches on top of the flames.

As they watched the fire, suddenly they heard heavy footsteps outside in the dark. There was a scraping sound at the door. Chas sprang up, her knife appearing in her hand like a magic trick. Si scrabbled to his feet and fumbled for his knife. A light beam flicked under the door and they could hear men's voices. The door was pulled open and three thickset men entered; one of them armed with a handgun. Handcuffed to another man was a boy. The man with the gun flashed his torch across Chas and Si.

'What do you want?' Chas demanded.

'Throw your weapons on the floor and kick them over here or I'll shoot you both before you can move,' he said.

Si looked at Chas. She remained as she was, holding out her knife ready to attack.

'Didn't you hear me?'

'He would,' said the man, handcuffed to the boy. 'You just ask this boy 'ere.' He pulled the boy forward. 'Tell 'em.'

The boy cowered. 'They killed my brother yesterday. He shot him straight out 'cos he resisted. You should do what he says.'

The man yanked him back.

Si dropped his knife and kicked it across the barn. Chas still didn't move. 'Chas!' he urged. 'Just do it!'

'Listen to him, he's obviously much smarter than you. You've got five seconds or I'll shoot him.' The man trained his gun on Si. 'Five... four...'

The boy cried out, trying to pull forward 'Please! He will do it and he won't miss!'

'Three...two...'

Chas flung the knife, purposefully, at the men, who had to dive apart to avoid it. It stuck in the barn wall, just behind the head of the ring leader.

'Bitch!'

The men moved forward, pulling the boy with them, and pushed Si and Chas roughly to the ground. Chas struggled to get up but was slapped back to the floor. Si struggled with one man.

'Don't be a fool, boy.' The man held a knife to Si's chin.

The gun man was holding Chas. She struggled ineffectually. 'Cuff her: tight!' he said. Then he threw some cuffs to knife man. 'And him.'

With their hands cuffed and feet tied they were roped together, back to back with the boy, then dumped in a draughty corner of the barn.

The men sat around the dwindling fire. They pulled bottles of beer from their packs. 'Well at least we'll have a bit of warmth tonight, eh,' one of them said, holding out his hands to the fire. 'Cheers!' He held up his bottle to Si and Chas, laughing. Chas spat in his direction.

'Aye: Bit of a bonus coming across this place tonight: Three to 'sell instead of one. That'll be good money,' said another man.

'They're going to sell us?' Si whispered. 'Who to?'

'You have led a sheltered life!' Chas said. 'They're slave traders. Rich people pay good money for slaves on the black market. Totally illegal but The Rulers turn a blind eye. You're scum now Si, like me, and this boy. What's your name?'

'Benevolence,' the boy whispered. He was small and thin; pale-skinned, with black hair and frightened black eyes. His clothes were tattered and makeshift. Everything about him was dirty. 'I was living with my brother in a shack not far from here. They ambushed us when we were out poaching pheasants. We thought it was game -keepers. Would've been better off if it had been. A few pellets in the backside is all we usually get from them. My brother wouldn't give in. He knew what they wanted us for. I kept telling him to back down but he was wild. Then Rory (the one with the gun), he just shot him. Didn't even give him a warning.' Ben started to sniffle.

The men were laughing and getting drunk around the fire.

'We'll think of a way to escape,' Si said. Then he added. 'I'm sorry about your brother. How old are you?'

'Ten.'

'Where are your parents?' Si asked.

'Dead. We'd been sent to the workhouse. Dad brought us to the tech-city to find work, but it didn't last long. We got rounded up into a workhouse. Within a few weeks of being there my parents got ill and died. Me and my brother had been separated from them. A wave of the New Plague was sweeping through the place. They were moving all the children out to another workhouse and that's when me and my brother escaped. It was a hell-hole that place. We said we'd rather die of starvation than live there.' He sniffled. 'And now he's dead too. I wish I was.'

'Don't say that,' Si said.

'Would be better than what's going to happen to us now.'

'He's right,' Chas said. 'We might as well be dead than slaves to some rich low-life.'

'What kind of talk is that?' Si said, anger brewing in his stomach. 'What about some fighting talk? I can't believe you're resigning yourself to this.'

'I'm not! I'm just saying...'

Si hissed in her ear. 'Well don't say it! We have to give this kid some hope.'

The boy's back was heaving against theirs. 'I can still hear you,' he said. 'I don't believe in hope any more. Everything just goes wrong.'

'No! You have to keep hoping – always. And you have to fight against the bad stuff. We will get out of this.'

Chas laughed her harsh laugh. 'You mean I'll get us out of this, don't you Si?'

'No, actually. We'll do it together. Ditch the arrogance, Chas!'

She didn't reply.

'Ben, do you believe me?' Si said.

'I want to.'

'Good. Keep it that way. Don't give up – ever!'

Chas sulked. Si was annoyed with himself for flaring up. She had been starting to open up to him and now he'd blown it.

'We do need you, Chas,' he said gently.

She turned her head to look at him. Then rolled her eyes and turned away.

*

Across the barn the fire was barely glowing and the men were settling down to sleep. They produced blankets from their pack. Rory, the leader, brought one over to Si, Chas and Ben. He pulled it round them and tied it in a knot.

'Don't want you freezing to death. You're valuable goods.' He bent down so he was face to face with Ben. Ben pulled back from his rank breath. 'See, I'm all heart, I am.' He laughed and went back to his gang.

'He's a monster,' Ben muttered.

'He won't be so smug when we escape and he's left with nothing,' said Si.

'Just go to sleep,' Chas said.

They leant against each other as best they could and slept fitfully. Chas was the most wakeful. Her instincts told her to stay vigilant, but the men were completely out of it, snoring their way through the dark hours. She was aware of Si twitching and jerking in his sleep. He kept muttering words that were hard to make out. And once he shouted, 'Get off me!' Chas nudged him, fearing he would wake the gang, but they didn't stir. Ben, however, did.

'What's up? Why's he shouting?'

'I don't know. Bad dream? Try and get back to sleep. '

*

Si was back in the Bastille, strapped to a medical trolley. He was ten years old and wearing the lab coat and the over-sized goggles his parents had given him. A man's face loomed over his, bulging like an image in a convex mirror.

'Tell us what they did with it,' the man demanded.

'I don't know what you're talking about.'

'We know you were there. You know where they hid it.'

'I don't. Who are you?'

The face swam in and out of view. The room spun and Si felt sick. He tried to move his limbs. Then his mother's voice whispered in his ear. 'You know nothing Si. We're proud of you. We love you.'

Then Bulging Face was back with a larger-than-life syringe.

'Get off me!' Si shouted, thrashing to escape.

'We need to find it. We're going in.'

The needle grew so large it filled Si's vision. His body convulsed. He screamed but no sound came.

*

Chas was shaking him. 'Si, wake up.'

He came round to find light splintering through cracks in the barn walls as dawn emerged.

'Are you okay? You've been acting all weird.'

Despite the cold, sweat was running down Si's forehead into his eyes. He tried to blink it away. 'I'm okay. Just a nightmare.'

'You were shouting and thrashing about.'

'Sorry. Did I frighten Ben?'

'No!' came the boy's voice. 'I'm not scared of you. At least you didn't wake the living dead over there.'

This made Si laugh. 'Well, we need to try and get away from those zombies.'

He tried pulling his hands out of the ropes but they wouldn't budge.

'Try harder, Mr. 'Don't worry we'll escape!' There's no getting out of this. Our knives are in our packs over there.'

'Can't you think of something?'

'I'm working on it, but nothing's going to happen 'til we're on the move. More chance of making a run for it then.'

Rory and his gang were stirring. There was a lot of groaning and swearing. One by one they went outside to relieve themselves.

'Let's get going. Got to get the goods tidied up in time for the Trading Floor tonight,' said Rory. He shuffled over to his captives. 'Mack, get over here. I'll take 'em one by one for a piss.' He untied them as Mack trained the gun on them. 'Don't try anything. Especially you,' he said, pulling Chas to her feet.

'You're not watching me take a leak,' she said.

'I'm not letting you out of my sight! So it's up to you!'

Chas was led out of the barn. Emerging into the cold light she looked around for an escape route, but the countryside was so open here, they wouldn't stand a chance. And what about that boy? How fast could he run? He was involved now and they couldn't leave him with these thugs.

The men donned official looking uniforms with ID cards to make them look like law-keepers. This was their passage through the tech-city gates with their prisoners. By lunchtime they were almost there. The Minster towered majestically above the tech-walls, its grand spires and turrets a tribute to the architectural craftsmanship of centuries past. Si remembered his parents bringing him here many times to marvel at everything this building represented. His father had loved to tell him of the men and women through the ages who had kept the faith alive under difficult circumstances. His parents had been faithful to the Way, despite all religion being outlawed as subversive since 2043. But their faith had driven them in their work. He knew they were trying to achieve something that would help the poorest people, but they had never told him exactly how.

As they approached the gates, Chas whispered,' Keep your head down. There'll be a reward out for you by now and the guards will know what you look like.'

Si hunched his shoulders and tried not to look dubious.

'Keep your mouths shut!' ordered Rory, as they approached the guards.

'State your business,' demanded a guard.

'Delivery of delinquents to the Master of Law,' said Rory.

'IDs?'

The men showed their cards to the guard, who scanned them in his machine. He nodded. 'Do these have IDs?'

'None of them. Workhouse runaways.'

The guard eyed them. Ben looked pleadingly at him but it made no impression. Chas kept her mouth shut. 'What's your name?' he said to Si. 'Have I come across you before?'

Suddenly Si began to shake and cough violently. His body jerked as though electric shocks were passing through it: So much so that the man he was handcuffed to stumbled and nearly fell.

'What the...'

'He's epileptic,' Chas said. 'You'd better get him inside. He's afraid of busy places. That's what's set him off - seeing the city.'

Si kept up the pretence of having a fit. Ben looked on, horrified. Two of the thugs pinned Si's arms to his side.

'Go on, get through. Hurry up.' They were inside the city. Si let his body relax and fall limply against his captors.

'That's all we need - a duff one.'

'It doesn't happen very often,' said Chas.

'I hope not, or we'll have to dispose of him. Pick him up, Mack. Let's get to The Tavern. Suzy should have our rooms ready.'

They walked through the districts of squalid high-rise flats where the poorest in the city lived. Then there were a few high-tech buildings housing various industries and leisure facilities. Si feigned coming round and Mack put him on his feet.

'Looks like he can walk now,' said one of the men.

'About time too. My back's killing me,' said the other.

'Can I have some water?' Si asked.

'Give him a swig of yours,' Rory indicated to Mack.

Si took a drink and they began to walk again. They passed through the ancient inner walls of York to the very heart of the city. The Tudor buildings leaned together like old men playing chess. Many of the streets were still cobbled and there was a 20th century market, selling flowers and produce, which had become more popular since the beginning of the new regime. The streets were crowded and there was a lot of jostling.

'Very creative at the gate,' Chas said, as she brushed against Si. 'I'm impressed.'

Si smiled.

7

When they arrived at The Tavern the landlady greeted the thugs like honoured guests. ' Rory! Boys. Good to see you. It's been a while.'

Rory kissed her full on the lips. 'Suzy, you old tart, the pleasure is always entirely mine!'

'That's what he thinks!' she said in a stage whisper to the rest of them.

The men laughed.

'I'll have tankards of ale waiting for you boys when you've got these upstairs.' She leaned forward and ruffled Ben's hair. He jerked away from her. 'Ah bless'im.' She looked at Chas and Si. 'Nice lookin' couple. You might do well to package them together.'

'They need a bit of polish,' said Rory.

'Don't worry, I'll have them lookin' grand, you'll see. Usual rooms boys?'

Upstairs, the room was clean but shabby. The wallpaper was covered in large garish flowers, peeling in places. There was a single bed, a dresser and a worn armchair. A small bathroom led off the main room. Si, Chas and Ben were un-cuffed for the first time.

'Suzy will be up shortly to clean you up ready for sale,' Rory said. As the men left the room, one of them took an old-fashioned key out of the key-hole and locked the door.

Ben went to the window. 'It's a long way down.' Even so, he tried rattling it. It had no lock but it was stuck fast. Si and Chas slumped on the bed.

'This is hopeless,' sighed Ben coming to join them.

'Didn't I tell you not to give up?' Si said.

'Si's right,' Chas admitted, reluctantly. 'We have to keep looking for opportunities to escape.'

Just then the door was unlocked and Suzy came in carrying a tray. She was accompanied by two of the thugs, who stood in the doorway.

'Here you are my lovelies. Get this down your necks. You'll need some energy for tonight.' She put the tray on the dresser and left, locking the door behind her. There were three bowls of steaming soup and crusty bread.

'What do you know about these slave markets?' Si asked Chas, as they ate hungrily.

'Not much. I met some kids once who were slaves to some of the rich people I skivvied for when I was in the workhouse. They were beaten and under-nourished. The girl was used for more than just chores! They tried to run but there was an electric fence around the property; dogs too.'

'I don't want that to happen to me,' said Ben. 'We've got to get out of here.' He rattled the window again.

Chas came over. 'Even if you could get it open, it's too far to jump and there's no way of climbing down.'

Si looked out. He tried the window. It was stuck. 'Help me, maybe if we all tried together ...'

'Why? Are you planning on flying?' said Chas.

Si gave her a dirty look.

'You don't understand,' she said. 'You have to wait for the right moment and that hasn't come yet.'

'So when will it come, Oh mighty Oracle?' said Si. 'We're running out of time.'

'You're wasting your energy.' She lay down on the bed and closed her eyes.

Si and Ben worked on the window but it wouldn't budge. Ben gave up first, throwing himself into a corner of the room. Eventually, Si admitted defeat, slamming his fists against the window pane. He waited for an 'I told you so!' from Chas, but she never opened her eyes. In fact, the way she was breathing indicated that she was asleep.

'What are we going to do now?' groaned Ben. Despite his talk of not giving up hope, Si felt useless. He shook his head.

At that moment the key turned in the lock. Chas sat bolt upright, her hand automatically reaching for a weapon that was no longer there. Suzy came in, carrying a bundle of clothes, followed by Mack, also carrying clothes.

'Okay my lovelies. Let's get this show on the road. You boys – out please. Mack here will escort you to the other room. I'm working on this pretty lady.'

Mack hustled them out of the door. Si tried a scuffle but Mack was far stronger than him. Ben looked back towards Chas.

'Go on,' she said, reassuringly.

Suzy ran a bath in the next room. 'You haven't had one of these in a long while, by the looks of you. You'll enjoy this. I've got bubbles and smellies, lotions and potions.' She chuckled as she came back into the bedroom. 'You're a healthy looking lass. You'll scrub up nicely. Now, get that filthy stuff off and get into that lovely hot water.'

Suzy was middle-aged. Her auburn hair was beautifully styled and looked a little incongruous combined with the garish make up and outlandish clothes. She had a constant smile plastered on her face.

'Well come on love, hurry up about it,' she said, as Chas sat on the bed and scowled at her.

'Why are you doing this? Is it money, sex, what?'

'Personal questions! And none of your business I might add. Now, it goes like this: you get undressed and get in that bath like a good girl or you do it for Rory. Oh, he'd enjoy that he would!' She laughed. 'But you...might not. Now come on, its not like I'm asking you to do anything nasty is it?' Suzy stood with her hands on her hips, still smiling, like a mother chiding her over a small disobedience. Chas still refused to get up. 'Oh dear, you are a stubborn one. Not attractive in a lady you know. I'll just pop and get Rory then, if that's what you want.'

Chas knew she was beaten. 'Okay, I'm doing it.' She went into the bathroom and shut the door.

'There's a good girl. But no shutting doors. I need to make sure you scrub up nicely.'

Self-consciously, Chas undressed behind the door. She had not had a bath for as long as she could remember. In the village they had a shower system using rain water and often she would swim in the river. As she lay down in the hot foamy water, she was shocked to find that her tense body automatically relaxed. The water enveloped her, and she closed her eyes, enjoying the feeling. She remembered her mother playing with her in the bath when she was little: blowing bubbles at her, playing with plastic ducks and boats and gently pouring the water over her head to wash her long blond hair. She was woken abruptly from her reverie by Suzy's hands moving over her body with a bar of soap.

'Hey!' Chas cried, jerking away and pushing Suzy's hands out of the water.

'Oh don't be modest. I know what you've got down there.'

'I'll do it myself!' Chas said. 'Just leave all the stuff you want me to use.'

'Okay love,' Suzy said, retreating to the door. 'But make sure you do a thorough job, or Rory won't be pleased!'

When Chas had bathed and washed her hair she had to admit that it felt good. She emerged from the bathroom wearing a towel round her body and one round her hair.

'I bet you feel better, don't you?' said Suzy.

Chas stared coldly back.

'Right. What to put you in? You're slim, a bit muscled for a girl, but I'm sure that will come in handy. New owners like a bit of glamour though. How about this?' She held a turquoise, strapless mini-dress against Chas' figure. 'Try it on then.'

Chas folded her arms.

'Okay, I'll turn away.'

Knowing she didn't have much choice, Chas slipped into the dress. The material was silky against her skin but it felt alien. She wanted her old combat trousers back and most of all, her knife. She struggled to do up the zip.

'Ah that's it!' Suzy cried. 'Bit of make up, glamorous hairstyle and you'll be perfect.'

Chas groaned inwardly. When Suzy had finished, Chas looked in the mirror, horrified by what she saw. Who was that person? Suzy had made her look like a younger version of herself: bright red lips and cheeks streaked with too much blusher. Her eyes had been matched to the dress and her hair was piled up with a few wispy ringlets framing her face.

'It's disgusting!' she snarled.

'Thanks for the compliment,' Suzy replied, still smiling.

'What's the point of all this? They just want us to do their dirty work.' 'Haven't you heard of 'eye candy? Men like something nice to look at. If you're lucky it might save you from the worst jobs. He won't want to ruin you.'

'I look hideous.'

'Nonsense! This is what they like. Now, stop whining. Enjoy being glamorous!' Suzy's permanent grin slipped momentarily. 'I'm off to see to those boys. Don't you go changing anything. You don't want to mess with Rory, believe me.' Chas saw the truth of this in Suzy's eyes.

In the other room Si and Ben waited, anxiously, wondering what was happening to Chas. Ben sat on the bed, hugging his knees. Sitting down next to him Si tried to think of something to say.

'You know, me and Chas are kind of in the same boat as you: Alone. Neither of us have had parents for years now, so we know how you're feeling. We can look after each other like a family now. Me and Chas can be like your big brother and sister.'

'Is she your sister?'

'No. We only met a few days ago. Bit of a long story. I'm looking for my parents. The Rulers kidnapped them, and Chas... well, she's helped me ...'

'She's smart – and brave too.'

'Yeah, she is,' Si agreed.

'You're not going to find them now. We're trapped. We'll

probably get split up. I'll never see you again after tonight.'

Si closed his eyes. He wanted to roar. What could he say now? 'Let's just keep our hopes up.' Then he did something that he hadn't done for a long time. He prayed silently.

*

'Well now, two fine young men to work on,' said Suzy, bustling through the door.

She enjoyed this part in her alliance with Rory. It made her feel like a fashion guru, especially when she got to watch the finished product on the catwalk tonight. She tried not to think of what happened to them when they were sold. She was well practiced in the art of self-deceit.

Si wondered if they could overpower her, grab the key and make a run for it. He watched closely as she put the key down her protruding cleavage. He didn't fancy going down there but these were desperate times!

'Can't take your eyes of me, eh? I know. Most men find me irresistible.' She threw back her head in uproarious laughter. Si saw his opportunity and braced himself to 'go in.' He jumped up from the bed and pounced.

'Hey! What you playing at?'

He knocked her to the floor. Ben was at his side in an instant. 'Get off me!' She screamed. 'You'll regret this.'

Ben put his hand over her mouth, but she bit his fingers and he withdrew them sharply. As Si fumbled for the key, the door burst open. Two of the gang instantly wrestled Si and Ben off Suzy and pinned them on the floor. One of them kicked Si in the stomach, knocking the air out of him. Ben cowered in a ball awaiting his turn.

'Idiots!' said one of the men, pulling out a gun.

'You all right Suzy?' asked the other, helping her up.

'Oh … yes, I'm fine,' she blustered, smoothing down her clothes and checking her hair. 'I think the boy was feeling amorous and got carried away!' A less certain smile appeared back on her face. 'But you'd better have this,' she said, reaching into her bosom and pulling out the key. 'It nearly got lost forever down there in all the excitement.'

'You keep your hands off Suzy, boy. Lay one more grubby little finger on her and you'll be sorry cos she's Rory's property. Comprendee? We'll be right outside the door. ' He gave Si another kick and they left the room.

Si lay groaning on the floor.

'Are you okay?' Ben asked, shuffling towards him.

Suzy moved towards Si. 'Oh dear! Those thugs! They've probably ruined the merchandise now. Here, let's get a look at you. Hope they haven't damaged your face.'

She and Ben pulled Si off the floor. He sat, doubled up, on the bed gasping for air. 'Get him some water from the bathroom,' she said to Ben. 'Now, no more of your shinanigans. I know what you were after, but they've got it now, so just cooperate. You don't have much choice. That's how it goes in this life.' Si raised his head to look at her and, for a moment, saw empathy.

In a flash she switched back to 'jolly' Suzy. 'I have two clean tuxedos. Should fit,' she said, looking Ben up and down, doubtfully. 'First though, you need baths.' She ran the water, pouring in plenty of bubble bath. 'Who's the cleanest? You I think, 'she said, indicating Si. 'You get in first, then the little 'un.'

He shuffled into the bathroom and tried to shut the door.

'No doors shut, but I won't look, I promise,' Suzy grinned, a twinkle in her eye.

Si turned away from her. He didn't really care. As Chas had unexpectedly relished the warm clean water, so did he. In the Bastille there were no baths only communal showers. Two minutes to get washed and out. He closed his eyes, feeling a stupid failure. Most of all he wanted to prove to Chas that he could get them out of this.

After Si and Ben had bathed, Suzy dressed them in the tuxedos. They felt awkward and uncomfortable. Their hair was combed and some foundation was smeared across their faces, which Ben found most alarming. He squirmed as Suzy tried to rub it in.

'Don't fuss lad. This is a big event. It's like being on HTV - almost!'

She stood them side-by-side. 'Yes. You look grand. You'd put any model to shame,' she said to Si, giving him a wink. 'You'll have to wait 'til tonight to see your friend. What a treat she looks.'

She banged on the door and was let out by one of the men, who wolf-whistled the boys before locking the door.

8

As Chas, Si and Ben waited, the Commander and his men pulled up at the city gates.

'ID, Sir,' said the guard.

The Commander rolled his eyes. 'Imbecile! You know who I am. Why do we have to go through this every time I enter a city? It's ridiculous.'

'With respect, Sir, these are your orders. No one enters without proper checks.'

'Yes, yes,' the Commander sighed. 'Here.' He and all his men handed over their devices to be scanned for ID. 'Have you had the holo-images of the fugitive we're pursuing?'

'Yes Sir, they came through this afternoon.'

'There's a girl with him too. Blond, about sixteen. Are all the gates alerted?'

'Of course, sir.'

Inside the city they made their way to the City Law-keeper's office where the Commander briefed his men and the local law-keepers. The obsequious Master of Law hung on the Commander's every word, emphatically repeating his orders to his men.

'We'll use this as a base. Make sure those HTV images are being broadcast; then get your men out on the streets. Report back to me any sightings. Check CCTV. They may be here already. Those ignorant gate guards pretend to be so vigilant, but I know how lax they can be.'

*

As night fell, Rory and Suzy prepared to transport their goods to the Trading floor. Everyone was dressed in evening wear. Si and Ben were brought down into the Tavern first, then Suzy and Chas made their entrance. Si's eyes widened as Chas tottered down the stairs in stilettos, gripping Suzy's arm for dear life. Suzy had wrapped a velvet shawl around her bare shoulders but her flabby upper arms still showed.

'You look different,' Si said.

'State the obvious, why don't you!'

'You look really pretty,' Ben added.

'I hate this,' she said, scowling.

'Quiet!' Rory ordered. 'Suzy, handcuff the kid to yourself. I'll take the girl and Mack will take the boy.' Each of them was secured to a captor.

Suzy had a horse and carriage into which Si, Chas and Ben were bundled, their handcuffs transferred to metal poles running from roof to floor in the carriage. Incongruously, inside the run-down looking vehicle there were plush velvet seats. Suzy climbed in beside them and Rory took the reigns up front. Two of his thugs stood on the back of the carriage.

'Now this is proper Cinderella,' Suzy said, grinning.

'Oh yeah! Prince Charming is waiting just around the corner!' said Chas.

'Ah don't be like that. Just enjoy the moment, that's what I always do when I get the chance.'

'Suzy," Si said. 'You know what's going to happen to us tonight.

Don't you care?'

'No more talk of that, boy. Enjoy the moment, that's what I say.'

'Shut up in there!' Rory shouted.

Suzy settled back into her seat and closed her eyes. Si wanted to shake her. Chas leaned back and stared out of the window. She had no knife, and no protection in this stupid outfit and ridiculous shoes. She could barely walk in them, let alone run anywhere. Ben looked from Si to Chas. Si tried to mouth that it would be all right, but he had no idea how to make it all right. Ben, sitting next to Chas, slid his hand into hers. For a moment she was startled. Then she remembered what this gesture meant and she squeezed his hand reassuringly.

The Trading Floor was a massive warehouse on the outskirts of the city. The tech-walls were metres away from it. Outside, all was dark; the place looked deserted. As Rory pulled their horse to a stop, another horse and cart drew up. Rory jumped down, grabbed the other man's hand and they slapped each other vigorously on the back.

'Dixie! Good to see you. What you got tonight?'

'Just a couple of lads. Bit scrawny, but aren't they all? Might get a decent price if I barter. You?'

'Mine are good. Young boy and two teens – one of them a good-looking girl. I expect to get a good price for them. Let's get 'em inside. Mack, you take the carriage.'

Chas, Si and Ben climbed out and the handcuffs were removed. The street lights in this part of town were dim. Several, Si noticed, had been broken near the warehouse.

'Don't try anything,' Rory said. 'You wouldn't stand a chance.'

The entrance hall to the warehouse was also dimly lit, but as they turned the corner and entered through some double swing doors bright lights stung their eyes. The place was suddenly buzzing with people and loud music. In the middle of an arena was a catwalk with seats either side of it. Wealthy people were standing around drinking champagne and being served canapés by young, scantily clad girls.

'Oh it's so exciting here.' Suzy squeezed Chas' arm in a girly sort of way. Chas immediately pulled away, but Suzy was too caught up in the atmosphere to notice. A young man with two assistants approached them. He wore heavy make-up and a flamboyant red and silver suit. His black and purple hair was gelled up like a skate ramp on one side of his head.

'Oh these are lovely darling,' he said, kissing Suzy on both cheeks.

'Oh thank you, Conscience, you're too kind,' Suzy replied, feigning modesty.

'I'll take them now. You go and make yourselves comfortable, for the show.' Chas, Si and Ben were handed over. 'Rory.' He nodded briefly, with a hint of distain in Rory's direction.

Rory curled his lip at him and leaned in towards his 'goods.' Grabbing Si and Chas roughly by the arms, he hissed, 'Anyone who tries to run gets shot. Bouncers on every entrance. Understand?'

They nodded.

'And Con, I want the teens packaged together. I think I'll get best price for them as a pair. They look good together.' The director of the show nodded without looking back at Rory.

'What about me?' Ben said.

'Shut it, runt!'

A lighter touch took hold of them and escorted them to a

backstage holding area. More make-up, perfume and deodorants were applied profusely.

'Haven't we got enough on already?' protested Si, coughing through the mists of spray.

'Hush, hush. It's all necessary,' fussed the assistant. A band was attached to each of their wrists. It stated the owner of the goods and how much the starting bid should be. On Chas and Si's band it also said 'pair.'

'Now what?' Si said to Chas.

She shrugged. 'Your guess is as good as mine. Opportunity needed.'

'Well, keep looking for it,' Si said. Chas gave him a sarcastic smile.

'Don't let them take me away,' Ben pleaded, almost in tears.

Chas shifted uneasily. This boy was getting to her and she knew why. She bent down to look him in the eye. 'Ben, I'll do whatever I can, I promise.'

Si called another assistant over. 'Hey, we need to talk to that Conscience guy.'

'You don't get to make requests,' said the assistant, sharply. 'Keep your mouth shut, if you know what's best for you. Goods don't talk.' He swept away.

Si didn't give up. He caught sight of the director across the holding bay. 'Hey! Hey! Conscience. We need to speak to you.'

Many heads turned. Conscience looked up from the goods he was attending.

'Be quiet!' demanded an assistant, coming to stand in front of Si, hands on hips.

Chas joined in. 'Hey there! Conscience. We need to talk to you.'

Despite rather flimsy efforts to make Chas and Si stop shouting, they continued until Conscience came bustling over.

'Okay. Stop now! I'm here. Do you want those thugs in here? They won't think twice about roughing you up, in places where it won't show. And they'll have a go at me. What do you want?'

'Can you swing things so that my brother here stays with us?' said Chas.

'Your brother?'

'Yes. I promised our mother, on her death-bed I'd look after him. Please, you can't separate us.' Chas held on to Conscience's arm, making puppy dog eyes up into his face. Si suppressed a smile; He'd never seen her act like this.

Conscience removed his arm from her grip and smoothed down his satin shirtsleeve. 'I was told only you two together.'

'Yes but I can see you're not heartless. Have a bit of compassion. I'm sure a man of your obvious talent could make it work with the three of us? We'll do whatever you need us to do.' Ben smiled as pathetically as he could, with marvellously effective tears brimming in his eyes.

Conscience hesitated, looking from one to the other. His hands fluttered to his hair. 'Oh, all right. When you get out there you need to act up the loving family bit. I'll talk up the advantages of having a family together.'

'Thank you. We knew you were all heart,' Chas gushed, throwing herself at Conscience and kissing him on the cheek. He blushed and blustered away to organise someone else.

Chas spat on the ground and wiped her lips. 'Jerk!'

'Great acting,' Si said.

'I've been taking lessons from you,' she replied.

Out front the traders and customers were taking their seats.

The main lights were switched off as powerful multi-coloured spotlights were directed at the catwalk. Strident music began to play and Conscience made his grand entrance onto the stage.

'Welcome ladies and gentlemen, to this month's Trading Floor extravaganza! Do we have a show for you! We have everything from young boys and girls, perfect for all those menial household chores, to the Teens, perfect for every kind of job and then some! Strapping young lads and nubile young women. What more could a master or mistress want?' There was laughter from the audience. 'So without further ado, let's see the first lot.'

By this time Ben was shaking and Chas felt sick. Si breathed deeply. 'Look let's go out there and really ham up the family thing in the hope that someone chooses all of us. Then we still may have a chance.'

Chas closed her eyes. 'You're one of a kind Si, I'll give you that!'

Many frightened children were paraded in front of the audience. People bid on them and there were shouts of jubilation as each lot was won and led off to be claimed by their new owners. These people were the real scum: The businessmen and politicians who had got rich from their bootlicking and fawning at the feet of The Rulers. Slavery was officially forbidden but no one was ever prosecuted for it.

'And now, an exclusive lot. Three for the price of...well, three. Ha ha!' Si, Chas and Ben were pushed onto the Catwalk. Ben and Chas froze, like unfortunate animals caught in car headlights.

'Smile!' urged Si. 'Do something... attractive.'

He grabbed their hands and tried to parade them confidently in front of the audience, like he'd seen real models do on HTV. At first the others could hardly move, but gradually their legs obeyed them.

'Come on!' hissed Si, through a fake smile. 'Help me here!'

Chas desperately tried not to twist her ankle in the awful stilettos she was wearing. How did people walk in these monstrosities?

'It's these bloody shoes!' she hissed back.

'Come on, Chas!'

The audience were sniggering and Si realised that they were aware of the argument. They were also laughing at Chas's attempts to walk. At the end of the catwalk Si, in desperation, put his arm round Chas and picked Ben up and hugged him.

'Don't overdo it!' muttered Chas.

'A family unit!' Conscience sung out, avoiding the scowling Rory's eye. 'A chance to get three new slaves, with such loyalty to each other that you'll never have any trouble. Just think how you could work that to your advantage, my friends. The small boy would be useful for all those dirty jobs you wouldn't dream of doing yourself. And the Teens: a strong handsome male at your beck and call (ladies) and a glamorous young lady to fulfil your every wish.' He winked at a fat man in the audience. Everyone laughed. 'Now who will start the bidding at £1000?'

There was a plethora of bids. It was hard to keep track; the bidding was incredibly fast but Conscience was impeccably in control. Ben, Si and Chas stood in the middle of the catwalk. Si began smiling and waving at some of the ladies in the audience, who tittered excitedly and urged their husbands to bid.

'Wave!' he hissed at the others. Ben hesitantly raised his hand. 'And for pity's sake, smile Chas!'

'I hate this!'

'I'm not expecting you to enjoy it!'

The bids started to peter out as the price got higher. '£3100.

Are there any higher bids?' No more hands went up. 'Going once, twice, sold to Mr. Joseph Kahn.'

Rory was on his feet punching the air and kissing Suzy. The three slaves were led off the catwalk to a waiting Mr. Kahn and his assistants. As they passed Rory and Suzy, Chas spat at him.

'You little...' Rory lunged at her.

Suzy pulled him back, carefully avoiding looking at Chas. 'It's done, Rory. You've got the best price ever! Leave it.'

He grunted and wiped the spit from his face.

Kahn handed his money to the collector. 'Secure the slaves,' he said to his assistant. 'Bring my vehicle round here and let's get out of this awful place.'

He didn't even look at Chas, Si and Ben. They were bundled into the back of a large magnetised vehicle with blacked out windows. The car sped off into the night, stopping briefly at the check-point. The guards didn't even ask to look in the back of the vehicle. It was obvious that Kahn held a lot of power. The car headed west out of the tech-city to Kahn's country estate.

*

It was gone midnight. The Commander was pacing the Law-keepers' office. His men had reported no sightings of Chas and Si. He had ordered them to stay out on the streets, questioning people until someone gave them a lead. The advert for Si's capture, promising a substantial reward, had only been showing since this evening due to incompetence from the HTV Company. Several people would soon lose their jobs, on the Commander's recommendation. Advertising screens around the city were also now playing the advert. At least the face of the boy would be well known in this city and nationally by morning. There was something niggling the Commander about the boy's companion but he couldn't seem to grasp clearly what it was. He was annoyed with himself. He called the Chief Law-keeper (who had not been allowed to go home) into his office.

'Do you actually know what's going on in this God-forsaken city? You are supposed to know everyone who comes and goes. Have you been through the CCTV, from all the gates, thoroughly?'

'Yes, Sir. Nothing unusual to report.'

'No one of the boy's description? Or the girl?'

'No, I ... I don't think so, Sir.'

'Download the footage to my tablet. Now! I'll go through it myself! If they get away because of you, it would have been better for you if you had been born a scrawny flee-ridden dog!'

'Yes, Sir. I'll send the footage now.' The man hurried away. The Commander paced some more, occasionally kicking furniture and muttering to himself about incompetence.

It was a menial and arduous job, with hours of footage to trawl through. The Commander cursed Si and the girl and the idiot at the Bastille for allowing Si to escape. He cursed his men and the law-keepers. If Si was not captured his chances of rising to greater power were gone. And, in fact, he would probably be demoted, or worse. He would not let that happen. His holophone flickered to life. As if his thoughts had summoned it up, an image of Premier Zephyr appeared.

'News.' was all he demanded.

'Nothing yet, Sir.'

'Commander Resolution, I do not need to remind you how serious this is, but I will. That boy holds the key to the possible destruction of all we have worked to achieve. If that technology gets into the hands of our enemies we lose control. Find him.'

'I will, sir. There's no question of that. My men are out in the city questioning everyone. We are examining the gate footage in fine detail.'

'Are you sure he came to York?'

'It's the next big city on the route that Alliston gave us.'

'But why would he risk the city?'

'He's looking for information about his parents sir.'

'Let me know when you find him, Resolution. And I expect news soon.'

'Absolutely, Sir.'

The image flickered away. The Commander cursed again and focused all his attention on the CCTV footage.

9

It wasn't a long journey, only about ten minutes once outside the city. Neither Chas nor Ben had been in a magnetic vehicle before but Si had been transported to the Bastille in one. The journey was completely smooth and noiseless and it was difficult to tell at what speed they were travelling. Kahn had paid for magnetic surface to be laid right up his driveway.

It was dark and no one spoke. A glass screen separated the captives from Kahn and his driver, who were in the front.

When the car stopped Kahn got out and said something to the driver, then he went into the house. A young black man, wearing a butler's uniform, opened the door.

'Master Kahn instructs you to come this way.'

They climbed out of the car and it was driven into the garage. Another slave led the way around the side of the well-lit mansion. Ben gazed at it in awe. Chas looked at it scornfully. It reminded Si of some of the places his parents had been invited to by their scientist colleagues who had been honoured by The Rulers. It had been built in the early 20th Century with several storeys. A modern garage and extended wing had been added. He took them inside a large utility room. 'You are to undress here. Someone will be down soon to dowse you and give you some work clothes.'

'Dowse us?' Si said.

'Yes. For fleas, lice etcetera. Please wait here.' He locked the outer door with a key card and went through to the kitchen, locking the utility door behind him.

'The room contained mainly domestic machines. In the corner was a large shower area. There were several windows. Si tried them all but of course they were locked.

'We could break one,' Ben suggested.

'Yes we've been good at that so far! We need to suss the place out. Find out what security they have,' said Chas.

The door opened and a less than friendly, older woman, in a domestic uniform marched in.

'Didn't he tell you to undress?' she barked. 'What you waitin' for? I want me bed. Grief! As if I 'aven't enough to do than be kept waiting up 'til all hours for new 'uns to arrive.' She stood in the doorway, arms folded over her ample chest.

'I'm not undressing in front of them,' Chas said, indicating Si and Ben.

'Just get on with it! Who do y' think you are, y' prissy little madam? There ent no room for airs and graces 'ere.'

Uncomfortably, they all started to undress. To afford Chas some modesty Si turned away and motioned for Ben to do the same. The woman however, did not. She watched them all closely until they stood naked in front of her.

'Throw those poncy clothes over here and get in that shower.'

They did as they were told. Si made sure he kept his eyes on the ground as he stood next to Chas in the shower. He could feel her embarrassment, as she tried in vain to cover herself up. The woman tutted and grumbled.

'Close your eyes and take a deep breath. Don't breathe 'til I tell you to if you don't want lungfuls of this.'

Suddenly she turned on a hose and they were blasted with white powder. 'Turn around,' she yelled. They obeyed. A cold white film lay heavily on their skin. They looked like three ghosts when she had finished. Ben began to cough.

'Keep still,' she barked and pressed a button. Chas let out an involuntary shriek as an explosion of icy water hit her body from all directions. Ben was nearly knocked off his feet. The temperature and force of the water sent waves of pain searing through their bodies. Inadvertently, Si turned towards Chas, his eyes wide. 'Sorry, sorry,' he said, turning away. But Chas could not speak. The icy water only lasted a minute but it was enough to turn their bodies blue. It ended abruptly and a strong burst of cold air hit them from all sides. Gradually, it began to warm up, but not enough to erase the goose pimples covering every part of their skin.

'Get out. Put these on.' The woman handed them some clothes. They were basic overalls. 'Come with me. I'll show you where you'll be sleepin'. On a normal day you're allowed five hours sleep. It may not be at night, dependin' on what Master Kahn gives you to do. I'm the housekeeper, Mrs. Ellisham and the butler is Mr. Nichols. You take orders from the Master via me and Mr. Nichols.'

As she was speaking she led the way through the vast kitchen and up three flights of narrow stairs. It was very quiet in the house. Chas had been listening and looking out for dogs, but had seen no evidence of any. She had noticed CCTV around the outside of the house, but couldn't see anything in the house, although this didn't mean there weren't hidden cameras.

Chas was shown a room on the third floor. 'This is where the females sleep. You might get a few hours. Master wants to see the lot of you at seven.' Mrs. Ellisham led Si and Ben up another flight of stairs to a long attic room. In it, were several beds, some of which were occupied. 'Yours are down the end,' she barked, not even bothering to keep her voice down. Then she turned and left without another word.

'Charming!' Si whispered to Ben. 'Come on, let's get some sleep. I need it.'

*

Commander Resolution held the city law-keeper's head firmly in his right hand and pressed his eyes hard against the screen.

'That's them, you fool! Didn't you study the footage?' He smacked the man's head hard off the desk and let him fall to the ground.

'I'm sorry Commander. I went through this so carefully. It is hard to tell that this is the boy, he's jerking around so much and his head is always down.'

'Your powers of observation are astounding!' He kicked the law-keeper. 'Get up! If I didn't need your help you'd be fired on the spot, but that'll have to wait. Get the gate keepers, who were on duty there this morning, in here now.'

'They'll be in bed, Sir.'

'What is wrong with you?' the Commander took hold of the man's shirtfront. 'Do you enjoy watching your life seep into the sewers drip by drip? Break their doors down if you have to but get them in here in the next half hour. Now get out of my sight.'

The city law-keeper hurried away. Resolution picked up his phone but as he did so it rang. An image of Sergeant Knowles appeared.

'Sir, we've got a guy here, says he saw the boy and a girl going into The Tavern with a group of men this afternoon. I'm on my way there now.'

'Excellent. I've just seen them on CCTV entering York late yesterday morning. They were with those men, but there was something wrong with Hunter. He was having some kind of fit. The girl was hard to see. She had her head down. I'll meet you at the Tavern. I've had enough of this stinking office.'

By the time Resolution had reached the Tavern, Rory's face was swollen and bloody. Suzy was weeping beside him, her lip cut and swollen. Both were handcuffed. There was no sign of the other men.

Resolution took one look at them and recoiled. He took Knowles aside. 'Was that necessary before I arrived?'

'They were being uncooperative, Sir. But they talked after a little persuasion. They're slavers. They sold Hunter, the girl and a child for £3100, this evening at a place called the Trading floor. The man who bought them was Joseph Kahn of Kahn Technologies Inc. He's highly regarded by the Premier.'

'Yes I know Kahn. Get him on the phone. Tell him we'll get his money back to him and the reward.'

The Commander forced himself to look at Suzy and Rory. 'I bet you wish you'd watched some HTV yesterday, eh? The reward for the capture of that boy is more than double what you got for all three of them.'

Rory looked disdainfully at the Commander through his swollen eyelids.

'What are you going to do with us?' Suzy whimpered.

Resolution turned to his sergeant. 'Arrest them. They're slavers.' He pushed his face into Suzy's. 'It's ILLEGAL!'

'Please,' Suzy begged. 'I have to do it. He makes me. I don't care to see those poor children sold as slaves.'

Resolution ignored her. 'Bring them to the law-keepers' building. Let him do something to earn his living.' He left the Tavern.

'Please!' Suzy shrieked after him.

'Shut up, woman!' Rory growled, as he and Suzy were bundled into the back of a vehicle.

*

Chas had hardly slept. Dawn light was creeping through the thin curtains. There were three other girls in her room, snoring quietly. She guessed it must be about 6am. She couldn't lie here any longer. The events of the previous two days had caught up with her and she feared being trapped here forever if she didn't do something proactive now. As silently as a breeze, she slipped on the soft shoes she had been given and picked her way across the room, slowly opening the door. There was no one about. She made her way towards the stairs, stepping on each one as if it might bite her. Her days of stalking animals had stood her in good stead.

The house was silent. She stopped and listened. Not a sound. Finding her way back to the kitchen, she expected that someone might already be in there preparing food. It was empty. She skittered across the marble floor and began pulling out drawers as quietly as she could. Finally, she found what she was looking for. It was only small, probably used for paring apples, but the blade was sharp and the cold steel was a comfort in her hands. Wrapping it in a cloth she found under the sink, she slid it carefully up her sleeve. She looked at the door leading to the utility room and outside. She was tempted to make a run for it but common sense told her that the doors were probably locked on a central system and alarmed. And besides, her conscience pricked her about Si and Ben.

There was a noise in the corridor: footsteps and voices coming towards the kitchen. There was nowhere to hide in such a short space of time. All she could do was pin herself to the wall behind the door. Two women and a young girl entered, nearly flattening Chas with the door. They were yawning and grumbling about their day's work. Before they had a chance to turn and see Chas, she fled through the door and back up the stairs to her room.

One of the beds was empty and another young woman was just dressing.

'So you're the new one. Where have you been?'

Chas tried to look sleepy, yawning and stretching. 'I had to go look for the bathroom.'

'You've been a long time.'

'Well I got lost. And then I got curious about the place. Went to have a look round.'

'You must be bonkers,' said the woman. 'If Kahn finds you snooping he'll string you up!'

'What do you mean?'

'He's harsh! He don't stand no nonsense. Beats us if we put a foot wrong. And I hear a rumour that he did literally string a boy up once (before my time) for stealing. Made everyone watch. Horrible!'

'Okay. Thanks for the warning,' Chas said.

The door of the room opened and Mrs. Ellisham bustled in. 'Hurry up, girl. You're on service today.'

'Yes ma'am,' said the woman, her eyes downcast. She fixed the last bit of her uniform and hurried from the room, giving Chas a tentative smile as she passed.

Mrs. Ellisham turned to Chas. 'The others you came with are already down in the Master's anti room. Come along.'

Downstairs Chas was shown to the room where Ben and Si were already waiting. Mrs. Ellisham said, 'The Master will call you into 'is breakfast room in a minute. And mind you behave yourselves if you know what's good for you!' She directed a warning look at Chas and left the room.

Si smiled at Chas. She scowled back at him, which made him grin.

'Lose the stupid grin! 'Chas said.

'Good morning to you too!' Si said.

'Oh shut up, Si! Do you think this is a holiday camp?'

'Of course not! But you don't have to carry on as if your friends are your enemies all the time.'

'Okay. I'm just tense. We've got to get out of here. This Kahn bloke will be on to you soon. You haven't told them your real name, have you?'

'No. I told them my name was Obedience.'

'Wonder of wonders!'

Ben spoke up. 'You should lay off him a bit. He's not as dumb as you make out!'

She actually smiled at Ben. 'I know. He's just a bit stupid sometimes.' She raised her eyebrows at Si. The tension eased.

'You won't leave me behind will you?' Ben asked.

'Of course not, little brother,' Si said, ruffling his hair. 'We're going together.'

'I only wish I knew how,' Chas said.

'You'll think of something,' Ben said, smiling up at her.

The door to the breakfast room opened and the butler appeared.

'The Master summons you. Step this way please.'

Si thought he was an odd man for a slave. His manners, even to them, were impeccable. He had an air of importance, but appeared humble at the same time.

They stepped inside the breakfast room where Kahn was seated at a table, surrounded by newspapers and empty breakfast dishes. The smell of bacon and toast tantalised their nostrils. Ben felt his stomach rumble. The butler cleared away the dishes.

'Thank you, Nichols, that will be all,' said Kahn in a deep heavy voice.

'Come here. Stand in front of me,' he demanded.

Kahn was a man in his fifties with a full head of jet-black hair. There were no signs of grey because he was meticulous about dying it. His stomach betrayed his love of rich food, but he was dressed immaculately in a dark suit and tie, as if he were about to attend a business meeting. As they approached the table he stood up and walked round to look at them. They were surprised to see how short he was, barely as tall as Chas. He studied them for some time.

'So you are ...?

No one spoke.

'Answer me. Address me as 'Sir." that will be fine.'

'Yes sir,' said Ben.

'Names? Proper names,' Kahn said.

'Benevolence, Chastity and Obedience, Sir,' Ben said.

'And you are a family?' Kahn said.

'Yes, Sir.'

Kahn laughed. 'Of course, I know that's not true, so you can drop the pretence now. You're here because I was looking for three new staff and you fitted the bill. All your prancing on the catwalk was very amusing.'

Kahn moved closer to Chas and brushed his torso against her. He ran his fingers through her blond hair. Her body tensed and she tightened her grip on the handle of the knife in her sleeve.

Lifting her hair up over her ear, he whispered, 'You'll do nicely for 'special tasks."

Si wanted to punch the sleaze-ball in his fat gut. Chas saw the fury in his face and shook her head slightly at him.

'Ah, protective, are we?' Kahn sneered. 'Well, you don't have to worry about her anymore, Silence Hunter. She and the boy are mine now and you are about to make me an awful lot of money.'

The colour drained from Si's face. Kahn pressed the button on his remote and the HTV sprang to life. He flicked through a few channels until at last an image of Silence Hunter - fugitive - stood eerily before them. A voice-over proclaimed that Si was a runaway from the Bastille, dangerous and very valuable to the person who turned him in. Then Chas was described as his companion but there was no image of her and no reward.

'The Commander is on his way here right now to take you back to the Bastille, Hunter. I have negotiated a much more substantial reward than that measly sum they were offering. Seems it was my lucky night last night.'

Si couldn't speak. They were trapped. They should have made a better attempt to escape from Rory and Suzy. Chaos enveloped him. Chas was not so immobilized. Kahn was standing in front of her facing the HTV. Quickly, she drew the knife from her sleeve and held it to his throat.

'He's not going back to the Bastille, and we're not staying here to be your slaves. Try anything and you're one hundred per cent dead! Ben, find something to tie his hands with. Si...'

She turned to see Si already going through the draws in Kahn's desk. She was pleased at his initiative. Si turned round with a revolver in his hand. He pointed it at Kahn, trying not to let his hands shake.

Ben had pulled the tie-back cord from the long plush curtains and was proficiently tying Kahn's hands behind his back.

'Don't be foolish, Chastity,' Kahn said, cajolingly. 'You can have a nice life here with me. I'll give you privileges, and the kid, if you want. Don't throw it away for this runaway. They'll hurt you for helping him.'

'Shut it!' Chas snapped.

'You'd better not, Mister,' said Ben. 'She's deadly with that knife.' She had told him a lot about her days in the forest while they were waiting at the Tavern.

'Now you're going to drive us back to York!' Chas said.

'Are you crazy? Everyone knows who he is now. You'll be caught immediately.'

'Shut up! Just do it!'

'My people won't let you out of here.'

'They will if they value your life. They may hate you but they know what will happen to them all if you die,' said Chas. 'Ben, open the door.'

'I'll follow behind,' said Si, gripping the gun firmly. 'Ben, keep close.'

Holding the knife to Kahn's throat, Chas stepped into the ante- room. There was no one about. 'Get us out the front door. Where's the car?'

'It'll be ready out front. I was expecting to go to an important meeting in Manchester. My chauffeur will be waiting for me.'

'Call him now and get rid of him,' Chas ordered.

'He'll want to know why,' said Kahn.

'Make a good excuse if you want to keep living!' Chas said.

Kahn called his chauffeur and made up a story about needing him to stay behind to drive the housekeeper into York in the other car, for groceries. They walked to the front door, Si covering their backs with the gun. As Kahn was dealing with the security to open the door, Nichols appeared at the top of the stairs. Si pointed the gun at him.

'Master!' Nichols shouted.

'Get down here now!' Si ordered. 'Don't even think of calling for help or you die and so does he.' The whole thing was surreal. Si felt like he was in some kind of gangster movie. He tried to keep his hand from trembling. Chas turned round with Kahn so that Nichols could see the knife at his throat. Nichols raised his hands, his eyes wide with fear.

Si looked around the hallway. There was a large chest by a marble bust of some long forgotten statesman. He edged his way to it, keeping the gun pointed at Nichols. He lifted the lid. 'Get in here,' he said. Nichols was a tall man and Si hoped he would fit inside.

'Master... I ...' he began to protest.

'Its okay, Nichols. Just do what the idiot says.'

The butler squashed himself into the chest.

'Ben, help me,' Si said.

Ben and Si lifted a heavy side table, flipped it over and placed it on top of the chest.

The front door opened. Chas pushed Kahn outside, her blade expertly against the flesh of his neck without making the slightest mark. As Si closed the door he could hear the butler banging on the chest. With a mixture of relief and fear he realised it wouldn't be long before someone found him.

The car was waiting and empty. Ben jumped into the back seat with Si. Chas pushed Kahn into the driver's seat and fumbled to untie his hands.

'Open the screen,' she demanded.

Kahn pressed a button and the screen slid open. Si pressed the gun into the back of Kahn's head. Chas shut the driver's door and ran round to get in the front seat. As she did so, a man appeared from the back of the house, shouting for them to stop and waving another gun.

'Drive!' Chas shouted.

Kahn made no move.

'Do it!' Si said, pressing the gun harder into his head.

'You don't have the guts to kill me, boy!' Kahn said, contemptuously.

Si gulped and closed his eyes briefly. Ben looked at Si, wondering whether he did, then he said, 'Yes he does, mister. You didn't see what he did to one of the thugs who sold us.'

'Just drive,' Si demanded.

'You know I would slash your fat guzzling throat in an instant, Kahn,' whispered Chas leaning in to him. 'Then I'd toss you out the door and drive this thing myself.' She pressed the knife slightly harder into his neck and slid it barely an inch. Blood oozed from the nick and Kahn flinched. He looked at Chas, fear and hatred dancing in his eyes.

He spoke to the car and it powered up quickly and silently. The man with the gun stopped, knowing it was pointless to shoot at this car with its high security spec. The car turned a neat 180 degrees on the spot and sped down the long drive. As they reached the end of the drive they saw the large security gates were closed.

'Get them opened!' Si said.

Kahn pressed a button on the steering wheel. The gates slid open, slowly. As they exited, Chas got Ben to get out of the car and smash the CCTV at the entrance to the estate so their direction would not be known. Si was growing impatient. How long would it be before the Commander and his troops were here?

The car turned left out of the driveway.

'Why are we going back to York?' whispered Ben. 'Surely it's crazy. Kahn was right.'

'They won't think we'd been stupid enough to go back to York and we need to find someone Chas knows who can help us. You don't have to come with us if you don't want to, Ben.'

'What else can I do? I've got nowhere to go and besides you've saved me from becoming a slave. I owe you both.'

*

The Commander was relieved. It hadn't taken them too long to track Silence Hunter down after all. His job would surely be safe and he was still in with a good chance of promotion. Although he was curious to see her, he had agreed to leave the girl with Kahn, as that had been part of the self-important fool's demands. And Resolution knew that it wasn't wise to mess with Kahn because of his associations with the Premier. On the road from York they passed only one or two cars going the opposite way.

10

Chas had noticed how the guards at the gate checkpoint had been lax in terms of security with Kahn. She hoped they would be again.

'Get them to let us though without a fuss,' she said to him, as they approached the gates. She scrabbled around in the glove compartment and found what she had hoped might be there – a pair of sunglasses. 'Tell them I'm your girlfriend and we're going shopping in town.'

'What about ID?' said Kahn.

'Get us in. And don't let them look in the back seat.' She turned to see Si and Ben already getting down on the floor. 'Close the screen.'

The screen slid shut. The car came to a halt at the gate. Chas took a deep breath and draped herself around Kahn's neck as if she was about to kiss him. Her arm hid the knife, but it still pressed firmly into Kahn's flesh. She was becoming a good actor.

Kahn slid the darkened window down. He recognised the guard.

'Morning Dryson,' he said.

The guard nodded at Kahn. 'Good morning, Sir.' He noticed Chas simpering around Kahn's neck. She was careful to keep her face buried in his shoulder. The guard grinned.

'Had a good evening, Sir?'

'Yes, thank you. We're going into town to buy my lady friend some new outfits.'

'Very good, Sir.'

'You want ID?' said Kahn, reaching for his phone. 'It's just my friend here has forgotten hers.'

'No problem, Sir.

'Thanks, Dryson.'

The guard nodded, Kahn slid his window up and they entered York. Chas pulled away sharply and prodded the knifepoint against his neck. 'Open the screen.'

Si and Ben sat up and the gun was once more in the back of Kahn's head.

'You kids are stupid,' said Kahn. 'They're going to find you soon, especially here. They've got eyes everywhere. Then God knows what will happen to you. The Commander doesn't have a reputation for leniency, let's put it that way.'

'Be quiet, 'said Chas. 'Pull over in that side street.'

Kahn brought the car to a halt where Chas had demanded.

'Leave it running and give us your wallet and your phone,' she demanded.

Kahn handed them over.

'Now get out - slowly. Si, cover him.'

Si slid out of the back door, watching in case anyone was coming. Kahn opened his door and Si kept the gun on him as he got out. Chas slid across to the driver's seat.

'Walk up the street and turn the corner. Keep walking,' Chas said.

Kahn looked at her as if humouring a child.

'Do it!' Si shouted. 'Or I'll shoot you.'

Kahn smiled sarcastically at him, then suddenly he leapt back into the driver's seat, knocking the knife from Chas's hand and grabbing her round the neck. Ben screamed and tried to climb through from the back. Si was on Kahn in an instant. Chas tried to escape but Kahn had a surprisingly strong grip. Ben had a handful of his hair. Si struggled with Kahn but his grip was tightening around Chas's neck. She could hardly breathe. Kahn kicked out at Si, landing a blow in his groin. He was on the ground for a moment. With one hand Kahn prised Ben's fingers out of his hair and pushed him forcefully into the back seat. At that moment Si leapt up, gun in his hand and smashed it against the side of Kahn's head. His grip on Chas loosened and he groaned, clutching his head. Si hit him again and this time he slumped to the ground, falling out of the car. Si pulled him away from the vehicle.

He jumped into the driver's seat, where Chas was gasping for air.

'Are you all right?'

'Yes, I'll be fine,' she croaked. 'Can you drive this thing?'

'I think so.'

'Let's get out of here before someone sees us.' They drove away, leaving Kahn unconscious by the side of the road.

'Pity we can't keep this, but they'll be on to us once someone finds Kahn. I know a place to dump it,' said Si. 'It's out at the old industrial estate over by Foss Islands. We used to drive past it on the way to my Gran's house.'

They arrived in a deserted car park behind derelict buildings. A sign said, 'Available for development.'

'You sure you're okay now?' Si asked Chas, putting his hand on her arm. 'Yeah.' She rubbed at her neck. 'He caught me off guard.

And you surprised me. You were ...good.'

'Sometimes I can be useful.'

They hid the car as best they could. In Kahn's wallet they found some money and credit cards. Si took the phone and threw it in the river.

'Why d'you do that? We could have used it,' Ben said.

'They'd be able to trace us,' Si replied. 'This person we're looking for better be useful, Chas. Kahn was right, it's crazy coming back here.'

'I told you, she knows lots of people and she'll help us. Let's face it, we're not doing too well on our own!'

'I'm hungry,' said Ben.

'Come on then. You can buy us some food. Chas and I need to keep out of any shops, away from CCTV. You should be okay. I doubt they know about you yet. You weren't on the HTV broadcast.' Si considered the gun for a moment then ditched that in the river too.

*

Kahn's household was in chaos. Some of the slaves were weeping; fearful of repercussions. Nichols and Mrs. Ellisham were trying to remain calm and in control. Along with Kahn's chauffeur, they were the only paid staff and they feared they would lose their jobs, at the very least. As soon as Nichols had managed to escape from the chest in the hallway, he raised the alarm, but he had no idea where the car had headed.

The Commander and Knowles arrived minutes after Kahn's car had entered York. He was beyond furious when he discovered that Si had eluded him yet again.

'Incompetent fools!' he yelled. 'That boy is a high priority fugitive! What kind of security does Kahn have around this place that a couple of kids can outwit it? And you, why didn't you stop them? They've kidnapped your Master! Your heads will roll for this.'

Mrs. Ellisham whimpered and tried to control herself. Nichols said, calmly, 'We are very sorry, Sir. We are at your disposal. How can we help?'

'I need an office, CCTV footage since they arrived and I want to interview all the sla... servants. Maybe one of them talked to Hunter or the girl.'

'There was a small boy with them too, Sir,' Mrs. Ellisham piped up.

'I know.'

'This way, Sir. You can use Master Kahn's office. I will organise for the staff to be brought to you,' said Nichols, polite as ever.

The Commander nodded. 'Knowles, get a shout out on Kahn's vehicle. And go frighten some people into talking.'

Knowles smiled and headed off to find his way round the house.

'They only arrived last night sir,' Mrs. Ellisham added. 'We knew nothing about them. I doubt they 'ad time to talk to anyone.'

'That is for me to decide, woman. Now go and get your staff ready to see me. I want to know any and every little thing they might have overheard or noticed about these three. And bring me some strong black coffee and bagels.'

'Yes, Sir,' she said, retreating, while Nichols showed him to Kahn's office.

Behind the closed door of the office The Commander cursed, slamming his fists into the desk. The Premier would have to be told. Resolution could see his ambitions fading before his eyes.

*

Chas, Ben and Si tucked into a large meat feast pizza, at Kahn's expense. They sat behind some industrial bins in a side alley.

'The next thing we need is something to hide our identity from the CCTV,' said Si. 'Ben, go back to that market we passed and find us some baseball caps and maybe some more sunglasses.' Chas still had the ones from Kahn's car. He gave Ben some money from the wallet.

'Be careful,' Chas said.

Ben smiled, gave her a little wink and was gone.

'What are we going to do with him?' she said. 'We can't take him. It's too dangerous.'

'We?' Si smiled. 'I thought you were going off to do your own thing once you'd got me this far.'

'Well...' she trailed off, looking down at her feet and kicking the dirt around. 'You need me. I can't leave you here. You'd be back in the Bastille by tomorrow night.'

'So! What does it matter to you?' Si asked, provocatively.

'I told you before. I can't let Plin's death be in vain. And besides, I'm curious about your parents and why you're so important to The Rulers.' She hesitated. 'I want to come with you Si.' She looked up at him then, an earnest expression on her face.

Si had the urge to touch her but he didn't dare. He felt a lump rising in his throat. 'Looking for your chance of revenge, eh?' he said, trying to be light-hearted.

'Of course,' she replied, with a tight lipped smile.

Ben was back in no time at all with three baseball caps.

'These were cheap and I though it would be best to get ones

without a logo.'

They ripped the tags off and donned the caps. 'Okay, Chas. Where do we find this woman?'

'It's a year or so since I was last here, but I think I can get my bearings from the Minster.'

'Let's go then,' said Si. 'Keep your heads down and don't talk to anyone.'

They weren't far from the Minster. Chas recognised the street that Plin had taken her down the few times she had been to York. It was still quite a walk from the centre of town. She led them over a bridge from which they could see luxury apartments lining the river banks on one side and shops and pubs on the other. They passed the magna-train station and the well preserved Railway Museum, where even electric trains were mostly consigned to history now. The area began to look more and more run down. There was a car dealership, struggling to sell magnetic cars and an old disused garage that had once sold diesel and petrol. There were one or two corner shops with peeling facades and luminous bargain price tags in the windows. Then they came to a district populated by old terraced houses and new tenement buildings made of depressing grey breezeblocks.

'She lives here,' Chas said, coming to a halt outside one of the tenements.

'Will she recognise you?' Si asked.

'We'll find out.'

'Ben, we need you to go find out if she's there first, before Si and I risk the CCTV. It's on the fifth floor. Number 102. She's called Meg. Tell her Plin sent you and that Chas is waiting downstairs. Tell her we need her help.'

'Okay,' Ben said and disappeared into the building. There was no security on the door. People who were housed here were not considered worthy of too much protection.

Chas and Si waited nervously. A group of boys passed them kicking an old football and shouting, totally oblivious to them. A middle-aged couple made their way slowly across the car park. He was coughing incessantly while she tried to hold him up.

She looked at Si and Chas. 'Not long for this life now. Bloody government!' Si and Chas recoiled involuntarily as the man looked up and coughed at them.

'Poor bloke,' Chas said.

'I guess these people don't have medical cover,' Si said.

Chas laughed. 'Of course they don't. No one wants them or cares if they die. He could have the plague for all we know.' Instinctively, they both wiped their faces. 'Scum, Si. Worthless scum; him, her ...me.'

'Do I qualify for that honour these days?' Si asked, with a half smile.

'Oh, no. You're far from worthless. There's a huge price on you – remember that. I'd love to know why.'

'So would I. I want to understand what this is all about.'

Ben reappeared, running towards them from the entrance to the building. 'She says to come up, but she was a bit suspicious.'

'At least she's going to see us,' said Chas.

Keeping their heads bowed, and caps pulled forward over their faces, they entered the building. Some of the CCTV cameras had been smashed but one or two looked like they might be operating.

'The lift doesn't work,' said Ben. They began climbing the stairs. On reaching the fifth floor Chas stopped.

'What's wrong?' asked Ben.

'I'll have to tell her about Plin.'

'Come on Chas. It'll be okay. It's me who should be worried. She might throw me out as soon as you tell her what happened,' Si said. He reached for her hand. She looked at him and shook her head, though a vague smile flickered across her mouth.

Ben knocked on the door. It was slightly open. 'Come on in,' said a husky voice. The hallway was narrow and dark. It smelled of damp clothes and burning dust. There were two rooms off the corridor and a third room at the end with the door ajar.

'In here,' came the voice.

They pushed the door open to find the woman sitting at a small table peeling carrots. The room was a very basic lounge/kitchen/diner. There was a small two bar electric heater, almost concealed by a clothes-horse containing a few items. The walls were shedding their floral wallpaper and the floor was carpeted with more faded, threadbare flowers. A small old-fashioned two-dimensional LCD screen stood in the corner and a radio was playing softly from the kitchen area. A tabby cat rose from the arm of a battered sofa, made a disdainful noise at them and padded from the room.

The woman chuckled and got up from the table. 'That's Mog. Meg and Mog!' She laughed again. 'Old children's book.' No one responded. Meg swatted the comment away with her hand. 'Grumpy old lady she is! Do you remember her, Chas?'

*

Chas looked at the woman. She tried to smile and nodded. Meg looked older than she remembered. The skin on her hands and face was sagging and wrinkled. She had long, grey-blond, wavy hair, which she had tied in child-like pigtails. On her head was a battered straw sun hat with a faded red ribbon running round the rim. She wore an old shell suit and carpet slippers. Across her mouth there was a smudge of bright red lipstick. She looked like a schoolgirl who had aged prematurely.

The four of them stood in silence for a moment, eyeing each other up.

'Well, can I get you a cup of tea? I've got biscuits too,' she said, smiling at Ben. 'Sit down, sit down. I'll just move me washing. Dear me, you don't want to be looking at my great big old pants, do you?' She chuckled again.

The three of them wedged themselves into the small sofa, leaving the battered old armchair for Meg. She brought them tea and biscuits. Despite having so recently eaten pizza they soon polished the lot off. Meg watched them patiently.

'So, what brings you to York, Chas? Where's Plin? Haven't seen him in ever such a time. March, I think it was. You didn't come with him that time did you?'

Chas shook her head. She didn't know what to say.

'Are you going to introduce me to your friends?' Meg said.

'Sorry. We've been really rude, 'Si said. This is Ben and I'm ...'

'Silence Hunter. Yes I've seen your picture on the TV. A wanted man, eh?'

Si gulped. 'Yes. We need help and we hoped you might be able to help us.'

'Well that depends on what you did. Why are they after you? You murder someone? They seem pretty desperate to get you back.'

'No it's nothing like that,' Si said. He began to tell his story. He didn't even know if she would help him but impulsively he felt he could trust her. The whole story took some time. Meg listened right to the end without comment. Even when he told her about the village and Plin being murdered, she just listened, her face impassive. All the while Chas bowed her head, afraid to look up, as the events of the past week were narrated like a fiction. Her emotions threatened to overcome her once more but she refused to let them. When Si had finished, no one spoke or moved for a very long time. He looked at the floor, unable to think of what to do or say next. Meg got up and went to the grubby window. She looked out over the city for a long time. Then she turned. Two lines of tears were zig-zagging their way down her crumpled cheeks.

'I'll help you Silence Hunter,' she said. 'Make yourselves some more tea and get some biscuits. I'll be back soon.'

Si got up, blocking the way. 'How do we know you won't come back with the law-keepers?'

Meg chucked him under the chin like a little boy. 'You don't. You'll just have to trust me if you want my help.'

Si looked at the others. Chas shrugged and Si moved out of the way. Meg adjusted her hat in the mirror, put on her old Barbour jacket and opened the door. 'Feed Mog, for me will you?' Then she was gone.

11

Si looked out of the window to see Meg emerge far below.

'She's a bit weird!' Ben said.

'I told you she was eccentric,' Chas replied, looking in the fridge. She found a lump of cheese, half a cucumber and an open tin of cat food. She took out the cat food and, from nowhere, Mog was meowing loudly round her feet as if she'd always loved her.

'Do you trust her?' Ben said.

'Yes,' Si and Chas said together.

'She wouldn't betray us. She hates The Rulers as much as we do. She loved Plin. He was like a son to her,' Chas said, a spoon of cat food poised in mid air.

'She might like the money better. Your friend Plin is dead. Maybe she hates Si for that,' Ben suggested.

Si frowned. 'Maybe she should hate me, but I don't get that impression.'

'Well, where's she gone then? Why didn't she tell us?'

'Wow, you are a suspicious kid,' Chas remarked. She resumed spooning the cat food, much to Mog's relief.

'Of course I am,' Ben said. 'but no more than you.'

'Yeah I know,' Chas placed the bowl on the floor; the cat detached itself from her leg and greedily tucked in. Si bent to stroke her. She ignored him.

Chas thumped down in the seat next to Ben. 'You remind me of someone.'

'Who?' Ben asked.

'My little brother.'

Si stood up. This was the first time she'd mentioned her family. He wanted to ask more but didn't dare.

Ben however, was not so cautious. 'So where is he now?'

'He's dead. He had leukaemia and of course there was no treatment for the likes of us.'

'How old was he when he died?'

'Seven.'

'That's awful. What was he called?'

'Endurance. How ironic eh?'

Ben wasn't sure what ironic meant but he said, 'Definitely.'

Si felt it might be safe to join in. He sat on the chair where Meg had been earlier. 'What happened to your parents, Chas?'

She looked at him warily, as if she had just realised he was there. Telling Ben about her brother seemed natural and she had let her guard down.

Si pushed a little into her hesitation. 'Chas, surely you can trust me by now.'

She sighed. 'My mother and father were illegal immigrants. They were always in fear of being deported. They were just agricultural labourers. They were so keen to tow the line that they used to beat us severely if we put a foot wrong. That's what The Rulers advocated, so they did it.'

'Did they beat your sick brother?' Ben asked, incredulously.

'No they went easy on him. I used to get into all sorts of bother, so eventually my parents asked the authorities to take me away. I ended up in the workhouse aged ten. I never saw my parents again and I never wanted to either. They betrayed me. I don't know what happened to them after that and I don't care.'

'Did you have any other brothers or sisters?' asked Si.

'I had two older brothers. Res was the eldest. He was the brains of the family and totally towed the line. He was the one who persuaded my mother and father to get rid of me. I heard him one night telling them that I was attracting the wrong kind of attention to the family. This made them even more scared. Then there was my brother Tel who I got on okay with. He wasn't interested in school but he didn't really make trouble either. He just did as he was told.'

'Why didn't he try to stop them taking you away?' asked Ben.

'He was only twelve at the time. He was powerless. But I remember the day they came for me. My eldest brother was full of smooth talk so that my parents' illegal status wouldn't be discovered. He stood there smirking as they dragged me kicking and screaming from the house. And you know the rest,' she said to Si.

Si nodded. There was a pause. She had made herself vulnerable to him. He felt honoured.

Chas rose to look out of the window. Ben began to stroke the cat, who had leapt up onto the arm of the sofa. Si wondered how long Meg had been away and what she was doing.

It was early evening when Meg returned. Dusk was turning into blackness. A few street lamps that still worked were flickering into life. Meg was carrying two shopping bags, filled with fresh vegetables, milk and other groceries. 'It's nice to have someone to cook for,' she said as she unloaded the bags, with Chas and Si helping.

'We're grateful for you kindness,' Si said.

'Think nothing of it boy. Now what is it they call you? I expect you don't like Silence.'

Si grinned.' No. It's just Si.'

'Well, get a peeler in your hand, Si, and peel some potatoes for me.'

Meg took off her coat but not her hat. It seemed as if this stayed permanently attached. On the sofa, Ben was sound asleep, curled into a little ball, cuddling Mog like a favourite teddy.

'Look at that little scrap,' she said, nodding her head in his direction. 'He's under-fed and worn out. Poor little mite.' She filled the kettle. 'Now one of you make a brew. We'll get an old fashioned shepherd's pie in the oven; then I've got something to show you.'

Chas, Si and Meg sat at the kitchen table, having cleared it of all the vegetables and put a tasty looking shepherd's pie in the oven. Meg poured more stewed tea from the pot. Then she reached in her bag and took out a folder. In it were photocopied newspaper clippings.

'This is why I was out so long. Took me a while to find these in the library.'

The clippings were from some years ago and related to the deaths of Kate and Morgan Hunter in a terrible lab fire in 2062. Si was fascinated by them. He hadn't read much about the incident at the time, as he had been too distressed. They ploughed through them for a long time looking for clues as to why they had been 'disposed of.'

'I remember the incident. It was big news here,' said Meg, 'especially since your father was from York.'

'Do you think they died in that fire?' Chas asked.

'At the time I thought so. I didn't have any reason not to. There seemed to have been a thorough investigation into the causes. But of course The Rulers could easily have carried out a big cover up.'

'I wonder if the other scientists who worked there suspected anything. But I wouldn't know where any of them were.'

'Pity. They might be able to help,' said Chas.

'All day I've been thinking that if your parents didn't die, where would they have been taken? Then it came to me – if they weren't in the Bastille it would be a place called The Priory. Have you heard of it?'

Chas shook her head.

'Can't say I have either,' said Si.

'I have,' said a voice behind them. Ben had emerged from the sofa, yawning and brushing cat hairs from his clothes. His hair was sticking to his face, which was red from the warmth of the fire and the cat.

'Good grief – the dead have arisen!' exclaimed Meg, hooting with laughter. The others laughed too. Ben stood with them at the table, as there were no more chairs left.

'So how do you know about the Priory young Ben?' asked Meg pulling him onto her knee. He didn't seem to mind her old chubby arms encircling him.

'My father used to be a fisherman in a port, nearby. We lived there until it all went wrong. He often used to talk about the Priory. There were lots of stories about what went on there. Sometimes the fishermen were paid to ferry mysterious people over to the island. They were threatened to keep quiet too.'

'The island? Where is this? What is it?' asked Si.

'The Priory is supposedly a top-secret detention centre for dangerous criminals. But it's used for all sorts of political prisoners in reality. People who 'disappear' often end up there,' said Meg.

'How do you know?' asked Chas.

'I have my sources,' Meg replied mysteriously.

'The island is called Lindisfarne, just off the coast of Northumberland,' Ben added.

'That's right. It is reachable by a causeway at low tide. The Rulers have tried to find a way to keep it surrounded by water.' She chuckled. 'But there are some things only God can control, even in this day and age. They built the Priory in 2050. I presume they thought it was reasonably remote and therefore a good place to detain 'the disappeared.''

'There are a few islands up there, just off the coast,' Ben said. ' Mainly small, with lots of birds living there: No people. My dad sometimes took me over there, bird watching.'

Meg nodded. 'The place used to be a draw for Christian pilgrims. But The Rulers destroyed what was left of the real priory. They sent the small population away and built the detention centre – ironically naming it The Priory.'

'And you think that's where my parents might be?' asked Si.

'There's a strong possibility,' Meg replied.

'Well that's where I'm headed then.'

'And how are you going to get in? Just walk across the causeway and ask to see your parents?' Chas gave him a sarcastic smile.

'Yes, of course!' said Si, giving her the same look back.

'Now, now you two,' said Meg, getting up to tend to their supper.

'I could help,' offered Ben.

'It's going to be really dangerous,' said Si. 'I was thinking you should stay here.'

'No!' he protested. 'I want to come. I know the area. You know I'd be useful.'

'We're not disputing that,' said Chas,' but we want you to be kept safe.'

'No, I'm not your little brother! I can look after myself. I want to come.'

Si looked at Ben. 'I think Chas is right. You would be safer here ...'

'But Si...'

'However, if you know the area it would be a huge advantage to have you with us. So, despite the danger, and because you want to come, I say you should come.'

'Yes!' Ben jumped up from Meg's knee and did a little victory dance round the room.

'Si – he's only a kid,' Chas pleaded.

'I agree, but he's determined and we might need him.'

Chas turned away in anger.

'Chas,' said Meg in soothing tones. 'Ben is welcome to stay with me, but maybe Si is right. Think what you were like at Ben's age. Would you have wanted to be left behind? You wouldn't have cared a jot about the danger.'

'Come on Chas - give me a chance. I want to come with you and Si. You're my family now.'

'I thought you just said you weren't my little brother,' she replied, half smiling.

'Yeah, well now I am again,' he grinned.

'Come on, let's eat. You lot need some good food inside your bellies,' said Meg, dishing out the shepherd's pie.

After they had eaten they sat by the fire and talked for a while, then Meg made up some beds for them on the sofa and the floor.

'Meg - thanks,' Si said.

She smiled at him and went to bed.

*

Si was back in the Bastille. He was strapped into a giant metal chair. His feet dangled over the edge. He was a little boy again. The room was bright and bare apart from a table in front of him containing various surgical implements. He could not move his limbs. He tried to turn his head to see if anyone else was in the room, but it was held tight. His stomach lurched and he felt sick.

'Mummy,' he murmered over and over again.

Then he heard a whimpering noise like that of a wounded animal. Gradually it turned into sobbing. At first he thought it must be his own until he realised it was coming from a corner behind him. It was a woman.

'Mummy?'

The sobbing continued.

'Mummy!' he cried, more urgently. The sobs grew louder. Si tried harder to break free from the bonds. He twisted and pulled and jerked. He groaned and strained and cried out. He couldn't do it. The sobbing continued.

A door opened opposite him. The man was back. He picked up a syringe from the table. Si squirmed. The sobbing turned to anguished howling. The man approached Si, a cruel smile on his face.

'Its time, Silence. Your mother has told us that you have it and now I am going to find it.'

The syringe grew out of all proportion with every step he took towards Si, as if he was part of some grotesque macabre cartoon.

Si strained at the bonds.

'No!' screamed the woman.

*

Si sat bolt upright. A faint orange glow from the streetlights seeped into the room. Chas and Ben were in deep sleep. Sweat poured down his back and neck. He was panting. 'Mum,' he whispered. 'What do they want?'

12

It was almost dawn. Outside, a slight frost glistened on the concrete. Si, Chas and Ben were ready to leave. Meg had given them as many provisions as she could. They now had a torch that worked, a map and warm (if somewhat ill fitting) clothes that Meg had collected over the years to sell at jumble sales. Meg had made them a loaf's worth of sandwiches and stuffed their pockets with chocolate bars. Each of them had a plastic bottle of water. They had some money left from Kahn's wallet and Meg gave them some more, despite their protests. Into Chas's rucksack she slipped her dead husband's Swiss Army knife.

'Thank you,' Chas said, feeling the security of a decent knife again and knowing how useful it would be.

Then Meg handed Si a piece of paper with a name and address on it. 'This is the name and address of a friend of mine in Durham. I know it's a long way up there, but it's on your route. It's a long time since I saw him, so I hope he's still there. Tell him I sent you and maybe he can help.'

'Thanks,' said Si, folding the paper and putting it into the zip pocket of his anorak.

'Who is he?' asked Chas.

'An old friend. I worked for him many years ago. Peter was a clever man. He had done well for himself by the time he was thirty.'

'What did he do?' Si asked.

'He was developing new technologies for the government.'

'He worked for the government?' asked Chas, suddenly on alert.

'He did. He loved his job, but he was no sympathiser, even then. He's a good man. I promise you.' She laid a reassuring hand on Chas's arm. 'Take the newspaper clippings, they might be useful and I don't want them here if anyone comes looking for you.'

'I hope they don't,' said Si. 'We've put you in danger.'

'Of course you have,' Meg laughed. 'But I can look after myself. Now, get going. Keep those woolly hats I've given you pulled down and hoods up. Keep off the main streets where possible and head for Bootham Bar. Follow the road straight through the bar. You need to get to the outer gate by seven. That's when the guards change over. It's your best chance to get out. They usually spend a few minutes talking in the guardhouse and the actual gate is rarely shut. If you're careful you should be able to slip through.'

'How do you know ...'

'Never you mind,' she said, winking at Ben.

The cat padded sleepily out of Meg's bedroom and began to meow loudly at her food bowl.

'Now get going. You haven't got long. Good luck.'

None of them knew what to say in return. They hugged her and were gone.

The streets of York were quiet. One or two early morning traders were up and about, but they weren't interested in the three travellers. They walked warily in silence, passing through Bootham Bar and up the straight road that led north. They could see the gate up ahead. There was no sign of change-over at the gate so far and they could see one guard, pacing the space between the walls, smoking a cigarette and looking bored. They moved into the doorway of a building to wait. Within a couple of minutes a van drew up and two more guards jumped out. They greeted the guard on duty and all three of them went into the guardhouse to join the other man on duty. This was their chance. Keeping in the shadow of the buildings, they moved quickly towards the entrance.

Si's heart thumped wildly. He looked at Chas who was as calm as if she was stalking wildlife in the woods. Despite his fear, this made him smile. He turned to Ben and gave him the thumbs up. Ben smiled back uncertainly. As they approached the gate Si motioned to the others to wait. There were CCTV cameras on the gate from all directions but there was no other way through the impenetrable walls of the city. Pulling down his hat, he slunk underneath the windows of the guardhouse. He could hear the men laughing and chatting. He beckoned Chas and Ben to follow him. Within moments they were through the outer gate and beyond the walls. For a few moments they tried to walk calmly away but as they rounded the nearest corner they began to run.

An opaque, grey dawn was breaking. There was no sun and it was cold but they were over-heating from the running and adrenalin.

'We've got to stop a minute,' Ben panted.

The other two slowed down and took the opportunity to drink.

'We made it,' Ben said, when he had recovered enough to speak again.

'Well I wouldn't say that. We got through the gate, but we

were caught on camera. There was no way round it. And if they examine the footage they're bound to know it was us,' said Si.

'We need to get parallel with the north road and cut back to it at some point,' said Chas. She got out the map. Thirsk is about twenty miles directly north. We could make it by nightfall and find somewhere to stay.'

Ben and Si looked at her. 'By nightfall?' Ben said.

'Let's just see how far we can get,' Si said.

*

The Commander was back in the law-keeper's office in York. He had been thoroughly dressed down by the Premier and was more furious than ever. He didn't take well to being humiliated and these fugitives would pay the price.

Last night he had returned to York to visit Kahn in a private hospital. He had slight concussion and a gash that had needed stitches. His car had been retrieved very easily with no damage to it. The only injury that concerned him was to his bank balance, having paid good money for three slaves who had now stolen his wallet and disappeared.

'I want compensation,' he demanded.

The Commander was doing his best to be polite in the light of Kahn's connections, but he disliked this greedy, arrogant man. 'Of course you will be generously compensated for this trauma Mr. Kahn. I will see to it myself.' He forced a smile.

'I'd expect nothing less Commander, if you don't want to be hearing from my lawyers. I'm holding you personally responsible.'

This irked Resolution even more, but he said, 'Of course. Now tell me exactly what you remember about Hunter and his friends.

Knowles, take notes.'

Kahn had overheard that they were going back to York to look for someone who might help them. It wasn't much to go on but at least Resolution now knew that they had returned to the city. Yet again the Commander, with the help of several coerced law-keepers, found himself trawling through all sorts of CCTV footage into the early hours of the morning.

After several hours, one of the law-keepers spotted three youths in baseball caps on the CCTV camera, entering a block of run-down tenement flats. Resolution was called to look at the footage. It was blurry and difficult to see, but any lead was better than none.

'Knowles, get down there and question every living being in that block. Hopefully they're still there, but if not, find out who they went to see. Get them down here for questioning.' Several men were dispatched with Knowles. 'The rest of you, keep looking at the CCTV. I want any more sightings reported to me immediately.'

It was pandemonium at the flats. Meg had been on the look out for them. She knew they would come and she had to admire the alacrity with which they'd found her. Si, Chas and Ben had left an hour ago. Since then Meg had been making her flat look as chaotic as possible. She deliberately spilled cereal on the floor and left dirty dishes lying on the surfaces and carpet. She spread dirty clothes from her linen basket around the flat. Her cover to the outside world had long been that of an eccentric old lady. She had made sure that there was no evidence of her three over-night visitors. Her only hope was that no one had seen the kids coming into her flat.

The law-keepers went systematically from door to door raiding flats and roughing people up. She knew how they enjoyed it. She had seen it many times over the years. There was much shouting and screaming going on. A lot of the tenants were old people like herself and Meg winced as she thought of the trouble brought upon them. It would take the law-keepers a while to reach her on the fifth floor. She settled into her armchair, in front of the TV with a cup of tea.

A loud pounding woke her from a doze. She sighed and braced herself. Slowly she rose and ambled to the door. More pounding.

'Open up. Law-keepers!'

'I'm coming, dearies,' she said. 'You got to give an old lady a minute.'

She opened the door a fraction and peered at them. 'Ooh you do make an awful racket you know. I was just having a nice doze.'

The man shoved the door open and, taking Meg by the scruff of her blouse, marched her back into the living room. Another man followed. He pushed her down into the armchair. The TV still blared. Aggravated, he scrabbled around for the remote and flicked it off.

'What you go and do that for? I was watching it. It's me favourite programme,' Meg whined.

'Don't be silly, you old bag. You said you were asleep.'

'Was I? Oh yes, maybe I was now. Would you like a nice cup of tea? I was just having one meself,' she said, struggling as if to get out of the chair.

'Sit still!' ordered the law-keeper. To the other man he said, 'Search the place.'

'What you looking for then? He better keep his hands off me silky drawers!' Meg cackled to herself.

'Shut it!' the law-keeper yelled, his patience already tried to the limit, having found nothing so far. 'What do you know about this boy?' he said, thrusting an tablet image of Si into her hands. 'He's got two other kids with him, girl and younger boy. Have you seen them?'

'Oh yes!' she beamed.

'When?' he demanded.

'Oh I seen this boy lots on the TV recently. But I haven't seen a girl or another boy. Just him. He's handsome, he is. Looks like my nephew. Billy he was called. He's dead now, bless his soul. He died...'

'Stop your rambling, old hag.' The man pulled Meg forward by her blouse until her face was almost touching his. 'I'm not interested in your annoying claptrap. Have you seen this boy - here – in the flats?' He threw her back into the chair.

'Oh no, I only seen my Billy when he was alive. He was a really good boy. Did ever so well at school. Such a pity...'

Suddenly the law-keeper lost his temper and slapped Meg across the face.

Slowly she raised her hand to her cheek and was silent.

'I don't want to know about stupid Billy!' He shouted every word in her face as if she was deaf.

The other man came back into the room. 'This place is a tip. Damn cat went and scratched me.' He held up his bleeding hand. Meg made a mental note to give Mog a treat this afternoon.

'Never mind about that. Anything?'

'Nothing.'

They stared at Meg. She had started rambling about her nephew again, quietly, as if to comfort herself.

The law-keeper shook his head. 'This is ridiculous. If you find out anything about *this* boy,' he said, pointing to the tablet, 'you call this number. Do you understand?' She nodded meekly.

'Fat chance!' he said to the other man as they left the flat, leaving the door open.

Meg sat still for sometime, nursing her cheek. She was relieved to have escaped with a mere slap. She had experienced worse.

*

'Sir, come and see this. It has to be them.'

The Commander watched as first Si, then Chas and Ben had easily slipped through the North Gate at 07:02 that morning. It was now midday. He was furious.

'Get those idiot so-called guards under arrest!' he screamed. 'Get Knowles back here. How long does it take to question a load of paupers? We need to get after them. They're headed north, at least I know that now.'

Knowles was soon back in the law-keeper's office, having found nothing of significance. His frustration was evident as he entered the room.

'Of course they're all going to deny harbouring the fugitives,' said Resolution. 'Anyway, we have a sighting now. Get the car ready. I've got a feeling Silence Hunter is on to the fact that his parents aren't dead. I also think he may know about the Priory. I want to intercept him before he gets to it. Also, I want to know more about that girl with him. Get the law-keeper to run a close scan of the CCTV and find out who she is. We've got a good description of her from Kahn and the slavers too. I want her alive, as well as Hunter.'

'What about the kid?' asked Knowles.

'Dispensable,' replied the Commander.

*

As night fell, Chas, Ben and Si found a sheltered place off the main road to sleep. It was a copse in the lee of a hill. They had tracked the main road north, keeping well back from it. Chas had kept them marching and they had made good progress, but now they were exhausted and most of their food supply was gone. The night air was cold and their bodies, sweaty from hiking, were beginning to cool down. They wrapped themselves in all the clothes they had available and burrowed down into piles of leaves, like hibernating animals.

'Can we light a fire?' asked Ben,

'Too dangerous,' Chas replied. 'Sorry.'

Ben's teeth chattered.

'Let's huddle together for warmth,' Si suggested. Ben immediately snuggled into Si.

Chas was less enthusiastic. 'I'm okay. I'm used to the cold.'

Si looked at her and shook his head. Their breath was making clouds of steam. She huddled into the smallest ball she could become. 'Suit yourself,' he said. 'But you can always change your mind.'

Ben soon fell asleep. It was black in the woods by now but no one turned on the torch. Both Si and Chas were well aware that their pursuers would not be far behind them. An owl hooted and there were soft scurrying noises in the distance.

'Are there wild animals out here?' Si asked.

'Yes,' Chas said.

'Should we be scared?'

'No!' she scoffed. 'They won't bother us. A few foxes and

badgers is all there'll be here.'

'So, that night when you found me and tied me to that tree, nothing was really going to eat me?'

She laughed into the darkness and Si wished he could see her face. 'No, Si. It was just to frighten you.'

'You did a good job.'

'Of course! Anyway, we're on the same side now. So never fear, I will protect you,' she said. He knew she was smiling.

'Maybe I'll get the chance to protect you.'

She made no reply.

The leaves rustled and she moved closer. Ben was asleep between them and Chas stroked his hair. Si felt her arm brushing his. He imagined her looking tenderly at Ben. Her silhouette was visible in the faint moonlight filtering through the trees. In the dark he felt braver. He reached out his fingers and brushed her cheek. She didn't recoil as he had expected her to. Instead her profile turned to face him. His fingers lingered on her face. She didn't say anything but they looked at each other in the darkness for what seemed a long time. Then she lay down beside Ben and went to sleep.

13

A vindictive, sprawling branch threw itself into his face, waking Si abruptly. He sat up, feeling cold and stiff. Ben and Chas were huddled round a small fire, eating the remains of the chocolate and drinking water that they had warmed in their mugs over the fire. They laughed as Si disentangled himself from his attacker.

'Oh yes, hilarious, having your eyes scratched out by a sadistic tree!' Si grouched.

'Drama queen!' Ben laughed.

Chas smiled. 'Come and have some chocolate before Ben eats it all.'

Chas handed him a cup of warm water. It tasted awful but he was glad of its warmth. He got the map out of his rucksack and studied it.

'We need to press on harder today,' Chas said.

'We could do with finding some transport. We'll never reach Lindisfarne before Christmas at this rate,' said Si.

'I'm sure the Commander will be onto us by now. We must keep a low profile,' said Chas. 'Have you still no idea why they're so obsessed with you?'

'It must be to do with Mum and Dad. I keep having these nightmares about the Bastille. There's always this man about to stick a syringe in me and telling me that I have something they want. He says my mum told him I had it. But I've no idea what it is? Maybe it's to do with Icthus. Mum and Dad were believers in the Way. If we get to the Priory I've no idea how we'll find out if my parents are there or how we'll get in.' Suddenly everything seemed hopeless and Si had an overwhelming urge to give himself up.

'Hey, don't go quitting on me now Silence Hunter,' Chas said. 'People have died for this; whatever it's all about. You and your parents are some kind of threat to The Rulers and that's a good enough reason to keep on. Maybe you should pray to your God if your parents were believers. He might help us.'

'Maybe,' Si said. Since his parents' disappearance the only times he ever offered feeble prayers were when he was in dire trouble. Right now he wished he had a stronger faith – something real that he felt deep in his soul.

'And remember, I can help once we get to Northumberland,' Ben said.

Si smiled at them. 'You're right. I'm glad you're here.'

They extinguished and covered over the fire, then set off towards Thirsk, which was directly north. This was still a thriving market town despite it having little protection from the open countryside.

'Can we risk going into the town to look for a real bed for the night? And some transport?' asked Si.

'I don't think so. It's too risky. If the Commander has seen us leaving York, which I'm sure he has by now, I expect he will already be in Thirsk asking questions,' said Chas.

*

She was right. Resolution and several of his men had arrived in Thirsk last night. This morning they were busy questioning market traders, shop owners and anyone they came into contact with. The local law-keepers had been alerted but so far there were no sightings of the three fugitives. The Commander was growing more impatient. He needed to be the one to catch Hunter. He wanted the glory. He wanted a higher position within The Rulers. At the moment this was slipping from his grasp. The Premier had been apoplectic last time he had spoken to him, threatening Resolution with all sorts of personal punishments if the boy was not found soon. He was terrified that the nanomedibot, developed by the Hunters, would get into the hands of someone else, who would clone it to cure the diseases that for now remained incurable to the poor. The New Plague, which had been engineered to 'decrease surplus population,' could become no more of a threat than the common cold. The boy had to be captured and the mother made to talk. Si was their only weapon against her. Even when they had tortured her, and killed her husband she had remained astonishingly silent about the information she held, which would enable the destruction of the nanomedibot. Only when they had threatened to kill Si had she relented and told them that he carried the proto-type in his body. They had promised her the boy's safety in return. The Premier himself had issued a signed statement, guaranteeing his immunity from harm. Promises were retractable. But then the boy had escaped.

Resolution was not surprised that there had been no sightings of Si and his accomplices yet. If they were on foot, as he suspected, they would not have reached Thirsk yet. There were no walls around this town, which made it harder to track those who entered and left, but the Commander posted men on every road into the town. He also sent men to the neighbouring villages to frighten people into cooperating should they discover anything. Once he had all the bases covered, all he could do was wait. But for how long?

*

Chas, Si and Ben were approaching Thirsk. They had kept to the fields and woods, as much out of sight of the main roads as possible. The houses of Thirsk rose like misshapen rocks out of the mist swirling over the landscape. They stopped to drink from a stream and fill their water bottles.

'I think they're waiting for us there,' Si said, nodding towards Thirsk. 'I can feel their eyes on us already.'

'What shall we do then?' asked Ben.

'I think we should look for some shelter out here again,' said Si, reluctantly. He had been daydreaming of a decent bed. 'We need to buy some food though. We've nothing left. And transport would be really useful. We've still got Kahn's money.'

'I think you'll find the reward on your head is greater than anything you could pay for a vehicle.' The voice came from behind a stout tree trunk, over the stream. A man slowly appeared, pointing a farmer's shotgun at them. Slowly they got to their feet and automatically raised their hands above their heads. This was it, he was either going to kill them or turn them in. Si wasn't sure right now, which would be worse.

'These two have nothing to do with it. Let them go,' said Si.

'I've seen this girl's picture with yours. She's wanted too. I'd get a massive reward if I turned you both in.'

'Well at least let the boy go,' Chas said.

'He wouldn't stand a chance. They'd find him. They don't do

mercy,' the man replied.

'He'd have more chance than if you turn him in with us. You know what they're going to do to us,' said Si.

'Who says I'm turning you in anyway?' the man said.

'You'd be a fool to shoot us when you could claim that reward,' Si said, realising that he didn't want to be shot here and now.

The man laughed. 'A fool! Yeah that's me! I hate The Rulers. I'm not going to hand you over. But before I lower this gun I need to be sure you're not about to slit my throat.'

'She could,' he nodded in Chas's direction, 'but she won't. We're more like outlaws really, cos I've got something The Rulers want. I don't know what it is, but they want it. It's a threat to them. She's wanted 'cos she's helping me. He's been unlucky enough to cross paths with us and fool enough to want to stay with us.'

Ben grinned up at Si. The man lowered his gun and splashed across the stream. Si, Chas and Ben lowered their hands, and Chas was ready to draw her knife in an instant. The man was dressed in old canvas trousers and a thick cardigan with patches on the elbows. His wild, white hair and staring blue eyes reminded Si of pictures he had seen of Einstein. He held out his hand to Si.

'Silence Hunter, I presume?' he said, smiling.

'Si.' He felt like some notorious celebrity from one of the HTV game shows. It was unnerving. 'This is Chas and Ben.'

'Pleased to meet you,' he said, putting out his hand to Chas, who took it warily, and to Ben who shook it with visible relief.

'THEY call me the Hermit, but my name is Aaron. You can stay with me if you like. No one ever comes down here. They think I'm a miserable old bugger, living on my own. They don't understand the bliss of solitude.'

They followed the Hermit to his home. It was an eco-friendly bungalow, built mainly from timber and glass, with solar panels in the roof, well hidden deep in the woods.

'I built this myself,' Aaron remarked. 'Took me a long time and a bit of resourcefulness, but I did it.'

'It's great,' said Ben.

'How long have you lived here?' asked Chas.

'Thirty years,' Aaron said, 'Before the Scum came to power. When that happened I was all the more determined to stay here and keep out of the way.'

A mangy dog came running out from behind the house. It didn't bark at them, just wagged his tail incessantly and bounced around, jumping up at Aaron.

'Hey Elvis. Good boy.'

The dog licked his face as he bent down to pet it. Ben immediately started to stroke him.

'Okay, so I'm not completely alone. Elvis here is my trusty companion and I have some chickens. Come in. Let's find you all something to eat and somewhere to sleep. You look worn out.'

'We are,' Si smiled. We've walked from York.'

'I know where you've come from. You're all over the news and they're playing the adverts with your picture on every half hour on the LCD.' Aaron gestured for them to sit down.

'Yes, it's making our journey all the more difficult.'

'You don't have to tell me anything you don't want to. They're being very mysterious about you on LCD, but they're making sure folk know you're dangerous and there's a huge reward on your head. And now they're talking more about you Chas. There's a reward for you too now, although you're not so expensive.'

'Dead or alive, or don't they specify?'

'Alive. Your status has obviously increased since you've been in this young man's company.'

'What about me?' Ben asked, rubbing Elvis vigorously on the tummy.

'They've mentioned you but there's no reward for you as yet.'

'Oh.'

The bungalow was a treasure trove of outdated equipment and memorabilia. Around the walls were pictures and posters of Elvis Presley. In the corner was an old CD player softly playing 'Are you lonesome tonight?' Next to that was an old LCD screen, like the one in Meg's house. Aaron had several old radios around the house and a telephone as big as a large chocolate bar with buttons that stuck out. In the corner was a computer with a small screen and hub. No one used such things now. Everyone used tablets. There were magazines and books lying around, depicting ancient pop icons in their prime. And an empty birdcage stood by the window, looking as if it had never been used.

Aaron flicked a switch and heavy blackout blinds automatically began to come down. He switched on the lights, powered by solar panels on his roof, and watched his visitors survey his home.

'I am a bit of a history freak,' he laughed. 'I love the old days of my boyhood and my grandfather was a great fan of the King of Rock and Roll. He got me into all this. I only have a computer and telephone so I can earn a living.'

'So why do people avoid you?' asked Si.

'Oh, everyone thinks you should move with the times. I like my peace and quiet so I keep up the pretence of being a bit hostile. People keep their distance, it's nice.'

'Have you always lived alone?' Chas asked, picking up a photo of a young boy from the window ledge. 'Is this you?'

The picture was faded. The boy in it was about fifteen and

looked very like a young version of the Hermit.

'That's my son, Carl. So no, I haven't always lived alone. He left not long after that picture was taken. He joined the law-keepers when The Rulers came into power. I've never heard from him since.'

'And your wife?' asked Si.

'Dead. A few years after Carl was born.' His face betrayed no emotion. 'Better to live alone. Hurts less.'

'And what about that bird cage? What kind of bird did you keep in there?' asked Ben.

'I don't believe in caging animals. My wife bought it to remind us of the joy of being free.' He looked wistfully at it for a moment. 'Let's find something to eat.'

The kitchen was pristine. This surprised Chas and Si after the jumble of the living area. Aaron had all his tins, jars and bottles organised in categories. There was a large old chest freezer in the corner. In the fridge he found a lump of cheese, some eggs, mushrooms and other vegetables.

'Grow some of my own out on a little plot of land I own, just past the wood. My garden. Occasionally it gets raided but I've put up a few deterrents now.'

'How do you get the rest of your food?' asked Chas.

'I go into town occasionally. Always in the guise of grumpy old hermit.' He chuckled to himself at the irony of it. 'Do you like omelettes?'

'We'd eat anything right now,' said Si.

The Hermit cooked up a wonderfully welcome meal. Then they sprawled in the comfy sofas. Ben was almost asleep as soon as they had eaten, so Aaron found him some blankets and put him to bed in another room on a pile of cushions.

He offered Si and Chas cans of cider. 'So how long do you need shelter? You can stay as long as you need to.'

'We don't want to put you in danger,' said Si.

'You're fine here. No one really knows about this place. They're not interested in me. They think I live in some hovel out in the woods so no one from the town bothers me. Now and then the odd vigilantes stumble on the house but I've taken precautions to defend myself against hostility. I've got cameras hidden in the trees about a mile away up by the road, so if anyone heads this way, I'll know about it. And I've got trip wires here and there in the woods that set off a warning alarm in the house. Mainly I give the odd wanderer some hospitality and they're on their way.'

'We're heading North. We're trying to reach the Priory. Have you heard of it?'

'The Priory? Have you lost your mind boy? You'll end up in there if you're not careful. Why on earth do you want to go there?'

Si related their story to Aaron. 'I have to find my parents. They hold the key to all this. I'm hoping I can get them out of there.'

Aaron looked at them as if they had announced that they were going to launch a coup on the Houses of Parliament tomorrow. 'You've got to be kidding, Si. The Priory is a high security prison for political prisoners, despite what they would have us believe about it. You don't stand a cat-in-hell's chance of getting into it, never mind getting back out!'

'Okay, that's encouraging. Thanks.' Si said.

' I'm only being realistic,' Aaron said, leaning forward to take another can of cider from the table.

'What else can I do? I can't just melt into the background. They're never going to let up on me and I'm convinced that my parents are alive. I've got to try and help them.'

I admire your loyalty son,' Aaron said. 'And what about you Chas, do you really think you can get in there and save his parents, presuming they're still alive?'

'I think we have to try,' she replied, softly. 'There's obviously something major going on here. I've got nothing to go back to, so I might as well go forward.' She looked up at Si. He no longer saw hostility and bitterness in her face. There was almost tenderness as she said, 'I'm doing this for Plin – and the others from the village. I'm doing it for my little brother, even for my stupid parents.' She paused as tears sprang to her eyes and she fought for control. Then she added quietly, 'I'm doing it for you, Si.'

Si was almost embarrassed at this open display of at least allegiance, if not affection. He'd never doubted that she was a loyal person; but loyalty to him, who had caused the deaths of her beloved Plin and her friends; this was unexpected. He stumbled over words and any sentence that he was trying to form petered out.

'Well, good luck to you both,' said Aaron, smiling at the scene being played out between them. He raised his can. 'To Chas and Si and your Mission Impossible.'

The other two raised their cans and laughed. 'Now, let's go to bed. You two can have my bed. I'll sleep on the sofa here.'

'No, I'll sleep out here too,' Si blustered. 'Chas can have the bed. We're not a ... she's not my...'

'I'm not his girlfriend, is what he's trying to say,' she looked at Si like he was some pathetic lost cause.

Aaron shrugged. 'Come give me a hand with blankets then, Si.'

14

The tantalising smell of bacon reached his nostrils as Si awoke the next morning. He was pleased that he had not had one of his nightmares. However, he was feeling nauseous and his head hurt. In the kitchen Aaron was cooking breakfast with Elvis lying at his feet. The dog wagged his tail and Si stroked his head. In the background Blue Suede Shoes was playing. Aaron was gyrating, frying pan in hand.

'Smells good,' Si said.

'It's a good wake up call, eh?' Aaron smiled. 'I can bet the other two won't be far behind you.'

As if on cue, Chas walked in. 'Good morning,' Aaron said.

'Hi,' she replied, yawning. Elvis got up to wag his tail at her and she petted him until he lay back down, contented.

'How did you sleep?' asked Aaron.

'Good,' she said.

'Want some breakfast? It's ready.'

He laid bacon, eggs, mushrooms and baked beans on a plate before them. Then he gave some bacon to Elvis, who wolfed it down in one slobbering gulp.

Si drew a long, luxurious breath in through his nose. It was a long time since he'd smelled or eaten anything so good.

'The little fella having a lie in?' Aaron asked.

'He's exhausted,' said Si. 'We keep trying to persuade him to stay behind, but he's determined to come with us.'

'Ah well, we'll let him sleep. I can rustle something up for him later. What do you want to do today?'

Si looked at Chas. 'We need to buy some more provisions and we could really do with some transport, as far north as it can get us. We can't go into the town though. It's too dangerous.'

Aaron chewed a piece of bacon. 'I could go into Thirsk and get provisions for you. I could try and find you some transport too.'

'That would be great. Thanks,' said Si.

'Be careful,' Chas added.

'I will,' said Aaron. I'm good at keeping a low profile. It's market day today and I occasionally go in to town for the odd thing.'

'Okay, thanks,' said Chas.'We could do with getting on our way as soon as possible.'

Aaron finished his breakfast. 'I don't shower if I'm going into town. In fact, I try to make myself more unkempt and wear my oldest sweaty clothes. If I stink and look the part, people avoid me.' He laughed. 'Feel free to use the shower and could you gather the eggs for me? Don't go out of the vicinity of the house. It's well hidden so you should be okay, but my shotgun is in the bedroom, if you need it. I'll only be three or four hours.' Aaron bent to ruffle Elvis behind the ears. The dog gave a satisfied groan. 'Stay here boy and keep them safe.'

Si took out a wad of money from Kahn's wallet and gave it to Aaron. 'Here, take this. Use whatever you need, to get us some transport.'

Aaron nodded. 'There are one or two people in town who know the real me and might be persuaded to help you.'

'Be careful,' said Chas.

Aaron smiled.

Si and Chas finished their breakfast. Through the window they watched Aaron, dressed as a tramp, shuffling towards the road. Chas went to look in on Ben.

'Well, he's still alive,' she said, coming back to the kitchen. Si was washing the dishes. 'He's snoring like a pneumatic drill!'

'It'll do him good,' said Si. Chas picked up a tea towel. 'Chas, is this pointless? Should I just give myself up?'

'No! You mustn't give up.'

Si was surprised at her conviction. 'But the Priory: It sounds impossible. That is if we actually make it that far. They're probably not far from us right now.'

'And so far we have outwitted them. We can do it Si.'

He turned to her. 'I don't really know why you're doing this.'

'I've told you why,' she said, not looking at him.

'Morning,' Ben said, breezing into the kitchen. Elvis jumped up, wagging his tail furiously. 'Hey there boy!' Ben threw his arms around the dog. 'Where's Aaron?'

'Gone in to town to find us some food and hopefully some transport,' said Chas. 'You slept well. Want some breakfast?'

'You bet. I'm starving,' Ben replied.

Si fried some bacon and eggs, which Ben ate almost as quickly as the dog had done. He gave Elvis more bacon. 'Can I take him outside to play?'

'Yes, but keep close to the house,' Chas said. As he left the kitchen she added, 'Wow, I sound like his mother!'

'I don't think he minds,' Si smiled. 'I'm going to collect the eggs.'

'I'll come with you.'

The sky was clear and the wind had an icy edge to it. Aaron made his way slowly into Thirsk, carrying an old shopping bag. He was wearing a dirty overcoat and woolly hat. His clothes, which he kept especially for his outings into town, had not been washed for years. Stale sweat clung to him. He always felt some anxiety at going into the crowded market square, which pleased him in a way and confirmed his decision to live a solitary life.

When he reached the town he noticed the law-keepers posted on the road. He thought about trying to cut through some back streets but they had probably seen him and it would look suspicious if he tried to make a detour now. As he approached at a slow amble one of them stepped up to him and immediately recoiled.

'Cor you stink!'

'Many thanks, young man,' Aaron replied, trying to pass.

'Wait,' commanded the law-keeper. 'We're looking for three kids: A teenage boy and girl and a younger boy.' He brought up a picture of Si on his tablet. 'Have you seen him? There's a reward out for them.'

Aaron studied the picture of Si. 'No I haven't seen them. I live on my own. Don't come into the town very often. Would they hurt me if I met them?'

'Yeah. You need to phone this number if you see them,' he said, thrusting a flyer into Aaron's hand.

'I don't have a mobile,' Aaron said.

'Well, use someone else's. Don't approach them. Now get going before I throw up!' The man pushed Aaron forward while his colleague flagged down a car that was approaching.

Aaron walked slowly into the town centre. There was a visible law-keeping presence everywhere. He went into his usual store. The shopkeeper was used to seeing him now and again, and tolerated him.

'Morning Hermit. You were only here last week. Forget something?'

Aaron grunted and the shopkeeper shrugged. He bought some extra things for Chas and Si to take on their journey: Chocolate, coke, crisps, water. As he served the Hermit, the man stood as far back from the counter as possible. He had long since given up advising him to take a shower. He didn't bother to try making conversation anymore.

Aaron made his way up Kirkgate to Cemetery Road where he found the Lion and Lamb, a chic gastro-pub, recently built. The landlord was the son of an old friend. If Aaron was in need he knew he could come here. He never went into the bar, where his incongruous presence would immediately attract attention. He knocked on the back door. A young woman opened it, raised her eyebrows and stepped back.

'If you're peddling something we don't want it.'

'Is Allegiance in?'

'What do you want with him?'

'Tell him Aaron is here. I'm his father's friend.'

She looked disbelievingly at him. 'Wait here.'

After a few minutes a young man appeared at the door. 'Come in old friend.' He didn't even flinch at the smell. 'Sorry about Maggie. She's new.'

Allegiance took Aaron into his sitting room and handed him a beer.'How's things?'

'Not bad. You?'

'Yeah, the pub is going well. Lots of young business types in the bar. New chef too.'

'Heard from your dad?'

'No, not since I last saw you. He's somewhere in Europe; that's all I know. I think he's scared of putting the family in danger if The Rulers think they can trace him through me.'

'He's a good man.'

'Yes, and he'd never have made it out of England if it weren't for you.'

Aaron shrugged.

'So what can I do for you?' Allegiance asked.

'I need a favour. It's risky.'

'Go on.'

'Have you seen the adverts about that boy, Silence Hunter?'

'Can't miss them and the law-keepers are swarming like flies.'

'Have they been here?'

'Yesterday.'

'I know where he is and I think he's worth helping. He needs a vehicle to get as far north as he can. He can pay.'

'What sort of vehicle?'

'Something discreet. Fast.'

Allegiance was silent. Aaron waited.

'I can ask around. When do you need it?'

'As soon as possible. Today?'

'I may know who'd be willing to risk it. How much money has he got?'

Aaron produced the wad of notes. 'He took this from Joseph Kahn. You've heard of him?'

'Of course. He's one of The Rulers' favourite businessmen: Donates a lot of money to their causes. I'm sure my contact would be happy to know he was depriving someone like that of his cash.

I'll need a few hours. Can I contact you?'

'Yes – you know the number. I need to get back.'

'They're at your house?'

'Yes,' said Aaron.

'Okay, leave it with me. You'll have some transport by the end of the day.'

'You're a good man Al. Your father would...'

'I know.'

Aaron stood up and gave Al the money. They hugged. 'Be careful old friend,' Al said.

Aaron ambled back down the street. He took a can of lager from his shopping bag and began to swig from it as if he were drunk. People whispered and pointed, while one or two crossed the street when they saw him approaching. Good. That was how he wanted it. He noticed several law-keepers in Market Square and, as he expected, he was stopped.

'Have you seen this boy?'

Aaron peered closely at the tablet as if it was hard to see, grunted and shook his head.

'Cor, you whiff, old man. Don't you shower?'

Aaron shook his head vigorously, like a mad dog.

'And you shouldn't be drinking on the street.' The law-keeper confiscated the can. Aaron tried to grab it back.

'If you cause any trouble old man, we'll have to arrest you for being drunk and disorderly.'

Aaron sniffed and wiped his face on the back of his sleeve.

'If you see this boy...'

'I know, I know,' Aaron slurred. 'I've heard it all before.'

The law-keeper gave him a shove. 'Just keep your eyes open for him and ... take a shower!'

Aaron shrugged off the man's touch, mumbling to himself as he shuffled away.

'Bloody vagrants!' the law-keeper said, wiping his contaminated hands on his uniform.

Aaron chuckled to himself. This felt like a good day's work. He found a way out of Thirsk through several gardens and into the fields, to avoid yet more questions. Soon he would be back home, safe in his cocoon. And he could take a shower!

*

Aaron had been away almost four hours. Si browsed his book collection. It was rare to see paper books these days. There was lots of biographical stuff and novels from as far back as the twentieth century. Some of the authors were classic writers that he had studied at school and some had long faded into literary insignificance. Chas played through Aaron's CD collection, having finally figured out what to do with them. At the moment Michael Jackson was blasting out 'Beat it! Just beat it!' Ben sat on the floor with Elvis, talking to him and stroking his stomach.

Suddenly Elvis sat to attention. He sniffed and stood up. Si grabbed the shotgun and Chas's hand went to her knife. She hit the stop button on the CD player. Elvis ran to the door, barking.

'Shall we let him out?' Si asked.

'No, he might get hurt,' Ben said.

Elvis was scrabbling at the door.

'It's okay,' Chas announced, looking through the window. 'It's Aaron.' They opened the door and Elvis bounded out to meet him.

'Hey boy,' Aaron said, bending to ruffle his dog's shaggy fur.

'How did you get on?' asked Si

'Good. Let me get out of these awful clothes and take a shower, then we can talk.'

When he emerged from the shower Aaron felt more like himself. Si, Chas and Ben were waiting for him in the living room. Chas had made a pot of herbal tea.

Aaron smiled at them. 'I feel much better now and you'll be grateful not to have to put up with that smell, I can tell you. I have to keep those old clothes in the shed, they stink so much!'

Chas poured the tea.

'Ah wonderful,' Aaron said, cupping the hot mug in his hands. 'Pity it's not a good strong pot of coffee. I miss it, now it's so hard to get hold of. I was addicted to it in my youth.' He looked wistfully out of the window, caught in a moment's reverie.

'So, any news?' Chas asked.

'I spoke to a friend. He's going to arrange something. I had to give him all the money.'

'Fine,' Si said. 'We need the transport.'

'Can you trust him? He won't turn us in will he?' asked Chas.

'If you can trust me, having known me for less than 24 hours, I think I can trust a man I've known since he was a child.'

She nodded. 'What was it like in the town?'

'Law-keepers everywhere. I was questioned a couple of times but I smelt so bad that they didn't keep me talking for long,' Aaron laughed. 'All we can do is wait now. I wasn't followed back here, but best keep alert.'

15

It was dark when the call came. Si, Chas and Ben gathered anxiously in the living room for news.

'You have a car. It's magnetic.'

'Wow. That's generous. There wasn't that much money in Kahn's wallet. I just hoped for an old petrol thing,' Si said.

'He hasn't taken the money. He hates The Rulers. His business started to go downhill when magnetic cars were introduced. He couldn't afford to buy many in. Then he lost his wife and daughter to the New Plague a few years ago. He couldn't afford private treatment. And you know how it is: can't pay - not worth saving.'

'There has to be a way to stop this,' said Si.

'It would be dangerous to try,' Aaron replied. 'You know they want it this way. Helps to ward off rebellion and keeps the population down. I think the New Plague was genetically engineered by The Rulers.'

'You think The Rulers introduced the plague to deliberately kill people?' asked Si.

'Yes. It didn't exist before they came into power and now it's rife in this country.'

'My parents were good people. Why would The Rulers want to kill them?' Ben asked.

'Your parents died from the Plague?' Aaron asked. Ben nodded. 'I'm sorry for you, lad. The Rulers don't target individuals. It's mass control, so they don't care who suffers for it.'

'What happened to Kahn's money if the car dealer didn't take it?' asked Chas.

'My friend is using it to bribe the law-keepers on the north road. There are two of them randomly stopping vehicles leaving Thirsk. The ones he has bribed are on duty from seven in the morning until two, tomorrow afternoon. They've been told what kind of vehicle you'll be in and will wave you through.'

Chas stood up and started pacing the floor. 'What? They're expecting us? That's crazy! They could take the bribe then hand us over anyway to get the reward money.'

'They don't qualify for reward money. It's their job to find you. This is easy money for them. There are no cameras on the roads leaving Thirsk so no one will be able to prove that they let you pass. They win.'

Chas was uneasy.

'Look, I'm not comfortable with it either Chas, but what choice do we have? We need the car,' Si said.

'Too many people to trust,' she muttered.

'I suggest we leave early in the morning,' Aaron said. 'I can get you into Thirsk unnoticed and take you to the car dealer's. The car will be ready for you in an unlocked garage at the side of the main building. If the worst comes to the worst, he can say it was stolen.'

'I wish we could thank him,' said Si.

'I'll make sure he knows you're grateful,' Aaron smiled. 'Now, food and an early night.

The shopkeeper was just hanging the closed sign when the law-keepers entered. He sighed. They had taken up enough of his time yesterday. Reluctantly, he let them in.

'Anything suspicious to report today?'

'No,' the shopkeeper said, wearily.

'Anything unusual happen? You know there's a reward for information leading to their arrest.'

'Nothing to report,' said the shopkeeper. The other law-keeper, who had been browsing round the shop, placed two bars of chocolate and a bottle of coke on the counter. As the shopkeeper served him he remembered the Hermit's shopping basket.

'A reward? Even for information?' he asked.

'Yes. You remembered something?'

'It might be relevant,' the shopkeeper said, hesitantly.

One of the law-keepers took out his tablet and began to tap the screen. 'Go on.'

It was too late to back out now, and a reward would help his business. 'There's this Hermit. He lives in the woods somewhere round here. He rarely comes into town more than once a month for a few provisions. Well, he was only here last week and then he appeared again today. And he bought all sorts of things he doesn't normally buy.'

'Do you know where he lives in the woods?'

'No. I doubt anyone does. He doesn't hang around. And he stinks. No one wants to go near him.'

'What does he look like?'

The shopkeeper described the tramp-like version of Aaron.

'Anything else you can remember? Did he say anything that made you suspicious?'

'No, he doesn't do conversation. He just grunts.'

'Right. We'll let you know if it leads to anything.'

As the shopkeeper locked his door, he was already planning what he would do with the money.

*

The Commander was pleased to finally have a lead, however tenuous. Several other law-keepers had seen the Hermit that morning. From the times they had given, he seemed to be in town for a long time.

'Get the men organised into search parties and find him,' he demanded of Knowles.

'You want them to go now, Sir? It's dark. Shouldn't we wait 'til first light?'

'For pity's sake Knowles, you have taken part in all sorts of night missions. This should be a walk in the park!'

'I know, Sir. But these are not military men. They're not used to it.'

'Well I'm not waiting 'til morning. If this is a genuine lead we could lose them by morning. Comb the countryside within a five-mile radius of the town. Call in reinforcements from neighbouring towns if you need to.'

'Yes Sir.' Knowles turned to go.

'And Knowles, I'm coming with you.'

Resolution had always loved the thrill of the chase. Before he became Commander he had been in anti-terrorism. His favourite part had always been the final moments when they moved in on the target. He wanted to be out there in the field when they located Silence Hunter. He got ready to move out.

It was five thirty when Elvis began to growl quietly. Aaron looked at his monitor that showed live pictures of the road. Si was also awake.

'What is it?' he asked.

'They've found you,' Aaron said, scrabbling out of his blankets. 'Look.' He pointed to the monitor. Si could make out three or four shapes, with flashlights, on foot, making their way into the woods.

'Wake Chas and Ben! You have to leave now! I'll give you directions to get to the garage.' He began scribbling on a piece of paper.

'Aren't you coming?'

'I have to stay. It will give you more time. They'll question me and I can mislead them. Hurry!'

Si turned to see Chas standing in the doorway with Ben and their rucksacks. He tried to persuade Aaron to come once more, but he refused.

'Head out the back and keep going in a straight line for about fifteen minutes. Chas, the trip wires are here and here in that direction.' He showed her a map on his wall. He had the wires marked. She could see the direction they needed to go. She nodded.

The blackness was beginning to subside into dull grey but they would not be able to use torches. Chas would need to use her hunting skills.

'Good luck,' Aaron said. He pushed a Swiss army knife into Chas's hand. 'Here. I want you to have it.'

An alarm sounded. 'Someone has stepped on a wire. They won't be long. Hurry!'

'Thank you,' Si said. 'Please, just ... don't get hurt.'

'Come on Si,' Chas urged. She kissed Aaron's wrinkled cheek, surprising him. 'Thank you.'

'Worth it,' he said winking at her. 'Take care of them, Ben, they need you.'

Ben bent to hug Elvis, then they ran into the woods and disappeared from sight. Aaron began gathering blankets and putting things back to normal. Within moments of heading into the trees, they heard Elvis barking furiously.

'What will they do to Aaron? We should help him,' Si said.

'No Si. We keep going,' Chas said.

Suddenly, there was a gunshot and a yelp from the direction of the house.

'Elvis!' cried Ben. He turned to go back. Si held him.

'Let me go!'

Chas grabbed him too. 'Ben, stop it. Don't be crazy. Elvis is dead. There's nothing you can do.'

'What about Aaron? Chas, we can't let them shoot him as well!' Si insisted.

She rounded on him. 'Okay, let's go back then and get caught. Is that what you want? It's not what Aaron wants. He's risked his life to help us. He told us he could defend himself.' She didn't believe it, but she knew they mustn't go back, whatever happened to Aaron. She felt the knife in her pocket and longed to go back and use it.

Si closed his eyes tightly. Chas could be hard-hearted. He felt sick at the people he had endangered and those who had already lost their lives because of him. He prayed it was not in vain.

*

Resolution looked around, as Knowles tied the Hermit to a kitchen chair.

'Not what I was expecting from the description we were given, I must admit,' said Resolution. 'Quite a sophisticated set up you have here Hermit, if a little turn-of-the-century.'

'You didn't have to kill my dog,' Aaron said, flatly.

'No, but he was annoying me,' the Commander said. 'Where are the fugitives?'

'Not here,' said Aaron.

Two law-keepers were searching the house. 'No, not anymore, but they were here. How long ago?'

'They've never been here.'

'You're lying,' said Resolution, slapping Aaron hard across the face.

'Why would I lie about it? I don't want trouble.'

'Why did you harbour them?'

'What makes you think I did?'

'Information,' said Resolution.

The law-keepers returned to the room. 'There's no one here, Sir, but we found this in the bedroom.'

He handed the Commander a child's sock. 'Do you have children Hermit?'

'I have a boy, yes.'

'Where is he then?'

Aaron hesitated. 'Left home.'

'And this is his sock, is it?'

'Yes.'

'Liar!' Resolution slapped Aaron again. 'Every time you lie, the punishment will get worse. And if you continue I'll let Knowles loose on you and that won't be a pretty sight.' He turned to the two law-keepers. 'Get out in the woods. Split up. They may still be in the vicinity. Contact me if you find them.' The men obeyed. Aaron hoped Chas had persuaded Si to keep going.

'When did they leave?' Resolution demanded.

'They were never here.'

The Commander punched him in the stomach. Aaron doubled up.

'Don't persist with this nonsense, Hermit. Last chance. Why protect them? You could claim the reward.'

Aaron lifted his head slowly. 'I'd rather join my dog!'

Resolution grabbed Aaron by the shoulders. 'You will tell us everything you know. Otherwise, be one hundred percent certain about this: you will join your dog!'

Aaron spat in Resolution's face. Resolution recoiled. Taking a pristine handkerchief from his pocket, he slowly wiped away the spittle. 'Knowles,' he said.

Knowles stepped forward.

'Call me when you're finished.' The Commander retreated to the kitchen. His phobia of blood was growing worse and had dogged his career, but he had never let it overcome his ambition to reach the top. And despite it he had got this far.

*

Chas stopped: listening.

'Someone's coming.'

Ben and Si turned. They could make out a flashlight swinging to-and-fro in the greyness

'You two go on. Take my rucksack. I'll catch you up.'

Si didn't protest. 'Be careful, Chas.'

Chas stalked back towards their pursuer. He was her prey

now: Easy to track. Careless. Pressing herself behind a tree, she prepared to pounce. Her breathing was scarcely audible; her muscles tensed in anticipation. As he passed the tree she leapt on him, her knife at his throat. He lashed out and managed to throw her to the ground. He was on top of her but she still gripped her knife tightly. Thumping her wrists into the ground, he tried to jolt it from her grip. He was much stronger than Chas, but she managed to bring her knee in between his legs and send him rolling onto his back. She sprang onto him, her knife poised. He grabbed her hand and they struggled to overcome one another. The man pushed her off and the knife flew across the ground. She scrabbled after it but he floored her again. Finally, he managed to reach for his gun. Chas tried to crawl away but she knew she was lost.

Suddenly the man gave a cry and fell to the ground. Si stood over him wielding a heavy branch.

'Can you stand?' he said to Chas.

Ben ran out of the shadows and they helped her get up.

'I'm okay. I ... you...'

'Saved your life again. Yeah, I know.'

'I told you to go on.'

'Good job I don't do everything you tell me then,' said Si. 'Come on, let's get going. There may be others nearby.'

'I need to find my knife.'

'It's here,' Ben said.

'Lead the way, Chas,' Si said.

*

Aaron held out for a long time. He took the violence as if he were forty years younger, but his body was weak and Knowles was ruthless. 'This is your last chance, Hermit, before I shoot you.' He held the gun to Aaron's temple. 'No one will miss you, not even your dog.'

Aaron knew if they shot him now, they would head back into Thirsk, and he wanted to give Chas, Ben and Si as much time as possible.

'Okay ... I'll tell you,' he rasped, through bleeding lips.

'Finally,' Knowles said, lowering the gun.

'Yesterday. I fed them. They left last night.'

'Where were they going?'

'They didn't tell me.'

'If you're lying...'

'Why would they tell me anything?'

'Which way did they go?'

He hesitated; stammered. 'I... I...'

'Come on, Hermit. We'll find them anyway and you'll have lost your life for nothing.'

Aaron stalled, deliberately.

'Come on, man!'

Knowles moved in once more. He pressed the gun to Aaron's temple.

Aaron waited for as long as he dared.

Knowles grew impatient. 'I've had enough of this!'

'They headed west,' Aaron blurted out.

'West? I don't believe you. They've been heading north all this time.'

'Believe what you like. I'm tired now.' Aaron's voice was almost a whisper.

Knowles went to consult Resolution.

'He must be lying. Why would they head west?' said the

Commander. 'Get more out of him.'

'Have you heard from the law-keepers in the woods?'

'Nothing.'

'You need to come in, Sir. You have to finish this.'

Resolution took a deep breath. 'How ... bad is he?'

'I've done my job, Sir.' Knowles knew Resolution hated blood and enjoyed forcing him to look at it.

Resolution stepped into the room. Aaron was in a pitiful state. The Commander closed his eyes and composed himself as the nausea rose in his throat.

'You have thirty seconds to tell us where they went or your life is over.'

'West! That's all I know! God forgive me. They're just kids. They don't have a clue why you're after them. They're just trying to survive.'

Resolution came towards Aaron and reached out to touch his swollen face. At the last moment he withdrew his almost imperceptibly trembling fingers.

'Knowles.'

As the Commander went outside, a shot was fired. A moment later Knowles joined him, kicking the dog's body as he passed.

16

The streets of Thirsk were virtually empty. The garage was easy to find and, as arranged, the car was waiting for them. This car wasn't voice activated and there was a key card on the driver's seat.

The car purred quietly to life. Si felt suddenly nauseous. His head was pounding, worse than the other morning. Chas looked at him. Beads of sweat were trickling down his face and his skin was white. He was shivering.

'You look awful,' she said. 'Are you sure you can drive?'

'Just a minute,' he said. He leapt from the car, just making it to the grass verge before throwing up.

'What's wrong?' Ben said, as Si got back into the car.

'I'm not sure. I felt odd the other day, but not as bad as this.'

'Its probably nerves,' said Chas. 'Or adrenalin.'

'Probably. I'll be okay.'

He eased the car out of the garage and followed the signs to the north road. They could see the checkpoint up ahead in the morning light.

'Here goes,' said Ben. 'I hope Aaron's plan works.'

'If they try to stop us, just keep driving ,' Chas said.

'I intended to.'

His stomach still churned. He touched the window to open it

and took deep breaths. A car was being stopped up ahead. A law-keeper leant in. The other law-keeper looked at their car as it approached. His face was impassive. Si prayed his familiar, one word prayer. In the car no one seemed to be breathing. The law-keeper waved them through and began to open the boot of the stationary car.

As Thirsk receded they let out a collective sigh of relief and burst out laughing.

'Thank God!' Chas exclaimed.

'That's what I'm doing!' said Si. 'And thank Aaron. I hope he's okay.'

'Do you think we'll ever see him again? Or Meg?' asked Ben.

I hope so,' said Chas.

It felt exhilarating to be driving the dual carriageway, after being on foot for so long. They silently watched the countryside shooting by. Neither Si nor Chas had ever been this far north before and Ben couldn't really remember it. To their right were the North Yorkshire Moors, rising sharply out of the mist over the fields. To the left were fields with a few farmhouses and ruined churches scattered about.

'Do you really believe in God, Si?' Ben asked.

'I think so.'

'Hmm,' Chas mumbled.

'My parents said that religion causes trouble,' said Ben.

'It can. We're in trouble,' said Si. 'Sometimes trouble is necessary.'

'I think you've got to look out for yourself,' Chas said.

'Yeah, well, I'm still trying to figure it out,' said Si.

'Are we going to find Meg's contact?' asked Ben.

'Yep,' said Si. The piece of paper felt like a precious object in his pocket. He felt for it now.

'Are you okay now?' Ben asked.

Si's stomach seemed to have settled but his head still ached and his skin felt like tiny spiders were crawling across it. 'I think Chas was right. It was just the adrenalin.'

A sign said: Durham eleven miles.

'Can I look at the paper with Meg's contact on?' Chas asked. Si handed her the crumpled sheet.

Peter Marsden

Eastfield House

Leamside

County Durham

'I wonder how long 'til they're back onto us?' Ben said.

'I hope this Peter guy can help us,' Chas said. 'Meg hasn't seen him for years. He could be dead for all we know or switched sides.'

'Optimistic,' Si teased.

She smiled sarcastically at him.

'Leamside. I wonder if that's a suburb of the tech-city?' Si said.

'We can't just drive in. We've got no ID and they've probably been alerted to look out for us,' said Chas.

As they turned off the dual carriageway a sign indicated Durham to the left.

'Leamside – right!' Ben yelled from the back.

'So, it's not in the city. That's good,' Si said.

'What's the house called?' Ben asked.

'Eastfield House,' Chas replied.

They looked intently for signs of a small settlement or village. They passed run down and derelict buildings dotted amidst trees and fields. An old filling station, long abandoned, gawped vacantly at them. They noticed one or two large houses set back in the trees, with heavy security and imposing iron gates, reminding them of Kahn's property. Chas felt the familiar sense of wariness kick in.

'It must be around here somewhere,' Ben said.

'Maybe we should park up and walk. It's hard to see what some of these places are called,' said Chas.

'And they're bound to have CCTV, so they're going to see us coming in the car. We could maybe avoid it more easily on foot,' said Si.

They found a lay-by, set back from the road and left the car.

'What are we going to tell him, even if he agrees to see us?' asked Si.

'I guess we just tell him we're friends of Meg's. See if we think we can trust him first,' Chas said.

As they looked around they could see a row of three disused terrace houses on the left hand side of the road. To their right was a rundown cottage and a deserted shop. Everyone knew it was madness to live undefended in the countryside. Scanning the fields and copses, Chas saw a bungalow, set back up a wooded driveway. Si and Ben saw it too and, without a word, they headed in the direction.

As they neared the, cottage a woman appeared in the door way. The actual door was missing, but there was a barn door leaning against the wall. The front windows were broken, but the apertures were shoddily patched up with plastic bags and bits of wood. Chas reprimanded herself for being careless. The woman leaned against the door post, with her arms folded, watching them vacantly. She was probably a druggie. A small girl appeared, winding herself around the woman's legs.

Si looked at Chas. Did they ignore her? He decided not.

'Hi,' he said, smiling at her.

She didn't answer.

'Come on!' Chas hissed. 'What are you doing, Si?'

'Just being friendly.'

'Well don't. Who knows who else is in there!'

The woman stood very still as they passed, almost looking through them, but Chas knew she was watching them.

The driveway wound its way up through a copse for about half a mile. There was no indication that this was the right house. Immediately, they noticed the CCTV attached to a tree at the entrance to the copse so they headed across the neighbouring field, rather than directly up the drive. They intended to show themselves at the gate but Chas didn't think it wise to give anyone too much notice of their arrival. When they could see the gates – heavy, wrought iron, security loaded, as they expected – they paused. A sign on the wall read 'Eastfield House.'

'Ben, you are the least famous of the three of us. I think you should press the intercom and do the talking. You okay with that?' Si asked.

'Sure,' Ben said, feeling important.

'Just tell him Meg sent you and that there are three of us. We need to see him alone,' said Chas.

'I hope this works,' Si said, chewing his lip. 'Ready?'

Ben nodded and stepped into view of the security cameras. He pressed the intercom. There was no answer. He tried several times but there appeared to be no one at home.

'Great!' said Si. 'Now what do we do?'

Just then a holo-image of a man appeared at the gate right

beside Ben. He nearly jumped out of his skin which made Si, and even Chas, stifle a laugh.

'Thanks for calling,' said the figure. 'As you've gathered by now, I'm not here. Call back later. If you're thinking of robbing me, think again, my security is unbeatable.'

As suddenly as it had appeared the image was gone.

'Do you think that was him?' asked Ben.

'Maybe. I'm surprised there's absolutely no one at home,' Si said.

'There might be. They could be onto the law-keepers as we speak,' Chas said. 'Come on let's scout around; see what we can find out.'

The wall stretched for about half a kilometre then turned sharp right. At intervals there were more CCTV cameras, camouflaged in bushes and trees. Some were pointed at the wall and others pointed out from the garden. Chas had eyes like a hawk though and kept ahead of the others so that they could avoid the range of each camera. The wall was about seven metres high, and they couldn't see over it. Along the top a blue tube of light, about five centimetres in diameter, hovered just above, making a very quiet hum. They turned the corner and followed the wall for about another half kilometre. This was the back of the property but they still couldn't see anything within the walls.

'Is that thing on top of the wall some kind of security thing?' Ben asked.

'Some kind of stun device. They used to have something similar at the Bastille. It senses body heat and movement: Stuns anything within a metre.'

'Wow!' Ben said.

'Yeah, except the one at the Bastille didn't look so sophisticated as that and sometimes it wasn't even powered up.'

The wall was well maintained. There was no damage or weak spots. They came full circle back to the front gates.

'Now what?' Ben asked.

Chas looked at Si. He had half expected her to make a decision for them. As if reading his mind she said, 'Your mission – your decision.'

He paused, thinking. 'We should wait and see if he comes back today. If not then we move on without him. Let's go back to the car in case we need to make a quick getaway.'

'I think we should move the car totally out of sight and come back here to wait. Got any food left? I'm starving. If not I could always catch a rabbit or two.'

'Oh and we'll light a fire here to cook it and let everyone know we're here!' said Si.

'Only joking! Anyway, you can talk!' Chas threw back.

'That woman was watching us anyway.'

'But you go and virtually introduce yourself to her!'

'I only said HI!' Si yelled.

'And gave her plenty of time to check us out!' Chas yelled back, taking a step closer to Si. 'She could have the law-keepers on their way out here already!'

'I doubt it,' Si countered. 'She looked like a druggie to me. She was stoned.'

'And what would you know about that? I'm surprised we've got this far with your idea of keeping a low profile!'

'Stop it!' Ben pushed in between them. 'What's the matter with you two? Someone might hear you!'

Chas and Si broke apart. 'Come on, let's go move the car,' Ben said, shaking his head.

Chas glowered at Si. He glared back and turned away, marching towards the car. Ben followed, then Chas, kicking at stones and clumps of grass as she went.

'You hungry?'

A man's voice startled Si and he looked across to the bungalow. The staring woman was standing at the door, but now a man was next to her. He was unshaven with a mop of jet black curly hair. He looked serious and a little threatening. Si hesitated and the others caught up with him.

'We've got enough. I hunt for my own meat – plenty of it round here – and I've just got back from Durham market.'

'No thanks,' said Si. 'We've got things to do.'

'That your car over there then?' the man asked.

'Er...yes,' Si answered. Chas dug him in the ribs.

'We've got to get going,' she said, pulling Si by the arm.

The man's face unexpectedly broke into a grin. 'You don't trust me. Well, the offer's there if you want it.' He gently put an arm round the woman and steered her inside the bungalow.

'Thanks,' Si shouted, as Chas marched him away from the bungalow.

'That's just the kind of thing I was going on about and you still take no notice of me. You're a liability.'

'Well why don't you just leave me alone then?' Si said.

'Please! Don't start all over again,' said Ben.

They ignored him. 'My face and your face are linked now, Silence Hunter – like it or not. If I quit now you're dead and so am I. Do you think they'll just let me go on with my life after helping you?'

'You could easily blend into the background – lose yourself in some forest again,' said Si.

Ben shook his head, growled at them and ran on ahead.

They walked on in silence, Chas a few paces ahead. Suddenly Si was angry with himself for provoking her. He knew she was right. He was careless. He found it hard that she always seemed to know more than him and he felt foolish. But he couldn't fault her loyalty to their 'mission' as she called it. He jogged a few paces and caught up with her.

'Chas, this is ridiculous.'

She marched purposefully on, refusing to look at him. He jogged in front of her, turned and took her by the arms. She tried to shake him off. He gripped more firmly.

'Chas! Just stop. I'm sorry! I'm sorry I keep messing up. I don't want to fight with you. Hey, you've been so amazing to me. I couldn't have done this without you.' He tried to look her in the eye, but she averted his attempts.

There was a silence. Chas closed her eyes and sighed. Then she looked at him. 'I want to come with you Si,' she said in a quiet voice.

He smiled and let go of her arms. 'Good.'

On an impulse he took her hands in his. To his surprise she didn't pull away. They stood for a moment like this, Chas looking down at her hands in Si's. He wanted to tell her that he wished he could take care of her; that he wanted her to feel safe, that he might be falling in love with her. He moved closer but she instantly stepped back and removed her hands from his grasp.

'Just try to be more... discreet.' She gave him a quirky smile. 'And don't be so sarcastic.'

He laughed. 'You can talk!'

17

When they reached the car, Ben was relieved to see them smiling. Si drove up the road until they found a dirt track surrounded by trees. Chas and Ben got out as he reversed as far as he could into a thicket. Branches screeched along the paintwork and the door opened just enough for Si to climb out. Taking their belongings they returned to the gate of Eastfield House to wait for someone to return. They had some food and water. Chas let Ben use her knife and he spent the hours whittling branches into spears and seeing how far he could throw them. She watched him, imagining her little brother doing this, or the children from the village. Si was quiet, thinking about his parents and wondering if this was all futile.

It was getting dark and cold so they put on an extra layer of clothing. Around the perimeter of the property floodlights started to flicker on, like eyes blinking awake. The dusky greyness was transformed into a false, clinical daylight.

'If no one comes we'll sleep in the car tonight,' Si said. Then we'll just have to go. We haven't got much money left either.'

Just then they saw car headlights. A few cars had passed by on the road, but this one was turning up the drive.

'Get down!' Chas ordered.

The silver Mercedes slowed. It had dark windows so it was

impossible to see inside. The gates opened and the car glided in. He worked for The Rulers and he had money. Were they insane to come here?

'I'm having second thoughts,' Chas said.

'Me too,' Ben agreed.

'Meg trusted him,' Si said.

'Yeah but should we? That was a long time ago,' Chas said.

There was a long pause.

'I'd like to try,' Ben said.

Chas looked him. 'Okay. You know what to say?'

'Yeah.'

Ben stepped out of the trees and up to the intercom. It was brighter here, under the security lights. He pressed the button. No one answered. He pressed again and waited.

'Doesn't this bloke have any servants?' Si said, in frustration.

Ben was about to give up when a voice came through the intercom.

'Who are you and what do you want?'

Ben knew that the man would be able to see a holo-image of him inside the house. 'My name's Ben. I've come to see Peter Marsden. Meg from York sent me.'

There was a silence. 'Hello?' Ben said.

'I'm still here. Meg, you say?'

'Yes she sent me to ask for Mr. Marsden's help?'

'I'm Peter Marsden. Are you alone? You'd better come in.'

'I'm not alone sir,' Ben said quickly. 'I have two friends with me. They're afraid to come in. They would rather you came to the gate to talk, if you're willing.'

'They need to show themselves.'

'Meg sent us to you 'cos we're in trouble and she reckoned

you'd help us.' Ben had said more than his remit. He was making up his own script now. Chas and Si could hear everything.

'I need to see them,' Marsden said.

'Promise you won't call the law-keepers,' Ben said.

There was a pause. 'It depends on what you've done,' said Marsden. 'There are some things I can't condone.'

'We haven't done anything wrong Mr. Marsden.'

Marsden paused. 'You have my word that I'll give you a chance to explain yourselves. Now, they need to come forward.'

Ben motioned for Chas and Si to come into the view of the cameras.

Marsden at once recognised Si. 'Silence Hunter and 'the girl'. According to the news you're dangerous criminals,' Marsden said.

'Do you think your friend Meg would have helped us if we were?' Si asked.

'Not willingly, but you could have forced her.'

This was difficult. All he had was their word against all the media propaganda.

'I guess you'll have to trust your instincts then,' Si said.

Marsden looked long and hard at their holo-images. 'Leave your bags there and turn out your pockets. Come to the front door.'

They looked at each other, uncertainly. 'Come on,' Chas said. 'We've got to move this forward one way or another.'

They dumped their bags in the bushes and showed Marsden all their pockets. Of course Chas had her knife tucked inside her clothes. There was no way she was going anywhere without that.

Marsden opened the gates and they walked the fifty metres up to the front door. It was a large, but unpretentious bungalow. The grounds were immaculately kept. As they reached the front door it was opened by a man. They recognised his voice from the intercom at the gate earlier on.

'I'm Peter Marsden.' He stretched out his hand. Si shook it.

Marsden turned to Chas. 'And you are?'

'Chas.' Marsden offered his hand but she wouldn't take it.

Unperturbed, he turned to Ben. 'And you are the brave Ben. Come in, all of you. My cook/house-keeper is on her day off but she'll be back later. I'll ask her to bring your bags in.'

They followed Peter Marsden into a spacious lounge with high backed leather sofas and soft lighting. Marsden was a tall man. He had jet black hair swept over to one side at the front and a moustache, which contained a sprinkling of grey. He looked to be in his fifties and fit, although Si assumed he was older from what Meg had told them. He was wearing corduroy trousers and a cardigan over a polo neck shirt.

'Sit down,' he offered. 'I was about to heat up a casserole. There'll be plenty to share. I'll make drinks and we'll talk.'

He went to the kitchen. Chas looked around for security cameras but she couldn't see any. They sat nervously not knowing what to make of Marsden. When he reappeared he brought a tray of drinks and biscuits.

'Help yourselves,' he said, laying the tray on an oak coffee table in front of them. 'So —the dangerous, highly prized criminal, Silence Hunter is in my house. Do you know I'm the company director of a government funded engineering firm developing new uses for nanotechnology?'

'Meg told us that you worked for the government. She also told us that we could trust you,' Si said.

'Nice to know she still thinks highly of me after all these years. I hope she's doing well. Is she still in York? I know she and Alastair moved there in the 20s.'

'She's still there,' Si said. 'But she's alone.'

'Yes, Alastair died about ten years after they moved there. They had a son but he was a good-for-nothing. Left home as soon as he could and never came back. She had principals and she stuck to them. She worked for me for a long time. Helped me to see a few things clearly when I was getting too caught up in my career.' There was a pause as Marsden reflected. 'So, what's your story?'

'It's a long one, if you want the whole thing,' Si said.

'I do,' Marsden replied. 'But first, let's eat. I've had a long journey today and I guess you might be hungry.'

Ben nodded enthusiastically. Marsden gave a command and some classical music began to play. He went to the kitchen to get the meals, thinking about his first impressions of these young people. Silence Hunter. The name seemed familiar, from an earlier time, but he couldn't quite put his finger on it. Maybe it was just a result of all the media attention. He knew however, that it was a serious offence to harbour fugitives. He was not averse to going against the law for a good cause, but it had been a long time.

They ate in the dining room at a grand mahogany table covered with an embroidered, white cloth. The cutlery was highly polished. Even though they were just eating casserole, Ben felt he was at a banquet and tried to eat as politely as he could remember.

'This is really good,' Ben said, trying not to speak with his mouth full. 'As good as my mum's cooking.' He wolfed it down even though it was very hot.

Marsden laughed. 'I'm glad.'

The other two nodded and made approving, grateful noises.

They ate mainly in silence and after dinner, moved back to the lounge. Marsden brought more coffee while Ben snuggled into a corner of the sofa, yawning contentedly. Chas watched him fondly as he closed his eyes.

'I guess Ben's not going to tell me much about himself tonight,' Marsden said, smiling. 'So, Si, let's start with you.'

Chas was silent for most of the time, only chipping in when she felt Si was not making something clear or if Marsden asked her a question. As Si named his parents a light came on in Marsden's memory.

'Of course,' he exclaimed. 'Kate and Morgan Hunter: I remember it.'

'Meg gave me some newspaper clippings. They're in my bag,' Si offered.

'It was a big story; the accident at the lab and the loss of two highly esteemed scientists. I met them once at a New Technologies convention in Birmingham.'

Si was amazed. He hadn't realised how well known his parents had been.

'And you think they're still alive?' Marsden said.

'Yes.'

Si even told him about the Bastille dreams he'd been having. Chas felt a tinge of jealousy that Si hadn't shared them with her.

'And Chas – why are you doing this? You've put yourself in serious danger. And what about him?' He gestured to Ben, snoring innocently on the sofa. 'What on earth are you doing involving a kid in this?'

Chas told Marsden the details about herself and Ben that were relevant to Si's story. 'And Ben wanted to come after we escaped from Kahn. We tried to leave him in York with Meg but he wouldn't stay.'

'And he could be useful when we get near the Priory. His father was a fisherman round there and Ben might know people who are familiar with the waters around the island.'

Marsden raised his eyebrows and shook his head. Then he blew out a long breath. 'And how did you hope I would help you?'

Chas and Si looked at each other for a moment. 'Not sure, to be honest. Meg suggested it and we're pretty desperate for any help we can get.'

There was a long silence as Marsden digested everything. Chas and Si waited anxiously for his response.

'I'm going to make more coffee,' he said, picking up the tray and heading for the kitchen.

'Can I use your bathroom?' Chas asked.

'Yes. This way.'

Si got up from the sofa to stretch his legs and pace the room. His impressions of Marsden were good so far, but there was still a finger of doubt prodding his mind. He felt trapped here in this walled fortress. If Marsden chose to hand them over they'd have little chance to escape, although Chas could probably find a way. He breathed deeply.

Chas sat on the side of the jacuzzi for a while. She too was unclear what to think of Marsden. He had told them little about himself. His defences were good here and he was clearly making great money working for The Rulers. Why would he risk it for them? It didn't add up. However, there was something about him, despite her misgivings. She stood up, splashed cold water on her face and dried it with the softest towel she had ever touched.

As she came out into the hallway, she could hear a muffled

voice coming from the kitchen. Marsden was on the phone. Immediately her senses were on high alert and she crept up to the door, which was slightly ajar.

'Thanks Eric. 'Sound advice, as always. I'll call you and let you know. I won't be in tomorrow though. Keep me up to date.'

There was a short pause. 'Fine. Thanks. Bye.'

Chas moved away from the door. What on earth did that mean? Cups clinked as Marsden picked up the tray and Chas retreated hastily to the lounge.

'Shall we put the boy to bed?' Marsden said. 'He's out of it.'

He picked up Ben, as if he was a blanket draped across his arms, and walked out of the room. Chas followed him. She needed to know where Ben was being taken. Marsden opened one of the many doors on the corridor and deposited Ben smoothly into a neatly made single bed. Chas watched as he tucked him in. Ben muttered something incoherent, and was silent again. Marsden smiled at Chas. She looked uncertain.

'You okay?' he asked.

She nodded, biting her lip.

'You really care about him, don't you?'

She nodded again.

'He'll get a good night's sleep there,' he said, moving towards the door.

Back in the lounge they drank hot chocolate. 'You look tired. I've got beds for you both. Harmony has just arrived back and she's picked up your bags.'

Chas and Si looked at each other apprehensively. 'And what have you decided about us?' Si asked.

'I've decided that you can stay here for now and I'll help you, as far as I can.'

'Thank you,' Si said, relief audible in his voice. 'And what about your housekeeper?'

'Harmony is loyal and trustworthy. She and I hold similar views and she would never betray me,' Marsden said.

Si nodded. 'Thank you. We're very grateful.'

Chas was silent.

'Come with me. I'll show you to your rooms. You'll meet Harmony in the morning. She's gone straight to bed.'

Marsden led the way down the corridor, which rounded two corners before it came to the bedrooms where Si and Chas were to sleep. They were in adjacent rooms, both small with a single bed and basic furniture; spotlessly clean and tidy as if waiting for guests to arrive. Their rucksacks had been placed by their beds with toothbrushes, towels and soap. There was a bathroom across the corridor for them to use.

'Harmony is so thoughtful, even on her day off. If you have everything you need, I'll say goodnight.'

'Goodnight. And thanks again Mr. Marsden,' Si said.

'Please – call me Peter.'

When he had gone, Chas pulled Si into her room and shut the door. She scanned this room for any kind of surveillance, but found none. Still, she whispered.

'Si, something's not right.'

She told him about the end of the phone call she had heard.

'That doesn't mean anything,' Si said, although his heart started to beat faster.

'It could mean everything,' she protested.

'Do you think they might come for us tonight?'

'Maybe... I don't know. We should be ready, just in case. I know where Ben is.'

Si wanted to trust Marsden. But he was conscious of the fact that Chas believed him to be naive. He bowed to her judgement.

'Sleep in your clothes. We'll sleep in shifts. You go first; I'll keep watch and wake you in a couple of hours.'

'Great!' Si said. 'I won't say goodnight then.' He yawned, retreating to his room.

Chas pulled out her knife and rolled it around in her fingers. She looked out of the window. This room seemed to face out towards the back of the house. She tried the window. It had a locking mechanism but it opened easily. At least they could get into the garden if they needed to. She thought about waking Ben and bringing him into her room to sleep.

'Si,' she whispered, putting her head round his door, 'I'm going to bring Ben up here.'

Si was in bed. 'Wait, I'll come with you. I could carry him.'

'Okay.'

'Let's give Peter time to get to sleep. We don't want anyone catching us snooping around.'

Half an hour later, the house was dead quiet. Chas remembered exactly which door led to Ben's room, even though there were many. Si gently lifted Ben in his arms. Making sure no one was about, they tiptoed back to Si's room, where Si laid him on the bed.

'You can put him in my bed, I'm not going to sleep much tonight,' Chas said.

'Neither am I,' Si replied. 'No, you have your bed and take what sleep you can get.'

'Honestly Si, you'll benefit more than me from a bed. I'm used to sleeping rough.'

'Yeah? Me too these days, so stop arguing and let me do

something for you for a change!'

She looked at him. A lop-sided smile appeared on her face, which she quickly erased. 'Well, why don't you have my bed while I'm on watch?'

'Chas!'

'Okay, okay Mr. Chivalry. I'm going!' She retreated.

Si made a makeshift bed on the floor with some cushions and his coat and lay down.

It was a fitful sleep, rife with snippets of dreams:

*

His mother's face, the man with the needle. There was no cohesion and no one spoke. His mother was crying over a body. He tried to speak to her; to comfort her. Then he bent over the body. It was his father. He recoiled. The body rose up and it was no longer his father, but Si himself. The man in the white coat materialized again. The needle appeared on its own, flying around like a rocket. His mother's face: crying, laughing manically, then screaming silently. An explosion! Newspaper headlines floating in the sky. A hand on his shoulder, shaking him.

He gasped and opened his eyes.

'Si, it's your turn,' Chas whispered. He was glad.

18

The men in the woods had reported losing the fugitives. The one with the sore head had admitted that he had engaged them but they had escaped. Resolution had commanded the other man to execute him in the woods, but Knowles had intervened.

Back in the Law-keeper's office Resolution and Knowles discussed what to do next.

'The hermit said they went west,' Knowles said. 'What do you make of that?'

'Ridiculous. That boy is on a course north. I'm convinced he's headed for The Priory. Someone must have tipped him off.'

'How? Who could possibly know?'

'I don't know. It was top secret. Only a handful knew that the Hunters' deaths had been staged. And their transportation to the Priory wasn't even documented.'

'We should put them on alert at the Priory and in the nearby towns. What about road blocks?'

'Yes. Get on to it. Every town and tech-city is on the look-out, but I want all law-keepers one hundred percent vigilant. Up the reward for the boy and harden the punishments for anyone found withholding information or helping them.'

'Yes Sir.'

'Get your men out in this town and find out if anyone's seen them today. What are the next towns and tech-cities?'

'There's Northallerton and Middlesborough on route, Sir. Sunderland, Durham...'

'Get them all on high alert. I want to be out of here by mid-afternoon.'

'Yes sir.'

Resolution paced the floor, furious and anxious. His position was in serious jeopardy now. He knew he should report in, but dreaded having to face Premier Zephyr again. He picked up his holophone; then put it down again. He'd give Knowles time to find out some information. Maybe he'd have something positive to report.

As if he had summoned it up, an image of Premier Zephyr manifested itself in front of him. Resolution winced and drew a sharp breath before hitting the button to bring the image to life.

'Commander Resolution. Have you apprehended the boy yet?' the Premier said.

'Not yet, Sir. We've been close and we have a few leads that we're following up.'

'Not good enough. This boy is a threat to national security. We need to find out what he knows.'

'We're very near to catching him Sir. We've upped the alerts and we know where he's headed.'

'Where would that be?' asked the Premier, unimpressed.

'The Priory, Sir.'

'Damn it!' the Premier yelled, slamming his fist down. 'The Priory? Are you certain? How does he know?'

'He can't know Sir, he's guessing.'

The Premier pointed a translucent finger in Resolution's

direction. 'You have three days to make a significant break-through and preferably apprehend the boy or you're off the case Commander. And that promotion I know you want will be out of the question. Three days!'

Before Resolution could reply the image self-terminated. He slumped in a chair with his head in his hands and cursed.

A few hours later, Knowles knocked on the door. 'Sir, we have a lead. Three people, fitting their descriptions, heading north, just south of Northallerton at around 08:30 hours this morning. A male fitting Silence Hunter's description was driving.'

'I knew it. Let's move out.'

He would be damned before he let Silence Hunter, some girl and a small boy rob him of his glorious ascent to power.

*

As dawn broke Si struggled to keep his eyes open. He was coming to the end of a two hour watch. Ben had barely moved all night. Si heard a door open in another part of the house and ventured out of his room to investigate. As he rounded the corner cautiously, he saw a slim young black girl heading to a bathroom in her dressing gown. He kept well back so she didn't see him. Harmony. He went back to his room as Chas emerged from hers.

'What is it?' she asked, alert as usual. Si wondered if she ever felt tired.

'It was just the housekeeper getting up. It's 6.30.' He yawned and rubbed the heels of his hands into his eyes.

'You go back to sleep, Si. I'll wake you if anything happens.'

'Thanks.'

As Si curled himself into his cushions, Ben woke up, stretched and yawned loudly. 'Morning Si. Wow! That was a good sleep.'

Si smiled ironically at him. 'Chas is next door.' He shut his eyes.

Ben knocked on Chas's door and went in. She explained their concerns.

'So you two have been up half the night?' he asked.

'Yes.'

'You should have woken me to do a shift.'

She smiled. 'You needed the sleep. You were out of it last night.'

'I want to be useful though.'

'You are.'

'Can we get some breakfast? I'm starving.'

*

Harmony greeted them as they made their way down the corridor. 'Good morning. Mr. Marsden is in the dining room, with the morning papers. Will you join him?'

'Thanks,' Chas said.

Harmony took them to the dining room.

'Good morning,' Peter said, rising from his chair. 'Have a seat and help yourself to some food. Did you sleep well?'

Ben looked at Chas. 'Yes thanks,' she replied.

'And where is Si?'

'Still sleeping,' Chas said.

'He can eat when he wakes up. Help yourselves. Harmony can bring you a cooked breakfast if you like. She does a fantastic fry up.'

He indicated the food on the sideboard and sat down to resume eating his toast and reading the news on his tablet.

There were croissants and toast, fresh fruit salad, orange juice, grapefruit and much more. Ben took a plate and helped himself to something from every platter. Chas had orange juice and fruit. Peter seemed very relaxed in their presence, as if they were merely friends staying for a few days. Chas felt uneasy. They ate silently for some time.

'You all get a good mention here,' he said, showing them the tablet. There was a photograph of Si and a description of their car.

'They know about the car?' Chas gasped. 'We can't stay here; they must be on to us.' She stood up.

'Not necessarily. It says here that a similar car with people of your description in it was seen heading North around eight thirty yesterday, near Northallerton. You could be anywhere. That's all they know. Where is the car? We'll get rid of it.'

Chas stared at him. Was he bluffing? Did he know that the Commander was on his way here right now? She was beginning to regret her decision to give Marsden a chance.

'Chas,' he said gently, 'I know you're afraid and you're not sure whether to trust me. I understand that. All I can tell you is that back when I knew Meg, I got involved in an underground movement, against the party that became The Rulers. I keep up my appearance of working for them as a cover. And it brings in good money, I have to admit, I like that. I have never been investigated for anything, so they have no reason to suspect you'd come here.'

'Unless they got Meg to talk,' she said.

Peter's face paled. 'I hope not. They're brutal.'

'I'm going to wake Si,' Chas said.

In about ten minutes she was back with Si. Peter couldn't help smiling as Si shuffled in, hair like a bush, yawning.

'Good morning Si.'

'Morning,' Si replied.

'You didn't sleep so well, eh?'

'Not really,' Si answered. 'Chas has told me about the news report.'

'Yes. Help yourself to breakfast first. Would any of you like cooked?'

Neither Si nor Chas did, but Ben nodded enthusiastically.

Peter laughed and went to inform Harmony.

Si helped himself to food, but he wasn't feeling too good again this morning. The same nausea and prickling under his skin had returned.

Chas was edgy, she couldn't sit down. 'I think we should leave.'

'I don't think so, Chas,' Si said. 'I believe him about the underground stuff you just told me. I like him.'

Chas gave him an exasperated look. 'It's not about liking him though is it? I felt the same when we got here. He does seem genuine but now I just don't know.'

'I like him too,' Ben said, his mouth full of toast. 'I don't think he'll give us away.'

Peter walked in. 'I won't. You have my word. I've just phoned one of my managers, Eric Myers. I trust him. He's going to get rid of your car once you tell me where you left it.'

Eric. It was the name Chas had heard on the phone last night. Another person who knew they were here.

'The car is in the bushes up a dirt track about a mile up the road to the left,' said Si.

'Okay. Well I'll get Eric to sort that out.'

Chas stood by the window, biting her lip. Her hand kept flicking to the knife under her jacket.

'Chas, it will be okay. Please try to trust me,' Peter said.

Si stood up and touched her lightly on the shoulder. He took her hand and led her to a chair. He crouched in front of her.

'Come on Chas,' he said gently. 'I think it will be okay. We're not going to stay here long anyway and we've already burnt our bridges by telling him everything last night.'

She nodded, resignedly.

Peter said,' Today we're going to work out what I can do for you. I can't come with you. I'm needed here and I can't risk the business. My office is the room right at the back of the house, very last door. Overlooks the garden. I like the peacefulness of it. In an hour come down there and we'll talk. I've got some business to attend to first. Make yourselves at home in the meantime. Have a shower, relax in the lounge. You're not going to be discovered here. Harmony will bring you whatever you want.'

He smiled at them and left the room.

'That Eric guy is the one he was talking to last night,' said Chas.

'There you go then. He was probably asking his help. He said he trusts him,' Si said. He was still feeling unwell. 'I think I'm going to have to go and lie down, I feel really bad.'

'Like yesterday?' Ben asked.

'Pretty similar.'

Si left the room as Harmony delivered an enormous breakfast to a wide-eyed Ben.

Si lay down. His head was throbbing and the nausea was growing. He closed his eyes and wished none of this was happening to him. He tried to focus on the time before his parents disappeared: A safe time, or so he had thought. He saw himself smiling and his mother and father hugging him. He saw days out at the beach when he was a toddler. He saw a visit to a zoo when he was about five and his father telling him all sorts of animal facts. He saw numerous birthdays and parties and friends. He remembered all the people at their underground gatherings of the Way. Nick, Lucy, Jenny, Michael – his parents' friends. And his friends: Honour, Bish and Teg. He wondered what they were doing now and if they ever thought of him. They must have seen the stories in the news. He wondered what they thought? As he concentrated on these images, the nausea subsided and he drifted back to sleep.

Chas sat with Ben in the dining room, watching him wolf down his meal. She was worried about Si. If he got really sick what would she do? Would she try to find his parents alone? She thought of her own parents and wondered where they were now and if they ever regretted giving her over to the workhouse. She dared to imagine what life might have been like with Kate and Morgan Hunter as her parents. Useless thoughts! She snapped her mind back to the present. Could Si have picked up the New-Plague? His symptoms were amongst the early ones associated with it. If he had it, they might all be infected by now and they'd soon know for sure if Si was infected. Once it had hold it was a slow and painful death, with no known cure. She glanced up at Ben, remembering that his parents had died of it. Maybe it wasn't too late to get Ben away. But she couldn't leave Si. She wouldn't. Maybe she should talk to Peter about Ben staying here. Did this mean she trusted him? Her head swam.

'You okay?' Ben asked, his mouth full of egg. 'You look white. You should eat more. Have some of this.' He held out his fork full of bacon.

Chas shook her head. 'I'm okay, honestly. Just thinking about things. You finish it.'

Ben sighed. He really liked Chas. He tucked the forkful into his mouth.

Harmony came in. 'Would you like anything else?' She smiled at Ben who had just cleared the last of the food into his mouth. 'Ah, you enjoyed that, I see.'

He grinned at her. 'It was amazing!'

She laughed. 'So, anything more for you?' she said to Chas.

Chas shook her head. 'No thanks.' Harmony nodded and turned to leave. 'What's it like being Peter Marsden's slave?'

Harmony stopped. Her smile was gone. 'Mr. Marsden does not have slaves. I am his cook and housekeeper. He pays me a good wage and I am free to leave if ever I want to. I live here because I have no family. He looks after me.' She paused. 'He rescued me when I was a child.'

Chas felt stupid. 'I'm sorry, I didn't mean any offence.'

'None taken,' Harmony said and left the room.

'See Chas, he is a good man,' Ben said.

Chas smiled at him. She still felt unsure.

*

The study, at the back of the house, was a light airy room that extended into a conservatory. There was a desk with a tablet in the corner. The walls were filled with novels and books about engineering, aeroplanes, and military history. There were also models of fighter jets on stands around the room. There was a large HTV on one wall. In the conservatory end of the room were two armchairs and a sofa. These were less formal than the ones in the lounge. When Chas and Ben knocked and entered, they found Si already there, talking with Peter about planes. Si was holding a model of an F-22 Raptor and Marsden was explaining how his company had produced the follow on version of the plane and been instrumental in developing its stealth technology.

'And the metamaterial cloak is a perfect working device. The device directs the flow of electromagnetic radiation (light) smoothly around an object, without reflection; like water flowing past a rock in a stream,. Hence no rays enter the eye, there is nothing to see, and it is without shadow. It's used for all kinds of security these days, not just military.'

Si was engrossed, turning the plane in his hands. 'Wow! I wish we could have learnt about this sort of stuff in school.'

Peter looked up at Chas and Ben who were watching them from the door. 'Come in. We were just talking science.'

They approached. 'Have a seat. Help yourself to drinks.' On the table was a pot of coffee, juice and biscuits.

'This is fascinating,' Si said.

'You feeling better?' Chas asked.

'I'm okay.' He had thrown up again when he had woken, but the sensation in his skin had died down and the nausea had all but gone now.

'I want to show you something,' said Peter, getting up and moving to a bookcase. He pressed a button. The book case opened out and behind it was a safe. He reached in and brought out a duffle bag.

'This is amazing! It's one of our latest developments and this is the prototype.'

'And you're showing it to us?' Si said.

'I trust you. I want you to trust me.' He glanced at Chas.

He undid the toggle string and brought out a metallic blanket. As he pulled more of it out, it was hard to tell what colour it was or in fact, where or what it was. It seemed to disappear. And not only that; as Peter stood up and held it over his hands, his hands suddenly disappeared too. Chas, Si and Ben let out a collective gasp.

Peter laughed. 'It's an invisibility cloak. I love demonstrating it. Watch.'

He pulled the cloak over his head and body and at once disappeared. They could only see the objects that had been behind him.

'Awesome! 'said Ben.

Marsden appeared again across the room. 'It's not perfect. Sometimes you can detect if the person moves because the background can distort slightly as the material moves. We're working on that.'

'I always thought this kind of stuff was only science-fiction,' said Chas.

'It was for a long time,' Peter said. He sat down and handed the cloak to Si. 'But invisibility technology has been under development for over fifty years. It's pretty similar to the stealth technology I was talking about with the planes. The cloak is made from metamaterials; tiny structures smaller than the wavelength of light. If properly constructed, the nanostructure of tiny rods in such a cloak can actually guide rays of visible light around an object. This is the first one that can truly do it in three dimensions, so that the object can't be seen from any angle. Put it on Si. There is an arrow on the inside where the crown of your head should go so that you face the right direction and can see through the cloak.'

Si pulled the cloak over his head and disappeared from view.

'Now, you two get up and walk around him. Can you tell he's there?'

Chas and Ben moved around where they had seen Si standing a moment ago. It was remarkable that even though their minds told them that Si was standing right in front of them, their eyes told them a different story.

'So cool!' Ben exclaimed.

'It is amazing!' Chas said, nodding her head.

'You can all try it,' Peter offered.

Ben was desperate to go next. He walked around the room in it. Sometimes they could see the background distorting when they followed the sound of Ben's giggling and exclamations.

'Yes, it doesn't make you all that invisible if you're noisy of course,' laughed Peter. 'It is only an optical illusion, after all.'

Chas tried it on. It felt as light as silk but not as slippery. The blue underside had two handles attached to it so that a person could stop it from slipping off. She moved around the room. It was hard to believe that the others couldn't see her. She was much harder to track as she had the stealth of a panther. They only realized where she was when the study door opened, ostensibly by itself. She took off the cloak and came to sit with the others, handing it back to Peter. He fed it back into its bag.

'I want you to have it,' he said.

'Why?' Si said, taken aback.

'I want you to find your parents. I think what you're doing is vitally important to the country.'

'But if they find out you've given us this, you're finished.'

'One hundred percent dead!' said Chas.

Si smiled at her use of the phrase with which she had greeted him. It felt like a lifetime ago, even though it was less than a week.

'I've done plenty of things The Rulers wouldn't like. I'm a dead man walking if they ever found out any of it,' he said.

They were all silent. Peter handed over the cloak to Si.

Si accepted it in stunned silence.

'Now what else do you need?'

They spent some time discussing their practical needs for the journey. Chas was beginning to relax a little. Peter gave them a lot of money. He offered them a car and provisions and gave Si a holophone.

'When do you want to leave?' he asked.

'We should go as soon as possible,' Si said.

'I can get you transport by tonight,' Peter said.

'Do you think it would be okay if Si and I went for a walk?' Chas asked.

Si thought this was an unusual request from Chas, who would be thinking as always, of keeping a low profile.

'Is there anywhere we wouldn't be seen?'

'I could let you out of the back wall.'

Si and Chas looked puzzled. Peter smiled. 'You missed the door in the wall then last night? It's well hidden, almost as good as being cloaked. There are fields and trees behind here for miles. You won't be seen.'

'Great.' Chas said.

'Take the phone so we can keep in touch,' Peter said.

'Can I come?' asked Ben.

'No, you stay here with Peter,' Chas said.

'I'll show you some of my planes,' Peter said. Ben liked the sound of that.

Peter showed them to the secret door in his back wall. It was cleverly constructed and used the camouflage of surrounding trees and shrubs very effectively.

'You're good at hiding things,' Si said.

Peter smiled. 'See you later. Be careful.'

'So, what is it?' Si asked, as they walked across the field in the pale, afternoon light.

I'm worried about you, Si. I'm worried about this sickness you keep getting.'

'Me too,' he admitted. 'It's not like anything I've had before. It's intense and then it's gone. My skin crawls but then it calms. Right now it just feels mildly itchy but there's no rash or anything.'

'Do you have any idea what it could be?'

'I've had thoughts,' he said.

'And?'

'Same ones as you, I suspect,' he said.

'Are you scared?'

'A little. If I'm infected with plague you might be too. That scares me more. And there's Ben.'

'I know. I was thinking of leaving him with Peter.'

'And me?' He hesitated. 'Will you leave me?'

'No, of course not. I meant you and me leaving together.'

'But what if I'm about to die?'

'Then so am I.'

Si stopped walking. Chas halted beside him. He looked at her, puzzled. He twined his fingers into hers. 'Chas I ...'

'Don't say it, Si.' She pulled away. 'We're friends. That's all it can be.'

'But I ..'

'That's all.'

It was early afternoon when Knowles received the phone call. He and Resolution were following up reported sightings of Si in Middlesborough. A boy matching his description, with a girl and younger boy had been sighted in a supermarket. Then there had been another similar report about a pizza place. In fact, sightings were coming in regularly now as people were keen to claim the substantial reward. They had all led to nothing.

This phone call was different. It was very specific, with good descriptions. The caller lived near the home of wealthy company director, Peter Marsden.

'Who is this Marsden, I've not heard of him?' the Commander remarked.

Knowles looked him up on the internet.

'He's the company director of a big technologies firm. They've developed a lot of stuff for The Rulers and their predecessors. They specialise in military and defence nano-technology.'

'So he's a big shot, eh? Like Kahn. Let's get up there. Let's put an end to this infuriating chase.'

19

The Commander, Knowles and several of his men approached Peter Marsden's house, stopping in front of the gates. Marsden and Ben were absorbed in models of fighter jets in the conservatory.

'Surround the perimeter,' the Commander ordered as they leapt out of their vehicles. 'Knowles, Richards, you're inside with me.'

Resolution pressed the intercom. It took a while for Marsden to answer, as he had instructed Harmony not to answer it. He looked at the images from his CCTV and knew at once who Resolution was, but his demeanour remained unshaken.

'Can I help you?' Marsden's voice said over the intercom.

'Open the gates immediately. We have a warrant to search the premises on the suspicion that you are harbouring three fugitives.'

'Utterly ridiculous,' said Marsden. 'Where did you get that idea?'

Marsden motioned to Ben to get the phone.

'Someone has informed on you Mr. Marsden. We know they're with you. Now open the gates.'

Peter showed Ben the number of the mobile phone he had given to Si and Chas. 'Go out of the room,' he said to Ben. 'Warn Si and Chas not to come back til we can get rid of them.' He looked at CCTV pictures from his other security camera. He saw four or five men moving around the outside of the garden wall, brandishing guns. 'Find Harmony. We need to hide you.'

Ben did what he was told, calmly, without showing his fear.

Peter pressed the intercom again. 'Let me see your warrant,' he demanded, stalling for time. He knew they would be coming in, he just had to hold them off as long as he could.

'Show yourself, Mr. Marsden,' Resolution retorted. 'Then we'll show you the warrant.'

Now that Ben was out of the room, Peter activated the holo-device on the intercom and his live image appeared in front of the Commander. 'The warrant,' he said again.

'You know we're coming in Mr. Marsden,' said Resolution, as Knowles scanned the warrant on his tablet via Peter's intercom.

'I need to speak to someone about this. I'm not happy about it,' Peter said.

'You can speak to Premier Zephyr if you like.' The Commander smiled. 'He has ordered me to do everything in my power to apprehend the fugitive, Silence Hunter. He is a dangerous criminal Mr. Marsden.'

Peter hoped that Ben had had enough time to get a message to Si and Chas and for Harmony to hide him.

'Why on earth then would I have him in my house? You can see I have security to keep out dangerous criminals.'

'Quit stalling Mr. Marsden. You have ten seconds to open your gates or my men will set an explosion and blow them off.'

*

Ben found Harmony in the kitchen. 'Harmony, the Commander is here. They've found us. Peter says can you find somewhere for me to hide and I need to get a message to Chas and Si.'

Harmony wiped the flour off her hands quickly. 'Come, this way. I know the best place. Here, let me have the phone.'

She dialled Marsden 2 and handed the phone to Ben, leading him down the corridor.

*

Chas stopped in her tracks about two hundred metres from the house. Across the field her keen eyes had spotted two men moving along the back wall. She pushed Si forward and dived into the soil herself.

'What is it?' Si gasped, spitting soil from his mouth.

'Look, two men, by the wall.'

He squinted across the field. The figures were almost imperceptible.

'I think they've got guns,' Chas said.

'How can you possibly see that?' Si asked, incredulously. Chas chose not to answer.

'Crawl on your belly towards the trees over there,' she said.

The mobile in Si's pocket bleeped. He grasped it and saw a picture of Peter Marsden come up. He pushed the button and kept crawling.

'Hello,' he said.

'Si, it's me Ben. The Commander is here. You mustn't come back. Get away as far as you can. Peter is trying to get rid of them but I think they're coming in. Don't come back for me. Just go.'

'Ben, we've seen some of the Commander's men out the back. We'll keep ourselves hidden. We can't leave you to them.'

'It's okay, Peter and Harmony are hiding me. You must leave. Please. I've got to go.'

The phone went dead as Si reached the trees.

'He says we should run. Leave him,' said Si.

'I know, I heard most of it.' She thought of what they had just been discussing.

'We can't,' Si said.

'I know.'

*

The gates opened. Resolution, Knowles and Richards drove in. Peter found Harmony.

'Are you all right?' he asked. She nodded. 'I'm sorry. I've put you in danger.'

She shook her head. 'Don't worry about me, Sir.'

'Where's Ben?'

'He's tucked into the space beneath the floor in the back bedroom.'

Marsden had made a trap door under the bed, covered with a large rug. The last time he had used it was ten years ago when he had entertained another visitor that The Rulers did not approve of.

'Did he get a message to Si and Chas?'

'Yes, Sir.'

'If only we could get him out,' Harmony said.

'It's too late now. The perimeter is swarming with troops. I don't want them to find you here. They won't be looking for you so hopefully they won't find you. Hide 'til I give the all clear. And if anything happens to me, just stay hidden 'til they've gone.'

'But, Sir, I want to help,' she protested.

'My dear Harmony, you have helped. But I don't want those animals getting their hands on you. No arguing. Go!' He kissed her on the forehead and she hurried towards the study and out into the garden.

The doorbell rang. Peter took his time getting to the door to give Harmony a chance to hide.

'Good evening Mr. Marsden,' Resolution said coldly. 'May we come in?'

'Do I have a choice?' Peter replied.

Resolution smiled sardonically at him. Peter stepped aside and the three men entered.

'Shall we go into the lounge?' Peter suggested.

They followed him. The house was quiet. Everyone sat down. Marsden did not offer them drinks.

'Where are the servants, Mr. Marsden?'

'I only have one, but she's visiting a friend.'

'Only one servant in such a large house?'

'Yes, I don't need any more. I have a gardener, of course, but he only comes once a fortnight. However, I'm sure you haven't come all this way to ask me questions about my staff, have you?'

Resolution had already taken a dislike to Peter Marsden. 'We are looking for Silence Hunter and his companions. We were tipped off that they are or were here with you.'

'And I don't suppose you'd tell me who told you that?'

'No. My men here will search your house.' Without waiting for permission the Commander waved Knowles and Richards out of the room. 'Search the place thoroughly.'

Peter Marsden held the stony stare of Commander Resolution. The two men weighed each other up. 'If they are or have been here Mr. Marsden it would be better for you to talk now. You could perhaps save something of your position, your career, if you tell us how they got into your house and forced you to help them.'

'I'm sure you'll believe whatever you want to believe Commander and don't give me that nonsense about leniency. I'm sure you'd love to take someone like me down. You see I know your history; where you came from and how desperate you are for power.'

A look of shock momentarily passed over Resolution's face. How could this man, whom he had never met before, possibly know his background? It was the Commander's most closely guarded secret and had the potential to wreck everything he had worked to achieve. He would have to be careful with Marsden.

Resolution's face resumed its mask of superiority, but Peter knew he had struck a crucial blow. 'Be careful how you speak to me Mr. Marsden. I could have you locked up for a very long time for insurrection.'

Marsden laughed. 'Rubbish! I've served The Rulers all my professional life. They have nothing against me. Why are they going to take the word of their jumped up general (who can't even catch a boy) over mine?'

Resolution boiled, but he had learnt to control his anger until the right moment. 'You'd be surprised. They know true loyalty over false.'

They faced each other in silence.

There was a scuffle in the corridor and, to his horror, Peter heard a child's voice, protesting loudly. He jumped up, as Ben was dragged into the room.

'Look what we found,' Knowles announced. Ben was being held between Knowles and Richards.

'There was a trap door, sir, under a bed. The boy was down there,' Richards added.

'No stone unturned,' Resolution said triumphantly. 'And so, Mr. Marsden, it looks like your good fortune just ran out. Can you explain the presence of this boy under a bed in your house? Or perhaps you didn't know he was there?' Resolution said sarcastically.

'I don't deny it. I put him there. But he's not important to you. I can tell you what you want to know if you let the boy go,' Marsden said.

'No!' Ben shouted. 'You can't betray Si and Chas! They can take me. I don't care.'

'Oh, you will care, believe me. What is your name?'

Ben refused to speak. Resolution nodded to Knowles. Knowles slapped Ben with such force he fell to his knees.

'Stop it!' Peter said, moving to intervene. Knowles drew out a gun and trained it on Marsden.

'Sit down!' Resolution commanded, 'unless you want to make it worse.'

To Knowles he said,' Get some cuffs on them both. You're under arrest Mr. Marsden for harbouring fugitives.'

'Now boy, your name?' Resolution said.

Ben's hands were being cuffed roughly behind his back. His face stung and his eyes had involuntarily filled with tears. He remained stubbornly silent.

'Oh come on. You don't want another slap from Knowles and I'm not exactly asking you for top secret information,' the Commander said.

'His name's Ben,' Peter said. Ben scowled at him.

'Short for ... Benevolence? Surname?'

Still no answer. Knowles moved to hit Ben again.

'Please, Ben,' Peter cried. 'Don't invite them to hit you for no good reason.'

'Benevolence Johnson,' Ben mumbled.

Richards was making notes on his tablet.

'Have you covered the whole house and gardens?'

'Not yet, Sir,' Richards replied.

'Look,' Resolution said, 'Let's make this less painful shall we? I know and you know that eventually you will tell us where Hunter and the girl are. Tell us now and avoid the pain. Simple.'

'I'll tell you,' Ben said forcefully. Peter looked at him in surprise. 'They're not here. They left ages ago. And they know you're here so they won't come back. I told them to leave me here.'

Resolution raised an eyebrow. 'How courageous! And how would they know we were here if they left ages ago?'

Ben bit his lip, realising that he had said too much.

'Bring me all the phones,' Resolution ordered.

Knowles found the phones. He found the last call, made only a few minutes ago, and handed that phone to Resolution. The Commander smiled and dialled the number. Ben and Peter could do nothing except wait in miserable silence.

*

The phone in Si's pocket began to vibrate. He and Chas were sitting amongst a small clump of trees not far from the house. They kept trying to pick out movements around the wall.

He looked at the number calling. It came up as 'home,' and the picture of Peter Marsden appeared. What should he do? He knew the house was probably swarming with troops by now.

'You have to answer it,' said Chas. 'Peter or Ben might need our help.'

Si answered it. 'Yes.'

'Silence Hunter. We speak at last. Do you know who this is?'

Si's heart began to race and he suddenly felt faint. Chas had her ear pressed up to the other side of the phone, trying to listen. She felt adrenalin course though her body like an injection of icy water.

'I think so,' said Si.

'I am going to wait in this house, very patiently, for five minutes. You are going to present yourself to me in that five minutes and we'll take it from there.' The Commander's voice was authoritative and calm. Si couldn't even formulate an answer. 'If you don't do as I tell you, Benevolence will die.'

'I'm too far away to get there in five minutes!' Si said; the panic rising in his throat.

'Don't play games with me Hunter. It's tedious. Five minutes. And bring the girl with you.'

'She's not here,' Si blurted out. 'She's gone on ahead of me. I can't contact her.' He was rambling now, trying to find any way to protect Chas.

Suddenly Chas pulled the phone from his hand.

'I am here, and he's not coming back,' she said boldly and ended the call.

'Chas, I have to!' Si cried, jumping to his feet. 'They'll kill Ben.'

She pulled him back down. 'And don't you think they'll do that anyway, when they have you? Do you think they'll just let him go? Or let him stay with Peter and live happily ever after?'

'Of course not!'

'Well then. We have to think this through. They won't kill him yet, because he's their hostage. He's their way of getting to you.'

'What about Peter? If they kill Ben, they still have Peter?'

'They won't kill Peter. He's too important. They wouldn't dare kill him here and now.'

'So, what are we going to do then?' Si said.

The phone vibrated again. Si answered it.

The Commander spoke. 'Your time is ticking by. You have three minutes left. Benevolence wishes to speak to you.'

'Si,' Ben voice was shaky. 'They have a gun in the side of my head. But I'm not afraid to die. Don't come back!' There was a terrible grunt as Knowles kicked Ben. Si heard Peter's voice protesting, then being suddenly silenced.

'Commander!' Si shouted into the phone.

'Yes,' said Resolution's voice.

'I'm coming. You have my word. Give me ten minutes. Please!'

'Ten minutes it is,' said Resolution, and the phone went dead.

'Si, you can't! You can't give it all up now. We have to find a way to get Ben out!'

'What? In ten minutes?' Si said. 'You don't think they'll kill him. I do! Think back to the village! They slaughtered loads of innocent people! They're ruthless.' He was angry. He felt helpless. Everything was crashing down, but he had to do something to save Ben.

Chas could see that she wasn't going to be able to stop Si. 'Okay. You're right. But let's get them to do an exchange. Ben for you. They send Ben out to me here and you go in.'

'He's not going to bargain with me!' Si said.

'No, he's going to bargain with me!' Chas dialled the number. The Commander picked it up.

'I won't let him come unless you give me Ben in exchange,' Chas said, as confidently as she could make it sound.

The Commander laughed. 'You want a deal. How naive.'

'You want Si. I've got him. You give me Ben, you can have Si. You kill Ben, you lose Si again.' She ended the call.

'Grief, Chas! You've got some nerve.'

'He'll call back.'

Several minutes passed, feeling like hours. They waited in agony. Si felt like he would throw up at any minute. He was praying that Ben would be all right. The phone vibrated.

'Okay. The boy is of no import. But you are an interesting young woman. I have a condition.'

'What?' said Chas.

'I want to know the name of my negotiator.'

'No.'

'No name, no deal.'

'That would be crazy.'

'Indeed, but that is my condition.'

There was a pause.

'Well,' said the Commander.

'Why?' asked Chas.

There was another pause before the Commander answered. 'You remind me of someone.'

'My name's Chas,' she said.

'And that is short for...? Charity, Chastity?'

'Chastity.'

'Surname?'

'No.'

'Tell me, or we'll kill Ben and keep pursuing you and Hunter.'

'You don't need to know who I am!' she shouted.

'You're wrong,' the Commander said, holding on to his self control.

Si watched in stunned silence as she fiercely tried to protect her identity. But he could see her resolve weakening in the face of the choice before her.

'Komchenski,' she growled.

Resolution felt a shiver run through him and his world jerked out of focus for a tiny moment, before he regained his poise.

'There, I've told you my name. Now, send Ben out of the back gate, over the field towards some trees to his right. When I see him walking towards them, I'll send Si out. Call off your men at the back of the house.'

'And you get to call the shots do you.... Chastity?'

She didn't like the way he drew out her name, like a curse.

'Yes I do.'

Surprisingly, Resolution gave a hearty laugh. 'Five minutes,' he said. The phone went dead.

Chas and Si watched, as the men from the back of the house began to retreat. Within two minutes they saw the gate opening in the back wall. Ben was pushed out, his hands on his head. Si and Chas couldn't see anyone else at first, but then another person emerged from the wall. He was pointing a gun at Ben.

The phone rang. Chas answered it. Before the voice could say anything, she demanded, 'Get rid of that gun, or Si won't be coming to you. I'm not having you shoot him - or Ben.'

'Let us see Hunter, then my man will lower his gun.'

'No!'

'Show us Hunter.' The Commander's voice was still calm but harsher than before.

Chas ended the call. She looked at Si. He stood up. Her heart felt like it was rising out of her chest and into her mouth. She suddenly wondered if she would ever see him again. He closed his eyes and inhaled deeply. When he opened them she was still staring up at him.

'This is it,' he said.

An unfamiliar urge gripped Chas. She stood up, put her hands around his face and kissed him. It was only the briefest of touches, but deep enough for Si to feel the pain of it in the pit of his stomach. She pulled away, but he pulled her back to him and she buried her face in his shoulder, as he kissed her hair.

After a moment she pulled back.

'This is not it,' she said firmly. 'I will find a way to get you back.'

'They're certain to take me to the Bastille,' he said.

'You've escaped from there before. I will come for you.'

'Chas, no. Get away. You and Ben - just go and find a life somewhere. Remind yourself that I caused the mass destruction of your village. That should help!'

She smiled her quirky smile at him and shook her head. The phone vibrated.

'Chastity. Send him out now. I am losing patience.'

Without another look at her, Si walked out into the open. He stood facing Ben, across the length of the field. Ben began to walk towards him. The man with the gun did not lower it.

'The gun!' Chas demanded, angrily, into the phone. 'Or me and Si are gone!'

The man with the gun did not move. Ben kept walking.

Without ending the call Chas shouted, 'Si, come on. They're not keeping their word. We're out of here!'

He looked back to her, then at Ben, walking towards him. Step forward, go back? What should he do? She beckoned frantically to him, her eyes wide.

They looked at each other once more. No words were spoken.

Si stepped forward and walked towards the house.

20

Chas watched as Ben and Si met in the middle of the field. Ben paused. Si knew he must keep walking, but Ben grabbed Si and hugged him. He began to cry. Si put his arms round him and closed his eyes tight, trying to control his own emotions.

The phone was still active in Chas's hand. 'Chastity!' the Commander barked. 'Call the boy forward. If Hunter tries to escape now, they're both dead. And you won't get far.'

Chas wasn't sure if she believed the Commander, but it was their only chance.

'Ben!' she shouted across the field. 'You have to let him go. Come on!'

'She's right Ben,' said Si. 'Go to her.'

Gently, Si prised Ben's grip from his waist. He looked into the boy's eyes. 'She needs you now. Go on.' He walked away towards the house.

Ben stood still in the middle of the field, watching Si.

'Ben!' Chas shouted. 'Come on!'

He took one last look at Si then ran towards Chas. She gripped him in her arms and pulled him into the trees.

'Are you all right? Did they hurt you?' she asked, looking him up and down.

'I'm fine,' he said. 'What are we going to do?'

'We're going to wait 'til they've gone, then we're going back to the house. We need some stuff if we're going to get Si back. What are they doing to Peter?'

'They handcuffed him. He's under arrest.'

'How did they know we were here? That guy on the phone. It must have been him. Where's Harmony?'

'I don't know,' Ben said. 'She helped me to hide; that was the last I saw of her.'

Chas didn't know what to think. 'They're certain to come looking for us. We need to hide now.' She flung the mobile phone to the ground. 'Keep close and do exactly as I tell you.'

*

As Si reached the wall, Richards grabbed him, twisted his arms behind his back and handcuffed him. Inside the wall, Si came face to face with the Commander. Si stared defiantly at him.

'So, we meet at last. You have led us a merry dance, Silence Hunter, as indeed did your parents. Now we can end this.'

'Are you going to kill me?'

'No. Not yet, at least. You have something we want. If you die, it dies. We're going back to the Bastille, where they can find it.'

'What is it?' Si asked.

Resolution sneered, then he turned to Richards. 'Get the car ready. Find out from Knowles if the law-keepers have arrived to take Marsden yet. Send out some men to find the other two. Kill them.'

'No!' Si screamed at him. 'You made a deal – me for him.'

Resolution waved his hand at Richards, who made his way back to the house.

'And now she has him and I have you. Deal is done. But I can't

203

'allow her to escape.'

'Why? She's nothing to you. You have me. You can take what you want from me. You've caused her enough suffering. You killed the people she loved in the village. Don't do this.'

Resolution moved in closer to Si. 'You know nothing boy! But she knows too much.'

'What do you mean? She hasn't a clue about any of this.'

'She knows too much about me, not you!' Resolution was losing his control.

'She's never met you! Are you out of your mind?'

'No, Hunter, I am not. Chastity Komchenski is my sister!'

Si was taken aback. This was her eldest brother: The one she had called Res. The one who had betrayed her and arranged for her to be taken away. He was the son of illegal immigrants and here he was Commander of the Secret Service. Si didn't let on he knew anything.

'She never talked about her past, but I knew there must be something rotten in it.'

Resolution felt the urge to slap Si, but he held back.

'Come on. We've got a long journey ahead of us. I want to reach the Bastille tonight.' He pushed Si ahead of him towards the house.

Inside, Si saw Peter, along the corridor, being led out of the front door.

He called out. 'Peter!'

Marsden turned. His face was bruised.

'I'm sorry.'

Unexpectedly, Peter smiled at him.

'No. I'm sorry,' he said. 'I let you down. Someone betrayed you. I don't know who.'

Before they could exchange more words, Peter was bundled out of the door.

'What are you going to do with him?' Si asked.

'He's in the law-keeper's hands. He'll go to prison for a long time I should think.'

Si shook his head. This was all his fault. How many lives were going to be ruined because of him? And he didn't even know why. He needed to know. He needed to find his parents. But how was that going to happen now?

The light outside was beginning to fade.

'Have you checked the rest of the house and grounds?' the Commander asked Knowles.

'Yes sir. It's clear.'

Si wondered about Harmony.

'Okay. Let's get going. Have you informed the Premier and the Bastille?'

'Yes Sir. The Premier said you should call him when you arrive at the Bastille. He was pleased.'

'And the reward?'

'Has been allocated,' said Knowles.

'You are very efficient, Knowles.'

'Thank you, Sir.'

*

Chas and Ben had managed to negotiate a route to the trees at the front of the house. Ben was full of admiration for Chas' amazing tracking skills, which had allowed them to circumnavigate any opposition. They had climbed a conifer and were well hidden from the ground. From their view point (too high up for Ben's liking) they could see over the wall into the front gardens of Marsden's house. They saw the tail end of the car, containing Peter, drive away. A few minutes later they watched as Si was bundled into the back of another car. Knowles got into the driver's seat and Resolution walked to the passenger door. As he pulled open the door, despite the fading light, Chas got a clear view of him. She had to grip the branches firmly, to keep her balance. She looked again. Her stomach lurched and sudden nausea rose in her throat. He hadn't changed much. There was no mistaking the face of her brother. How had she not recognised his voice? She was all the more determined to get Si back now.

*

As Knowles drove away, Si saw the cottage they had passed. The man was standing on the doorstep with his vacant-looking wife. He smiled and shouted something as they passed. Resolution gave a barely distinguishable nod. Si wished he had listened to Chas. He closed his eyes and leaned his head against the darkened window. He was resigned to his fate as the Bastille loomed into his mind. An almost guilty relief washed over him, as if he was releasing Chas and Ben from their ties to him. He hoped Chas would be sensible and get away with Ben. Then again...he didn't.

*

There were still men looking for Chas and Ben. One of them had stopped underneath the tree in which they were hiding. They heard him speaking to the others on his phone.

'Once we've searched the vicinity, move out. We'll cover a mile radius. Shoot on sight.'

Fear slid its fingers around Ben yet again as he tried his hardest not to slip from his position in the tree. He felt as if the man had only to look up and he would be seen. Chas was not surprised by the order from her brother to kill them. She understood that she was a threat to his powerful life. Resolution had never let anything or anyone stand in his way. He was afraid. And fear had once driven him to hand her over to the authorities. She had her suspicions about what he might have done to their parents and her other brother.

The man spoke again. 'I know. I've had enough of this bloody chasing about. He's got Hunter. Who cares about the others.'

He moved off into the growing darkness. This time there was no flashlight and Chas presumed they must have night vision goggles. This would make her and Ben much easier to find. They pressed themselves into the tree trunk and barely breathed until he was gone.

'We have to wait til we're sure they're gone' she said to Ben. He nodded. Despite the darkness and the creeping cold, he was sweating.

*

In the garden, Harmony prised herself out of her hiding place. Her limbs ached from the confines of the space. She had heard and witnessed some of what had gone on nearby. Cautiously, she moved back towards the study doors. They had been left open. A light was on in the hallway and security lights blazed around the grounds. She kept in the shadows; afraid. But she had to find out what had happened to Peter. She had to get help.

*

After a couple of hours, Chas and Ben heard the men returning to the front gates where their vehicle was parked.

'Should we take a last look in the house and garden?' one of them said.

'No, they wouldn't come back here would they!'

'What will you tell the Commander?'

'I'll tell him what he wants to hear: We killed them and got rid of the bodies. Come on, let's get out of here.'

After the car disappeared into the night, Chas began to climb down the tree with Ben following. The security lights gave them some guidance but it was still difficult after sitting there in the cold for so long. For Ben, coming down was much harder than getting up.

'You okay?' Chas asked, climbing through the branches behind him.

'I think so,' he said.

They made their way to the hidden entrance in the back wall. It had been left open. Keeping in the shadows, they entered the garden and scouted across to the study doors. They were now locked and the light was off.

'We'll have to find another way in,' Chas said, leading the way round the side of the bungalow. 'We need to get our stuff and the invisibility cloak.'

'Then what are we going to do?' asked Ben.

'I'm going after Si,' Chas said.

'And me?'

Chas stopped and looked at him. 'I'm going to the Bastille. I need you on the outside. You will have to stay with Meg, if she's okay with that.'

'She's not going to be happy when she finds out about Peter,' Ben said.

'I know, but we'll just have to deal with it.'

The only light that was now on in the bungalow, was the lounge. The curtains were drawn. All the doors and windows Chas tried were locked. Chas thought this strange. Why would Resolution's men switch lights off and lock doors?

'There's someone in there,' she whispered to Ben. 'We need to find out who.'

At that moment they heard a vehicle pulling up to the gates. They were already open and the car glided up the driveway. Chas and Ben quickly hid.

A man got out of a black Porsche. He was wearing a suit and tie. He looked around anxiously, but within moments a light came on in the passage, the front door was opened and they heard a female voice. Harmony.

'Who do you think that is?' Ben whispered.

'I dunno. Maybe it's her boyfriend. Maybe it's whoever gave us away. We need to be careful, but we have to get in. We need a vehicle too if I'm going to have any chance of getting Si back.'

They were almost back to the study when they came across an open window. It was a very small aperture, to a cloakroom, about five feet off the ground.

'This is your moment Ben,' Chas said. 'I'll give you a leg up and you squeeze in there. Silently! Get to the study and open the doors. Can you do it?'

'Sure.'

He stood in her grip and heaved himself up to the opening. It was very narrow, even for Ben's slight form. He squeezed himself through gradually. Even though it hurt his back as he tried to contort his body though the window, he didn't make a sound. His body felt like it was being sawn in half as he levered himself down and tried to find something to lower his hands onto. The toilet cistern was directly below him. Gently, and as skilfully as a gymnast, he placed his hands on it. He looked for some space and as his legs followed through the window he deftly flung himself onto the floor. There was a minor clatter as he sprang off the back of the toilet. Chas was impressed but tensed herself, in case anyone had heard. Ben thought this too and quickly hid himself behind the toilet door.

*

'Did you hear something?' Harmony asked, getting to her feet.

'No,' Eric said.

Harmony dried her eyes with a tissue. She had explained to Eric over the phone what had happened and he had said he would come immediately. Sheer relief, at seeing him arrive had sent Harmony (who up until then had remained as calm as she could) into floods of tears.

'I'm probably just jumpy. I locked everything up!'

'Are you sure?' Eric asked. 'I'll go and check if you like.'

'No. It's fine. What are we going to do Mr. Myers?' Harmony asked.

'Try not to worry Harmony. I'll sort this out. I'll pull all the strings I can to get Peter out of this. He is foolish sometimes, but, he's a good man. We need to get you out of here for now. Pack some things and you can stay with Elaine and I 'til we sort this out.'

'Thank you,' she said, managing a brief smile.

*

Ben waited for a few minutes, his heart racing. He tried to slow his breathing so that it wasn't noisy. Then he ventured out of the small cloakroom. He was only about three metres from the study door. He pressed down the handle and went in, closing the door behind him. There was plenty of light flooding in from the security lights. He unlocked the French doors and peered out. He was relieved when Chas moved out of the shadows and came into the room.

They spoke in whispers. 'Where did Si put the invisibility cloak?' Chas asked.

'After you went out Peter put it over here.' Ben led her to a cabinet by the wall. She picked it up. 'Let's get our rucksacks.'

'What are you going to do about transport? Steal Peter's car?'

'Not exactly steal it. I'll bring it back as soon as I can. And anyway, he's not going to need it for a while.'

'I hope he gets away,' Ben said, biting his lip.

Chas wasn't hopeful. She wished she could help, but right now Si was her priority. She looked at Ben and felt the need to reassure him. 'He'll be okay. They won't harm him. He's an important man.'

'Yes, but he's a traitor now.'

'He'll have a good lawyer. At least they won't be able to do anything illegal to him. Let's make his sacrifice worthwhile. Let's get Si back.'

They moved into the hall. It was darker in here as there was no light filtering through. They could hear muffled voices from the lounge at the front of the house. Their bedrooms were not far down the corridor. Suddenly, the lounge door opened. Opening a door now would cause light to come into the hall and they would be discovered. Chas threw Ben and herself against the wall and they edged round the corner, just as Eric switched on the hall light.

'Just pack a few essentials,' he said. 'I'll phone Elaine now.'

Harmony came out of the door and headed towards her bedroom. Eric was pacing about near the front door. Chas and Ben couldn't get to their bedrooms.

'I'll just check everything's locked,' Harmony said, coming out of her room.

She walked up the corridor towards the back of the house. Round the corner, where Chas and Ben were waiting, the corridor led to two more rooms. Harmony was going into every room on her way through the house. Ben looked expectantly at Chas. They were trapped. Chas pulled Ben into the first room behind them. It was a small bedroom. Neat and tidy, as all the others had been. In it there was only a bed, a wardrobe and a chest of drawers. There was no room under the bed. Chas opened the wardrobe to find it full of boxes. Harmony's footsteps were approaching. All they could do was to crouch down behind the bed.

The door opened and the light went on. Harmony looked around the room and came towards the window. There was no way she could miss the two of them on the floor. She looked as though she might be about to scream but no sound came from her gaping mouth. Ben stood quickly to his feet and took two steps towards her, smiling.

'Harmony, we just need our things, then we'll be gone.'

Chas was on her feet now. She had been preparing to defend them, or silence Harmony, but she could see it wouldn't be necessary now.

Harmony drew a shuddering breath. 'You frightened me, that's all. Like seeing ghosts. I didn't know what had happened to you.

I thought you'd have been long gone by now. I overheard the exchange.'

Ben looked puzzled.

'I was hiding in the garden. I'm just thankful they didn't realise I was there.'

'We're going after Si,' Chas said. 'That's why we came back to get our things. We need some transport too.'

Harmony looked quizzically at her. 'You were going to steal a car?'

Chas looked uncomfortable. She hesitated. Ben interjected. 'Not steal exactly, just borrow.' He tried smiling winsomely at Harmony.

'Who's the man in the lounge,' Ben said.

'Eric Myers? I called him. He's Mr. Marsden's associate and closest friend. I'd trust him with my life. He's going to help get Mr. Marsden out.'

'How can you be certain he isn't the one who gave us away?' asked Chas.

Harmony let out a short choked laugh. 'Mr. Myers is as trustworthy as Mr. Marsden. He would never betray him, even when he disagrees with him.'

'About helping us?' Chas said.

'Yes.' Harmony made to leave the room. 'You don't need to sneak around now. I'll tell him you're here and you can go get your things. I'll get some food together for you and we'll think about transport. Do you know where they've taken Si then?'

'Pretty sure. The Bastille,' said Chas.

Harmony looked shocked. 'How can you possibly get him out of there?'

'I don't know, but I can't abandon him. Not now.'

Harmony smiled. 'I like you.' She turned to Ben. 'Come and show me how you got in. I need to secure the house.'

Ben took her to the cloakroom and she secured the window, admonishing herself for leaving it open. Chas offered to make sure the French doors were locked but Harmony insisted on checking them herself. Then she led them down the corridor to meet Eric Myers.

Myers was a very tall, broad shouldered man with receding but neatly trimmed blond hair. Harmony explained who they were and what they wanted. Despite the circumstances Myers proffered his hand politely. Ben took it and accepted the firm handshake. Chas was wary and didn't reciprocate. Eric Myers shrugged.

'The Bastille? You don't stand a chance of getting him out of there.'

'He escaped before.'

'Don't you think that will make them all the more vigilant this time?'

Chas looked sulkily at him.

'Why don't you two just get out of here? You should just drop it now and get away while you've got the chance.'

'No!' Chas cried. 'Come on Ben, we'll get our things and go.' She turned to the door.

Myers sighed loudly. 'Wait. We had a car ready for you. I can have it here in ten minutes. Can you drive?' He looked sceptically at Chas.

'Yes,' she said defensively. She had driven a couple of times, joyriding, when she was a child. 'Why would you still give us the car?'

'It's what Peter would want. I may not agree with some of the things he gets mixed up in, but he has this magnanimous heart and I respect that. What about Ben? Are you taking him to the Bastille?'

'No. I have a safe person to leave him with.'

Myers nodded.

'Will you be able to help Peter?' Ben asked.

Myers pulled out his mobile. 'I hope so. I've got a few strings to pull, but he's got himself in deep water this time. Go get together what you need.'

'I'll get some food for you,' Harmony offered.

Eric was already speaking to someone about the car as Chas and Ben went to get their things. She took Si's rucksack and repacked the contents between hers and Ben's. She didn't like doing it. She felt like Si was already dead. It made her anxious to be on her way. They already had a few hours head start on her and how long would Si be able to hold out in that torture house?

As she and Ben emerged from the bedroom, a car was pulling up on the drive. Eric opened the door and went out. There was a brief exchange between him and the driver.

'It's all yours. Do you have any money?'

They had very little left of Kahn's money. She shook her head. Myers took out his wallet and offered her a substantial sum. 'This should help.'

Chas was suddenly overwhelmed. 'I can't take it. Why would you give us this?'

'It's for The Cause. Peter believed that Si was important. You believe he is important. Take it.' He pushed it into her hands.

'Okay... Thank you.' She stuffed it into a zip pocket on her jacket.

Harmony came forward. 'Here, can you fit this food into your packs?'

Ben and Chas took it.

'I want to thank you both,' she said, looking awkwardly at her feet, then slowly making eye contact with each of them. She wasn't used to being indebted to anyone.

Myers nodded. Harmony hugged Ben. 'Will Peter be all right?' he said.

'Don't worry about him,' Myers said. 'I'll sort it out. I don't think it would be safe for you to contact us again.'

'Come on, Ben,' Chas said. 'We should go.'

'And so should we,' Myers said to Harmony. 'Are you ready?'

21

Si sat in the back of the car, his head slumped against the window. His hands had been uncuffed. Resolution and Knowles were in the front and a glass screen had been raised between them and Si. The Commander was on the phone to the Premier. The car had a screen in the dash and Si could see the Premier's face, but the conversation was muffled. The Commander laughed now and again and the Premier looked very pleased. Si wondered, yet again, why he was so important to them.

He had spent the first hour of the journey thinking about Chas. He wavered between hoping she would get away with Ben, and hoping she would come and find him. But the more he thought about the Bastille, the more hopeless he felt. If she came, she would probably end up 'one hundred per cent dead,' as she liked to phrase it. He closed his eyes and willed her not to come. Stupid! He would probably never see her again and he hated this thought more than he feared being back in the Bastille. And he did fear it.

He looked at the blackness speeding past him; thrusting him onwards towards his fate. He knew that they were not going to pretend that he was a 'guest.' He knew that there would be no 'freedoms' to wander the grounds, sit in the common room with the other 'guests,' go to the school wing or use the gym and pool.

He would be confined to what they called 'medical.' That was the euphemism for the wing where people were held in isolation, experimented on and tortured. Some were treated for medical conditions, but few returned without horror stories to tell: Muffled screams, gibbering wrecks in wheelchairs and doctors with distinctly unethical bedside manners.

Si had spent some time there before he had escaped. How had he managed to escape? He couldn't quite fathom it now. A bubble of hope floated into his mind, but he burst it quickly. They would watch him like their lives depended on it this time – and maybe they did.

He hoped they would find out he had the New Plague and that before he died they would all have been infected. But that would mean Chas and Ben were likely to have it, not to mention Peter and Harmony. He closed his eyes again and tried to clear his mind.

His mother's face swam in and out of his consciousness; smiling, soothing him with words that he couldn't hear. He felt her hand stroke his hair, like she used to do when he was small. Then she was speaking to him urgently, her face lined and worried, but with no audible words. He tried to touch her, he tried to ask her what she was saying; to tell her he couldn't hear her. Then she was gone. Black mist swirled around him; its tendrils hooked around his head, his arms, his torso, his legs. The mist became solid tentacles, pinning him down. He was back on the slab in the Bastille. This time it was distinctly the Commander's face looming over him with the syringe. He could hear the woman sobbing in the corner. His mother? He cried out to her but no sound came. He tried to pull his limbs from the straps that held him, but as he looked down they were black moving tentacles. His heart raced and he tasted salt in his mouth. The Commander's leering face loomed closer with the larger than life syringe. The woman was still sobbing. Si cried out to her. The Commander held the syringe above his chest, with two hands, like a dagger. Si braced himself; terrified. Suddenly, the woman screamed and roared, like a wild animal. She lurched herself at the Commander. It was not his mother. It was Chas.

*

The car pulled into the Bastille compound. The floodlights were brighter than daylight. Si steeled himself to face whatever was coming. He must not betray his parents or anything that they stood for. As Knowles and Resolution got out of the car, they were met by the Bastille Master. Si recalled the rotund figure, who used to make the odd appearance in the school room or the dining hall to bark orders and throw his weight around. The guards and teachers acquiesced, but it was obvious that even they had little respect for him.

The obsequious little man greeted the Commander. Si had never seen the Master behave like this with anyone else and, despite his circumstances, this amused him. After a brief discourse, Knowles came back to the car and pulled Si out. As he stood up, Si looked ominously at the building. He breathed deeply, trying to remain composed, but his stomach lurched and suddenly he was throwing up.

Knowles uttered profanities, wiping spatters of vomit from his clothes, and dragged Si away.

'I'll get that cleaned up,' the Master said. He threw Si a disgusted glance. Si smiled sarcastically, as Knowles ushered him into the building.

The Bastille was a Victorian mansion set in its own grounds. It had three floors and, over the last twenty years, two anachronistic wings had been added, like awkward prosthetic limbs. The house itself had once been a handsome place. Its sandstone facade was perfectly symmetrical and many windows looked out onto a south facing garden. People had once laughed and played and enjoyed many pleasures here. The garden remained a well-kept tribute to its Victorian creators. Despite being set on the moors, the Victorians had managed to cultivate the ground and make things grow, behind tall brick walls, constructed to shelter the place. It had been an oasis of peace and beauty: The antithesis of everything the Bastille had become.

Si was checked in and Knowles led him through the imposing hallway and down a dark, high ceilinged corridor, dimly lit by the night security lights. Si knew where they were going. Their footsteps echoed on the concrete floor. Behind the closed doors Si pictured the rooms they were passing. Most were bedrooms. He could hear people coughing, snoring, shouting in their sleep. As they turned a corner, a gaunt man in pyjamas limped towards them. He was unshaven and his hair wild. His eyes were vacant and he swayed from side to side, mumbling to himself. Knowles pulled Si to one side to let him pass. Si was feeling so ill he didn't even look up.

'Bloody imbecile!' Knowles muttered.

An orderly came rushing up the corridor. 'Sorry, Sir,' he said, addressing Knowles. 'He sleepwalks.'

Knowles rolled his eyes.

They came to a modern door. It was locked and Knowles punched in a code. It swung open and they entered one of the modern wings of the Bastille: Medical.

'What are you going to do to me?' Si's mouth was dry and his voice cracked.

'Nothing tonight.' Knowles didn't look at him but kept his grip firmly around Si's upper arm. He led him into a reception area. There was a male nurse on duty and Knowles checked Si into room twenty. The nurse led them to it, punched in another code and Si entered a sparse room with a bed, cabinet and chair. There was nothing overtly medical in the room and nothing with which Si could hurt himself or do any damage to anything. Another door led into a bathroom.

'Get some sleep,' Knowles said, dumping Si on the bed.

'Can I have some water?' Si asked the nurse.

The nurse looked at Knowles, who nodded. A jug of water was fetched and placed with a plastic cup on the cabinet. Si took a few gulps.

The door was locked and Si was alone. He glanced around him at the all too familiar setting. It wasn't that long since he had been here. Now he was back it felt like he'd never been away. The whole of the last few weeks felt unreal; so much had happened. The cold familiarity of this place was ironically comforting. He lay down, and slept.

It seemed like only a few minutes later when the door opened. A different nurse, female this time, brought in a tray of food. She didn't look at Si, or speak, just placed the tray on the cabinet and left. He rolled over and squinted at the breakfast. He was hungry but his body felt like lead. He heaved himself to a sitting position and reached out for the bread. There were sachets of marmalade, jam and butter. He couldn't be bothered with any of it and bit into the roll in his hand, chewing it with his eyes closed. After a few mouthfuls he had to reach for the water to help him swallow it. He felt the now familiar nausea rising in his stomach and the feeling of tiny insects crawling inside his skin. It made him twitch and scratch. The nausea was growing, his head began to swim and he lay back down with a groan, not wanting to have to rush to the toilet to throw up. He lay on his side, still chewing a last mouthful of bread, willing the sickness to leave him alone. Somewhere in his mind he began a half-hearted prayer, but it petered out as he drifted back to sleep.

*

Chas easily got used to the car. Eric had arranged for three fake IDs for her, Ben and Si: Peter's last present to them. These got her into York again. It had been hard dropping Ben at Meg's and explaining all that had happened. Chas thought at one point that Meg was going to kick them out, but she had surprised them by agreeing to look after Ben. They made arrangements to meet at a disused warehouse on the North road, outside the city. Meg and Ben were to come there every other morning at ten for a week.

'If we don't turn up within a week, you have to make a new life here, Ben. Promise?'

Ben held her gaze intently. He didn't want to promise, but he nodded. She hugged him tightly and was gone.

22

As Chas drove towards the Bastille, Si was waking up for the second time. He still felt nauseous and his head was throbbing. The tray of food was gone and only a jug of water remained. He sat up, regretting it instantly. His head swam and the throbbing intensified. He lay back down. What was wrong with him? His knowledge of plague symptoms was only hearsay, having never come into contact with anyone who had contracted it. He lay on the bed, hoping he might die before the Commander had the chance to do whatever he was intending to do. There was a window in the room and Si looked longingly at it, wondering if there might be a way out of here. He laughed at himself. Of course it would be locked. He wondered how long it would be before they came back for him. Then his thoughts turned to Chas and Ben. What had become of them? If he knew Chas at all, she would be on her way here right now. He wished he had been more insistent that she should go her own way and forget about him. There was no way she could get him out of here.

*

How could she get him out of there? This thought hammered Chas's brain as she drove towards the moors. The on-board navigation system gave precise directions, so she didn't have to think too hard about her route. The motorway was busy but never congested.

*

Until now, determination alone had driven her this far. She needed a plan to get into the Bastille and out again. So far everything she thought of had flaws and she was becoming increasingly frustrated. Her best idea was to use the invisibility cloak that Peter had given them. She was cynical about its power to convincingly hide her. She could still be detected by noise or someone could still bump into her. Also, she didn't 'feel' invisible underneath it, because you could still see yourself. It was weird. But, there seemed no alternative. She would wait by the gates to the Bastille, under the cloak, until a vehicle came through. Then she would move in with it. She turned off the motorway onto the moors.

Si was surprised that no one had come to interrogate him yet. No nurses had come to attend him. He had sipped the water, trying to refresh himself, but it had not worked. He decided to attempt a shower. As he swung his legs over the side of the bed the urge to be sick overwhelmed him. He dashed to the bathroom and threw up. It made him feel a little better. He should have done it ages ago. The shower was nice and hot. He stood under it for a long time, enjoying the jets of water on his skin, soothing away the crawling sensation.

As he was drying himself he heard the door being unlocked. He quickly pulled on his clothes. A man he had never seen before was waiting for him in the bedroom. He wore a white coat and was of medium build, with black hair and a neatly trimmed goatee beard. Si presumed he was a 'doctor': A term used liberally at the

Bastille to cover a multitude of tenuous medical roles.

'Come with me.'

'Where are we going?' Si asked, as he was escorted from the room.

The doctor made no reply.

'Do you like working here?' Si persisted. 'I bet you get a kick from tormenting people, don't you?'

Still the man made no reply. Si shrugged and gave up.

They reached another room. Inside was a long table, with straps attached for arms and legs. Around the room were various trolleys containing medical equipment. Si froze in the doorway. This was the room from his nightmare. This was where it was going to end. Icy cold flushed through his body and a wave of new nausea swept over him. His feet wouldn't move.

The doctor pulled at his arm and he stumbled forward into the room.

'Get onto the table,' the doctor ordered.

Si stood still, panic rising.

'Get onto the table,' the doctor repeated.

Si was not going to do anything voluntarily. He thought about attacking the doctor.

'Security can be here in an instant. You really don't have a choice.' There was no emotion in the doctor's voice. Si continued to stand still. His feet would not allow him to get onto the table where his worst nightmares had occurred. The doctor glanced at him and moved to a panel on the wall. Suddenly Si leapt on him. He grabbed him around the neck and wrestled him to the floor. The doctor was taken by surprise, but he fought back. He elbowed Si in the groin and struggled to his feet, as Si doubled over. He reached for the red button on the panel. Si lunged forward to stop him but he was too late. Within seconds, two security guards burst into the room. They hauled Si up; as if he were a scrawny chicken wrestled from the coop, and threw him onto the table. They strapped down his limbs. He struggled hopelessly. The guards never said a word. Once he was secured, they nodded to the doctor and left.

Si stopped struggling. He knew it was futile. The doctor spoke to him as if he were a naughty child. 'That was unnecessary, don't you think?'

Si turned his face away. All his energy had been sapped and he awaited his fate. He wondered if the Commander himself would be coming or if this doctor was going to carry out the procedure. He remembered the times before he had escaped when he had lain, half drugged on a similar table, being poked, prodded, injected and opened up under local anaesthetic.

'Is the Commander coming?'

No reply.

'What are you looking for?'

The doctor continued to ignore him and Si roared in frustration. The doctor didn't flinch, but left the room and once more Si was alone with his thoughts. He hoped the Commander would come soon and get it over with. He felt the nausea rising in his throat again and expected to hear a woman crying at any minute.

*

Chas arrived at a cross roads up on the moors. The car told her that the Bastille was one kilometre straight ahead. She turned left and looked for somewhere to hide the car. Finding a rocky outcrop, she manoeuvred the car behind it. She estimated it would take them about ten minutes to get back here on foot, depending on what state Si was in. But she didn't dare drive within sight of the Bastille. She picked up her rucksack and took out the water, taking several gulps. She pulled out an extra jumper and wriggled into it, putting a jacket on over the top. Then she reached for the pack that contained the invisibility cloak. Opening it up, she held it against her body and watched as half of her torso seemed to disappear. She still felt dubious about its power to truly conceal her, but she folded it up and tucked it under her arm. She patted her knife, in which she did have confidence, and set off in the direction of the Bastille.

The moors were barren and bleak, especially at this time of year, and dark clouds scudded across the wind-swept sky. She pulled her jacket tight around her neck, feeling exposed. A few barren trees, bent in the direction of the prevailing wind, afforded her little concealment. Feeling vulnerable, she could see the Bastille ahead of her. It towered boldly over the landscape, daring anyone to approach. Chas strode on defiantly.

She took out the cloak and wrestled with it for a couple of minutes, finally managing to put it on, so that she could still see. She walked carefully forward to avoid tripping over it. When she was within a few metres of the Bastille gates she began to look for ways to get inside. The walls reminded her of Peter Marsden's garden, although on a grander scale. They had the same kind of security field hovering on top of them. She walked around the perimeter. The Victorian walls didn't go all the way round. Where the new wings had been grafted on, the walls had been knocked out and replaced by high wire fences. She guessed they were electrified. Eventually she decided there was no way over, under or through and headed back to the main gates, hoping that some vehicle would arrive soon and she could slip through undetected.

*

Si waited. No one came. He wondered if this was part of the torture; leaving him to fear what lay ahead. He fought hard to control the nausea, which this time, was mainly fear generated. Finally a door opened.

'Good morning, Silence.' The Commander entered with another doctor. His demeanour was business-like. He was wearing a shirt, tie and smart grey trousers, as if he had arrived for a day in the office. Si studied his face. Now that he knew who Resolution was, he could see some resemblance to Chas in the man's face. Behind the spectacles, his eyes were the same shape and the same piercing blue. His face, though more hollow cheeked, was the same angular shape. Si felt a pang of longing to see her again.

The doctor busied himself with some equipment on a bench at the side of the room, while the Commander fiddled with a remote control, projecting holo-images into the room.

'Are we watching a movie then?' Si asked, sardonically.

'You might say that,' the Commander replied. 'I have some questions for you. We don't necessarily need to hurt you, Silence. It depends on whether we can easily locate what we are looking for and how much you ...and your mother cooperate.'

At the mention of his mother cold adrenalin flooded Si's veins. 'My mother? Is she here?'

'No. I think you know where she is. That's where you were trying to reach, wasn't it?'

'The Priory?'

The Commander nodded. 'Indeed.' He gave a short, ironic laugh. 'How you were proposing to 'rescue' her, I've no idea. The security there is one hundred percent better than it is here.'

Again, an echo of Chas, in that stupid phrase. He almost laughed. 'Thanks for the warning. I'll remember that when I next visit.'

The Commander smiled patronisingly.

'If you've hurt my mother I'll...'

The Commander raised an eyebrow. 'You'll ....'

Si yanked at the straps that were holding him and let out a frustrated growl.

'Yes, nice sentiments Silence, but in fact, you'll do nothing, because you can't. Your family are much too loyal to one another and to certain causes. And that is your downfall.'

'It's better than the selfishness that's driven you all your life,' Si yelled.

The Commander frowned at him. 'Self-preservation is a better description. I serve my country and my government. That's hardly selfish now, is it?'

Si was about to blurt out what he knew of Chas and her family but he stopped himself. He had to use that weapon at the right time, and this was not it.

'What about my father?' Si said. 'Am I going to see him?'

'No. Your mother is all we need for now.'

The Commander pressed another button on the remote and an image flickered into life. An empty room came into view. It looked like an interrogation room; bare walls, a chair, with restraints dangling from its limbs.

'Doctor Fredrikson, are you there?' After a short pause a man came into the room. 'Doctor Fredrikson?' The Commander repeated.

The man looked into the camera. 'Yes. Good morning

Commander.' His face was lifeless and serious.

'Do you have the prisoner ready? Where is she?'

'She is on her way down Commander.'

Resolution shuffled impatiently. 'I said ten thirty doctor. It is now ten thirty two.'

'Yes, Commander and she will be here any second.'

The Commander folded his arms. The doctor on the screen moved away to the door and opened it, looking up the corridor. Si felt the muscles tighten all over his body in fear and anticipation. He hadn't seen his mother for over three years. Maybe he would be able to talk to her. His limbs began to tremble and he had to breathe deeply.

As Si watched, a small thin woman was brought into the room. She was wearing a grey pinafore dress, a white T-shirt and pumps. Her legs were bare. Her head was bowed and shoulder length hair fell across her face. She looked like a child in school uniform. The guard who brought her did not touch her and neither were her limbs restrained in any other way. She came meekly and obediently into the room and sat on the chair. For a moment Si forgot who this was, so transfixed was he by this child-like figure. Then she looked up. He gasped. Her cheeks were pale and drawn. The beautiful brown eyes Si remembered, blankly stared into the middle distance. Si bit his lip to prevent a whimper from escaping. He wanted to get to her. He wanted to cry out that he was coming for her. He wanted to hug her and be hugged. Instead he remained silent, trying hard to keep his emotions in check. It wouldn't help if the Commander saw how much this was affecting him.

His mother clearly had no idea why she had been brought to the room. She couldn't see Si; that was evident. She wasn't really looking at anything. The doctor moved around her and began to place electrodes on Kate's temples and chest. She didn't even flinch as he put his hand inside her T-shirt. Finally, the leather restraints were secured around her wrists and feet.

'What are they doing to her? Can they see or hear us?' Si asked.

'They can hear us and when that incompetent idiot gets his act together they will be able to see us.'

'Doctor Fredrickson, are you ready?' His voice was impatient.

'Yes, Commander. Kate, look over here, please.' He addressed Si's mother almost gently, as one would a vulnerable child.

Kate Hunter looked at the doctor, momentarily confused.

'Is she drugged?' Si said. Aggression was collecting in his stomach. He looked at his own restraints. His fists clenched, and he slammed them into the table.

'I doubt it,' the Commander said. 'They rarely need drugs with long term inmates at the Priory.'

'Over here, Kate,' the doctor was saying, as he motioned to Kate to turn her head.

Finally she turned her head. The camera fixed in on her face. Her eyes widened and a whisper escaped her lips. 'Si.'

'Mum!' his voice was urgent, he couldn't help it. 'Are you all right? What have they done to you?'

Suddenly, her face was alive. It was like her spirit had just been injected with adrenalin. A little more colour flushed her cheeks. She was focused.

'No questions!' Resolution ordered. 'Silence, you need to know that the electrodes fitted to your mother's body will give her increasingly powerful electric shocks if you or she do not comply or cooperate.'

Si looked at the Commander with distain.

'I thought you were dead. They told me you were.' A sob caught in her throat.

'I escaped, but they caught me. I knew you were alive, Mum. Where's Dad?'

'No questions! Didn't you hear me? I meant what I said. Doctor Fredrickson?'

Fredrickson looked at Kate.

'No!' Si cried. 'I won't ask any more. Stop. Don't hurt her.'

The Commander was not about to relent. 'Doctor,' he said again.

Fredrickson pressed something on the remote he held. Kate cried out and doubled over. It only lasted a few seconds but Si couldn't stand it.

'Stop it!' he screamed, yanking at his restraints, in vain.

'That was only a small burst.'

Kate sat up. Her face was pale once again, her eyes were closed. She opened them slowly and smiled faintly. 'Si, it's okay. They've done this before. I can take it.'

Resolution frowned. 'This time we are going to keep on until you tell us how to extract the nanomedibot from the boy without destroying it.'

'Why?' Kate said. 'Why don't you just destroy it?'

'We can use the technology for other things. You and your husband made some ground-breaking developments. We cannot waste them and our scientists have so far failed to come close. Why do you think you are still alive?'

'And when you get what you want?' Kate said.

'I've told you before – the boy's life and yours will be spared and you can be reunited.'

'In prison?'

'What would you rather? That, or eternity?'

Kate smiled.

'Tell us the procedure,' Resolution demanded.

'Wait – I want to know what this nanomedibot is before you cut me open,' Si said.

The Commander rolled his eyes behind his tiny spectacles. He folded his arms and looked at the screen. 'You might as well tell him how you've been using him as a human storage container all this time.'

Kate took a deep breath. 'Si – your father and I knew we were in danger just before they staged our deaths. We panicked, I have to admit that now. One night we sedated you and injected you with the prototype for the first nanomedibot capable of repairing cells damaged by the New Plague. NMBs have been in development for years, but never had anyone been successful in making them function fully, without fatal consequences to the patient. We were confident that we had done it. All the tests we had carried out were conclusive. We had to hide the NMB, so we injected it onto your bloodstream.' She paused. 'Si, the New Plague is a manufactured virus. It ...'

She was cut off by Resolution. 'Enough!'

Si had a thousand questions buzzing around his head and he couldn't ask any of them. Suddenly he guessed why he was feeling ill every day. Resolution watched him, a sadistic smile playing across his lips. 'It looks like your son is lost for words. Now, shall we begin?' He turned to the doctor in the room with him. The man nodded.

'Tell us how to extract the NMB.'

She hesitated, looking intently at Si's image in front of her.

'Mum, I don't want you to give it to them. I don't care what happens to me.'

'But she cares,' Resolution said in a mocking voice. 'And you care what we do to her – and therein lies the rub. You both care about each other. It's touching – and highly effective.'

'Please Mum. I don't care if I die. You know it will be all right. You know where I'll be waiting.'

'But you do care if we hurt your mother, don't you?' He turned. 'Fredrikson.'

The doctor moved forward. Si thought he hesitated just a fraction.

'Don't do it!' Si yelled, but the doctor pressed a button and Kate doubled over once again. This time it was more prolonged and her cry was agony to Si's ears.

'Mum,' he wailed, losing what little grip he had on his self-control. Tears were running down his cheeks and he thrashed about ineffectively. 'Mum! He's right. I can't bear them hurting you.'

Her face was limp as she came round from a short blackout. 'Si, I love you. They won't harm you while they can still use the NMB.' She almost laughed. 'Let them kill me, then they'll never get to it.'

Resolution slammed his fist into the table on which Si lay. 'Damn you woman. Do I have to get Knowles in here? We can hurt the boy, believe me, we will.'

'You touch him – you get nothing,' she snarled with a ferocity Si wouldn't have believed she was capable of from her initial appearance. Si was shocked by her vehemence. Resolution's impatience was growing. Suddenly, he turned off the holo-image. 'Doctor,' he said. 'Come with me.'

'Where are you going? What's happening to my mother?'

23

Outside the Bastille Chas waited. The wind was biting and there was no shelter near the entrance gates. The invisibility cloak did not offer her any protection from the elements. She was restless, agitated. Was no one going to drive through these gates today? She kept trying to formulate another plan to get in but everything she thought of ended in frustration. She decided to walk around the perimeter once more. She had seen a stream near the wire fence and she needed more water. If a vehicle approached she would still be able to hear it and run back to the gates before it went inside. This annoying cloak would have to be hitched up though, in order to run. Unexpectedly, she laughed out loud at the thought of how ludicrous that would look.

As she moved along the wall and into a different position, the building afforded her more shelter from the wind. She found the stream and bent down to fill her bottle. For some reason her thoughts turned to Peter Marsden. She wondered what was happening to him and if his friend Eric had managed to get him released.

Strangely, at that moment, Si was thinking of Peter too. Not only of him, but all the other people who had suffered for this NMB. His thoughts inevitably ended up with Chas. He pictured her cool blue eyes, her frowning face. He heard her cutting remarks at various points in their journey. He closed his eyes and imagined that kiss as they had parted for the last time. Finally he opened his eyes, wishing he could still see his mother. He ached to know what was happening to her. She had been in this room and yet she was hundreds of miles away. How was he ever going to help her now? A sense of hopelessness settled on him like a storm cloud.

*

Resolution was in conference with the Premier. Knowles and the doctor were also present.

'Just get the woman to talk, Commander. How hard can it be?' the Premier was saying. 'You have the boy. Do whatever it takes. As long as he's still alive when the NMB is extracted it will still function, won't it, doctor?'

'Yes Premier, as far as I'm aware, it will.'

'What do you mean – as far as you're aware? Don't you know for certain man?'

'Yes, Premier. Yes. It will function as long as the boy is alive when we extract it. If he dies before we take it out it will shut down in a matter of seconds. Its only purpose is to save life and once the heart stops it will also shut down.'

'Well, even if you have to take him to the edge of death to get that damn woman to talk – just do it. I presume Knowles here has the necessary tools to make Kate Hunter talk when she sees her son?'

'Of course, Premier,' Knowles said.

'Let them stew for a few hours before you start. Fear is good preparation for surrender.'

The holo-image flickered away. Resolution was impatient to

finish the process. He paced the room shaking his head.

'We don't have to wait that long, Commander. We can start back on them in an hour maybe,' Knowles said.

Resolution looked at him and shook his head. He glanced at the doctor. 'Things get back to the Premier, Knowles. Let's schedule it for...' he looked at his watch, '1400 hours. Get someone to put water in there for the boy and loosen one wrist so he can drink. I don't want him dehydrating.... yet.'

The doctor and Knowles stood up to leave. 'And Knowles, find out what happened to Hunter's companions. I presume you haven't heard from the men we left to hunt them down?'

Knowles shook his head. 'No Sir. I'll chase it up.'

Resolution nodded and sat down at the desk in the corner of the room. His thoughts returned to his sister. He hadn't had time to think about her since they arrived at the Bastille. He needed to know she was out of his way - permanently. All those years ago, when he had watched her being dragged off to a workhouse, he had thought he was rid of her. She had been trouble for him and the family back then. Always doing something that drew attention to them, which was not what they needed, being illegal immigrants.

Chastity didn't even exist when they had come to Britain. The two boys' names were quickly changed to fit in with the new regime. Forged birth certificates and legal immigrant certificates were bought, at an extortionate price, on the black market. They were meticulously taught English by their father, until Resolution had forgotten how to speak Slovak. Sometime later, when Chastity was born, she was an official British citizen. Resolution had been envious of her status over the years. He wanted to be British. He was the one who deserved it. He was the one who worked hard at school; fell in line with all the rules and regulations set down by the Government. He was the one with ambitions to serve this country. And yet she had British citizenship, which she couldn't care less about; which she flaunted and abused; which she kicked against – all the time. And then the youngest had come along, and he was also a British citizen. But he was weak and hadn't bothered Resolution so much.

Chastity had always been a thorn in his side. It was her rebelliousness that had caused him to arrange for her removal to the workhouse. It was her rebelliousness that had caused a beady eye to fall on the family and force him to eventually inform on his parents and cause their deportation. In doing this he earned himself some amnesty for his loyalty to The Rulers. However, it was always a precarious relationship, despite his status now, and he could not have his troublesome little sister ruining things.

Impatiently he picked up his phone and called Knowles. 'News?'

Knowles was a highly efficient man, used to the Commander's demands for prompt service. 'They are dead, Sir.'

'And? What did they do with the bodies?'

'Burned them, Sir.'

A sense of relief washed over Resolution and he breathed deeply.

*

Contrition Wright was only twenty one. He had been working as an orderly for three months at the Bastille. He knew most of the inmates were here for political reasons and he had made an effort to get to know most of their names. Sometimes he smuggled little luxuries in for them: Nice shower gel for one lady, sweets for some of the teenagers, certain magazines for a couple of the men. He even risked a book for one lady. He often sat chatting to the inmates, long after he should have moved on to another task and had been reprimanded once for his attentions to the prisoners, but he considered this an honour.

He had been given the task of taking water to Silence Hunter. Contrition had known Si from before his escape. He liked him. He was friendly and funny. Despite the rumours about Si, he was not afraid of taking him water and unfastening his hand from the leather strap. He was curious to see him, in fact, and to know why he was such an important prisoner.

As he was in a kitchen filling a jug with water, a hand shot over his mouth and an arm anchored around his neck. The jug clattered into the sink as Contrition struggled with his assailant. He was unsuccessful and soon lay unconscious on the floor.

'Sorry kid,' the assailant whispered.

The assailant stripped the boy of his orderly's uniform and put it on. Orderlies had ID chips in their hands, which also opened most doors, but Contrition also had a pass card for the high security rooms. The uniform was a bit tight and the trousers were slightly too long, but it would do. Filling the jug and putting it on a tray with a glass, the assailant glanced one last time at the boy on the floor. He would come round in a while and be none the worse for it.

The imposter cautiously exited the room and headed down the corridor, trying to walk confidently. Two nurses were at their station. They had their backs turned and were laughing about some story one of them was recounting. There had been lots of speculation about what was going to happen to Si and why he'd been brought here at dead of night. The assailant had an inkling where Si would be, but wasn't sure exactly which room. Overhearing Contrition being told to take water to Si in medical room two, was a stroke of luck.

Standing outside the door of medical room two, there was a moment of wavering. Who might be inside? How would Si react? The pass card opened the locking device.

Si opened his eyes and took a deep breath. This was it. They were back to finish torturing him. At least he would see his mother one last time. He stared at the ceiling, not even turning as the door opened.

'Si?'

He turned at the unexpected voice.

'Temp!'

He recognised Temp, but only just. His hair was neatly smoothed down and he had shaved. He looked so much younger in the orderly's uniform. Temp put the tray down and began loosening the straps around Si's limbs. 'We haven't got much time.'

'I've been waiting in here for hours. I saw my mother.'

Temp looked at him in confusion.

'Holo-image. They're holding her at the Priory. We were half way there.'

Si's ankles were now free and Temp was working on his hands.

'How did you know I was here?'

Temp shook his head. 'I saw you in the corridor last night, didn't I? I was 'sleepwalking.'' He laughed. 'I don't really sleepwalk. I just get up. I can't sleep well here. I go for a walk to relieve the boredom. They think I'm sleepwalking. It's quite funny really. I saw you, but obviously didn't show any recognition.'

Si rubbed his wrists and jumped down from the table. He took the glass, filled it with water and gulped it down. Then he refilled it and did the same again.

'Let's get out of here,' Temp said.

'What's the plan?' Si asked.

'I haven't had time to think of one. Let's see if we can get out of the building. I've got this pass card.'

'What about the security cameras?'

'I know where they are.'

Si didn't hold out much hope of escaping, without a decent plan.

'Are you sure you want to get mixed up in all this?' Si said.

'I've got nothing to lose.'

'When I escaped before, I climbed over the fence when the power was off, 'cos they were doing repairs. I just seized my chance.'

'Let's go for it now,' Temp said. He listened at the door. There was no sound in the corridor. Slowly he opened it. Si glanced around the room. The feeling that he was leaving his mother behind tried to hold him, but in reality this was his slim second chance to reach her. They slid out of the room.

The corridor was empty. They headed in the opposite direction to the nurse's station. At the corner they stopped and peered round. Clear.

'There's a door into the main building up here, then we can make for the exit through the back of the house,' Temp said.

They came to another corner. As Temp peered round he saw two orderlies coming towards him. He pushed Si back along the corridor they had come, down searching for somewhere to hide. There was nowhere. All they could do was press themselves against the wall around a corner and hope the orderlies went straight past.

*

In the kitchen Contrition Wright opened his eyes to find himself on the floor. He remembered the arm around his neck and rubbed his throat. The jug, the tray and glass were gone. He should notify the Master immediately.

*

Temp and Si reached the inner door into the main building. There was a camera here.

'Wait,' Temp said. He jogged back up the corridor before Si had the chance to protest. There was nowhere to hide if anyone came. This was a junction of three corridors. Someone could come down any one of them at any moment. He would just have to run. His heart and head pounded. But the adrenalin was keeping any sickness at bay. At least now he was sure the sickness was not the plague. The relief of that was almost as good as a cure, despite the fact that he didn't really understand what the NMB was doing to him.

His eyes darted in every direction. An orderly turned the corner behind him, pushing an empty wheelchair. His heart leapt and he looked for somewhere to run, until he realised it was Temp.

'Get in,' he said, pushing the wheelchair up behind Si. 'Put this blanket around you, cover most of your head and keep your face down.'

Si did as he was told, the panic subsiding, as he sat down in the chair. Keeping his head down, Temp pressed the pass card to the door panel, hoping it worked like a chip. It opened. They were through into the main building.

24

Chas had returned to the main gate and was almost screaming with the frustration that not one single vehicle had approached the Bastille. She paced back and forth like a wild cat, in an enclosure. She knew it would be dark soon. It was becoming unbearably cold and she needed shelter. The best she could do was huddle by the wall. She wasn't sure how much longer she could wait without getting hypothermia.

*

When Resolution heard the report from the Master he threw back his head and roared.

Knowles and the doctor stared, wide eyed. It was very rare for the Commander to show emotion and this was an extreme outburst. He picked up the jug, still half full of water, and hurled it across the room. It smashed against the far wall. The glass and tray followed it.

'Commander!' began the doctor, his voice shaking, 'I really don't think...'

'Shut up, you idiot!' Resolution screamed, grabbing the doctor by his coat lapels and throwing him to the floor.

Knowles stepped forward to intervene. 'Sir.' He picked up the doctor and pushed the quivering man behind him. Knowles looked Resolution in the eye. 'Sir, we will find them. They can't have got far. The Master has the security guards looking at CCTV and searching the building. Everyone is on high alert. They cannot escape.'

The Commander's face was purple with rage, but his breathing began to slow and he deliberately started to take deeper breaths. He nodded to Knowles, not trusting himself to speak and annoyed at his loss of control.

'Let's see what the Master found out. He's questioning the orderly who was assaulted.'

The doctor stepped aside to let Knowles and Resolution out of the room. Then he began clearing up the broken glass.

*

'Do you have any idea who assaulted you? What did you see?' The Master was standing over Contrition, who was sitting in the Master's office, sipping a glass of water. He didn't feel shaken anymore but when the water and a chair had been offered to him, he felt it his duty to accept.

He shook his head. 'It all happened very suddenly. And he was so quiet, I didn't even hear the door open behind me.'

'But you know it was a man?'

'Hairy arms. I'm guessing it wasn't a woman. And he was strong.'

The Master nodded. He was about to ask another question when the Commander and Knowles entered the room, without knocking. He smiled ingratiatingly at Resolution. 'Commander.'

Contrition involuntarily froze at the sight of the man he had heard so many horror stories about.

'Have you found him yet?' Resolution demanded.

'Not yet, Commander,' said the Master.

'Who is this?' Resolution asked, looking intently at Contrition.

'This is the orderly who was assaulted, Sir. His name is Contrition Wright. He knows it was a man who assaulted him.'

'Oh very helpful! And?'

'And not much else I'm afraid.' The Master wrung his hands nervously. Contrition stared, wide eyes at the Commander, waiting for something nasty to happen to him.

The Commander just rolled his eyes. 'What about security?'

'Still looking, Sir,' the Master said.

'It must be at least ten minutes since the alarm was raised. And how long before that while this boy was unconscious?' Resolution was trying to keep control of his anger. 'I want news as soon as you find them. Knowles and I are going to look ourselves. Keep me informed.'

'Yes, Commander.'

There was a knock on the door and another orderly entered. He looked nervously at the Commander and Knowles, then turned to the Master. 'Sir,' he said, 'Temperance Alliston is missing.'

'Of course!' Resolution said, throwing up his hands. 'Of course, Alliston knows him from the village. But how did he know Hunter was here?'

'Everyone knows,' said the orderly.

'What?' said Resolution, shaking his head in disbelief.

'Yes Sir. News travels fast here.' He smiled nervously at the Master, who glared at him.

'And the sleepwalker?' Knowles asked.

'Yes Sir, Temp is well known for his sleepwalking,' Contrition added.

'What are you talking about Knowles?' the Commander asked.

'Last night, when I brought Hunter through the corridor, a man in pyjamas walked past us. It must have been him, it was hard to tell in the dim lights.'

Resolution drew a long, angry breath, then marched from the room, Knowles following.

*

There were more people about in the main building. Temp kept his head down and hoped no one would stop him. Si hunched himself up into a bundle of blankets. Temp noticed that they were starting to get curious looks. He headed for the corridor that led to the back entrance, where goods were brought in for the kitchen. There would be few people about in the kitchen at this time. He turned the corner and saw the back door straight ahead of him.

'Not far now,' he whispered to Si.

Si looked up briefly and saw the exit ahead of them. What were they going to do once they were out of the building? He didn't dare ask.

'Stop!' A voice called from behind them. Temp turned to see two security guards, armed with tazers.

'We know who you are. Put your hands behind your heads and get down on the floor.'

One of them spoke into his communication device to inform the Master that they had found them.

Si got out of the chair and put his hands behind his head. He had thought all along that this would happen. Temp was not so keen to give in. Suddenly, he pulled out a knife, grabbed Si from behind and held the knife to his throat.

'Back off or I'll slit the boy's throat,' Temp yelled.

Si was taken aback. He struggled but Temp was strong. He had him in a vice-like grip.

The security guards were uncertain how to proceed. They had been told that Hunter must be taken unharmed.

'Put the knife down. You can't escape. Give it up now and you won't get hurt.'

'I'm not giving anything up. You come at me and he's dead. Then I'll be dead too. I'm not staying in this place any longer. I want a car ready in ten minutes or the boy dies. Give me the car and when I'm safely away from here I'll dump the boy out on the moor and you can have him.'

Si pulled at Temp's arms. He could hardly breathe. Temp tightened his hold as Si struggled, making a choking noise.

'Keep still boy,' he said loudly, 'Unless you want to die right now.'

Si was confused. Was Temp really just doing this to secure a passage out of here? After all, he had no reason to be a real friend of Si's, after what had happened at the village. He must blame Si for that.

'Tell my demands to the Commander,' Temp said. 'You've got nine minutes.'

The security guard relayed the message.

The Commander and Knowles were on their way there. 'Just keep him there and don't provoke him,' Resolution said. 'We'll be there in a minute.'

'What do you propose?' Knowles asked, as they hurried on.

'There are more security guards outside the back door. He can't go anywhere. We talk him down, grab the boy and get rid of Alliston.'

*

'Seven minutes,' Temp said.

Si wondered what Temp was going to do when it got to zero minutes.

When the Commander and Knowles arrived on the scene, Temp regarded them with hatred.

'Put the boy down, Alliston.' Resolution spoke to him like a naughty child, caught stealing biscuits. 'Do it now and I will be lenient with you.'

'Six minutes,' Temp said.

'You're not really going to hurt him. Stop playing games and give us the boy,' Knowles said.

'No. You give me a car and you'll get the boy back in half an hour. Don't give me the car and he dies. And I know you need him alive, don't you?'

The Commander fumed inwardly. His lip curled up ever so slightly.

'You're bluffing,' Resolution smiled, folding his arms.

'You think I'm not capable of hurting him? You should know me better.' Temp moved the knife away from the main artery in Si's neck and slashed the knife across Si's arm.

Si's eyes bulged and he cried out, as pain coursed up his arm, across his chest and through his whole body. Temp was a mad man!

Resolution cursed. 'What the hell are you doing!'

Temp placed the bloody knife back against Si's neck. Si clutched at his bleeding arm.

'I don't give a toss about Silence Hunter and I care even less about what you want. In fact I'd love to stop you getting what you want from him, but most of all I want to get out of here.'

'You idiot, Alliston! You must know that this is futile!' the Commander screamed, losing his self-control for the second time in an hour.

'Five minutes,' Temp said.

Resolution ran his hand through his hair. 'Get him a car!' he barked at the security guard. The man looked at him in confusion.

'Do it!' Knowles ordered.

'If you harm the boy again or try to take him with you, you will die a horrible death Alliston,' the Commander snarled.

Temp laughed. 'I don't want the boy. Why would I? He's out on the moor in an hour. You're welcome to him when I'm gone. All my friends are dead because of him.'

'A car is waiting round the front Sir,' one of the guards said.

'Give us Hunter now and you can go,' Resolution said.

Temp laughed. 'You're joking! He's my security. Let us through.'

'Let them pass,' the Commander snarled at the guards outside the door.

'Throw your weapons away from you and move. You try to stop me...'

The Commander signalled impatiently for them to comply.

'Give me an hour before you send anyone out to pick him up,' Temp said, 'or he dies and you don't get what you want.'

Holding Si in his vice like grip, the knife at his throat, he moved towards the door. It was a few minutes' walk to the front of the building, but Temp kept a firm grip on Si the whole time, looking around in case anyone was going to attack them. Hoping there were no snipers on the roof. Si stumbled forward, blood seeping through his fingers and dribbling down his arm.

'Why did you do this?' he rasped.

Temp didn't answer. Rage surged through Si and he struggled in vain.

Dusk was gathering. The light was now a pale grey. Si saw the car waiting for them, with open doors. Temp pushed him into the passenger seat and shut the door. Looking all around, he quickly got into the driver's seat. He started the car. It hovered into action just above the car park. The gates at the end of the drive were opening and Temp drove determinedly towards them.

He glanced across at Si. 'I'm sorry about the wound. I had to make it look like I meant it,' he said. 'It's not deep. Rip some material off your shirt and make a tourniquet. That should stop the bleeding.'

Si looked incredulously at him. He began to rip some material off his shirt.

They were coming up to the gates. The car slipped through. No one was following them so far. He looked across at Si. 'I'm sorry, if I worried you. I'll take you to a safe place, then you're on your own. What happened to Chas?'

Si pulled the strip of shirt tight around his bleeding arm. 'She could be dead for all I know. She was with me when they took me and there was a boy with us too. I hope they got away.' This was only a half-truth. Si was torn between wanting Chas to be safe and wanting her to be with him. It was selfish, he knew, but he didn't want to do any of this without her.

They were about a mile from the Bastille. Suddenly Temp

slammed on the brakes and turned the steering wheel hard to the left. The car skidded to a halt at a forty-five degree angle to the road. Si was catapulted forward, his seat belt preventing him from smashing through the windscreen.

'What the...' Temp grabbed the knife from the floor and leapt out of the car.

A head and torso, with no legs had appeared out of nowhere, hovering in the middle of the road, like a ghostly apparition picked out by the headlights. Si hadn't even seen it. He had been too busy making the tourniquet.

'Stop!' Chas shouted, not moving from the spot in the middle of the road.

Temp looked on in wonder as the rest of her body appeared. 'Chas? How on earth? There was no one about. Then suddenly half a person appears, floating above the road, like a spirit! Scared the hell out of me!'

'And you're the last person I expected. I was going to steal this car and drive it back into the Bastille to find Si.'

Si got out of the car. 'Chas!'

Her eyes widened but still she didn't move. 'Si, you're alive.'

He moved towards her, wanting to grab hold of her, but he held back. He just stood in front of her, grinning. Glancing down at her hand, he saw the crumpled blue material.

He laughed. 'The invisibility cloak!'

'Bloody nuisance!' she said. 'What happened to your arm?' She touched the blood-stained tourniquet. 'What else have they done to you?' Her eyes searched his body for other signs of injury.

Temp shook his head. 'Just get in. Long story. We need to get away from here as quickly as we can.'

From the back seat Chas said,' I've got a car, hidden just down there when you come to that cross roads.'

'Even better,' Temp said. 'You two take that. When the Commander comes after me I can be a decoy. Si can explain everything once you get going.'

'But what will you do, Temp? You need to ditch the car, or they'll find you,' Si said.

'No I need to keep going, keep leading them on for as long as possible. Lots of sightings of the car will lead them away from you and give you a head start.'

He pulled up as Chas indicated where her car was.

'I'm sorry I doubted you,' Si said to Temp, as they got out of the car.

'I'm glad I was convincing,' Temp said, smiling. 'Sorry about the arm.'

'You did that?' Chas said.

'I'll explain. It's okay. ' Si said. 'Thanks for everything, Temp. I'm sorry... about the village and everything.'

Temp nodded. 'You've got to go help your parents to do whatever it is The Rulers don't want them to do.' Temp said.

'I know.'

'Bye again, Chas,' Temp said. 'One day I hope we'll meet again in better circumstances. Then we'll have a memorial ceremony for Plin and all the others.'

She nodded. Hesitantly she stepped towards him. They looked at each other for a few seconds then she hugged him. Temp was taken aback. He held her for a few moments and kissed the top of her head. Then he jumped back into the car, turned it round and was gone into the night.

'Come on,' Si said, 'We need to go.'

They drove off in the opposite direction to Temp.

'I can't believe he cut you and you're okay with it,' Chas said.

'Hey, it got us out of there. Hurts like crazy though. I can't believe you came after me. You are crazy! How did you think you'd get me out of there?'

'That thing,' she replied, indicating the invisibility cloak, tossed on the back seat. 'But it was so annoying to wear. Peter needs to sort that out!'

'What happened to him? And where's Ben?' Si hardly dared to ask.

'Peter was taken. His friend, Eric, was going to try and get him released. Ben is safe. He's with Meg.'

'Meg? You went back to York? Was she okay? How did she take it about Peter?'

'Too many questions!' Chas glanced at him and let a smile slip. 'It was tough on her, especially about Peter. I said I'd go back for Ben, but I'm not sure what we should do now. What's the deal with Temp? How did you get out?'

As Chas drove, Si explained what had happened to him since they had parted. He told her about his mother and the thing that he hoped was still inside him. The only detail he left out was the revelation that the Commander was her brother. He didn't know if she could take that. Or it might make her do something foolish and impulsive.

'You saw your mother. That's good. Now we know for certain where she is.'

'Yes, but watching them torture her, that was too much. I'm scared Chas. They know I'll go after her and what if they kill them both before we can get there?'

'I don't know. They'll certainly know where we're headed now, and they'll be ready for us.'

'D'you think it's impossible?'

'Probably, but that doesn't stop us trying. What have we got to lose?'

'Me? Nothing. I have to try to save my mother. But you? This is not your destiny. You could have a life somewhere else.' He looked intently at her.

She stared ahead, in silence, for a long time. Theirs was the only car around. The headlights picked out the rocks at the side of the road, in an otherwise vast blackness. She wanted to tell him what she knew about her brother and that she'd do anything to have the chance for revenge, but she didn't want Si to know that. Somehow she didn't think Si approved of revenge and he might think she would jeopardize their plans. Besides, there was another, stronger reason she wanted to go with him.

Her voice came quietly. 'I've told you before Si, I want to come with you. If this is your destiny, then it's mine too.'

He looked back at her. She kept her eyes on the road ahead. He leaned over and kissed her cheek.

25

Si awoke to find that they were driving through streets filled with ambient light. His head had begun to throb, as well as his arm.

'Where are we? How long have I been asleep?'

Chas grinned at him. 'You've been out of it for a couple of hours. We're getting close to York. I've not seen anything suspicious.'

'You must be shattered. Shall I drive?'

'I'm fine. We need a plan. Are we going back for Ben or are we driving straight to the Priory?'

Si was tempted to leave Ben with Meg. He would be safer with her. If they took him with them there was a good chance he'd end up dead. It wasn't right. But on the other hand they had promised to take him and he could have some useful contacts on the coast.

'I know what you're thinking. I have the same dilemma,' Chas said.

'And? Any conclusions?'

'I'd rather leave him with Meg, but we'd be letting him down. He'd never forgive us.'

'But at least he'd be alive to decide whether to or not.'

'I know but...'

'So how are we going to get him out of York? I can't go into town. They'll be looking for me again.'

Chas told him the plan.

'Wow you had it all worked out, didn't you?'

'I wish I had. I hadn't a clue how I was going to get you out of the Bastille. How's the arm?'

Si looked at the tourniquet and gingerly lifted it. Through the gash in his shirt he could see that it had stopped bleeding. 'I'll survive,' he said.

'You're not such a wimp after all, Silence Hunter,' Chas said, grinning at him.

'I never thought I'd hear the fearless Chas say that to me!'

'We're not far from York, so the warehouse should be coming up soon.'

In a few minutes they pulled up to the building. Chas drove onto the parking area and round the back. She turned off the car and her eyes closed.

'Good idea. We could sleep for a couple of hours before they get here,' he said.

She turned her head slowly towards him, then she was out like a power cut. Si pushed a few strands of hair back from her face and stroked it for a few seconds. Then he twined his fingers through hers, closed his eyes and fell asleep.

*

'We've had several sightings of the car in service stations and from motorway security cameras, Sir,' Knowles said to the Commander. They were heading along the motorway towards Manchester. Resolution was in the foulest mood Knowles had ever witnessed. He wouldn't dream of voicing his opinion that the Commander had made a stupid decision in letting Temperance have the car in the first place. Why hadn't he just ordered the security guards to attack Alliston with the tazers? Of course he was desperate to keep the boy alive. Knowles doubted that Temp would have killed the boy, and now he had been proved right. There was no sign of Silence Hunter on the Moor. Temperance had taken him and escaped. Resolution should have called his bluff. He was furious with himself.

He was well aware of his abjectly foolish decision. He was beginning to doubt his own ability to command this operation. He had never doubted himself before. But the pressure was getting to him. He knew if he failed here that his head was on the block in more ways than one.

Knowles spoke to several of his men in other cars. He turned to the Commander and, as if reading his thoughts, he said, 'Don't worry Sir, this time he won't get away, I'll make sure of that.'

Resolution didn't reply. His pride had suffered and Knowles was just making it worse.

*

Si woke up with a jolt. Someone was tapping on the top of the car. He looked around but saw no one. Was someone else wearing an invisibility cloak? Adrenalin surged through his body. He couldn't focus his mind and his head hurt. He turned this way and that trying to see someone, which made him feel dizzy and nauseous. Chas, incredibly, was still sleeping. He reached into the back of the car for the rucksack, where there was a weapon.

'It's a bird,' Chas said, without opening her eyes.

Si opened his door and got out. Sure enough a huge seagull was strutting across the roof. He shooed it away in irritation and got back into the car. He leaned across Chas to look at the

257

clock. Ten past ten. His stomach was churning. He felt bad. The familiar sensation of crawling inside his skin had started again. This actually made him smile. The Nanomedibot was still in his bloodstream. He had worried that with all the blood loss it might have somehow seeped out.

'They should be here,' he said, getting out of the car again. 'I'm going to look.' As he stood up, his stomach lurched and he retched violently a few times. There wasn't much in his stomach and it was painful. He swayed and steadied himself against the car.

Chas jumped out of the car. 'Si, are you okay?'

'I'll be fine, it'll pass. At least we know it's still game on. I'm going to look around.'

'Wait, I'll come with you.' Chas began yawning and stretching.

'You okay? You haven't had much sleep lately,' Si said.

'I told you before, I can survive on a few hours here and there,' she replied.

Cautiously, they moved to the entrance of the warehouse. The heavy steel door was partially open. Si peered inside. It was a big empty space and surprisingly light from all the large windows. There was no sign of Meg and Ben.

'Let's split up and look around, maybe they're hiding somewhere 'til they see us,' Si suggested.

Chas doubted it, but she agreed to have a look. 'Will you be okay on your own?' He looked very pale.

'Yes, I'll be fine.'

She looked dubiously at him.

'I'm okay,' he reassured her.

Chas took the outside and Si ventured into the warehouse. He didn't dare shout their names in case he drew attention to their presence. There wasn't really anywhere to hide. A few dilapidated offices led off the main space but there was no one in them.

They met back at the car. 'No sign of them,' she said.

'Me neither. How long should we wait? Why aren't they here?'

'I think we give them 'til twelve then we have to go.'

'What if something's happened to them?' Si asked.

'I don't know. If we go looking for them in York we're likely to get caught. We can't risk it.'

Si bit his lip. He didn't like the thought of leaving, not knowing if Meg and Ben were in trouble.

'I know what you're thinking Si, but we have to make a decision. We can come back - when you've found your mother.' She didn't sound convinced and Si knew it was more of an 'if' than a 'when.'

A small voice made them jump.

'Chas.'

They turned to see Ben standing at the door of the warehouse, looking dishevelled and weary.

'Ben!' Chas yelled and ran to him. She grabbed his arms and bent down to look at him. Si followed.

'You look terrible. Where's Meg? Are you all right?' Chas said.

'I saw Si, when he was in the warehouse. You didn't see us. We were in some boxes.'

'Is Meg there?' Si interrupted.

'Yes. She's sick; really sick. We came yesterday and she wasn't feeling well and when we got here and you didn't turn up, she lay down and couldn't get up again. I built the boxes around us for warmth and to hide us. She's burning up.'

Ben led them to where Meg was. Her body was slumped in a

heap and her familiar straw hat lay crumpled beneath her head. She moaned as they approached.

'Meg,' Ben said gently, kneeling in the straw beside her. 'Meg, it's Chas and Si; they're here.' He touched her arm and she moaned again. She tried to look up at the two shadowy figures.

'Meg,' Si said, bending next to her. 'What's wrong?' Chas knelt on the other side of her. Si felt her forehead. It was very hot and clammy. Her hair and clothes were sticking to her, despite the autumn chill. 'Have you got any water Ben?'

'No. I thought about leaving her to go and find some but I didn't dare. I knew I had to go this morning though, if you didn't come. I was going to get help.'

'There's a bottle of water in my rucksack,' Chas said. 'I'll go and get it.'

Meg tried to speak. 'Si,' she croaked. 'So good to see you. I'll be all right. Just a temperature. Help me sit up.'

Si and Ben put their arms around her and heaved. She was a large lady and it was hard work. Meg groaned and winced as they tried.

Chas arrived back with the water and some clothing that she had dampened. She handed Si the water, which he put to Meg's lips as Ben lifted her head. She knelt and laid the clothes over Meg's forehead and on her wrists.

'It might help with the temperature,' she said.

'She needs a doctor,' Si said.

'Stay with her Ben, keep giving her sips of water,' Si said. 'Chas, come outside for a minute.'

Once outside, he said, 'What are we going to do now? We can't abandon her like this. We'll have to get help.'

'Are you crazy?' Chas shook her head. 'You can't risk it and time is running out. We need to go. We'll have to leave Ben here to get help for her.'

Si ran his hands through his hair, pacing up and down. 'I don't know. That's a big responsibility for him. What if she dies? She looks really ill. We have to get her to a doctor or do something.'

Chas didn't say anything. She kicked the wall in frustration.

'We should take her with us,' Ben said, coming outside. 'We could find help on the way.'

'Don't be ridiculous Ben!' Chas snapped. 'That would be a death wish for us all. We can't take a sick person on the rescue mission from Hell!' She glanced at Si, thinking of his condition.

'When we get to Seahouses I know people. They'll help us and they'll take Meg in – look after her - I know they will.'

'I don't think so, when they find out who we are and what we're doing there,' Si said. 'They'll be scared. And she could have Plague. They'll probably want to turn us in themselves.'

'No, they're not like that!' Ben protested. 'They're good people. They suffered because of The Rulers. They hate them, like most of us do.'

'Yeah, but not everyone is prepared to risk their lives for what they feel, Ben,' Chas said. She threw her hands up in frustration and marched across the yard. Ben and Si stood silently watching her for a few moments.

'She's not mad at you, Ben, just the situation. How is Meg?' Si asked.

'She's taken some water. She can speak a little, but she really needs help Si.'

'I know. We're going to help her. Chas wants to help her too. That's why she's so frustrated.'

Si and Ben went back into the warehouse. 'Don't worry Meg,

we're going to help you,' Si said. 'We won't leave you.'

She nodded.

Chas came in.

'We're taking her,' Si said, firmly. 'We can find a chemist on the way and get some aspirin. That should take her temperature down.'

He expected a protest, but Chas just nodded.

With considerable effort, they heaved Meg into a sitting position and onto her feet. She did her best to help them, but she was still very heavy. She moaned as she stood up. Si ducked under one arm and Chas the other, while Ben supported her from behind.

'My hat,' she croaked.

Ben picked up the crumpled straw hat and placed it on the old lady's head. Slowly and awkwardly, they made their way to the car and gently bundled Meg into the back seat. There was just enough room for Ben to squeeze in beside her. Si fastened a seat belt around her plump figure and she slumped against Ben, who kindly took her weight.

'You'll be feeling much better soon, Meg,' Si said. He patted her hand. 'I'll drive for a while, if you like,' he said to Chas.

She looked at him. The colour had returned to his cheeks. He smiled, reading her thoughts. 'I feel fine.'

They got into the car and headed north for the second time. Si's thoughts turned to the people they had already met on this route: Aaron, Peter, Harmony. He hoped they were all right.

*

Resolution and Knowles stood in the car park of a car dealership. They watched as the fire service dealt efficiently with the car fire. The law keepers and security guards were also on the scene. Resolution was incandescent with rage. Temp had managed to set the car alight and get away before anyone realised he had been there. A member of the public had reported the car fire on his phone, but he had made no mention of Temp or any passenger. A small crowd of onlookers had gathered. The Commander had ordered all CCTV footage to be looked through immediately.

The manager of the car dealership hurried out to talk to the Commander. He had also been suitably admonished.

'Sir, we have the footage of the car being set on fire if you'd like to see it.'

'Of course,' Resolution replied. 'Knowles.' He gestured for Knowles to follow him.

The car had been parked quite a distance from the security cameras so the image was small. But it was obvious that a person was setting fire to it with a can of fuel. Then the person ran off in the direction of some trees. There was only one person in the footage.

The Commander slammed his fist into the table, making the mugs and papers jump. 'How did he get petrol? Why did this idiot have petrol here? No one uses petrol these days! What has he done with Hunter? Is he burnt alive in the car? Has he dumped him somewhere? Has he escaped? Damn it Knowles! Get out there and ascertain whether there's a body in there or not.'

There was no body in the car.

'So, we know he was alone when he got here. Maybe he did dump Hunter on the moors and we just haven't found him yet,' Knowles said. 'We've got people searching.'

'And maybe he didn't dump him. Maybe he let him out

somewhere on the way here. What was I thinking?' Resolution was pacing and raking his hands through his hair.

Knowles gritted his teeth and shook his head, as he wondered the same thing for the nth time.

'Get another bulletin out on him. All authorities on high alert, TV adverts again etc,' said the Commander.

'Already onto it, Sir,' Knowles replied. He walked away, speaking into his phone. Resolution sat down at the desk in the manager's office. His holophone began to ring. He checked the caller. It was the Premier. Resolution groaned. He was tempted not to answer, but knew he would have to speak to him sometime. The holophone flickered into being and an image of Premier Zephyr, at his desk, appeared in front of Resolution.

'I have been informed that somehow Silence Hunter has escaped from the Bastille again! Explain.'

Resolution felt his heart pounding. He didn't scare easily but he knew his career depended on how he handled this.

'It was a tactical move, Sir. Another prisoner had Hunter as a hostage. He was going to kill him if we didn't let them go. He took Hunter with him but told us he would dump him on the moors, just outside the gates.'

'And you believed him! You are one of my highest ranking officers. Why would you believe that?'

'This man, Temperance Alliston, had been part of the commune where we killed everyone. He witnessed the slaughter of his village because of Hunter. I thought he hated him. I thought ...'

'You thought! Well you have made a serious, serious error of judgement. Furthermore, you have failed at every turn to apprehend Hunter and retrieve the NMB. You are removed from the case, pending investigation.'

Resolution stood up and moved towards the holo-image as if the Premier were really in the room. 'Sir, please, that would be a mistake. I know the case, I know the boy. I can find him.'

'Damn it Resolution, I have given you too many chances! A car will pick you up from the Bastille and bring you to London, in a couple of hours. Be ready. And bring Knowles with you.'

The image flickered and died. Resolution let out an animal roar. He would not give up the chase. He had to prove to the Premier that he could do this. It was his only hope now of attaining the power he craved. If he failed, all was lost and he'd probably spend the rest of his life in prison, or worse, end up being deported – like his parents. He knew that Si would try to get into the Priory – fool that he was. So that was where he would wait, out of sight, hunted himself now. But he would bring Silence Hunter in. It was his only hope.

He called Knowles. 'Get the car ready. You and I are driving to Northumberland. I'll explain as we go.'

26

'Here take this,' Ben said, gently holding a bottle to Meg's lips. In it they had dissolved some soluble aspirin. She sipped the water and managed a smile. She was still hot and clammy.

'The aspirin should help your temperature,' Si said, patting her hand.

She smiled again. Ben got on to the back seat beside her and put his arm around her.

Si was also feeling queasy again. His head throbbed, his arm throbbed, but he didn't want to use up any of the aspirin. He had a feeling Meg might need it all.

They were about fifty miles north of York. Chas looked at Si's pale face. 'I'll drive now,' she said.

'I can keep going Chas, honestly if you need to rest ...'

'Don't be a martyr, Si. Get in.' She slid into the driver's seat. 'How far do you think it is?'

'I'm not sure. I'm guessing about another hundred miles.'

'Let's get going then,' Chas said. 'I hope you're right about people helping us in this fishing town, Ben.'

'They will. I know them. I know who we'll call on: our old neighbours, Ethan and Sarah.

Chas glanced worriedly at Si and then in the mirror at Meg. Her body was slumped against Ben's. He caught Chas's eye in the mirror and smiled at her. She looked away. This mission was becoming crazier by the day: A sick woman, a kid and a sick (even if he wouldn't admit it) teenager. She was the only one with any chance of making a rescue attempt. She had some skills, at least, that would be useful. But it was madness, none-the-less, to think that they could infiltrate the Priory. Even the Bastille was allegedly not even close in terms of security. The Priory was on an island, which was tidal, crossable only by a causeway at certain times of the day.

Meg coughed and shuddered. Ben took the lid from a water bottle and gently tipped it to her lips. Chas was worried. The Plague was never far from people's minds when someone exhibited unexplained feverish symptoms. They really needed a doctor.

Meg tried to speak. He voice was husky, but stronger than before. 'Take me to Peter's house, please.'

Chas looked at her in the mirror. 'Meg, we can't go there. What if it's being watched? And Peter was arrested, remember. We don't know what ... if ...'

'Please – I need to know what has happened to him. His housekeeper might be there.'

'Harmony?' Chas could actually picture Harmony going back to look after the house even if Peter had not returned. She didn't strike Chas as a timid woman. 'Does she know you? I don't think she'd welcome us back, and, no offence, especially with a sick person in tow.'

'I met her a few times. She seemed kind. Please Chas, I ...' Meg broke into another fit of coughing. Ben brought the bottle to her lips again.

Chas glanced at Si but his eyes were closed, despite the noise.

As the coughing subsided she said, 'I'll have to talk to Si about it. We'll be near Peter's house soon. I'll stop and we'll talk about it. Now you try and get some rest.'

*

Si woke up as the car stopped. They had pulled off the dual carriageway onto a country road. His head felt fuzzy.

'Everything okay?' he asked Chas.

Chas stretched. 'Let's go for a walk.'

Si looked at her; puzzled, but followed her out of the car. He was a little unsteady and felt nauseous, but he tried not to show it. He took some gulps of the autumn air. The sky was clear and the sunshine warmed their faces. The road was lined with trees that were almost bare. Chas told him of Meg's request. Si was as reluctant as she was to go back there, even though he desperately wanted to find out about Peter.

'I know it's mad to go back but I think she needs medical help and we can't take her with us, Si. What can we do with a sick old woman in tow? We could leave her at Peter's if Harmony is there. She could get help for her. And what about your arm? Does it need attention?'

Si's arm had stopped bleeding and he was trying to ignore it. 'She might not be there and even if she is, she's not likely to want anything to do with us,' Si said.

'I don't think she's like that. And I don't think the Commander, if he's onto you again yet, would think even you are stupid enough to call back there. He knows where you're headed, and anyway, what reason would you have to go back to Peter's?'

Si mused on her words. 'Okay, we'll do it. It kind of makes sense in a bizarre way.' They stopped walking. He turned to her and smiled. He took his hands out of his pockets and slid one of them into hers. She looked down at their fingers intertwined. He looked questioningly into her eyes. She didn't take her hand away and they walked back to the car in silence.

Ben was awake. 'What have you decided?'

'We're going back to Peter's,' Chas said. 'I'll go on foot, through the fields and in through that hidden entrance at the back. If everything's okay, I'll come back and we'll bring Meg up in the car.'

'We can't go the same way we went last time. We mustn't go past that cottage,' Si said.

'Why?' asked Ben.

'Because they were the ones who turned us in,' Si said.

'How do you know?' Ben said.

'Because as they drove me away to the Bastille, the man was there watching us and he nodded to the Commander.'

'Some people will do anything for money,' Chas said.

'I'm coming with you,' Si said. 'In case there's trouble.'

'No offence; but you're not up to it. You can't hide it from me. I know you're feeling ill.'

'I'll be okay. I'm not letting you go alone.'

'Ben can come with me,' she said. 'You stay here with Meg.'

Before Si could protest some more she said, 'Come on Ben. Hand me that pack. There's a weapon in there for you.' She put her hand on her own knife that never left her side. Si was annoyed. 'Besides,' she said, 'if the worst happens and something goes wrong, you need to get away. It's important that you stay here.' She silenced him before he could say anything else. 'I'm going, you're staying. Don't argue.'

He sighed. 'Okay, I'll stay. You should use the cloak.'

'No. I hate that thing. Besides, we won't both fit under it. Give us an hour. If we're not back, we're in trouble and you have to leave.' She looked back to Meg, who had opened her eyes. 'How are you doing?'

Meg managed a smile but her face was grey and sweaty. 'I'll be all right.'

Ben kissed her on the forehead and got out of the car.

'One hour, Si, then you go,' Chas said.

Si looked away from her.

'Promise me!' she said, urgently, gripping his good arm.

He glowered at her and nodded.

*

Chas found the hidden entrance easily. It seemed so obvious to her now. She wondered if it would be locked but as she pushed, it opened without much force. This made her wonder if anyone was here. Surely they would have locked it. She and Ben crouched in the bushes around the entrance. She knew there was CCTV in the garden so she needed to be cautious, even if it did seem odd that the hidden entrance was not locked. Keeping in amongst the shrubs and bushes, she and Ben crept along by the wall. Chas knew that she would be picked up by the cameras at some point but wanted to give herself as much time as possible if anyone was monitoring it. So far she had seen no signs of life in the house. Choosing her moment, she darted across the lawn towards the study doors. Ben followed. The doors were mainly glass and the room had two large windows to let in the sunlight. They pinned themselves against the wall under a window and Chas peered into the room. It was empty. She feared to try the door in case it was alarmed.

'There might be a window open like last time,' Ben suggested.

'Let's look,' Chas said.

They crept around the outside of the house, keeping their bodies low and close to the walls. There was no window open. There was, however, a car in the drive. A fresh dose of adrenalin surged through Chas's body. There was someone here. Did Harmony drive? Was Eric here?

'What shall we do?' Ben asked.

'You should put your hands behind your head, stand up and turn around,' came a voice from behind them.

*

Si was keeping a close eye on the clock. Chas and Ben had been gone half an hour. He was feeling very queasy now and, although he was trying to ignore it, his skin tingled and his eyes kept blurring. He tried to keep focused, but he knew he couldn't escape from the thing that was inside him, making him ill. He was scared. At the same time he was mopping Meg's brow with a damp cloth and giving her regular sips of water. She was starting to look a little better and she was able to talk more.

'You're a good boy, Si,' she said. Her voice was still faint and her breathing shallow. 'You're all good kids.'

'Shhh. You shouldn't try to talk,' Si soothed.

She ignored him. 'I want to. It's such a shame you're mixed up in all this mess.'

'I know. I'd like a quiet life really, but this has its plus points.'

'Oh? Would those plus points come in the form of a young lady called Chas?'

He smiled.

'Thought so,' Meg said, closing her eyes again. The short

conversation had worn her out.

Forty minutes.

Si had no intention of leaving without them.

*

As they turned around, Chas and Ben looked into the face of Eric Myers, who was pointing a shot gun in their direction. When he recognised them he lowered the gun. 'What the hell are you two doing back here?'

Keeping her hands on her head, Chas said, 'We need your help – again.'

Eric sighed. 'You've got a nerve! Put your hands down and come in.'

They followed him into the hallway. Harmony was there waiting anxiously to see who Eric had found. Her dark face turned a shade paler when she saw who it was. But her hospitality kicked in.

'Come into the lounge. I presume your mission failed? What happened?'

In the lounge they sat down as Chas summed up the events of the last few days. It seemed like an age since they had left here. 'So, Si is waiting in the car with Meg. She pleaded with us to come here. She hoped to find out about Peter, and that maybe, if there was anyone here you might look after her 'til she's well again. She needs a doctor. And Si has a big gash in his arm.'

'We don't have much time,' Chas said. 'I told Si that if we weren't back in an hour, he should leave, because something must have gone wrong. What has happened to Peter?'

'He's here,' Eric said.

Chas and Ben were shocked. 'But how?' Ben said.

Eric swept his hand through his hair 'A lot of negotiating with people in high places, some blackmail and lots of money changing hands.'

'Where is he? We're putting him in danger again, aren't we?' Ben said.

'He's resting. He's had quite an ordeal – interrogations and the like. I'm not sure you can stay, or your friend. It is highly dangerous for Peter to be associated with you. The authorities will be on the lookout for Si again. We may get a visit.'

At that moment Peter came into the room, looking pale and haggard. 'Bring Meg to the house.'

'Peter!' Ben ran to him and hugged him tightly.

Taken by surprise, Peter staggered backwards a little. Then he put his arms around Ben and smiled. Chas stood up. 'We don't want to put you in more danger. I didn't want to come here, but Meg ... she's really sick and she was desperate to know about you.'

'It's okay,' Peter said. 'Bring her here. I can't really let you stay though.'

'No. We don't want to cause more trouble.'

'Peter, this isn't wise,' Eric said. 'You know how hard it was to get you out. If you harbour them again there will be no reprieve.'

'I can't abandon Meg. She's an old friend. If you knew how she'd helped me in the past...'

'This is serious!' Eric stood up, his voice was raised almost to a shout. Frustration was written in his face. 'Peter, let me take her to a hospital or something. You can't risk having her here.'

'She's come to me for help. I've spent too long these past few years building my career, ignoring the wrongs I've seen around me and forgetting some important people in my past.' He lowered his voice. 'Being a selfish coward. Not anymore.'

There was a short silence; no one seemed to know what to say. Eric broke it. 'And what about us, Peter? The people who work for you now? The people who recently risked everything to get you out of prison. Don't we count?'

Peter came towards Eric. He put his hands on Eric's arms. 'Eric, you are more than my employee. You are more than my second in command. You are my friend. I would do anything to help you, as you have for me. I owe you my life right now. However, Meg has also saved me from harm in the past and I can't abandon her.'

'You won't be abandoning her. Just let me take her to a hospital, somewhere away from here. She'll be better off in hospital if she's so sick anyway.'

'He may be right,' Chas said. 'Look, I really have to get back and tell Si what's happening. We've been gone nearly an hour, but if I run I can make it.'

Eric and Peter stood still, their eyes were locked. Peter sighed and closed his eyes for a moment.

'Bring her here Chas ....'

'Peter, please!' Eric said.

'Then - I'll let you take over. I'll bow to your judgement. You are a faithful friend Eric.'

Eric shook his head. He was not comfortable with having Si or Meg in the house.

Chas stood at the door. 'I'll be back soon.' Her hour would be up in two minutes. She was desperate not to lose Si again.

27

Si was in the back of the car with Meg. She was holding his hand, her eyes closed. He was keeping her cool by any means possible. The windows were down, he kept putting cold damp cloths on her head and blowing cool air on her face. She smiled every time he did this and told him he was a 'good boy.' But the hour was up and there was no sign of Chas. He should leave, but his dilemma was whether to leave Meg and go to look for Chas or wait here indeterminately. His stomach churned and the nausea grew worse.

'Meg, I need to go and find out what's happened to Chas and Ben, they've been too long. Will you be all right?'

'Of course,' she said, opening her eyes.

Si looked dubiously at her. Then he withdrew his hand gently from her clasp and began searching in a rucksack for something to defend himself with. Chas and Ben had taken their only weapons. He couldn't find anything of much use and felt his chest tightening at the thought of a confrontation. He could hardly rely on brute strength. He remembered how he had saved Chas in the woods from her attacker and hoped that sheer adrenalin would be enough.

As he emerged from the car his legs almost gave way. A tidal wave of nausea swept over him and he retched. There was nothing in his stomach and he couldn't remember the last time he had eaten. Hot acid bile burnt his throat. He reached back into the car for the water bottle and drained the last few drops.

'I'll be back soon, Meg.' He glanced at her. She nodded. He headed off in the direction Chas had taken.

*

She was running through the wooded area that stretched from the side of Peter's house along the fields, towards the car. Light on her feet, she easily negotiated obstacles in her path. Si was walking towards her, his head down as he tried not to trip over anything and struggled to keep himself from retching again. She saw him first. Relief flooded her. He hadn't gone, but more than this, he was coming to find her. He looked up and broke into a grin.

'Why have you left Meg on her own?' she demanded, as they came together.

The smile dropped from his face. 'I was coming to find you. I thought you might be in trouble.'

'I told you to leave after an hour.'

'I know, but I couldn't go without you, Chas – you must know that.'

'Come on. Peter's there. He told me to bring Meg.'

'Peter is there? How?'

'Come on. Let's get back to the car. I'll explain on the way. We need to get Meg to the house. Let's hope those people in the cottage don't see us.'

'I'll keep my hood up to drive and you just keep low.'

Chas noticed how pale Si looked. His features were drawn and he had dark rings forming beneath his eyes. 'Si, are you okay?'

'I'll be fine,' he said.

'You look awful.'

'I said I'll be fine. Don't worry.'

They drove to the house. As they came up the drive, Peter, Eric and Harmony came out to meet them.

Si emerged from the car. 'Peter, it's so good to see you.'

'Likewise,' Peter smiled and hugged him.

Harmony and Eric began to gently lift Meg from the back of the car. Amidst the groans she tried to smile at them and thank them. Then she saw Peter.

'My dear Meg. It's so good to see you. We'll have you well again in no time.' He kissed her clammy brow.

'Thank you for helping us again,' Si said. 'I know we're putting you in more danger. I must admit, we didn't expect to see you. We'd just hoped Harmony might be here.'

He glanced at Harmony and Eric as they tried to help Meg to walk into the house. Ben was trying to help too. They were half carrying her, but she was not a light woman and it was with some effort that they made it to one of the spare bedrooms. Harmony and Chas helped her out of her clothes, which were dirty and smelt of stale sweat. Harmony found a large night dress of her own, which just about fitted around Meg. They propped her up on the soft pillows. Meg closed her eyes and smiled. Harmony had already put a jug of iced water on the bedside cabinet. She reached for a glass now and tenderly helped Meg to sip the water.

'We gave her aspirin,' Chas said.

'That's probably helped,' Harmony replied. 'I will have some in our medicine cupboard.'

'When can I see Peter?' Meg asked.

'I'm sure he'll be along soon,' Harmony said.

*

Harmony took freshly brewed coffee and sandwiches to the lounge, where she and Chas joined the others. Ben tucked in hungrily, Chas had something but Si couldn't face it. His stomach was lurching and he was finding it hard to concentrate. His palms were clammy, but he didn't want to give in to the growing feeling of panic rising inside him. He had to get to the Priory and rescue his mother.

'You'll have to leave as soon as you've had something to eat,' Eric said. He hadn't sat down and was pacing the room.

'Eric, don't hassle them,' Peter said. 'They've been through a lot. I want to know what has happened.'

'Peter, its madness them even being here! The Rulers are bound to be on their trail again and if it leads here you're not going to be able to play the 'get out of jail free' card twice.'

'Well, it was hardly free, was it Eric?' Peter raised his eyebrows, knowing how much money had been paid as a blatant bribe.

'We'll be gone within half an hour, I promise you,' Si said. 'You've done enough. All we wanted was for someone to take care of Meg, and she was asking for you so much.'

'Don't worry about her. She's safe now. I'll get my doctor to her. He's good. Now tell me how you escaped from the Bastille - twice in a matter of weeks! I doubt anyone else can claim that.'

Between them, Chas and Si related the escape to everyone.

'I knew the invisibility cloak would prove useful,' Peter laughed when Chas described how she had jumped out of the gloom at the car.

'Well it was a bit of a pain to wear,' Chas said.

Peter laughed again. 'Yes, needs modifications. Still in the early stages, like I told you.'

Harmony came into the room. 'Peter, Meg is asking for you.'

'Of course. I must go and see her.' He stood up.

'And we should get going,' Chas said, also standing.

'I'll make you some extra food to take,' Harmony offered.

'Thanks,' Chas said.

'I'll make sure your car is fit for the journey,' Eric said.

Si stood. 'Thank you Eric. I'm sorry ....'

The room suddenly turned upside down and everything went out of focus. Eric reached to grab Si, as a wave of extreme nausea surged through him and his body lurched sideways. He heard Chas call his name; her voice sounding like it was coming from inside a distant cave. Blackness seeped into the edge of his vision and he was quickly engulfed by it as he lost consciousness.

'Si!' Chas screamed again, leaping over to him.

Everyone crowded around him. Peter bent to check that he was breathing and take a pulse. 'What on earth is wrong with him?'

'Is he dead?' asked Ben.

'No, he's got a faint pulse,' Peter said.

'It's the thing inside him,' Chas said. 'It's been making him more and more ill. And he's lost a lot of blood. He keeps fighting it though; saying he's fine.'

'The thing? What do you mean? Has he got a disease? Plague?' Eric said, alarmed.

'No, no! His mother and father implanted a nano...thingy inside him, (before they were kidnapped) to protect their research. And now it's malfunctioning or something. It's the whole reason why The Rulers are after him. They want it.'

'What can we do? Is it going to kill him?' asked Peter.

'I don't know,' Chas said. 'I think it was designed for healing people but something's gone wrong with it.'

Eric was beside himself. 'Peter, he really can't stay here!'

Peter picked Si up and, for the first time, Chas and Ben witnessed his anger. 'What shall I do with him then, Eric? Throw him in the back seat of the car and get this girl to drive off with him, knowing he might die?'

'She can find help.'

'Don't be ridiculous! She doesn't know anyone. I do. Harmony, let's get him to a bed.'

'You can't get the doctor to him, Peter. He'll know who he is and he'll turn you in, no matter how friendly you think he is. Most people are scared of The Rulers, remember.'

'I've got to help him,' Peter said, struggling with Si's body.

'Please, save him!' Ben begged, appealing to Eric. Despite herself, Chas found her cheeks were wet with tears.

Eric took Si from Peter, who was still in a weakened state from his ordeal.

'You said you'd bow to my judgement,' he said to Peter, over his shoulder, as he followed Harmony to a bedroom.

'I know, I know, but I can't throw him out.'

They laid him on the bed. Chas sat next to him. His body was limp and his breathing shallow. He was covered in a film of fevered sweat.

'I'll get some cool cloths,' Harmony said. 'Maybe he's caught a bug from Meg.'

'No! This is serious. It's not some bug!' Chas shouted.

'Ben, come and help me,' Harmony said, ignoring Chas's outburst.

'I'm going to make a phone call,' Peter said. 'Don't worry, help will be here fast.' He left the room and Chas could hear Eric pleading with him not to take any more risks.

Chas couldn't speak. All the pain of losing those she loved was flooding her like a raging torrent. She held Si's clammy hand and willed him not to die. She thought of the God Si's parents believed in. She had never believed in any supernatural power, but her lips silently formed the words 'help him.' She closed her eyes and repeated them over and over again.

*

This time Si was not in the Bastille, he was in a cold, dark place by himself. He traced his eyes with his fingers to make sure they were open, because it didn't seem to make any difference; the blackness was more complete than he could ever have imagined darkness to be. He was lying on his back on the ground, his whole body shivering, and he realised he was naked. He got to his knees and crawled painfully, slowly, stretching out his hand in front of him to feel his way. The ground was uneven and wet. His hand touched a solid mass. It was a rock face with thin streams of water trickling down it. Feeling his way along it, around every corner, he realised he was trapped in an area of about three square metres. He slumped back against the wall.

And then he heard it: A quiet scuttling sound. His body tensed as the sound was magnified by the utter silence. It began to multiply as if whatever had made the sound in the first place had just reproduced itself many times over. His stomach clenched and bile rose in his throat. He edged along the wall but there was nowhere to go. The scuttling drew closer and closer. Then he felt them. Long, spider legs began climbing across his feet and hands. He shook his limbs violently and breath caught in his throat as he let out a frightened whimper. The creatures kept coming; more and more of them, climbing his body, reaching his torso, his forearms, his collar bone. He tried to claw them off his flesh, but now they were streaming up his neck and onto his face. He closed his eyes; he wanted to scream but didn't dare open his mouth. He tried to swat them off but more took their place. He put his hands to his ears to stop them crawling inside. Finally, he thrashed his body around the floor of the cave, scraping his raw flesh against the jagged surfaces.

*

'Si, Si!' Chas was crying as Si's body convulsed on the bed. She ran to the door of the room. 'Peter!' she screamed. 'Please hurry! He's having a fit.' She glanced back at the bed as Si threw himself to the floor, then ran down the corridor in search of help.

*

Knowles was not happy about the position the Commander was putting him in. He had always been completely loyal to Resolution. He didn't like the man, but he had worked under him for a long time and this was his job, no questions asked – until now. Knowles was driving and Resolution was in the passenger seat, ranting about his service to the Premier, the Premier's ingratitude and the trouble Silence Hunter had caused him. He had been on a mission before, but now his need to apprehend Silence Hunter himself had become an obsession. Knowles listened. All he wanted was not to lose his job or worse, to be tried and imprisoned for crimes against The Rulers. But here he was, a renegade now with the Commander. He had no misconceptions that he could just walk away though. The Commander would not let that happen. He had always needed Knowles when it came to the rough stuff. Resolution could easily shoot someone and walk away, but he didn't have the stomach for torture and blood; it was his Achilles heel and only Knowles really knew the extent of it.

Resolution had not even given Knowles the option of waiting for the escort to London, he had just decided that Knowles would remain with him, like a conjoined sibling. Knowles had thought about protesting but he knew the Commander too well. He could come willingly or with a gun in his back. He decided to do without the gun. The Commander may not have been able to carry out torture but Knowles knew Resolution could take him down in an instant. His combat training had been exceptional. And so, he drove in silence, towards the island of Lindisfarne, as the Commander talked on and on, making plans for the final, triumphant capture of Silence Hunter.

28

'We're going with him,' Chas insisted as Si's limp body was lifted into the back of the car.

'That's fine,' the man said. 'But hurry, I need to get him to my surgery as quickly as possible.'

'Peter, can we take the car again?' Chas said. 'We might need it.'

'Of course,' Peter said. 'Go!'

The man was Doctor Nick Reece. He was not Peter's GP, but a friend Peter knew through his past connections with the Way. In desperation, not knowing what to do to help Si, he had rung Nick. To the man's great credit, he had been at the house within half an hour, despite the personal risks of getting involved. Si had still been convulsing much to everyone's distress. Chas was frantic; convinced he was about to die.

The doctor had injected Si with a muscle relaxant that had stopped the convulsions. He had also sealed up Si's arm. His surgery was in the city of Durham. Chas and Ben had no choice but to leave their car outside the walls and climb into the boot of the doctor's car. The doctor turned on his flashing light and siren. As he approached the gates, other cars made way for him and he sped through without having to stop for security checks. When they arrived at the surgery it was late. Nick took out his key card and gave it to Chas.

'Unlock the doors, then on the wall over by the reception desk is the security keypad. Key in the number 2850 to shut off the alarm.'

'Help me with Silence,' the doctor said to Ben. They pulled him from the car and Nick carried him like a child into the surgery. Chas found some lights. 'Open that door,' Nick told Ben. 'Now, third door on the left. It's a small operating theatre.'

Chas flung open the door and turned on the lights. Nick laid Si on the table.

'Tell me again – about the nanomedibot,' he said.

'I don't know much, just that his parents injected it into him to preserve it. It's meant to save lives.'

'Well, this is killing him.'

'Can you get it out without destroying it? This is everything the Hunters worked for and the reason Si is on the run.' Chas couldn't believe she was hesitating, when Si's life was in jeopardy.

'I doubt it. I don't know enough about the subject. I've read about the research in various medical journals. That's how I heard of The Hunters. But no one knew that they'd gone this far. I don't even know how to get it out. All I can do is try to stabilize him.'

'If Chas and I could get the Hunters out of the Priory, they could help Si,' Ben said.

'Maybe,' Nick said.

He began opening a packet that contained a syringe. He attached Si to a machine to monitor his heartbeat, which was very erratic. He tapped the syringe and injected liquid in to Si's arm. They watched the monitor, as gradually the heart rate began to regulate and his breathing became calmer.

'Now we have to wait. I'll monitor his temperature and stay with him. You go make some drinks and find something sweet to eat. You're both in shock. Turn right, three doors down is our staffroom. Mine's a hot chocolate.'

'I'm staying here,' Chas said firmly.

'Go, please. You can't do anything now. I'll let you know of any changes, good or bad.'

She sat down on a plastic chair and folded her arms, refusing to meet anyone's eye.

'Chas ...'

'It's no use doctor,' Ben said. 'You won't budge her. She's made up her mind. I'll go.'

'Well, make yourself useful and get some blankets out of that cupboard over there,' Nick told her.

Chas moved obediently to the cupboard and pulled down several woollen blankets. Nick took one and covered Si with it. 'This one's for you,' he said, handing one back to her. 'So I know very little about how you came to be involved with Si.'

Chas shrugged, not looking at him. She still couldn't bring herself to let down her guard easily. They watched Si, breathing normally now. The monitor beeped steadily and the sound was as soothing as the ticking of the old fashioned clock that Chas's parents used to keep on the mantelpiece. In rare moments of peace, she had enjoyed the reassurance of its soft, steady tick.

Ben came back in with a tray containing three hot chocolates, a plate of biscuits and a few brightly wrapped chocolates he had found on the table in the staff room.

'Any change?' he asked, putting the tray down, his eyes darting to the monitor.

'He's stable,' Nick said. 'That's good.'

'Will he wake up soon?' Ben asked.

'I don't know. We'll just have to wait.'

'Are we safe here?' Ben asked.

'It is a bit unusual for surgery lights to be on at this time of night. I should call someone and let them know I'm here. Occasionally I stay late to do some paper work. I'll do that now, then no one will suspect anything.'

Nick left the room.

'What are we going to do now, Chas?' Ben asked, sitting down in the empty chair. Chas shared her blanket with him.

'Depends on Si, doesn't it?'

'Is he going to be okay?' Ben asked.

She looked at him and shrugged.

'Stupid question.' There was a pause. 'I think we should finish what we started, come what may,' he said, expecting Chas to agree straight away, but she didn't. She continued staring across the room. 'I mean, Si would want us to rescue his mum. Even if he... well... you know,' he trailed off, unable to voice his worst fears.

Chas turned to him. 'It would be pointless to risk our lives for his mum if he dies,' she said bluntly.

Ben was shocked. 'But Si would want us to!'

'But if he's dead, what's the point? For all we know, she could already be dead. And we're more than likely to end up the same way ourselves.'

Ben was silent. The monitor beeped its regular rhythm. He looked hopefully at Si for a glimmer of movement. There was none.

'But you'd do it if Si was going to be okay,' he said, not looking at her.

'Yes.'

'Why?'

'Because, if Si is alive then there's a point to it all.'

The doctor re-entered the room. He glanced at them, sitting in silence, then he moved to the table to look more closely at Si. He picked up an instrument with a tiny light on it and opened Si's eyelids to peer into his eyes. He then checked his blood pressure and temperature.

'His temperature is returning to normal.'

'Does that mean he's going to be all right?' Ben asked.

'It's looking more likely,' Nick said.

'Can you bring him round?' Chas asked.

'Well... yes, possibly. But you risk destabilizing him again. Let's wait. Look, you should get some sleep, you're both exhausted. You could kip down on the sofas in the waiting room. I can keep an eye on Si and if he wakes I'll come and get you.'

'I'm okay here thanks,' Chas said. 'You go Ben. You can go too doctor, I'll let you know if he wakes. How about that?'

Nick was about to protest, but already he had learned the meaning of that determined look in her eyes. 'Fine. Come and get me if there's any change. And if you're falling asleep, I'll take over.'

'Okay,' Chas agreed.

Ben and the doctor left Chas alone with Si and her own thoughts. She walked over to the table. At least he looked like he was sleeping peacefully now. Her mind wandered back over past events and she felt angry with herself for getting this close to Si. But there was something so engaging about him. In a strange way he had inspired her, he'd given her a purpose again. She liked being able to help him too. She touched his hand. It was no longer hot and clammy. She traced a line along the palm with her index finger. It trailed up his arm and to his lips, but as she touched his lips she pulled back her finger as if it had been electrocuted. What was she doing? She slumped back in the plastic chair and waited. She was exhausted, but her eyes never left Si's face for a minute.

It was almost dawn when she heard the noise. A soft groan. At first she didn't realise what it was and looked towards the door. Then he moved his head.

'Si!' She jumped up. He groaned again. 'Si, can you hear me?'

'Water,' he croaked. 'Can I have some water?'

She looked around and saw a sink and a glass next to it. She filled it and gently lifted Si's head to sip the water.

He took a few sips. 'Thanks.' He tried to push himself up to a sitting position.

'Careful. I should go and get the doctor. Wait a minute. Stay lying down.'

'Where am I?'

'I'll tell you in a minute. Keep still.'

She ran from the room and in less than a minute she was back with Nick and Ben.

'How are you feeling?' Nick said, smiling down at him.

'Could be better,' Si said. 'Where am I?'

'You're in my surgery. I'm Doctor Nick Reece, an old friend of Peter's. You can trust me. I knew of your parents. They were amazing scientists.'

'What happened to me?' Si asked.

'You collapsed at Peter's house. We got you here. You were convulsing and I managed to stop that, but the NMB is still inside you and it's malfunctioning. I don't know how to get it out safely.

Only your mother and father know that. But I don't know what it will do next, or if you might have more severe fits.'

'Good news then,' Si said. 'Can I have more water?'

Chas handed him the glass.

'I need to get my mother out of the Priory,' Si said. No one spoke at first.

Nick broke the silence. 'It's really your best hope of getting the NMB out, but...' he shook his head.

'Well, we've got this far,' Ben said.

'And we've overcome some pretty tough obstacles,' Chas added.

'So are you saying, you still want to come with me?' Si managed one if his infectious grins.

Chas gave him one of her sarcastic smiles back. 'Maybe Ben and I should go alone.'

'No! I'm coming!'

Everyone looked at him anxiously.

'I have to go!' Si insisted.

'Of course we're going with you then,' Ben said. 'You need us.'

'Yeah, you're right about that,' Si said.

'I'm going to give you these.' Nick turned to the counter behind him and prepared some syringes. 'This is what I used to stop the fit tonight. If it happens again they might buy you some more time. I'll show you how to administer them.'

They watched carefully, then Chas put them in her rucksack.

'Can you get us out of the city?' Chas asked.

'Yes. It will have to be the same way you came in for you and Ben, I'm afraid.'

Si looked quizzically at them.

'In the boot,' Ben said.

'Si, put this blanket over your head in the car. I'm going to wear a contamination suit, as if I'm transporting an emergency plague victim to isolation. A few flashing lights and sirens and we'll be fine.'

As they emerged from the surgery a cold, grey dawn was breaking. There were some cars moving through the streets. Ben and Chas climbed into the boot. Nick was wearing a blue isolation suit and mask. He got into the driver's seat and Si sat in the back with the blanket pulled up around his shoulders and over his head.

As they drove through the morning traffic, Si stared at the ancient cathedral looming majestically above them, on the hill. He thought about all the people who had sought sanctuary in that place, down the centuries. His father had been fascinated by cathedrals. He'd told him stories about most of them. They had spent many hours trawling around York Minster. Si had visited Durham once, when he was about six or seven. His father had told him how the Monks had brought the body of St. Cuthbert here from Lindisfarne to escape the Viking invaders. It was reported that many pilgrims had come to Cuthbert's shrine and been healed by the power in the bones of the dead saint. How ironic that Lindisfarne was now the site of The Priory, a place of torture and pain. His parents' faces swam into his mind.

'I'm coming,' he whispered, closing his eyes and seeing their faces drawn on the inside of his eyelids.

The car flew through the checkpoint.

'Knew that would work,' Nick said, a note of triumph in his voice.

'Thank you,' Si said. 'You probably don't know what you've got involved in.'

'I know some of it. And my instincts tell me I'm doing the right thing.'

Within a few minutes they reached the spot where they had abandoned their car. Ben and Chas were released from the boot. Si was still shaky on his feet.

'Do you feel sick?' Nick asked him, anxiously looking him up and down.

'A little, yes, but I'll be fine.'

'Remember, use the syringes if necessary. Take these with you too.' He handed Si some anti-sickness tablets. 'Take one now. And if... when you get out of the Priory, contact me. Here's my number. We can try again to get the NMB out. Your parents will know how to do it.'

'Thank you again,' Si said, shaking the doctor's hand.

'God keep you,' Nick offered, holding Si's hand between his for a moment.

Si looked at him. It was an expression that Si had heard from his past, by other members of the Way.

'You're turning into some kind of Messiah,' Chas said, keeping her eyes on the road as they headed North again.

'What do you mean?'

'Everyone you meet wants to help you. You're their hope Si; their hope that someone can fight back against The Rulers, and maybe, just maybe, win.'

29

08.53am was the first opportunity Resolution and Knowles had to drive across the causeway to the island that was the home of the Priory. It was a beautiful place but Knowles and Resolution didn't have time for aesthetics. The tide had turned and now the causeway was dry enough for them to get across. Vast expanses of sand stretched out on either side of the causeway like huge angel wings. The sand was too wet to ever get a vehicle across and a high fence had been erected along the edge of the coast for miles and miles to keep out any curious 'pilgrims!' There was a check point as they reached the island and their drive across was monitored by CCTV.

'Commander.' The guard at the checkpoint gave him a brief salute. 'Sir, I can't let you pass. There is a warrant out for your arrest.'

'What? That's ridiculous!' Knowles protested.

'Sir, our orders are to apprehend you both on sight.'

Guards began to close in on their car, pointing rifles at them.

'And who has issued this ludicrous order?' Resolution asked calmly.

'The Premier, Sir. It came through, in a message, a few hours ago.'

'Can I see it? What would I be doing here if I was a wanted

man? Do you think I'd come to the highest security detention centre if I was going to be arrested?'

'Well, I don't know Sir, I just know my orders.'

'Let us see them then,' Knowles insisted.

The guard went back into his station and came back with a tablet computer.

Knowles took it through the open window and handed it to the Commander.

'This is clearly fabricated: Part of the vendetta that has been going on against me in government. I can assure you that I am authorised by the Premier himself to come here with regards the Hunter case. Here, take a look at this.'

He reached into his pocket and brought out his holophone. He scrolled through the recordings of his conversations and found one in which the Premier was giving him instructions to apprehend Silence Hunter. He handed the phone to the guard. 'Check this.' He flicked the message to play and watched as a holo-image of the Premier appeared beside the car. The guards watched the conversation between the Premier and the Commander. Knowles and Resolution looked straight ahead, saying nothing as it played out.

The guard was uncertain.

'Would you like me to call him now?' Resolution asked confidently, taking the phone back. 'I'm sure he'd like to learn how we are being treated at a crucial point in this operation.'

'Erm, no Sir, that won't be necessary. You can pass. I'll phone ahead and let them know to have the gates to the compound open ready for you.'

Resolution nodded. Knowles tutted, touching the window to raise it, and drove on.

'First obstacle negotiated,' the Commander said, smiling.

Knowles said nothing.

They drove along the edge of the island, coming into what was left of the old village. It was all but a ghost town now. The main street remained intact: A line of stone built houses, a shop and a pub stretching out mournfully before them. The rest of the village had been obliterated. The churches and the true, ancient priory, were rubble. No one lived here anymore. Everyone had been forcibly removed and re-housed on the mainland. In the distance the castle remained, high on its rocky outcrop. Until recently it had been used as a military barracks, but was no longer in use. Resolution had never been here before and he marvelled, not at the dignity of the castle, but at the brilliance of the modern giant structure that dominated the landscape beyond the cowed houses.

The building was made of steel and reinforced glass. If the sun had been out it would have sparkled like a glorious diamond. It took up the whole of the centre of the island and looked nothing like a prison.

'That's too good for the scum it holds,' Resolution said, as if to himself.

'It's impressive,' Knowles agreed.

'It looks like a high class hotel. Should be in the Capital, not hidden away in this time forsaken place.'

'Sir, what are we going to say to the governor?' Knowles asked.

'What's his name again?' asked the Commander.

'Mark Aspen. By all accounts he was sent here because he's good at what he does, but he lost face some years ago and they wanted him out of the way here.'

'Okay. We'll handle him the same as we did those idiots at the checkpoint. I'm just buying us time, Knowles. It can't be long before the boy tries his rescue attempt. That's all I need. Then we'll prove our worth once and for all to the Premier.'

'Yes sir.' Knowles was not convinced. He could see his career unfurling before him.

30

Si, Ben and Chas reached the outskirts of the little fishing village of Seahouses not long after Knowles and Resolution had got on to the island. They found somewhere inconspicuous to leave the car. Magnetised vehicles were not common in rural communities. The people here did not travel far and their forms of transport were very basic. There was an old-fashioned car dotted here and there in a driveway or at the side of the road. A horse and cart rumbled past them and Chas felt herself longing for her village. It seemed so long ago that she had been immersed in that life, and yet it was such a short time since she had stumbled across Silence Hunter, in the woods. She looked at him and wondered how different things would have been had he taken a different route. But here she was, stuck with him, involved with him, drawn to him.

'What?' asked Si.

Chas pulled herself back to the present. 'Huh?'

'What? You're staring at me. I'm all right you know.'

'Well, you don't look it,' she said, glad that he didn't know what she had really been thinking.

'You don't,' said Ben. 'Here, have some water. Do you need another tablet?'

'No, honestly, I'm fine. Just the water.' Si took several gulps; then handed the bottle to Chas, who also drank deeply. He was not feeling well. The anti-sickness tablets had reduced the nausea but his head ached, and the crawling sensation beneath his skin was getting worse. He was determined to ignore it though, because the others were already too anxious for him.

'I think we should go round the back of the main street,' Ben said. 'I know a way through the fields, right into the back gardens of the fishermen's cottages.'

'Lead the way,' Chas said, gesturing with the water bottle.

Ben took them along a narrow muddy footpath along the side of a field. They were about a hundred metres from the back gardens of the main street. It felt strangely comforting to him to be back here. He remembered himself and his brother running through these fields, chasing rabbits, when they were younger. The sea was to the right of them. It was drizzling and the water was choppy; a dirty grey colour. The smell of fish grew stronger and stronger as they approached the backs of the houses, near the harbour.

Ben stopped. 'You wait here. I'll go and see if the Carters still live here and if they'll help us.'

'Are you sure this is a good idea?' asked Chas.

'We were neighbours. My father worked with Ethan.'

'Okay. But be careful. If you're not back within the hour, we're coming to find you,' Chas said.

Ben saluted her and grinned. 'Yes sir.'

Chas and Si settled themselves under a bush to wait and shelter from the rain.

Ben walked towards the middle cottage in a row of three. It was about 150 years old and had taken many a battering from the wild winds that whipped the shores here. A curl of smoke escaped from the chimney, indicating that someone was home.

Ethan and his wife, Sarah, had always been fond of him and his brother. He remembered how Sarah had cried when Ben's father had decided to move them to the city to find a job that paid better. What a disastrous decision that had been! He wondered if their children, Grace and Honour, would remember him. It had been three years now. Grace would be nine and Honour was the same age as Ben. They had especially doted on his brother Deter. He gulped back a sob and tears pricked the back of his eyes. He swiped them away. This was definitely not the time to be getting sentimental about his last moments with Deter before that thug, Rory, had shot him.

He found the hole in the high hedge that he, Deter and Honour had made. It was still there: That was hopeful. Surely a new family would have repaired it. The garden was littered with an old climbing frame, goal posts, a doll's pram and various other toys. These looked familiar. He approached the back door, then decided he should go to the front, so as not to startle them. It would be enough of a surprise seeing him again after all these years.

The front door was painted blue, as was the one to the left. That had been the only place he had ever called home. His father and Ethan had painted the doors with some leftover paint from the boats. The fishing boats had been their pride and joy. His father had been heart broken when he had been forced to sell his. Ben looked out over the harbour. The cottages were up on a small rise, overlooking the water. A few fishing boats bobbed rhythmically in the harbour, nestling in relative safety like baby birds in a nest. The sight, and pungent smell of lobster pots and fish, was almost too nostalgic to bear. He turned away, steeling himself for the task ahead of him. He lifted his hand and rapped on the door.

It was Sarah who opened it. She was in her mid-forties, thin and haggard looking, with bags under her eyes and no make-up. Her mousy hair was caught up in a knot at the back of her head, but wisps fell around her face and neck. She had flour on her hands and cheeks and wore an apron over her dress.

'Hello Sarah.' It was all Ben could manage, to get those two words out.

Her eyes widened and her hands shot to her cheeks. 'Oh my goodness! Ben? What are you doing here?' She looked up and down the street. Immediately Ben assumed she had seen something suspicious. He looked behind him. The street was empty. 'Where are your parents and Deter? Are they in the village?' Her face had broken into a smile now.

'No, they're...not here.' He didn't want to tell the whole story on the doorstep. 'Can I come in?'

'Of course, love,' she said, her smile turning into a concerned frown. Putting her arm round him she ushered him inside.

She led him up a narrow passageway into a small living room. A log fire burned in the grate. It was a mirror image of the house next door. He sank down into the battered settee, without being asked to sit. He ached to turn back the clock a few years. The pain was so physical that he had to sit for a moment taking gulps of air, to steady himself.

Sarah sat opposite, looking worriedly into his face. It was clear to her that this was not a social visit to old friends. 'Honour and Grace are at school. How are things with you and... the family?'

Ben couldn't answer. He gripped the sofa, his fingers clawing at the material. He kept swallowing back the saliva that threatened to turn into something else and spew out onto the carpet.

'I'll get you a drink,' Sarah offered, patting him on the leg and rising to go to the kitchen.

Wide eyed, Ben looked around the room. It was sparsely decorated; shabby even. But smiling photographs of Honour and Grace stood on the sideboard and a wedding portrait of Sarah and Ethan took pride of place on the mantelpiece.

Sarah returned with a glass of water and put it in Ben's hands. Then she sat opposite him again, taking in his shabby, unkempt appearance.

'Can you tell me what happened Ben? Take your time.'

Slowly, he was able to relate what had happened to his parents and to Deter. Tears brimmed over as he talked, and when he got to the part about Deter he began to sob. Sarah moved to the sofa and put her arm around him.

'Oh Ben, you poor, poor boy.' She hugged him until the sobs ceased. 'You've come to the right place though. I'm glad you came back here. You can stay with us.'

He began to sob again. He hadn't got to the reason he had really come back yet and he had to fight the urge to just snuggle into these motherly arms, obliterating Chas and Si from his mind. But they were waiting, and if he didn't carry out his task within the hour he had been given, they would be here, crashing through the back door to 'save him.' He pulled away from her.

'Where's Ethan?'

'Down at the boat. He should be back soon. He has this sixth sense when I'm making scones and he can't resist them for long.'

'Can you go and bring him back now? I need to ask him something really important.'

She smiled and frowned at the same time. 'Well, yes, I could.

He won't be long though.'

'It's just that I haven't got much time,' Ben said.

She shook her head. 'What do you mean?'

'Can we just get Ethan? Then I can tell you both together.'

'Okay love. You take some more sips of that water. I'll be back in five minutes.'

He wanted to run down to the harbour with her, but he knew he couldn't talk about any of this out in the open. Guilt surged through him, knowing that he was putting this family in danger.

Sarah came back into the house looking flustered. Ethan followed behind, leaving his boots on the doormat. He was a tall, muscular man. A typical looking fisherman with a square jaw and balding head. He was wearing a chunky jumper and jeans.

'Ben! What a surprise,' he beamed, a detectable note of caution in his voice. Ben stood to greet him. Ethan took the boy tenderly by the shoulders. His features changed. 'I can't believe what's happened. It's awful.' He pulled Ben to him in a bear hug, muffling his face in the jumper. 'We'll do anything we can to help you. You know you can stay here. Sarah said you wanted to talk to me. What is it?'

They all sat down. Ben took a deep breath and took up his story from the point where Rory killed Deter and he met Si and Chas in the barn. He continued, watching the recognition on their faces as he talked about Silence Hunter and the looks of anxiety that passed between them. He stopped just before he got to the fact that Chas and Si were only a few metres away, depending on him to secure them a means of getting onto Lindisfarne. He looked from Sarah to Ethan, wavering between pressing on with the plan and just leaving them in peace and safety.

'How does he plan to get his mother out of the Priory?' Ethan wasn't stupid. He already knew what it was Ben was unable to ask him.

'I …I don't know. We… don't have a plan as such, just…I…had an idea.'

Ethan raised his eyebrows but said nothing. Ben bit his top lip.

'I came to ask you to take us to the island in the boat.' There was silence, then Ben was talking fast. 'You know the waters Ethan; better than anyone. You know all about that island. You and dad used to talk about going there when you were boys, with your dads, before they wrecked it and built the Priory. I know you hate The Rulers too.' He paused again, then said more quietly, 'I know I've no right to ask this and that you'd be putting yourselves in danger, but I don't know what else to do.'

No one spoke. Ethan and Sarah exchanged glances, and she, almost imperceptibly, shook her head.

Ben said, 'If I don't get back in a few minutes they'll come looking for me. I'd rather go and bring them to meet you. Please, at least meet them, then you can decide.'

Ethan looked again at Sarah. She spoke. 'We've heard news reports about Silence Hunter. He sounds dangerous. He's wanted for several crimes, including assaults on innocent people. According to the News his accomplices are dead. Were they talking about you?'

'It's all rubbish! Si is a good person and so is Chas. You believe me, don't you?' He turned to Ethan.

'The children are at school Sarah. I'll go out to the field with Ben and meet them. I won't bring them back here unless I feel confident it's the right thing to do. And I'm not promising anything, Ben. Okay?' Ben nodded. 'You trust me, don't you love?' He stepped towards Sarah and took her by the shoulders, looking into her eyes.

She pursed her lips and nodded. He kissed her on the forehead and followed Ben out of the house.

31

Chas stood up ready to move out and find Ben, when she saw him heading towards them over the field.

'He's coming back – with a man.' Her hand tightened around her knife. 'Get ready Si.'

Si stood up, swaying as he tried to regain his balance. He squinted down the field towards the sea. His vision blurred, then Ben and the man came into focus.

'He doesn't look like a threat to Ben. Hopefully it's this Ethan guy.'

'Hopefully. But be ready just in case it's a trap.'

She was ever his guardian. Si smiled. 'Yes sir,' he said, mimicking Ben.

Ben was with them in minutes. 'This is Ethan. Ethan - Si and Chas.'

Si held out his hand to Ethan. 'Hi.'

Ethan shook it. 'Hi.'

Chas nodded warily at him.

'We can't really talk out here,' Si said.

'Well, you're going to have to if you want my help. There's no one around and we can see if anyone comes within a hundred metres of us. My wife is understandably nervous about you coming to the house.'

Si nodded. 'Of course.' He looked at Chas.

'I've told him everything, Si,' Ben said. 'You need to tell him what we want him to do.'

'Ben's told you we need to get to the Priory to get my parents out? I've seen my mother by holo-image, and talked to her, when I was in the Bastille. I haven't seen my father, but I know they've been tortured. I don't really know what state they're in. I know this must seem foolishness to you, but I have to try and get them out.'

'And he might die if he doesn't rescue them,' Ben blurted out. 'He's got this thing inside him and its killing him and the only one who can get it out of him is his mum.'

'What do you want me to do?' Ethan asked.

'Can you take Chas and I to the island by boat? And can Ben stay here?'

'No!' Ben protested. 'I'm coming. You're not leaving me behind again!'

'I'm not risking your life, Ben. Nor Chas's, if she's sensible enough to let me go alone.'

Chas snorted in derision. Si took this to mean, 'You are joking!' and didn't protest.

'I would rather you stayed with this family, Ben. They can care for you if anything happens to us. You can make a home here.'

'He's right,' Ethan said.

Ben was furious. 'Is that the real reason you let me come this far? I'm not staying here without you and Chas. Forget it. This is not my home anymore.'

'Ben, it could be,' Ethan coaxed.

Ben looked up at him. 'I can't. These two are my family now.'

For a moment they all looked at him in silence. Ben looked

defiantly at Chas and Si, his arms folded, an expression of determination on his face.

'I will help you,' Ethan said, 'but I can't have you at the house. I want to keep my wife and children out of it as much as possible. The Priory is high security, as you know. I don't fancy your chances of getting in and certainly not of getting out alive with two prisoners. Do you have weapons?'

'There's Chas,' Si offered, half in jest.

'We've got my knife but that's it,' Chas said, speaking up for the first time.

'And we have an invisibility cloak,' Ben said, eagerly.

'A what?'

'Invisibility cloak. It was given to us by a friend who works with advanced technology. It's a proto-type.'

Ethan looked dubious. 'I could take you around the back of the island – to the North Shore. The waters are rough, especially at this time of year. However, you can't take a boat within 200 metres of the island. They use radar and threaten to blow up anything that penetrates the limit.'

'So, what are you suggesting?' asked Chas.

'You'll have to swim the last part. I've got wet suits.'

'Enough for my parents too?' Si asked, looking doubtful.

'I can get my hands on four – yes. You'll have to carry them across and leave them somewhere ready for your return.'

'What if my parents are in a bad way and unable to swim?'

'Then you'll have to find an alternative means of escape,' Ethan said.

Si leaned forward, his hands on his knees and began breathing heavily.

'Si? Are you all right?' Chas said, putting her hand on his

back.

Si's stomach had just lurched as if he was going to be sick. 'I'll be fine.'

Chas shook her head. 'This is crazy. You're ill. You could have another fit at any time. What if it happens when we're swimming or when we're in the Priory?'

'What if it does?' Si said, shooting up angrily and wishing he hadn't. His head swam. 'Chas, you know I'm going to do this somehow, whether you come or not, I won't give up now.'

'I know, I know - and of course I'm coming.'

'And me,' Ben said.

They all looked at him again. 'You can come on the boat, but you have to stay on it with Ethan. You'll be more use to us that way,' Si said.

'I will need help out there,' Ethan said.

'Okay,' Ben muttered.

'I'll get some supplies together Meet me down at the harbour at five. Be careful though. People have seen images of you. They know who you are, especially you, Si.'

'What about your wife – is she going to be okay with you helping us?' asked Si.

'Leave that to me.'

'We're in your debt. Thank you,' Si said.

'I must get back. Ben, why don't you come with me? Sarah would think it odd if you didn't come back. You can help me allay her fears.' Ben agreed. Ethan turned to Si and Chas. 'Five o'clock.'

Chas and Si watched them grow smaller and smaller. Both felt a tug at their heart strings as Ben left in the company of someone who clearly cared for him. They crawled back beneath the bush to shelter from the drizzle. They ate the food in their back packs that Harmony had prepared.

'We have to persuade Ben to stay here,' Chas said.

'I agree. He'd have a proper family here again.'

They huddled close together under the bush for warmth as much as concealment. Both were thinking about what lay ahead in the next few hours. Si couldn't let go of the guilt he felt for all that he had drawn Chas into. And now, it was coming to a conclusion. What would become of them? And if, by some miracle, they got out of this alive, what would she decide to do? Surely that would be the moment she would leave to find another commune. Hadn't she talked about that as they walked to York?

Instinctively, he slid his arm around her. She glanced at him. He continued to stare out at the rain coming down, soaking the fields. He thought she would move away, but instead she inched closer.

'Do you trust me Chas?' he asked.

'Yes,' she replied, simply.

'I might not be able to protect you.'

'I know.'

'I'm scared.'

'I know. So am I.'

'You're not scared of anything, are you? You're the girl who threatened to kill me the first time we met,' he laughed.

There was a pause. 'I'm scared of losing you Si,' she said.

He looked at her in surprise, then, putting his hand gently behind her head, he pulled her into him. She didn't resist, as he thought she might. She let him put his lips against hers. He kissed her tenderly, but briefly, still afraid of overwhelming her, but as he made to pull away, she hooked her hand around his neck and pulled him back towards her. And she was kissing him. Hard. Desperately. Si kissed her back, his whole body aching to be in a different place, a different circumstance with her. Their kisses were infused with desire, fear, need. When they pulled away, their eyes locked. No words were necessary. They held hands until it was time to go to the boat.

At half past four, Ethan and Ben left the cottage. Sarah had gone to pick up the children from school. Ethan didn't think it wise for Ben to meet the children again until everything that had to happen had happened. Sarah had been upset about the arrangements and begged him to change his mind. But Ethan was a determined man. He told her he was doing it for Ben's parents and Deter. He tried to reassure her that he was not putting himself in danger, but she wasn't fooled and stormed off to meet the children.

Ethan reminded Ben how to prepare the boat for the journey out to sea. It was not going to be smooth sailing. The rain had set in and the sea was getting rougher. The St. Cuthbert had a blue hull and cab. She was from a bygone era, when Ethan's father and grandfather had fished with her and he believed the craft brought him luck: After all he was still making a living from fishing, when others, like Ben's father had failed. Ben was warned to be careful of the myriad of wires, rigging and machinery on the boat, especially when they were out at sea and the boat was likely to pitch from side to side in this weather.

'Here, put these on. They'll be massive on you, they belong to my fishing partner, but you'll be soaked to the skin in no time if you don't wear them.' Ethan handed him a coverall suit with an elasticised hood to pull up. Both Ethan's and his own suit were bright orange.

'Won't these suits attract attention?'

'They're meant to, under normal circumstances. If a man falls overboard, he'd be more easily seen. It'll be okay. It's not unusual to be wearing them.'

The suit was too long in the arm and leg but Ben managed to make it wearable by rolling up sleeves and legs. It felt cumbersome.

'You'll do,' Ethan said, smiling at him. 'At least you'll be warm and dry.'

'What will the others wear?' Ben asked.

'I've got the wet suits and waterproof coats. And there are a few heavy duty blankets in the storage boxes at the stern, if they make it back with his parents.'

'Look, they're coming.' Ben watched Chas and Si approach the harbour, coming down past Ethan's cottage. Si had his hood pulled up and his head down. Chas had her hands in her pockets, shoulders hunched against the rain, but constantly checking around them for danger.

Ethan greeted them. 'Here put these on. They might even warm you up.' Si was shivering. They were both already wet through. 'I've got flasks of hot tea in the cab. You look like you could do with one already.'

They changed in the cab, although there was not much room and the wet suits were tricky to get on. They helped each other and ended up falling over a few times, which, in their heightened state of nervousness, made them both giggle uncontrollably.

'Are you okay?' Ben asked, popping his head inside.

Chas was sitting on the floor, tears streaming down her face. She couldn't remember the last time she had laughed like this. 'We're fine,' Si said. 'I've finally found something she's not good at – putting on a wet suit.'

'Hey, I've never done it before,' she protested, pretending to sulk.

Ben was glad to see her laughing. 'Ethan wants to talk to you when you're ready. He says did you find the flasks?'

'Not yet,' Si answered.

'They're over there, inside that box seat.'

'Okay, thanks. We won't be much longer,' Si said.

The light was fading rapidly as they emerged from the cab, clutching steaming cups of tea. Si was glad to be feeling the warmth of the wet suit and coat. Chas was not so enamoured with the wet suit. It felt restrictive and awkward.

'Thanks for the tea,' Si said.

'You're welcome. I'm all set to move out,' Ethan said. 'We should get going. I don't want to attract attention to the fact that there are four people on the boat. Are you ready?'

They nodded, although Si's stomach heaved at the thought of what they were about to embark on.

'I've got a waterproof backpack that you can put essentials in.' It already contained two other wet suits. They transferred a head-torch that Ethan had given them, Si's medication, Chas's knife and the invisibility cloak. The back pack just about closed and sealed, but it was heavy.

'It's going to be a bit rough in this weather for you. If you're going to throw up please do it overboard.' Ethan smiled at them. They looked green already.

Take one of your pills Si,' Ben said.

'Good idea. Anyone else for one?'

'To be honest – I don't think they'll help much. You take one, but don't waste them on the others,' Ethan laughed.

'Great!' Chas muttered.

Ethan went into the cab, started the motor and backed the St. Cuthbert away from the wall. He turned her round and chugged slowly out of the harbour. The others sat in the stern of the boat, on the port side, watching the white crests of water breaking across the bow as she ploughed out into the darkness. In the distance they could just pick out the shapes of rocky islands protruding from the sea. There was a lighthouse, still pulsing out its light, on one of them.

'That can't be the Priory,' Si said.

'No, they're the Farne Islands,' Ben said. 'The boats used to take people out to visit them in the old days but that all stopped before my time. I think the only people who go over there now are fishermen and the maintenance people for the lighthouse.'

As the boat left the safety of the harbour, the ride became rougher. Ethan stood at the helm inside the cab, calmly directing the boat out to sea. The three friends sat in silence, holding on to the side of the boat. Rain lashed their faces and the wind tried to steal their breath. The lighthouse continued to pulse, unperturbed. Both Chas and Si were fighting the rising feeling of nausea as the boat pitched more violently in the mounting waves. The thought of having to swim in this was uppermost in their minds. If they made it to dry land it would be a miracle, never mind what they had to do when they got there. Si began to say the only prayer he used these days – 'Help!'

'Lindisfarne is over there,' Ben shouted, battling against the wind to be heard.

He pointed into the darkness. At first it was difficult to see anything, but eventually Si saw a tiny blob of light. 'That's the Priory, all lit up,' Ben said.

Chas had seen it too. 'At least we won't have any trouble finding it once we're on the island Si,' she shouted, somewhat sarcastically.

'I feel terrible,' Chas said.

Si reached for her hand. 'That makes two of us then.'

All of a sudden, Chas stood up and retched over the side of the boat. When she had finished she sat back down, her head in her hands, groaning. Si rubbed her back.

'I'm never ever going on a boat again!' she said.

It seemed to take forever to reach the island. The blob of light from the Priory was growing larger. Then Si saw a tiny white pyramid, seemingly jutting out of the sea, illuminated rhythmically by the lighthouse beam.

Ethan came out of the cab. 'That's Emmanuel Head; where we're headed,' he shouted. 'That pyramid is an old marker to show ships where the rocks are off the North Shore of the island. We'll be cutting the engines as soon as we're near enough. That's what you need to swim towards. Is Chas okay?'

'No! I'm so bloody not okay!'

'What are you going to do?' Ethan said.

'We're going to swim into the blackness in that hideously rough sea and Si is going to pray to his God that we somehow reach the shore!' she replied.

'That's about right,' Si said, shrugging his shoulders.

Ethan looked dubious. 'This is crazy. I must be insane to have brought you. You're likely to die out there.'

'Don't beat yourself up about it. It's our choice. We won't haunt you from our watery grave,' Chas said.

'Si attempted to stand up. 'It's okay, Ethan. You've done more than enough for us. Like I said before, I have to do this.' He looked down at Chas. He'd never seen her looking so ill. 'Chas, you don't have to come. Stay here and wait for me.'

'You are joking! I have to get off this awful boat as soon as possible. I'd rather die in that black sea than stay on this thing a moment longer than I have to!'

Si and Ben laughed and even Ethan had to smile. 'I'm going back to the cab. It won't be much longer, I promise.'

Si couldn't believe that he was not feeling too sick himself. The anti-nausea tablets must really be helping – and adrenalin, he guessed. He began checking their things. Everything was packed into the waterproof rucksack. He took out the head-torch and fastened it onto himself. As the little boat bounced nearer to the island, his heart pounded. Everything ahead of him now was perilous in the extreme and he seriously doubted their chances. He looked at Chas who was concentrating all her efforts into not being sick again. Was she even a strong swimmer?

Suddenly the engine cut out and they realised that this was as far as the boat would be taking them. Yet the white pyramid still seemed very far away. Behind it, the lights from the Priory were an extra beacon to guide them. Ethan came out of the cab.

'This is it Chas,' Si said. 'Are you ready?'

She stood up, swayed and promptly threw up again. 'Just get me off this thing,' she groaned.

'Here,' Ethan said. 'He handed them a length of rope. 'Let me tie this round you, so you can't lose each other in the sea.' He tied the rope around their waists. 'Keep your eyes on that marker but swim to the right of it to reach the beach. I'll wait for you until just before dawn. If you're not back, you understand that I'll have to return without you.'

Si nodded and switched on the torch. Ben flung himself at Chas and hugged her. Then he pulled Si into the embrace and the three of them stood, huddled together for a moment.

Si pulled away. 'We've got to go. Are you ready Chas?'

They positioned themselves on the edge of the boat and looked down into the black swirling sea. The waves were hitting the hull with some force. Chas gripped Si's hand. Their eyes met.

'Jump!' Si shouted, and they were gone.

32

The icy fingers of the sea closed around them and squeezed all the air out of their lungs. Chas surfaced first, gasping for breath, her head pounding from the sudden cold.

'Si?' she panted. She couldn't get anything else out.

Where was he? She looked frantically around, as waves slapped her in the face. She began to panic that the weight of the backpack had been too much for him. She tugged at the rope as she felt it pull against her.

Suddenly, his head broke the surface a couple of metres away.

'Si!' she screamed.

'I'm okay,' he replied.

They began to swim in the direction of the white pyramid. Once the initial shock of the freezing water passed, the wet suits did their job of regulating body temperature. The rope tugged between them, feeling like it was cutting them in half, but it was a lifeline and they understood now that without it they would never be able to keep together. They swam as hard as they could, but it was exhausting and the pyramid never seemed to get any nearer. Their limbs flailed about in the water. Si had always thought himself a good swimmer, but the weight of the backpack and the icy water were factors he had never had to deal with previously. He did however, find himself pulling Chas along at times and it dawned on him that Chas was not a strong swimmer. It was sheer determination that was propelling her forwards at all. Panic began to flood Si's mind, but he pushed it aside and ploughed on.

Slapping them in the face every few seconds, the salt water stung their eyes. They were tossed violently by the waves, one moment moving forwards, the next, drowning. The rope tugged around their waists. They would certainly be bruised, but better that than separated, Chas thought.

Remembering what Ethan had said, Si tried to direct them to the right of the pyramid. It felt hopeless. It would have been easy to stop swimming and let the inky blackness drag them down; the waters close over their heads – the end of all this. It took extreme effort to keep going.

As if reading his thoughts, Chas shouted, 'Keep going Si. We're almost there.'

Somehow, they reached shallow waters. High sand dunes rose up in front of them blocking out any light from the Priory. They had rounded the corner from the pyramid, which meant that even the intermittent beam from the lighthouse was no longer any use. Except for the tiny shaft from Si's head torch (which, remarkably, had stayed firmly attached to him) it was pitch black. They felt their knees hit sand and staggered to their feet, wading through the breakers to the beach, where they collapsed in a breathless heap. Neither of them moved for some time.

'Are we dead?' Chas whispered.

'Feels like it,' Si replied.

'I always knew I'd end up in Hell,' she said.

Si sat up. 'We're not there yet. Come on, let's try and figure out where we are and how to get out of this black hole.'

He pulled hard at the rope knots to untie himself and stood up. The torch beam was truly pathetic against this blackout. He could see fragments of strange shapes illuminated in the beam. Walking towards one of them, he found it to be a large twisted branch of a tree, discoloured by much lashing from the sea. The only sound to be heard was the rhythmic crashing of waves into the silent beach. It was eerie and soothing at the same time. He looked into the sky and sighed.

'If you're there, I could really do with some help. Oh... and thanks for getting us out of the water by the way.'

He shone the torch towards Chas and walked back to help her up. As she stood, the clouds began to part, revealing the moon. The landscape was suddenly bathed in silvery light.

'Wow, that makes a difference,' Chas said, looking around.

'Yeah,' Si said, smiling.

He scanned the beach, which was a cove, surrounded by high sand dunes. To the left he could still see the tip of the pyramid, peeping out over the grass. To the right, in the distance, the dunes seemed to slope down towards the sea.

'I'd say we try that way to get round these dunes,' he said. 'Are you up for it yet?'

'Yeah. Let's get moving. I wish we could get out of these wet suits though.'

'Well, if you want to go naked, we can.' He grinned at her and she scowled back.

'Where are you going to leave the rucksack?'

'Somewhere here, on the beach. Let's look for a place where we can hopefully find it again.'

Despite being out of the freezing waters, they both felt colder now, than when they were swimming.

Si dumped the backpack and heaved a sigh of relief. They took out Chas's knife and the invisibility cloak. Si slipped the syringes into a small pocket in his wet suit. Lost in their own thoughts, they kept on towards the slope where they could climb up and over the dunes towards what they hoped was the centre of the island.

As they came up over the ridge, disappointment hit them. All they could see in the dim light was grassland surrounded by more dunes, stretching out as far as they could see. The water lay behind them and ahead to their right.

'How do we know which way to go?' asked Si.

In the distance, Chas noticed a faint halo of white light, around the dunes. 'That glow over there is probably from the Priory. Let's head in that direction.'

Si led the way, as he had the torch. In places it was difficult to navigate a way around the boggy patches. Clouds kept covering the moon, making the darkness almost overwhelming. The glow from the floodlights was all that guided them. After what seemed like hours they reached a small valley between two sand dunes. Here the bog had turned into a small lake, with no way around it. Through the valley they got their first glimpse of the Priory. It was an imposing building, luminous white against the black sky.

'We'll have to go through this,' Si said.

They waded gingerly into the water, which came up to their knees, clambering out over uneven ground to an old stile. From here they had a clear view of the Priory. It was only about a kilometre away now. They paused. Floodlights illuminated the dark fields. The building was surrounded by a high wire fence and there were guard posts high up in each corner of the square perimeter. It reminded Si of pictures he had seen of concentration camps from the Second World War in the twentieth century. He shivered, not from the cold. Chas felt him shake. She too felt daunted by the enormity of their task. She was a hunter and a fighter but this was way out of her comfort zone. As they stared silently at the monstrosity before them, Si slipped his arm around her shoulder. She moved in closer to him, but it was difficult to feel any warmth when they were clad in wet suits that squeaked as they rubbed together. It made Si laugh.

'I don't know why I'm laughing,' he said. 'I'm scared stiff.'

'Me too. But we can do this, Si. Think of your parents. You could be seeing them very soon.'

'Don't worry, I'm not thinking of giving up now. I'm not going back in that freezing sea without them. We're going to have to use the invisibility cloak to avoid those search lights. There's virtually no tree cover near the fence.'

'There is a line of trees over there.' She pointed to the right. 'That might get us a bit closer.'

Si turned off the torch and they made their way towards the trees. The ground was uneven and they stumbled frequently. Searchlights were sweeping a 10 metre radius from the fence. When they could go no nearer under the cover of the trees Si unfolded the cloak and draped it over them both. It was not a good fit and their feet were uncovered from the ankles down.

'This is stupid,' Chas said. 'They're going to see us. And it's really difficult to walk together like this. I feel like a pantomime horse!'

'Well, have you got any better suggestions?'

'No,' she admitted, reluctantly. 'When we get to the fence, how do you propose to get in?'

'I've been thinking about that. We need to attract attention so that someone opens the gate and comes to investigate what's happening. Then we sneak in undetected under this.'

'Oh, simple! And how do we attract attention without getting shot?'

'Stones,' Si said.

'Stones? Any more clues?'

'We throw stones at the fence. Those kind of fences will have sensors and be able to pinpoint any disruption to their forcefield. We throw lots of stones at different points on the fence. Someone will hopefully come out of the gate and we get in as they come out.'

'Brilliant plan, O Great One!'

Si frowned at her. 'Well, it's all I can think of, so if you've got a better idea - feel free!'

'Come on, let's just do it. Are you feeling all right?' Chas asked.

Si hadn't felt any nausea since plunging into the sea. Maybe the shock of the icy water had done some good. 'I'm fine. Not felt this good for a long time actually.'

She looked at him quizzically, trying to make out whether he was being sarcastic or not. 'That's good. Let's go.'

They broke cover of the trees, crouching and walking at the same time to try and keep as much of themselves covered as possible. Only Si could see out of the cloak, which was incredibly frustrating for Chas. As they came into the range of the search lights Si began to pick up stones. He also noticed small shapes moving in the field. 'Sheep!' he said. 'There must be another fence, stopping them from reaching the electrified fence.'

'Let me see,' Chas said, clawing at the cloak to reach the mesh which allowed them to see out. 'I can see it. It's just a small wooden thing but we'll have to climb over it.'

The sheep were totally oblivious to the cloaked shape moving through their field, until Si bumped into one, scattering a frightened group across the field bleating loudly. A spotlight immediately shone on them. Si and Chas crouched to the floor, motionless. The light passed over them.

'Wow, they're good,' Si said.

'Very. Be more careful!'

They moved towards the wooden fence. Negotiating it was interesting. They waited until the spotlights were elsewhere (although they didn't know how long it would be until they came round again). Quickly, without the cover of the cloak, they both climbed over; then pulled the cloak back over themselves.

'This is it, we need to start getting their attention,' Si said.

They threw handfuls of stones, dirt, rocks - anything they could find - at the fence, all the time moving towards the tall, steel entrance gates. Immediately searchlights, like hungry birds of prey, came swooping to the spots where the debris hit the fence. Si and Chas crouched as low as they could under the cloak, moving only slowly and sporadically in patches of darkness; only throwing more stones when the lights had moved away. They were nearing the entrance. Suddenly they heard a vehicle start up inside the compound. Three men, with rifles, jumped into a jeep.

'We'll only have a few seconds to get in,' Si said.

The gates began to swing open outwardly. The jeep revved its engine and sped out into the relative darkness. The gates began to swing back immediately. Si and Chas broke into a run, the cloak flying out behind them, their legs and arms exposed. They would surely be seen, Chas thought. But they made it, through a narrow gap as the gates closed behind them. They stopped, fell to their knees and adjusted the cloak over them.

'How could they possibly not have seen us now?' Chas panted. 'They must have CCTV on this gate.'

'Hopefully no one will register a couple of pairs of hands and feet randomly moving by themselves,' Si said. 'And at least the wet suits are black.'

'I hope you're right. Now what?'

'We get inside, find my parents and leave.'

Chas rolled her eyes. 'Ah yes, simple again! Silly me!'

*

Mark Aspen, Priory Chief, had not been so easily taken in by Resolution and Knowles. He had put them in a holding room, much to the Commander's disgusted protests. He had then called the Premier to find out what was going on. The Premier told him that a helicopter would be sent to pick them up. In the meantime he was to treat them as guests and play along with their deception. The Premier knew that Resolution would put up a fight if he thought he was about to be arrested. Aspen already knew that Silence Hunter could be planning some kind of rescue mission. No one knew that Chas was still alive. If Hunter came near the Priory he would be apprehended without any difficulty.

'Perhaps you will be loading him on the same helicopter as the Commander and Knowles. Now that would be ironic,' said the Premier.

Aspen released the lock on the holding room door and entered, to find Resolution pacing the room and Knowles sat at a table.

'Commander, there has been a terrible mistake. I apologise. I have not been able to reach the Premier at present and having spoken again to my men at the checkpoint, I am inclined to believe you. Your record is impeccable and I am very sorry for the treatment you have received.' It had taken every ounce of will power to deliver such a humiliating speech.

Resolution walked up to Aspen, putting his face a few centimetres in front of the other man's. 'You will regret treating me like this,' he spat.

Aspen had never met the Commander before, but his dislike of him was instant. He smiled inwardly to himself at the man's arrogance. 'I can only apologise again, Commander.' He took a step back and indicated that they should leave the room. 'Quarters have been prepared for your stay with us.' A man in uniform was waiting by the door. 'This is Peace. He will show you where they are. Please ask for anything you need. Refreshments are on their way.' Resolution and Knowles followed the man and Aspen walked away in the other direction, without another word.

'I don't trust him,' Resolution said, as he and Knowles sat in their quarters.

'No sir. He still thinks he's a somebody.'

'We need to find out what he knows and be ready for Hunter. Call him and let him know we want to be shown around immediately. I want to see Kate Hunter as soon as possible.'

'Yes, sir.' Knowles spoke into the holocom. A small three dimensional image of a receptionist appeared before him. She then redirected him to Aspen's office.

Aspen did not want them messing about with any of his prisoners. He had let them interrogate Kate Hunter enough, and now that they were technically his prisoners themselves, he wanted to keep them away from her. He refused them permission;

politely of course, making lots of excuses why Kate wasn't available. Resolution was furious and took over the conversation. 'I think you'll find I outrank you Aspen, so you'll let me see her immediately.'

'With all due respect, Commander, I am in charge here at the Priory and I think you'll find that my decisions are final.'

The image disappeared, leaving Knowles to bear the brunt of Resolution's anger and frustration. He was used to it.

33

'So, how do we get inside?' Chas said.

'Do I have to be the guy with all the ideas tonight?

Chas just shrugged, as they stood by an entrance huddled under the cloak. Cameras were trained on the door, but they trusted the cloak now to mask them.

'I guess we could knock?' Si suggested, playfully.

'Si, take this seriously!'

'I am, I am! Sorry!'

As they were speaking, an orderly came out of the door. They were too late to rush in as the door swung closed again. The orderly was walking towards them, looking straight at them, and for a brief moment Si thought he could see them. Suddenly, he realised he couldn't see them at all and that he was going to walk straight into them. Quickly, he pulled Chas to one side. The man walked past, unaware of their presence, and lit a cigarette. Si gestured to Chas that they should follow the man when he went back inside. He stood there for ages, dragging on his cigarette and blowing rings of smoke into the cold night air. It was hard to keep still under the cloak. Finally, he stamped it out and walked towards the door. They followed so closely behind that they couldn't understand how he wasn't aware of their presence. They managed to get through the door just as it was closing, but a corner of the cloak got caught, almost revealing them.

They stopped abruptly. Si yanked at the cloak, aware of the cameras monitoring this area. The cloak was trapped. Becoming more and more irritated, Chas gave it one enormous tug and it came free, with an ominous ripping sound. Si looked at her, wide eyed with frustration. If they hadn't needed to be quiet he would have shouted at her. Instead, he gestured impatiently for her to follow.

Navigating the corridors, in the cloak, was difficult. There weren't many people about, but there were some security guards, orderlies and people behind desks. Unlike the Bastille none of the inmates were allowed in the corridors; they were all behind locked doors. The corridors were dimly lit at night. Every time Si saw someone, he flinched and came to a halt, making Chas bump into him. She was growing more and more annoyed.

'Si!' she hissed. 'Don't keep stopping suddenly. No one can see us. Let me do the looking now.' She pulled him out of the way so that she could see. 'We have to get out of this cloak, its driving me crazy and we're going to do something stupid soon if we're not careful.' She advanced slowly, looking at signs on the doors. After a few minutes she saw what she was looking for and pushed open the door. It was a walk-in cupboard containing general supplies. As the door closed behind them she flicked on the light and pulled the cloak off, exhaling with relief.

'What exactly are we doing?' Si demanded.

'Well, what's your plan?' Chas said. 'This is crazy, Si!'

'You knew that already. You didn't have to come!'

'You'd be dead by now if I hadn't!'

'You think you're so wonderful, don't you? And that I'm some kind of feeble wimp you have to protect! I've never understood why you didn't kill me on the road after what happened at your village. I never got it. Why you stuck with me. But now I do. It's an ego trip for you, isn't it? You're smarter than me. You're my protector. I'd be dead without you. I'm just ...'

She slapped him across the face. He reeled back in surprise.

'Shut it, you idiot! No, this is not an ego trip, thanks! I've got scores to settle remember. And for some insane reason I want to help you find your parents.' She turned away from him and began to rummage through the supplies on the shelves. 'This is what I want.' She pulled out an orderly's uniform and began to take off her wet suit. Si turned away. 'I'm going to dress as an orderly and you can keep under the cloak. No one is looking for me anymore, so I don't think I'll be recognised.'

'You'll need that wet suit for the swim back,' Si said.

'I'll come back for it, or I'll do without it,' she said, struggling to pull it off.

'What if you get stopped. You've got no ID. Orderlies have ID chips implanted under the skin in their hands in these places; at least they did in the Bastille. They can be scanned at any time.'

'We'll just have to risk it. I can't bear another moment under that cloak.' She pulled the uniform over her head and wriggled into the too large trousers. 'Right, come on.'

'Si looked at her dubiously. He had a sudden impulse to laugh. 'I'm sorry,' he said, swallowing back the urge. 'I'm sorry for what I said about you. It was stupid.'

'Forget it,' she said and pushed past him to open the door, her hand checking for her knife, under the uniform.

Si was back under the cloak, the corridor was clear and they slipped out. Chas was impressed once more at the total invisibility afforded by the cloak, and hoped he was following her. Now they had to focus on finding the Hunters, but hadn't a clue where to start.

34

The Commander had had enough waiting. He and Knowles had been formally shown around the prison by a security officer, but only areas carefully chosen by Aspen. As expected, he wasn't taken anywhere near the wing where Kate was being housed. Knowles had downloaded a plan of the Priory to his phone when Resolution had distracted the security guards in one of the control rooms.

'It looks like we need to head over to this wing,' Knowles said, showing Resolution the plan. They headed out of their room in that direction.

*

Chas held a plastic cup of hot chocolate from a drinks dispenser in the corridor. She walked boldly up to another orderly. 'Excuse me.' He turned and looked her up and down inquisitively. 'I've been asked to take a drink to Kate Morgan, but I'm new here and I'm kind of lost.'

The man looked at her disparagingly. 'Where's your tablet? That's got a floor plan on it? You're supposed to carry it at all times.' He pulled his tablet from his pocket.

'I know. I feel really stupid. I left it in my room when I came on duty.'

'Go back and get it then,' he said, turning away from her.

'Give me a break. Just let me have directions. It'll take me ages to go all the way back to my quarters.' She hoped that this was true.

'Maybe you'll remember it next time if you have to go back for it,' he shot back, without even looking at her, and moved away down the corridor.

'Idiot!' Chas muttered.

He had only taken a few steps when he stumbled and fell apparently over nothing. Chas grinned to herself as she saw Si's foot slip back under the cloak. Another orderly, who was coming up the corridor, held out her hand to help him up.

'You want to watch where you're going,' the girl said.

The man ignored her and got up. He scowled back at Chas suspiciously, and limped away. The girl came towards Chas, grinning. She was not much older than her.

'You want to watch him. He thinks he's better than the rest of us. I'm Patience – my friends call me Patty. How long have you been here? Not seen you before.'

'Just started today,' Chas said, keeping her eyes on the floor.

'What's your name? Could do with a few decent people round here. Gets really tedious.'

'I'm ... Harmony,' Chas replied. 'Can you tell me where I should take this? It's for Kate Hunter.' She held out the hot chocolate.

'Yeah, I'll take you if you like. You're not far from it. Must admit, they don't usually do prisoner requests. It's usually drinks at set times. No one gets anything else.'

'I'm just following orders. Point me in the right direction, you don't need to come with me. You've probably got stuff to do.' Chas tried to shuffle past her but Patty started walking with her.

'Actually I was just going off duty, so it's no bother. What time do you get off?' Chas wished she wasn't so annoyingly friendly. She was beginning to prefer the rude guy.

'I've just come on.'

'Oh. Which block are your quarters in? We could maybe hang out together if we get the chance.'

'Er... yeah. Which block are you in?'

'X2.'

'Oh right, me too,' Chas said, with a fake smile.

Si was following them, feeling more and more apprehensive as Chas deflected question after question. At least no one was taking any notice of them, as Chas had become inconspicuous talking to Patty.

They rounded a corner and went through some double doors. This corridor was slightly different, as all the doors either side of it had electronic pads beside them on the wall. These were obviously prisoners' rooms. Si's heart began to beat very fast at the thought that he would be with his mother soon.

'It's not far now, just round this corner,' Patty said.

'Great,' Chas replied.

As they rounded the corner they saw two men standing by the door of one of the prisoner's rooms at the far end of the corridor.

'Wow, Kate is popular tonight. I wonder what they're doing,' Patty said.

Chas recognised her brother almost instantly. She lowered her head and swore under her breath. Her heart began to race.

The Commander shouted down the corridor to them. 'Ah at last! I've been waiting for assistance with this door. Hurry up!'

Patty looked at Chas and raised her eyebrows. 'Just coming, Sir,' Patty said, hurrying her pace.

Chas pretended to stumble, spilling the drink all over the floor. She swore more loudly this time. Patty stopped. Chas turned her back to the Commander. 'I'd best go and find something to mop this with and get another drink. You go and help them.'

'Okay,' Patty said, looking anxiously in their direction.

Chas turned and walked, as calmly as possible in the opposite direction, followed by Si. She found the nearest unlocked room and peered in. It was an office – empty, fortunately. Si followed her in. She turned her back to the door and lent on it, breathing heavily. He took off the cloak.

'Did you see who that was?' she asked.

'Yes,' he replied. 'And I'm guessing that was my mother's room they were trying to get into. We have to get to her before they do.'

'That's impossible now. We have to wait until they're gone.'

'But they might hurt her.'

'They won't. They're waiting for you, aren't they? Come on, we go back and watch for them coming out.'

'And how do we get in?'

'We use Patty.'

'How?'

'Get her to swipe her chip across the panel. Now, stop asking questions. Come on.'

'What about the hot chocolate?'

Chas glared at him, so he put the cloak back on and followed her out of the room.

*

Knowles and Resolution had no trouble bluffing their way into Kate Morgan's room. Patty left them to it and headed back down the corridor. She saw that the spillage was still there and decided to come back and mop it up herself. As she turned the corner she bumped into Chas.

'Didn't you find anything to mop up the drink with?'

'Oh, no, sorry. I'm still not used to where everything is.'

'Come on, I'll show you.'

'Who were those men? They looked important?' Chas asked.

'Apparently he's Commander Komchenski. I've heard of him. He arrived today. Something to do with Kate Morgan.'

'Did he say what?'

'No. Why would he tell me?' Patty laughed. 'Orderlies are just one step up from prisoners you know.'

'Do you think he'll be long in there? I really want to get my job done.'

'Who knows? Why don't you just go in, leave the drink and then we can go? Didn't you get another one?'

'Was just about to. I don't think I should go in while he's in there.'

'Well, let's just leave it then. It's only a drink. She can do without.'

Chas hesitated. 'Look, you go. Thanks for your help. I'll ...meet you later. I think I should do everything I've been told to do since it's my first day here.'

Patty shrugged and smiled. 'Okay. See you later then. Don't get lost again.'

'What's the code to get in?'

'All you need to do is swipe your ID chip across the panel.'

'I... erm... it seems to be malfunctioning. I couldn't get it to work earlier.'

Patty looked quizzically at her. 'You should get it checked out.

You could be arrested as an intruder if you get scanned. Come on, let's just leave it.'

'No, really, I've got to do it!' Chas insisted, with more force than she meant to.

Patty took a step back from Chas.

'Sorry. I didn't mean to scare you. I want to get things right and after what you've told me, I'm ... just nervous. I'll go get the drink. Will you let me in? Then you just go.'

Patty looked dubious. 'Okay. There's a drinks facility down the corridor, turn right at the junction, then left.'

While Chas headed off to get the drink Si stayed with Patty, watching her and watching the door to his mother's room. Patty fiddled with her sleeves and kept glancing up and down the corridor. Si was frustrated at the necessity of involving her. Then he began to hear what he'd dreaded – whimpering sounds coming from behind the door. He wanted to rip off the cloak and break the door down. It took all his will power to hold himself back. Patty heard the noises too. She began to look about her, more frantically, as if wondering what to do.

Chas returned with the drink. 'Have they come out yet?' She asked, hopefully.

'No, they're still in there. I wonder if I should call security. I'm sure they're hurting her and that's not right.'

'No! Don't do that!' Chas protested.

'Why not? I think I should.'

'Hang on. Let me in there. They might stop if someone goes in.'

Si was desperate to get into the room, but afraid that Chas would be instantly recognised by her brother. He wanted to tell her to let Patty go in so that he could sneak in behind her.

'I really don't think you should,' Patty said. 'I'm going to call security.'

'No! Just swipe the panel, will you! Then you can get out of here.' She grabbed Patty's hand and slammed her palm against the panel.

'Hey! You're crazy!' She pulled her hand away from Chas. The door remained shut. Chas grabbed her hand again. 'Open the door!' she insisted.

'You're hurting me!' Patty protested, but she turned her hand over and swiped the back of it across the face of the panel. The door clicked open. 'I'm out of here!' She pulled back her hand and stormed off down the corridor. Chas cursed as her eyes followed the retreating figure. Then she steeled herself to enter.

'You ready?' she said to her invisible companion.

Yes,' he replied. They entered the room.

'What do you want? Get out!' the Commander shouted, without turning from Kate. Chas kept her head lowered so that he wouldn't see her face. Si could see his mother hunched up in the corner of her bed. She looked frightened but she wasn't crying. Knowles had been bending over her and straightened up to look at Chas as they entered the room.

'I just brought this, Sir. Requested by the prisoner.'

Kate looked confused, but didn't contradict her.

'Just get out! I'm not to be disturbed,' Resolution roared.

Instead Chas walked towards them. 'I'll just leave this for her.' She met Kate's eyes, briefly. Kate looked at her curiously. Resolution turned to Chas, fury in his eyes, about to launch into a tirade on insolence. In an instant he recognised her. His eyes widened and his face reddened as if it would explode.

'You!' he cried. 'You're supposed to be dead!'

He looked around the room, expecting to see Si. Suddenly Chas threw the hot liquid in his face. He flinched and cried out, automatically bringing his hands up to his face. At once she drew out the Swiss army knife, jumped on his back and put the knife to his throat before Knowles had even realised what was happening. Si threw off the invisibility cloak as Knowles was reaching for his gun. Kate gasped at the sudden appearance of her son from nowhere. Knowles wheeled round. Kate screamed, but Si jumped on him, taking him by surprise. The gun fell to the floor and Knowles staggered across the room. Kate jumped off the bed and threw herself after the gun. Resolution was struggling with Chas but she was strong and held on.

'I'm going to kill you Resolution! You're scum. You betrayed our family!'

'Get off me sewer rat! It's you who is going to lose here. We are not family!'

Chas tightened her grip around Resolution's throat, causing gurgling, gasping noises instead of words. Still he could not throw her off. Her fury was greater than his. This was suddenly very personal for Chas. She hadn't realised just how long she had been waiting for this moment.

'You robbed me of my real family and then you had Plin and the others killed. And you *will* pay!' She pulled back hard around his throat and brought them both tumbling to the floor.

Knowles kicked at the gun, which slid under the bed. Kate ran at him and between them she and Si managed to knock Knowles to the floor.

'I will slit his throat!' Chas yelled, manically.

Resolution gripped her hand that held the knife. He was amazed at how strong she was. As he wrestled with her, the knife made a gash in his cheek. He automatically put his hand to it and drew bloody fingers away from his face. Looking in horror at the blood on his hands, he loosened his grip on Chas. She tightened her grip around his neck.

Meanwhile, Knowles was still wrestling with Kate and Si. He managed to throw off Kate, sending her flying into the table in the middle of the room, hitting her head and dazing her.

'Mum!' Si yelled.

In the instant Si was distracted, Knowles managed to twist around and get Si on the floor underneath him in an arm lock. He pulled Si's head back by the hair. 'Drop the knife, girl or I'll snap his puny neck!'

Chas hesitated. Inwardly, she screamed at Si. She badly wanted her revenge - now. She could slit Resolution's throat in an instant, but she knew Knowles wasn't bluffing. Her personal vendetta raged strongly against her feelings for Si, but it would have to wait. She threw down the knife in frustration.

'You little bitch!' Resolution turned on her, his hands round her throat. Chas gagged and automatically gripped his wrists.

'Chas!' Si yelled.

'Commander, stop!' Knowles said, still holding Si in a firm grip. 'We need them, to get out of here and to get our reputations back!'

Resolution threw Chas onto the bed, smacking her head off the wall in the process. She fell limply on to the bed, unconscious.

Knowles released his grip on Si's hair, but kept him in the arm lock. Si struggled to get to Chas but it was useless.

He looked at his mother. 'Mum, are you all right?'

'Yes, I think so.'

Resolution pulled Kate roughly off the floor, still fingering his bloody cheek with distaste. 'We have to get these two to the Premier, but we can get rid of her.' He looked over at his unconscious sister.

At that moment, security guards burst through the doors, pointing tazers at them all. 'Drop your weapons!' one of them yelled.

The Commander looked at them. 'Surely you don't mean us?'

'All of you!' said a voice from behind the guard. Mark Aspen stepped into the room. 'And put your hands on your head.'

Knowles looked at Resolution; the Commander gave the faintest shake of his head. Knowles said, 'Drop your weapons, or I take out your prisoners.' He then hit Si forcefully in the mouth with the butt of his gun. Si reeled and fell to his knees, blood seeping from his lips. Resolution closed his eyes briefly. Kate cried out and tried to pull away from him. Knowles grabbed her, putting the barrel of the gun to her head. 'We know how important they are to the government.'

Dazed, Si began to get to his feet. 'Get off her!' he snarled. Knowles kicked him away. 'Stay there, boy, if you don't want to lose your mother. I've had just about enough of this!' Knowles snarled back.

Aspen signalled his men not to shoot, but they did not lower their guns.

Resolution spoke. 'We only want the same as you, Aspen. We want to hand these prisoners over to the Premier. Let us go and that's what we'll do.'

'They are already captives of the government here, as are you,' Aspen retorted.

'I need to take them to the Premier myself. I have to prove to him that I have completed this mission.' His voice was rising in pitch. 'I deserve to be promoted. I will not be thrown off like an old pair of shoes to rot in the gutter!' Resolution's face was bulbous and red; his eyes bulged like a madman's.

'It's too late, Commander. You are under arrest, just like the others,' Aspen said, calmly.

'If you don't let us walk out of here with them, Knowles will shoot Kate Hunter, then the boy and that girl.'

'He won't get the chance,' Aspen said.

Resolution laughed. 'You don't know Knowles. He doesn't mess about or hesitate. I give the command, he carries it out – instantly.'

'You should just shoot them both now,' came a groggy voice from the bed, as Chas came to.

Resolution turned to Chas in distaste. He raised his fist to her but Aspen stopped him. 'Don't move, Commander, or I might just take her advice.' He moved to the door and, turning to his men, said, 'Keep watch over them.' He retreated from the room, locking the door behind him.

35

'What are you going to do now, brother?' Chas said, spitting out the last word as if it were poisonous. 'Looks like your precious career is over.'

Resolution turned on her, his eyes blazing. 'Shut up! Don't call me that. It is not over for me.'

'How fantastically ironic that it should be me who helps to take you down,' she said. Then she leaned forward and spat on him.

Resolution went to hit her again. Si leapt up from the floor to defend her.

'Keep still!' ordered the guard. 'Nobody move.'

Knowles still had the gun to Kate's temple. Si slumped back against the foot of the bed and Resolution sat down on the chair at the table. Knowles knew that even if he took out these guards, they would still be captive.

Aspen came back into the room holding a holophone. 'The Premier wishes to speak with you, Commander.'

The holophone was placed on the table, where it projected the Premier into the room. 'Well Commander, you have got yourself into a spot of bother. And dragged Knowles into it with you,' he said. 'Why don't you get Knowles to let Mrs. Hunter go and give yourselves up to Aspen, without a fight? Things will be simpler that way.'

Resolution bristled. He didn't like being spoken to in such a patronising manner, even if it was by the Premier, and especially in front of all these witnesses.

'Premier, may I speak with you in private?' he said.

'I don't think that will be necessary, Commander. Now I am ordering you Knowles to put down your weapon and end this peacefully.'

Knowles barely hesitated. He had already decided his career was finished and his freedom would be taken as soon as he surrendered. He looked at Resolution, whose breathing had become quick and shallow. He raised his eyebrows and shot one of the guards in the knee. Blood spattered everywhere. The other guard tried to stun Knowles but he was too fast. He pushed Kate to the floor and flung himself towards the man's legs, taking him down. Aspen launched himself towards Resolution, knocking the holophone on the floor, making the Premier disappear. There was a scuffle between the two men, which resulted in Resolution overpowering Aspen.

'We're getting out of here, get moving,' he shouted at them all. 'We're taking Aspen with us. He is our passage.'

Chas jumped off the bed, wincing at the pain in her head. Si was on his feet immediately, but felt his own head swimming and a bout of nausea take hold of him. Kate stood up. 'Si, are you all right?'

As another wave of nausea hit him, Si doubled over and threw up.

'It's the NMB. He's been getting worse and worse,' Chas said.

'Come on, get him out of here,' Resolution shouted. 'Knowles, keep hold of Kate. We don't want these two trying anything on.'

'What's the point in taking them now, Commander? We're finished. Let's just get ourselves out of here,' Knowles protested.

'We are not finished!' Resolution shouted. 'I do not give up. We are taking them.'

342

Knowles grabbed Kate again and held the gun to her.

'Leave her alone!' Si yelled, moving to attack Knowles, but doubling up in pain again.

'Si, wait!' Chas said, grabbing his arm to steady him and speaking so that only he could hear her. 'He's right. They are our only passage out of here. We have to go along with them for now.'

Chas helped Si to stand. Resolution picked up the tazers and, to her astonishment, handed one to her and one to Si. He took out his own gun and they moved out of the room. Patty was waiting by the door, with several more security guards. She stared in disbelief as Chas came out of the room. Chas gave her a cold stare and she looked away.

'Put your weapons down and let us pass or Aspen dies,' Resolution said. He and Chas trained their guns on the guards. There was a stand-off for several seconds. Resolution pressed his gun hard into Aspen's temple. 'We want safe passage out of here.'

'Do it!' Aspen yelled.

The guards put down their weapons.

The band of disparate allies made their way down the corridor, Resolution and Chas leading the way, with Knowles and Si covering their backs. They used Aspen's security chip to pass all security points, knowing they were being watched at every turn on CCTV.

'Get us a car!' ordered Resolution as they neared the entrance.

'You're insane, Commander!' Aspen cried. 'You can't possibly think the Premier is going to show you any mercy after this. He'll have you hung for treason!'

'Shut up! Get us a car!'

Aspen led them to a vehicle, just big enough to take all six of them at a push.

'Get in the front,' He ordered, pushing Aspen across into the passenger's seat and climbing in beside him. The others clambered into the back.

'Give me your weapons,' Knowles demanded as he got in beside them, training his gun on them all.

Si looked at Chas. She hesitated.

'Come on, don't be foolish,' Knowles said. 'You know I'll kill you first girl. I want to get out of here as much as you do!'

Si handed his tazer over. 'Do it Chas. I want to keep you in one piece.' Reluctantly Chas handed over the gun. Knowles held his gun to the back of Aspen's head. The vehicle began moving towards the gates. Si slumped forward.

'Are you okay, Si?' Kate said, taking hold of his hand.

'What about Dad? We can't leave without him.'

There was a silence. Kate squeezed his hand hard. Knowles glanced at her. He knew. 'You never told him?' she said to Knowles.

'We had no reason to. He didn't even know for certain that you were alive until a few days ago.'

'What are you talking about?' Si asked.

'Your father died here Si. I don't know what happened to him. They told me he committed suicide, but he would never have done that.' She looked bitterly across to Knowles.

'No! When?' Si cried.

'About seven months ago.'

Si buried his head in his mother's chest. She enfolded him in her arms and he wept. Fear, grief, relief – a whole host of emotions flooded out. Chas laid a hand on his arm.

'Shut him up!' Resolution growled.

'No!' Kate growled back.

Resolution mumbled something to himself and turned his attention fully to the road.

They emerged through the Priory gates on to the road leading to the old village. It grew darker and darker as they moved out of range of the security lights. The village was deserted and run down now. The buildings had been robbed of their stone and stood like eerie monuments to a time when people had come here for sanctuary. The ruins of the true Priory of Lindisfarne towered behind the village; once majestic and powerful, now dejected and powerless to defend the island against the evil that had overtaken it.

'This is where you leave us,' Resolution said to Aspen, slowing the car. He turned to Knowles. 'Give me one of their weapons.' Knowles handed him a tazer. He stunned Aspen. Resolution opened the passenger door and pushed him out into the darkness of the dilapidated streets. Then he drove towards the causeway.

'Now what?' said Chas

Suddenly a volley of shots was heard from behind them and headlights appeared from round a corner. Resolution hit the accelerator.

'Get down!' Knowles shouted automatically. He knew his weapon was inadequate but he opened a window and began to fire back. More shots came from behind. Crying out, Knowles fell back into the car. He had been shot in the neck; his gun was lost. He slumped against Kate, who muffled a scream, as blood from the wound in his neck began to seep all over her.

'He's been shot!' Si shouted at Resolution.

'Here.' Resolution tossed Si his gun. 'Keep firing at them.'

'No, Si,' Kate cried. 'Keep down. You'll get shot.' She pulled him down with her and Chas.

'Is he dead?' Chas asked.

'Hard to tell,' said Kate. 'He's badly wounded. We need to find something to stop the bleeding.'

More shots were fired. The back windscreen shattered and pieces of glass rained over the passengers.

'Why the hell isn't this bullet-proof glass!' Resolution shouted. More shots and Resolution cried out. The car swerved violently and Si, Chas and Kate braced themselves for impact. However, they felt the car swerve back onto the road and keep moving.

Resolution managed to gasp, 'I'm hit in the shoulder. Silence, fire back at them or they'll be on us any minute!'

'No Si!' Kate said, urgently pulling him to stay down. Si pulled away, leaned across the shattered glass, and fired at the vehicle, which was now frighteningly close. Miraculously, it swerved violently to the right. There was another vehicle following too close behind. It hit the swerving one in front and both veered into the sand dunes, the second one turning over spectacularly onto its roof in only a few seconds. Si couldn't believe his eyes.

The others sat up amidst the broken glass, Kate pushing Knowles over to one side. They peered at the stranded vehicles, disappearing rapidly into the night behind them.

'Well done. I'd never have believed it if I hadn't seen it happen,' Resolution rasped. His breathing was sharp and shallow, but he was still driving. They were on the causeway now. Water was lapping around the car wheels and Resolution had to slow down. 'We've only just made the tide. How bad is Knowles?'

Kate felt for a pulse in his wrist. He was blood soaked and she wasn't much better. She couldn't feel one. She tried his neck. Her hand moved over the wound where the bullet had gone in. The blood was sticky and warm but already starting to congeal. There was no pulse in his neck either.

'He's dead,' she said.

'We need to get rid of this car,' Resolution replied, matter-of-factly. 'They will be searching for it with helicopters soon.'

'We should look at your wound,' Kate said, leaning forward and seeing profuse bleeding coming from the top of Resolution's arm. 'You can't drive for much longer; you're losing too much blood.'

'We must keep going. We have to get through the check point somehow.'

'How are we going to do that?' Chas said.

'No idea,' Resolution replied, 'but there it is.'

They were expected. Floodlights blazed and a welcome party, guns at the ready, awaited them. A voice through a loud speaker ordered them to stop. There were three guards.

'Get right down!' Resolution commanded.

A barrage of bullets hit the car. The front windscreen shattered. Resolution couldn't see where he was going but his foot was hard on the accelerator. The men leapt out of the way and there was a short reprieve in the firing. It wouldn't be long before more vehicles were on their trail.

The road twisted in front of them up a hill. Ahead of them, just over the railway line, they saw a farm.

'Pull in up here,' Si said. 'We'll go and see if we can find another vehicle.'

Resolution stopped the car at the side of the road and fell back into the seat, his energy almost drained through loss of blood. Everyone else jumped out of the back seat, leaving the body of Knowles lying across the broken glass. Kate opened the front door and moved Resolution to look at his arm.

'All I can do, for now, is try to stem the bleeding. He needs a hospital fast.'

Resolution was barely conscious now.

'I say we dump him and Knowles here. We don't need them anymore,' Chas said.

'I'm not leaving anyone who's alive,' Kate replied firmly, looking into Chas's face. 'He's still a human being and he's still your brother.'

Resolution pulled Kate's face down to his ear with his good arm. 'She is nothing to me,' he rasped. Then he blacked out.

Kate began tearing at material from her clothing to make the tourniquet. 'Hurry!' she said to Chas and Si.

They ran to the gate entrance to the farm. The place seemed deserted but Si wondered if there would be dogs guarding the premises. People in the countryside needed to protect themselves. Cautiously, they undid the rope around the gate and pushed at it. It began to groan loudly so they stopped, waiting for any signs of life. Surely if there were dogs they would have come barking by now. The silence was threatening. Si didn't like it and his flesh began to creep. He braced himself for another bout of nausea but it didn't come. He stood still, taking deep breaths.

'Come on, what are you waiting for? Are you okay?' Chas said.

He nodded.

They moved forward towards one of the huge barns. There were no lights on anywhere and it was hard to tell whether the place was still inhabited. Heaving open the door of the first barn they found it empty. The floor was strewn with straw, but there were no animals except for a few rats that scuttled into darker corners. The second barn was the same, except for a large tractor. They walked over to it and examined it by the light spilling in from the moon. It felt rusty to touch and had a broken window on the left.

'This hasn't been used in a while,' Chas said.

'Not a great getaway vehicle anyway,' Si said. 'I don't think this farm is inhabited you know. No animals, no dogs to see us off, rusty old tractor ...'

They didn't hold out much hope of finding anything useful but as they were leaving, Chas caught sight of something sticking out from the side of the house. They ran over to it. It was a car. Quite an old one, probably not magnetised, but if they could get it going...

Chas tried the door and it opened. She jumped inside. It was key operated. Keys would have been a nice little miracle, but there were none. 'We'll have to hot-wire it,' she said to Si.

'And you know how to do that?'

'Of course!'

Within minutes the car came to life. Si looked around in case there were any signs of movement, but no lights came on in the house and still there were no dogs. He breathed again. 'I'm going to get Mum. We'll drive the other car up here and hide it in the barn. Hope this has enough fuel.'

When he got back to the other car, Kate had secured the tourniquet around Resolution's arm. He was still unconscious. 'We've found a car and it works. We can hide this car up in the barn there. The place seems to be abandoned. We can leave Knowles there too. I'll drive. Are you okay to get in the back again?'

Chas was waiting for them. They manoeuvred the car into the barn and between them, hauled Resolution across to the new vehicle. Chas sat behind the wheel, Kate took the seat next to her and Si climbed into the back with Resolution slumped across him. It was a strange feeling to have the man who had been hunting them all this time, laid helplessly across his knee. He wondered if Ethan and Ben were still waiting for them out at sea. At least Ethan would give up just before dawn and return to

Seahouses. Then a thought occurred to him. Maybe it would be best for Ethan and for Ben if they thought that Si and Chas had failed. Ben could stay with Ethan and his wife and none of them would be in danger. As they drove, he explained his idea about Ben to Chas and Kate.

'We can't just abandon him!' Chas protested. 'He'll feel betrayed.'

'But he'll be safer with Ethan. Surely that's more important. For all he knows, we could have drowned or been killed in the Priory. We should think of protecting him. This is not over for us yet.'

Chas was silent. She knew Si was right. After a while she asked, 'What do we do now?'

Kate replied. 'We need to get Resolution some help. And we need to get the nanomedibot out of Si.' She turned to the back of the car. 'From what you've told me and what I've seen, it's malfunctioning badly. I'm sorry we did that to you without your consent. We panicked when we knew they were onto us.'

'It's okay,' Si said.

'I still think we should dump Resolution. We are putting ourselves in more danger carrying him with us,' Chas said.

'I can't do it,' Kate replied.

'I don't understand you,' Chas said. 'After all they've done to you. They killed your husband, they kidnapped you and locked you up for years; they experimented on your son! And now you have a small chance to get even.'

'Isn't it really you who wants to get even?' Kate suggested.

'Of course I do. I'd shoot him myself if you'd let me. He's evil. He destroyed my family.'

'Ever heard of mercy, Chas?'

'Yeah. He doesn't deserve it.'

'We all need a bit of it. Maybe it will do him some good.'

'Yeah right! And maybe it will do us a lot of harm!'

In the back seat, Si groaned and doubled up.

'Si, are you all right?' Chas asked.

Suddenly, his skin was burning up but he felt as if ice cold water was being poured through his veins. He was shaking violently. He tried to speak, to tell them where to find the syringes, but he couldn't form the words. He slumped back in the seat.

Kate leaned into the back of the car and touched his hand. It was clammy. She felt his pulse. It was shallow. 'Chas, we need to get help really quickly.'

'There's a doctor who helped us before. He said he would help us get the nanomedibot out. He gave us a number but I don't think we still have it. I could try to get us to his surgery. He gave Si some syringes to help with the fits, but I think we left them in the rucksack on the beach.'

Si grasped his mother's wrist and pulled it toward the small pocket in the front of his wetsuit. She could feel the small cylinders against his chest. Quickly ripping open the pocket, she tore the packaging off. 'They're here!' she cried, in relief. She climbed into the back seat and heaved Resolution's body off Si. Then she began pulling the wet suit off him in order to give him the shot of adrenalin. As soon as she had given it, his body began to calm and he slept.

'Just drive as fast as you dare,' Kate said. Chas's foot was already to the floor.

36

Ben sat huddled by the fire in the cottage, a mug of hot chocolate grasped between his hands. When Ethan had turned the boat back towards Seahouses Ben had been frantic. He had tried everything to persuade Ethan to stay. He had even threatened to jump in the sea himself, but Ethan had finally talked him round. Ben had sat in the cab at Ethan's feet, sobbing.

Now he stared into the fire, unable to believe that Si and Chas were gone, and wishing he was with them.

*

The great old cathedral at Durham loomed out of the misty dawn light up ahead. Chas had no idea how they would get into the city. Resolution had not stirred. She hoped he was dead. Kate sat in the back, dozing and holding Si in her arms. His breathing was becoming shallower and he shivered every now and then, talking incoherently. Chas had told her what she knew of the dreams he had had.

There was blood all over the back seat of the car. They were wanted for all sorts of reasons. And they had a senior member of the government, half dead in the back seat. Chas couldn't see them making it through a check-point.

'Look, I think we need to use Resolution as a decoy to get us into the city. All I can think to do is slow down, turf him out and ram the barrier. The shock of a body falling out of the car might give us the few seconds head start we need,' Chas said.

'He's very weak. He might not survive the fall,' Kate said.

'Kate – it's either him or your son! Come on – I know which one I choose to save.'

Kate shook her head. 'Okay. I don't have any other ideas.'

'You'll have to push him out with some force. Can you do it?' Chas said.

'Yes.' Kate shifted her position and moved between Si and Resolution. She checked Resolution's pulse. It was barely evident.

As they approached the check-point she felt her own pulse quicken. She waited until there were no other cars in front of her and the way ahead was clear. She pulled up to the guard and lowered her window. As he bent to check her details she punched him in the face. He reeled back. At the same time, Kate flung open the back door and kicked Resolution onto the tarmac. Another two guards came running. Without delay Chas backed up a few metres and floored the accelerator, smashing through the barrier.

'Get down!' she yelled at Kate, as gunfire rang out behind her. In the mirror she saw one man bent over Resolution and two pointing guns at their car.

'They'll have someone chasing us in no time. We have to dump this and go on foot from here,' Chas said.

'We'll never make it,' Kate cried. 'We look totally ridiculous and we'd have to virtually carry Si.'

'Got any better ideas?' Chas shouted, impatiently.

They abandoned the car in a side street as soon as they could and dragged Si out. He was conscious enough to walk if they held him between them.

'Can you remember where this surgery is?' asked Kate.

'Trust me. I've got a good memory for places. I used to track things in the woods. If I can tell one tree from another, a city is easy.'

They were well aware that the main streets were riddled with CCTV, so the journey to the surgery took a lot longer than they would have liked. Si was struggling and so were they under his weight. But, to Kate's immense gratitude, Chas was a determined young woman.

The door was locked. Kate banged on it. 'Help us. Please.' There were no signs of life, although lights were on inside.

'Come round the back,' Chas said. 'Let's see if we can see anyone inside.'

There were several office windows. Chas peered cautiously into them all. Then, she saw him. Nick was bent over his desk. She banged on the window, making him jump. It took him a few seconds to register who she was.

'Come to the fire exit,' Nick said, indicating that they should follow the building round to the right.

'I never dreamed you'd make it out of the Priory – not for one instant,' Nick said, as he let them in.

'Thanks,' Chas said, dragging Si into the corridor with Kate on his other side. 'Kate – Nick. Nick – Kate.'

'Thank you for helping Si,' Kate said. 'We have to get the NMB out of him. He's dying.'

'Do you know what to do?' Nick asked, showing them into the small operating room that Chas remembered from before.

Kate nodded. 'Yes, if you have the instruments I can hopefully get it out.'

They laid Si on the table. 'Where is everyone?' asked Chas.

'Most of the staff start arriving from 8.15, so we don't have long.'

They laid Si on the table. Nick began to cut the wet suit off him. He sent Chas out of the room to find towels and fresh clothes for Si; then he locked the door behind her.

*

'I'm hoping you have an ultrasound machine,' Kate said.

'Yes,' he replied.

'Good. I can use it to locate the NMB. It carries an ultrasonic signal. I suspect that it has started to break down inside Si's body and the poison it carried for targeting plague mutated cells, has started to leak out. We had hoped that the NMB would be perfectly safe, no matter how long it remained inside the person.'

'I can't believe the government are so anti this technology. It could save so many lives eventually,' Nick said, as Kate began to scan Si's body.

'Oh they do want it. Don't be mistaken about that. But they don't want it available to the masses. That's why they were so keen to get hold of what Morgan and I had developed. Here it is. Look, there... on the monitor.'

Nick couldn't see anything. 'Where?'

'There. See that vein? It's heading for the right atrium. We need to move quickly.'

Nick still couldn't see anything.

'You need to take blood from this vein.'

'It's dangerously close to his heart.'

'I know, but if we don't try and the NMB reaches the right atrium we won't have a hope of saving him.'

'You want me to do it?' he asked.

'Of course. You're the doctor, I'm only a scientist. You will be much more accurate than I could be. This is my son's life. I want it in the most capable hands.'

'How will we know if I've got it?'

'There won't be any more signal in his body.'

Chas rattled the door handle. 'Hang on,' Nick said.

The process was swift. Nick placed the syringe of blood on the table. Kate took up the ultrasound scanner and waved it over the syringe. The signal was there. 'You did it!' she cried, hugging Nick.

They opened the door and Chas rushed to the table. 'Is he okay?'

'He will be,' Kate said, relief lighting up her face. Chas let out the breath, which it felt like she had been holding since Si had first started to get sick. Kate took her in her arms and hugged her. 'Thank you.'

'What are we going to do now?' Chas asked.

Nick looked at the clock. 'My colleagues will be arriving any minute. I need to make some phone calls. I have contacts in Amsterdam: People sympathetic to your cause Kate. I could try to arrange safe travel for you, documents and everything. Meanwhile, here are the keys to my apartment. It is three streets from here. Turn left at the lights. Number 17A Brunswick Court. Go through the back garden and in through the French doors. There is no security at the back. Wait there. I will be home at six. Help yourself to anything.'

Si was coming round. Nick gave him another shot of adrenalin so that he would be able to make it to the apartment.

'Why are you helping us?' Chas said.

'You've inspired me: Brought back memories of old loyalties.' Nick smiled, looking at Kate.

'We owe you so much,' she said.

'What happened?' Si asked, still groggy.

'You're going to be well now. The NMB is out,' Kate said.

'But is it intact? Can you use it?' Si said.

'It was a bit of a maverick, Si. I need to start again and make modifications. But this one will help.' She emptied the syringe into a sample pot and sealed it, then put it in her pocket.

She and Chas supported him as he tried to stand. His legs buckled slightly. 'Can you do it?' Chas said.

'Of course,' he replied, attempting to grin at her. 'What kind of weakling do you take me for?'

*

At six Nick returned to his flat to find all three of them asleep. Chas was the first to jump up at the sound of the door opening.

'I'll wake the others,' she said.

'No need,' he replied. 'Let them sleep. I can't get you out until tomorrow night, but everything will be sorted and you will travel to Amsterdam as planned.'

Chas wasn't so sure about leaving England, but she knew they had very little choice.

*

At 22:00 hours the next night, from the deck of the ferry, Chas, Si and Kate watched the east coast shore line recede. Everything had gone so smoothly that Chas had been suspicious.

'Will we ever be able to come back, do you think?' Si asked.

'I hope so,' Kate said, as they leaned on the railings, watching the winking lights on the shoreline become as tiny as stars. She pulled the small pot out of her pocket. 'I have the NMB in here. I'm hoping they'll be able to help me make adjustments to it and continue to develop the technology. Then –I'm coming back. I'm not abandoning this country. I was born here. I have good memories from my childhood. And Morgan died here trying to bring healing. I'm not prepared to let that go to waste.'

Si put his arm around his mother and she leaned her head on his shoulder. They stood, for a few more minutes, watching the black ocean churning at the back of the boat. 'Well, I'm going inside. It's getting cold out here.' Kate kissed Si on the cheek and touched Chas gently on the back before wandering away.

'I wonder what Ben's doing?' Chas said.

'I've been asking myself the same thing,' Si replied. 'I hope he's happy. I've got a feeling he will be – in time.'

'Yeah, I guess,' Chas said. 'If we make it back here, we should go and see him – explain.'

'Or maybe we shouldn't stir things up for him again,' Si said. Chas didn't reply. 'I'm glad you assaulted me in the woods that night. I'd be dead now if you hadn't threatened to kill me.'

Chas laughed. 'Yeah, you definitely would.'

'I'm sorry Chas... for everything bad that's happened to you ... because of me.'

She turned and looked at him then. 'We'll come back one day – with your mum, won't we?'

'Definitely,' he said.

She took his hand and laced her fingers into his. He held them to his lips and kissed them. 'Good,' she said. 'There are some people I want to catch up with.'

Si squeezed her hand. 'Come on. It's cold up here.'

Turn the page to read the beginning of Part II, **Breaking Lies.**
Coming in 2017...

Kate came up from behind, putting her arm around her son's shoulders, as he stood on the deck of the ship. He was leaning on the rail, staring ahead into the darkness. The icy wind sliced through his hair and burned his cheeks, but he was glad of it. Kate pulled the hood of her Parka closer round her face.

'Can't sleep?'

Si shook his head.

'Me neither,' she said.

They were heading back to England, just over a year since they had fled to Amsterdam.

'Nervous?' Kate asked.

Si shrugged.

'I am,' she offered. She rubbed his back, like she used to when he was a little boy. He still didn't respond. 'You want me to go?' she asked.

He shrugged again. 'Don't mind.'

They stood in silence, allowing the blackness to slide around them. It was a strange feeling, standing here in the dark, ploughing through black water, not knowing what lay ahead of them.

'You miss her,' Kate said.

Si pursed his lips. His mother was good at reading his mind. He did miss her, but he was also angry with her. Why did she have to go back so soon? Why couldn't she have waited with him?

'No point dwelling on it,' Si said. 'Chas will always do what Chas wants.'

'Don't be angry with her. She did what she needed to do,' Kate said.

'She's selfish!' He thumped his palms on the rail of the ship.

'Come on Si. Not really. She's been through a lot. And she stuck by you all that time. Saved your life and little things like that,'

Kate said, trying to lighten his mood.

'She only stuck by me because she wanted to get close to her brother and take revenge. Selfish! And now that's where she'll be headed. Back to find him.'

'She said she wanted to find Ben,' Kate said.

'An excuse. Most of all - she wants to kill Resolution.'

The idea of revenge troubled Kate. 'Well, it's you and me now kiddo. And we need to focus on the path ahead of us. Tobias and Mikel are just what we need. I'm so glad they wanted to come with us. Without their help in Amsterdam this would have taken a lot longer.'

'Is Nick meeting us at the port?' asked Si.

'He should be there when we dock. It was good that he managed to get the new phones to us with our new IDs on them. He's taking us straight to a plague camp somewhere.'

'I can't believe how much worse it's got since we've been away,' Si said.

We can't prove the Rulers are behind it... yet.'

'You will though.'

'We will. But for now, the Nanomedibots are primed and ready to help those infected. We can finally do what your father and I intended, way back. We can save people's lives.' They stared silently into the distance for a while. 'Your dad would be pleased to know that you're fulfilling his role now.'

Si hugged his mum. 'You miss him,' he said.

'Every day.' She squeezed his hand and went back below deck.

The story continues in Part II of the Breaking trilogy
Breaking Lies

Look out for the sequel on Amazon and Amazon Kindle
To be informed, in advance, of availability contact Karen Langtree

www.karenlangtree.com/contact

For more information, go to:

www.monkeyislandpublishing.com

MONKEY ISLAND
PUBLISHING

About Karen ...

Karen is a teacher, musician and writer who lives in York with her children and husband. She has been writing children's books for 10 years and has finally made the transition into Young Adult fiction – something she has always enjoyed reading and always wanted to write.

Writing Breaking Silence was a totally different experience to writing for younger readers. She enjoyed doing the research into new technology – something she never thought would inspire her!

The characters have become part of her life and she is keen to explore what they will do next...

Karen loves to hear from readers and always replies to emails. Please contact her on her website:

www.monkeyislandpublishing.com

Other books by Karen:

Knights of the Wobbly Table
My Wicked Stepmother
Fairy Rescuers
Return to Elysia
Angel Small
Angel Small Follows the Star

Musicals by Karen:

Angel Small
The Rainboat
Go Grace Darling
School for Angels